M000304602

OPHIDIAN

OPHIDIAN

A GREGORY MACNEE / MI6 NOVEL

W. G. ROWAN

This book is a work of fiction. References to real people, events, establishments, organizations, or locales are intended only to provide a sense of authenticity, and are used fictitiously.

Copyright 2020 by William G. Rowan

ISBN 978-0-578-80735-5

Dedicated to the two lovely women in my life,
My wife Kimberly, and my daughter Jillian.
Without their love and encouragement, this book would never have been finished.

Also, of course, to my chef Anatole, without whose culinary creations, life simply wouldn't be worth living.

PROLOGUE

NORTH ATLANTIC

Flying at forty thousand feet above the North Atlantic, MI6 special agent Gregory MacNee, is returning to London after a two week long joint MI6 – CIA training conference held at Camp Peary near Williamsburg Virginia, lovingly referred to as The Farm. Reclining in the first class section of Global flight seven, from Washington Dulles to London Heathrow, he sips a fine cognac while reading over the more important points of the conference. It had been a grueling two weeks both mentally and physically and he was beginning to feel the strain. Finishing the last of his cognac, he put the report back in his brief case, switched off the reading lamp, and drifted off to sleep, dreaming of his beautiful Octavia and their son William during the happy days before the accident that took them from him.

It was late afternoon on Christmas Day, little William was by the tree playing with one of his new toys under the watchful eyes of Steppings, the kindly octogenarian who had taken care of the MacNee family for decades and raised young Gregory after his parents had been killed in a car crash two weeks after his tenth birthday. Gregory and Octavia were in the library sampling an exquisite bottle of Chateau Mouton Rothschild vintage

1961 that was a gift from Mobius, Gregory's head of section at MI6. Sitting on the worn leather sofa before a crackling fire, with Octavia's head on his shoulder, enjoying the warmth of her body, the fragrance of her thick auburn hair and the smooth richness of the wine, he was at peace.

Gregory was ripped out of his peaceful dream by a massive explosion. The airliner pitched forward violently out of control, plunging down to the dark sea and certain death. He was being pressed into his seat as if by a giant hand, unable to move or grab the wildly swinging oxygen mask just out of reach. The explosion tore a large hole in the jet's fuselage towards the front of the main cabin, sucking several flight attendants and passengers out into the night for the long fall to the sea.

The noise was deafening from the screams of the terrified passengers, the wind, and howling engines trying in vain to overcome the dive to the sea. Soon everything in the freezing cold cabin began to move in slow motion, becoming quieter as the fog of unconsciousness from the lack of oxygen swept over him. The big jetliner impacted the waves hard and began to break up and sink. Gregory was aware of a heavy impact to his head, and a searing pain in his back and legs. Intensely cold water poured over him as the first class section sank into the depths. Everything was cold, dark and quiet now, the freezing cold began to dissipate, there was no more fear, there was no more pain, and he was being drawn to the peace of death, like a moths drawn to a flickering flame.

Suddenly, he was wrenched from his seat and shot to the surface like a cork as the seat belt broke free of its frame. He floated in and out of consciousness, until a light, brighter than the sun, enveloped him. He had always heard people who had near death experiences say that they were "drawn to a bright light". Expecting peace and serenity in the light of God, he was instead being stabbed by thousands of freezing knives. Out of the light came hands that carried him up to the heavenly light, but there was no peace. He was being stabbed and battered until all was darkness again. Semi-conscious now, he thought "What a strange place". Everything was hard, cold and confused. The lights he could see where red and fuzzy, like balls of red cotton candy. The noise of a thousand banshees screamed in his ears, then blackness.

Lieutenant Mike O'Leary increased Gregory's morphine drip as the Royal Navy Super Sea King helicopter touched down on the aircraft carrier HMS Invincible. Medics ran to the chopper and carried the few survivors to sick bay. Three of the ten survivors of the crash died on the way to HMS Invincible. Gregory was suffering from hypothermia, severe concussion, deep lacerations all over his body, broken right femur, broken left arm at the wrist, and six compressed thoracic vertebrae. The doctors and nurses in Invincible's sick bay stopped the bleeding from the many lacerations and set his broken leg and arm. They stabilized him for transport to a nearby hospital ship, HMS Hydra, where the facilities were far better for a man in such a serious condition.

For six weeks Gregory lay unconscious, in a drug induced coma, while the swelling in his brain from the impact with the airframe subsided. The bones in his leg and arm were healing nicely as were the deep cuts. The lights above his bed swam in and out of focus, sounds were muffled and undistinguishable. It took some time before he could focus enough to recognize what he was seeing and where he was. "I'm in a hospital bed. A hospital bed? How the hell did I get here, and why can't I move anything"? Then he was asleep again. When he woke up he was surrounded by doctors and nurses monitoring all the tubes and scanners he was hooked up to. After performing a multitude of tests, they told him he would live, and walk again, but his complete recovery could take months.

"Given months or never, I'll take months every time" he said in a weak gravelly voice.

Later that day Mobius, MI6 head of section, and his lovely assistant Kimberly Trent came to see him. Gregory was very anxious to find out what had happened to him.

Mobius said "Ok, take it easy mate, don't get upset, just be calm and listen. You were in a plane crash coming home from Langley a little over six weeks ago. They had to place you in a drug induced coma to allow your head injuries to heal".

"Oh God Gregory, I was so afraid you'd never wake up." Kimberly said, gently holding his hand.

Mobius said, "The flight recorder was recovered and it seems a terrorist bomb exploded on the right side of the main cabin. The plane immediately depressurized, sucking several of the crew and passengers out of the hole, then plunged almost straight down, crashing into the North Atlantic eight hundred miles South West of Iceland. There were only seven survivors and you were the only one to survive in the whole forward section. Luckily HMS Invincible and HMS Hydra were on maneuvers only thirty miles from the crash site. They saw it as it happened on their radar and scrambled three rescue helicopters to the scene. No one would have survived in that freezing water for more than five minutes. It looks as though our friends from The Islamic Brotherhood for Jihad are claiming responsibility. You don't appear to have been the target, just in the wrong place at the wrong time. Looks like they're trying to show the world what they're willing to do to achieve their goddamn political ends. It seems the bomber was wearing the bomb, killing himself along with almost everyone on the plane.

These fuckers get crazier by the goddamn day. First they shoot women and children, and then blow up ice cream parlors. Now they blow up a fucking airliner full of people that don't even know The Islamic Brotherhood for Jihad exists. This is fucking crazy, and..." Mobius saw Miss Trent glaring at him. Looking at the floor he said, "Sorry, Kim. I promised her I wouldn't get upset and make you worse. Sorry mate, it just gets me going."

The nurse came in and said "I'm sorry, the patient needs to rest now, and you'll have to go." As she began to hustle them towards the door, Kimberly went to Gregory and kissed his forehead whispering, "Get well soon, darling".

He wanted to reach for her, but he was hooked up to so many damn tubes and monitors, it was impossible.

Mobius said "Later this evening I'm meeting with the director at Whitehall, and the CIA station chief, to get more intelligence on this Islamic Brotherhood for Jihad group. You rest now my friend, and I'll talk to you again in a few days".

The MI6 driver held the door as they slipped into the back of Mobius's big Jaguar XJ-L sedan and Kimberly said, "I can't believe he survived the crash. He's a mass of bruises and looks so weak." Mobius just gave her a fatherly look, squeezing her shoulder and said "He's going to be just fine Kim, don't worry".

Alone again, Gregory lay in his hospital bed, listening to the monitors beep and watching God knows what, dripping from bags into the tubes he was attached to. As he lay there, he began to think about the long and complicated mission that started many months ago on a small island off the cost of Sicily.

CHAPTER ONE

VAUXHALL CROSS LONDON

I n early December, Gregory received a message from Mobius, requesting his presence at Vauxhall Cross, as soon as possible on
a matter of some urgency.

Gregory had his chauffeur, Pierre, drive him to Vauxhall Cross
immediately. His pulse quickened as it always did at the thought
of a mission.

Miss Trent escorted Gregory into Mobius's office. Mobius rose
from his desk and came around to shake Gregory's hand, waving him to one of the leather chairs in front of his desk. "Gregory,
thank you for coming so quickly. We have a dangerous situation
ongoing in Italy. Our agent, John Holloway, went missing eight
days ago, while assisting two Mossad agents. They had been investigating a scheme to covertly raise money for a rogue Russian
group attempting to purchase weapons of mass destruction from
one of the breakaway Soviet Republics, and then sell them to any
Islamic terrorist group with the cash. Since many of these groups
are funded by Arab oil money, they can pay huge amounts for
these weapons. Agent Holloway's body was found in the nets of a
fishing boat off the coast of Isola di Pantelleria, a small island located off the southern tip of Sicily, with a bullet hole in his skull.
The Mossad agents have not been heard from and are presumed

dead. I've been in touch with Mossad's Director in Tel Aviv, and he told me that his agents had been investigating the actions of one Valerio Drago. Drago is Don Marco Conti's Capo, who they suspected of passing millions of Euros to the Russians through his casino operation on Isola di Pantelleria.

"I'm sorry sir, Capo? I'm not familiar with that title". Gregory said.

"Capo is Italian for boss. Drago's the boss of all the Conti's business dealings, including their casino on the island'. Mobius told him.

Continuing, Mobus said "The Mossad agents investigated Don Marco and said he has no involvement in the scheme. However, the Don thinks Drago may be planning to kill him, and take over the Conti Cosca with the help of these Russians.

It looks like Drago is doing this strictly for money and power over the other families on the island. Drago thinks that with the covert support from Russians, he can kill Don Marco. As the new head of the Conti Copa, he can destroy the other families competing with the Conti Copa, leaving him in total power in the area. It is imperative that we keep Don Marco from being killed by Drago."

"Sir, if I might ask, why would MI6 want to help a Mafia crime boss like Don Marco maintain his power base in Sicily?"

"Don Marco has been the power in Sicily for decades. He was instrumental in helping the Allies during operation Husky during the invasion of Sicily in July 1943. The Don was in hiding from Mussolini's,"Iron Prefect of Palermo" Cesare Mori, at that time. In 1925 Mori was given special powers by Mussolini's National Fascist Party, to use any means possible to destroy the Cosa Nostra, what we call the Mafia, in Sicily. Mori used murder, torture and took women and children hostage, in order to get the members of the local Mafia cells to become informants. Don Marco went into hiding in a fourteenth century monastery in the high mountains near

Mount Cammarata above San Giovanni, a hundred kilometers or so away from Palermo. Dressed as a monk, and with the help of the Abbot at the monastery, he was able to avoid capture by Mori's forces. The Don formed groups of underground fighters to disrupt the Fascist Italians and German Nazis before the invasion. After the war, he was helpful to the allies in establishing local governments, to restore order in Sicily and help fight the Communist takeover in the late forty's. The Don is seen as a patriot by the people in Sicily. Because of his help during and after the war, it's to our best interest to keep him in power. Are you familiar with the Mafia rules of Omerta?"

"No sir, all I really know about the Mafia is from the cinema, if I'm honest".

The rules of Omerta strictly forbid any member of the Cosa Nostra, or Mafia, from co-operating with, or giving any information to, Governments or law enforcement. Though he can't openly work with us, to do so would violate the rules of Omerta and cost him his life, the Don has provided us with very useful information over the years and is a secret friend to us. So you can understand why his co-operation must be kept secret." Mobis explained.

"Yes sir I can see that now. As to the Russians, do we have any idea who they are and whether their working alone or with an organization?" Gregory asked.

"At this time we don't know anything about them. We haven't heard of any official Russian operation, or of any new covert criminal organizations in Russia. But, with the instability in Russia at the moment, and the emergence of what is called the Russian Mafia, anything is possible. We do know that Drago has no concern for the tens of thousands of people who would die if the terrorist attack Israel, which of course is their most likely target if they can acquire such weapons. If the terrorist can acquire an atomic device, detonate it in Israel, and make it look like it was done by Iran or Iraq, Israel would retaliate and pull the world in to an atomic war. Your mission is to stop the flow of funds to the Russians immediately. Discover who's responsible for Holloway's death, identify and eliminate all parties associated with this operation and do it quickly, while concealing the Don's assistance and any MI6 involvement".

"Yes sir. I'll review this report and get my team of special operators ready to get underway within a few days. I'll keep you informed of our progress." Gregory said.

Back at his home in Highgate London, Gregory sat by the fire in his study, sipping a fine 18 year old Glenlivet single malt; reading both the MI6 and Interpol reports on Velario Drago. For the most part Drago seemed typical of the current Mafioso types in control since the war ended. In trouble with the law since he was a boy, Drago was suspected of several brutal murders, but there was never enough evidence to convict him. He did a short stint in Pagliarell prison in Palermo for armed robbery of a bank and the death of a guard. Don Marco used his influence to get Drago released early, and Drago had been his strong right arm ever since. The reports made it clear that Drago was always heavily armed, and had a personal guard unknown to the Don. "Drago will be difficult to take down without a serious blood bath, and the subsequent investigation would show MI6 involvement. I'll have to come up with a plan to remove Drago with minimum collateral damage and remain under cover". He thought.

The next afternoon Gregory called together the MI6 special operators he had selected for this mission. Byron Hill, expert with explosives, speaks Italian and Russian, and agent Connell Baines, specialist in hand to hand combat, electronic espionage, all types of firearms, speaks Italian, Russian and Yiddish. Byron Hill had served with SAS Forces in the Falkland Islands War, as well as Afghanistan. His expertise with precision explosives was extensive, and may be useful on this mission. Connell Baines was an electronics genius, who earned his Doctorate in Electrical Engineering from Cambridge. He served with the Royal Marines as a counterinsurgency specialist for six years, seeing action in Afghanistan. Gregory had worked with both Hill and Baines on several missions and knew that both were professionals. Mobius told him they would be working with one specialist from the Israeli Intelligence agency, Mossad, Guy Zussman. Zussman is a very experienced agent, speaks Italian and Russian, Yiddish, and is currently working undercover on Isola di Pantelleria as a bartender at the Casino Degli Dei.

Briefing the team at Vauxhall Cross, Gregory explained, "We received intelligence from Holloway, that's been verified by the Mossad Director in Tel Aviv, that a man called Valerio Drago, has been using a gang of hustlers to rip off the 21 tables, at the Casino Degli Dei, on the island of Isola di Pantelleria, off the southern coast of Sicily. Casino Degli Dei, is an ultimate high roller casino, catering to the wealthiest people in Europe and the Middle East. The hustlers cheat the tables wining hundreds of thousands of Euros, turning the money over to Drago for a small percentage. Drago funnels the money to the rouge Russian agents to fund their weapons deals, with the promise of support when he moves against the Don. As the Soviet Union continues to crumble, they've become the super store for all types of weapons, including atomic and chemical weapons.

They've retired many of their military officers due to budget concerns, with no pensions, or pushed them out with charges of miss-conduct, or crimes against the State. Many of these officers have gone into business for themselves, acquiring weapons and selling them to anyone with the cash. Don Marco Conti would not tolerate dealing with the Russians, so he believes that Drago is out to kill him and take over the Conti Cosca, with the help of the Russians. If Drago is successful in killing Don Macro Conti, and taking over the Conti Cosca, these Russians would have a conduit to all the money they need to purchase weapons.

"Do we know who these Russians are? Are they official or free lance operators?" Byron Hill asked.

"So far we don't know. We haven't discovered any official operation, and we haven't heard of any new criminal organizations, but they pop up almost daily now in Russia." Gregory told him.

Continuing, Gregory told them," Drago and his chief enforcer, Tito Abrami, have a long history of using sadistic violence, torture and killing to achieve their goals. They're into all the usual things of course, drugs, prostitution, murder for hire, and they have a total disregard for human life. We're told they've threatened the families of dealers at the casino, to force the dealers go along with the cheating scheme. If they go along, they're paid, if they refused to go along, they're wives, children and other family members would be killed in a most vicious way. They're given a choice; take "*Piombo O Argento*" Lead or Silver. We suspect Drago and Abrami of killing Holloway and the missing Mossad agents. These guys are very bad news and need to be eliminated quickly. We've been in touch, covertly, with Don Marco Conti on the island. The Don suspects that Drago, and the Russians, are working together and planning to kill him and take over the Cosca, but he doesn't know when or how they plan to move against him. The *Casino Degli Dei* is part of the vast Conti Cosca holdings. The rules of Omerta, prohibit the Don from openly working with law enforcement, however, he secretly worked with MI6 during the war against the Germans and the Fascist, and is willing to accept our help, using his influence to assist our team on this mission. I'll head for Isola di Pantelleria today to get a feel for what's happening, and meet with Zussman. Connell, you and Byron fly to Sicily the day after tomorrow, and pick up whatever you think you'll need from our contacts there. Come over to the island on the ferry. We'll meet on the sport fishing boat, "*Contessa*" next Friday as tourist on a fishing holiday. We won't have any direct contact with Don Marco directly. I'll be meeting with an informant known only as Romano.

CHAPTER TWO

SOUTHERN ITALY

Arriving on the island early in the morning, Gregory checked into a large suite at the elegant "*Hotel Bela Vista*". "What a magnificent view of the Mediterranean Sea. Such a beautiful place for such a dark purpose" he thought. After showering, he went for a walk around the quaint old village to get a lay of the land. Upon his return to the hotel, the lovely young woman at the desk gave him a sealed message, along with a cheery smile, that actually seemed genuine. "Thank you Miss Caruso" Gregory said.

Gregory went to his suite and ordered a Continental breakfast of strong black coffee, assorted pastries and fresh fruit, then opened the message. It was short and to the point.

"Meet me at Café La Cale at seven this evening." signed Romano.

Gregory dressed casually with a light weight suede jacket, soft Bally moccasins, with grippe soles, excellent for fighting, and his Walther PPK just in case, he never trusted informants.

He met Romano in the bar of Café Le Cale that evening, and took an immediately dislike to the man. Romano was of medium height, thin with a hawk like nose, slicked back hair, shiny suit, pointed shoes, sitting with his back to the wall drinking wine, and leering at the women as they passed by.

"What an oily little worm this guy is. This son of a bitch would sell his mother for a five pound note" Gregory thought.

Approaching the table and saying softly, "Mr. Romano? I'm Mr. MacNee, an author researching a book on corruption in the local economy and law enforcement. Thank you for taking time to speak with me".

Romano looked around nervously when Gregory took a seat at his table. "Look, the Don told me to talk to you, ok let's talk so I can get the hell out of here. I don't want to be seen talking to you so I'll get right to the point. I think they're cheating the 21 tables using signals and body language but I can't be sure, their very difficult to spot". Romano said."

"What kind of signals? Gregory asked.

"The dealer will shift his weight slightly to his right foot when he has a nine, ten, or picture card down, and to his left when he had a low card. The Picciotto would then bet big or double down when he went left. There are many ways dealers can signal the Picciotto to let him know what their hold card is, but it looked like body signals to me". Romano explained.

"I'm sorry Mr. Romano, what are Picciotto"?

"Just low street gang punks, who work for Ambrami."

"How long has this group been working the Casino Degli Dei?"

"On and off for several months now."

"Do you have any idea who the brain behind the scheme is?"

"As to who the top man is, I don't know, but there are rumors that it's Don Marco Conti's Capo, Velario Drago and Drago's enforcer Tito Abrami, but I'm not sure. The Picciotto work the tables on Friday and Saturday nights, usually from around 8:00 to midnight. The days, times, and Picciotto vary so they're not obvious. I'd be damn careful asking too many questions about Drago and Tito If I were you. They're not the kind of guys you want piss off, if you know what I mean"

"I think I do, violent types are they"?

"Violent, yeah, you could say that. People disappear and are never heard from again who piss those two off. They're both very bad news. Be careful around both of them, but especially Drago, he's dangerous and paranoid".

"Have any of the dealers or Picciotto involved tried to quit" Gregory asked?

"No way, once they cheat the house, Drago has them by the balls. If they wanted out, Drago would say, "Fine, we'll just let the Don know that you've been ripping off his casino, and you'll be out, all the way out."

"Has anyone contacted the local Polizia?" Gregory asked.

"Not a chance. The Polizia belong to the Don" Romano said.

Rising from the table, Gregory shook hands with Romano saying, "Thank you Mr. Romano, for your time and your insight, and also for the warning about Drago and Abrami".

Gregory slid an envelope with five hundred Euros across the table.

Romano nervously pocked the envelope without opening it, stood up, and walked out through the kitchen disappearing into the night.

Gregory returned to his suite to work on a plan of action against Drago, Abrami and the rogue Russian team. Looking out over the peaceful sea he thought, "I'll need to study the layout of the Casino, the surrounding area and Dragos's movements so I can develop a plan to take them all out. When we move, we move fast, execute the plan and get out of the country."

He rented a small non-descript sedan, and drove several routes to the airfield from the casino. Once the opposition was eliminated, each of the team members would take a different route to the airfield and go to different airlines. Gregory would head for

the executive terminal where a private MI6 plane would fly him
back to London." He noticed that Drago parked his large Alfa, in a
covered parking space, with his name on it at the Casino and the
car was unguarded. "This could be an opportunity" He thought.
Using a pay phone on the side of the road, Gregory phoned Byron
Hill, and told him about Drago's Alfa, and that he could access the
car without being seen. "If you elect to use the car for Drago's removal, you'll find it in the parking space every night from five p.m.
on." Gregory told him.

The *Casino Degli Dei* (*Casino of the Gods*) was opulent in the extreme, and befitting its name. The thick carpets were rich, in a deep
burgundy color, with the casino logo embroidered in gold. Looking
over the casino floor, Gregory saw plush, butter soft leather chairs,
at the highly polished dark wood gaming tables. Most of the tables
had no limit signs in gold. The waitresses carried trays with cut
crystal glasses rimmed in gold, and wore long golden silk gowns,
slit high to the thigh, with the casino logo in deep burgundy on
the shoulder.

"This is definitely a high roller casino, with very big money
changing hands" Gregory thought.

Using the house phone, Gregory phoned Drago's office, asking
to arrange a time to meet with Mr. Drago, to get his insight on corruption on the island. He was told curtly "That might not be convenient for some time. Mr. Drago's a very busy man."

Gregory played some poker, in the beautiful poker room that
looked out over the 21 tables. This gave him a good vantage point,
to watch the well dressed crowd, and the action at the tables without being observed. He watched for the signals Romano had de-
scribed. He notice that when the dealer shifted slightly to the left,
an elderly gentleman in a deep blue tuxedo, at one end of the table,
and a strikingly beautiful, and very sexy young woman wearing a

black low cut silk gown, tight in all the right places, at the other end of the table, would double down and win big. She'd cheer and wave her arms about, clapping her hands and sip some champagne. Considering her figure, and the gown, everyone close by was watching her. The elderly gentleman just smiled. He seemed be enjoying her show more than winning. Her routine brought a crowd of the curious around the table, screening the dealer from the unwanted eyes of the floor supervisor, and making her just seem lucky when she won. The elderly gentleman went un-noticed.

Gregory played for a couple hours, and then went to the bar for a talk with the undercover Mossad agent, Guy Zussman.

Zussman said "See the tall muscular guy in the tux? That's Drago, the other two are the Russian agents. Tel Aviv identified them as Alexei Petrov, former Lieutenant Colonel with the Russian Speznaz. Real bad ass, but he crossed the wrong comrade and got booted out. The other guy is Boris Kozlov, Russian Navy Captain 1st rank in their ballistic missile program, pushed out with no pension due to budget downsizing. Both decided to roll over on Mother Russia, and have gone into business for themselves; selling weapons acquired from Belarus and Ukraine. Mostly small stuff, until now. Mortars, AKs, SAMs that sort of thing. Tel Aviv says they believe they're working a deal to acquire and sell a small atomic devise, perhaps atomic artillery shells, or worse, a suit case nuke".

"A suit case nuke, I've heard the expression, but I'm not really sure what it is or how it works. Wouldn't any nuclear bomb have to be large and very heavy? Gregory asked.

"No not really. A small amount of Uranium or Plutonium, just a ten pound ball would do. They build a lattice work of explosives around the fissionable material, in a very specific way, when the explosives are triggered, the explosion compresses the fissionable material then it explodes. I'm no expert, but that's the basic concept. The bomb would be small but particularly dirty releasing tons of radiation.

Even a forty pound suit case nuke would devastate a couple mile radius, releasing enough radiation to kill tens of thousands people in the months after the initial blast. I've heard whispers that something big is going down this Saturday. Both Drago and Tito seem more agitated and paranoid than normal, and I've see a lot of Alexei and Boris over the past week. Maybe they're going to move on the Don sooner than we expected. That may give them the money they need, I don't really know, but it seems big and might be an opportunity for us to make our move".

Valerio Drago was in his mid-thirty's, six feet, muscular, thick black hair, impeccably dressed in a black tuxedo with deep burgundy cummerbund, jewelry all gold. His attire suggested elegance, his demeanor suggested violence.

"Drago looks like a charming, easy going chap from here" Gregory said with a sarcastic grin.

"Zussman said, "Yeah, charming and easy going like a bull, until someone pisses him off, and then he'll kill everyone in the room in fit of rage. Trust me Gregory, I've see him go off. Pure psycho, he'd kill anyone and not give it another thought".

"Where's his other half, Abrami?" Gregory asked.

"I don't know, hasn't been in tonight. He's probably shacked up with one of his whores, he'll be in sooner or later" Zussman said.

"What do you make of the two at the 21 table, the old guy in the blue tux, and the stunner in the black silk"? Gregory asked.

"Him, I've never seen before. But the woman is Sophia Gambini, the latest rising star of the cinema in Rome. I saw her at a theater party in Rome about a year ago; she's kind of hard to forget.

"I think I'll go play with Miss Gambini for a bit" Gregory said. Gregory slid into the chair next to Sophia, and started to bet with her. After a few hands their eyes met, and he casually said, "Good evening, you're Sophia Gambini, the famous actress aren't you"?

"Why yes I am, but I wouldn't go so far as to call myself famous." Sophia said modestly"

"Your performance in *"Love on the Rocks"* was wonderful. It made the whole film for me" Gregory said.

"Grazie Mille Segnore" she said, with a flashing smile"

"My name is Gregory MacNee, I'm an author, researching a new book about corruption in government and law enforcement in Europe since the war ended "Gregory said extending his hand.

"Nice to meet you, Mr. MacNee." Sophia said taking his hand.

"How warm, soft and smooth her hand felt, but with a firm grip." He thought

"Sounds like interesting work, I'm sure you'll have plenty to research here in Italy alone." She said.

"Indeed, I was trying to get to interview Mr. Drago, to get his opinions, but was told he would not be available for some time." Gregory noticed that at the mention of Drago's name, Sophia's demeanor and beautiful smiling eyes went hard for a moment, but quickly recovered. "It seems like she doesn't like Drago at all." he thought.

"So, when will you be staring in another film Miss Gambini?"

"Oh we're already in production in Cortina d' Ampezzo. I play the love interest of the star downhill skier" she said with a sexy smile.

"Ah, lucky downhill skier" he said with a grin.

"Here comes the waitress; can I order you another glass of champagne Miss Gambini?"

"Yes, that would be lovely, but only if you'll call me Sophia, Gregory".

"I would be delighted Sophia." Signaling the waitress, Gregory said, "Mumms Imperial for the lady, and I'll have a very dry Tanqueray Martini, up with two olives please".

Their drinks arrived, and sitting closely at the 21 table, he could smell her exquisite perfume and feel the warmth of her body. It was a bit difficult to concentrate on the game, so Gregory just bet with her. When she would bet big or double, Gregory would do the same. Just a few hands later he was up ten thousand Euros, when the pit boss touched his shoulder and said "Mr. Drago can spare you a few minutes now". It was more a command than an invitation.

"I'm sorry Sophia; I really must see Mr. Drago. Will you be staying here on the island for long?"

"No, I must head to Rome tomorrow for about three weeks, before going back to Cortina".

"I'll be in Rome in just over a week; perhaps we could meet for a cocktail or dinner. I'd love get to know you better, and hear more about your exciting career." Gregory said.

"I'd like that very much Gregory", reaching into her purse, she handed him her card with her phone number in Rome. "I'll look forward to it."

"Enjoy the rest of your stay Sophia, and best of luck here in the casino" Gregory said.

Following the pit boss, Gregory was shown to the office of Valerio Drago, Managing Director of Casino Degli Dei. The pit boss knocked once then showed Gregory in.

Drago didn't stand when Gregory was shown in; saying curtly, "Have a seat Mr. MacNee, I can only spare a few minutes". The look in his eyes was not a friendly one.

"Thank you for taking time from your busy schedule to see me Mr. Drago. Since you're obviously quite busy, I'll come straight to the point. As one of the community's leading businessmen, I was hoping you could tell me about the corruption in the business community, and local law enforcement, here on the island". Gregory said.

Looking at Gregory with disgust in his eyes, Drago said "What I can tell you, is that you are misguided Mr. MacNee. We have no corruption in our business community or law enforcement. Also that we in the business community won't appreciate you starting rumors that we do have such problems. Yes, I would recommend that you spend a few days enjoying our island, and then go home to England".

Gregory saw a very hostile demeanor in his posture and his eyes. "This guy is telling me to get the hell off his island and stop asking questions".

Rising, Gregory said, "Well thank you for seeing me Mr. Drago." extending his hand. Drago did not take it. He sat there looking like he would just as soon shoot this Limey prick here and now.

Gregory headed back to the bar and ordered a Tanqueray martini, very dry. Sipping his drink he told Zussman that the meeting with Drago was actually about what he expected. "That's one nasty piece of work" Gregory said.

"That's the way he seems to me too." Zussman said. "While you were away, Sophia and the old guy have been cleaning up; check out that stack of five thousand Euro chips".

About two hours later, Gregory saw Sophia cash in her chips and head for the door. Following her at a discrete distance, he strolled casually down the boulevard appearing to check out the high end shops but kept his eyes on Sophia. She went into a small restaurant on the corner, so he went into a cigar store across the street and bought some Cubans while keeping an eye on the restaurant door.

After about ten minutes he went into the restaurant, unnoticed by her, and took a seat in a quiet corner. Ordering some pasta, with shrimp and scallops, in a garlic white wine cream sauce, and a glass of local Pinot Grigio, he sat eating and watched her.

Sophia sat at the bar drinking a white wine, when the old man from the 21 table came in carrying a black briefcase, and headed straight for the men's room. No one but Gregory seemed to notice, that an old man went in and a young man came out. The young man walked up to Sophia and kissed her neck; she giggled and kissed him on the cheek. He sat next to her ordering a Perrier sparkling water with a slice of lemon. They enjoyed their drinks and ordered another round. Sophia passed a large envelope to him and said, "This is the last time Tony, I'm out, do you understand, out".

About half an hour later, Sophia left the restaurant alone, and shortly after her, the young man left carrying a briefcase with the package she gave him in it. Gregory assumed it was the money both of them had won from the 21 table.

"I wonder how Sophia and this guy are connected with Drago. What would a very successful movie star be doing cheating a casino for a gangster? I can't believe she knows about Drago's scheme to kill the Don, or the Russians weapons deal. I'll just have to see where she fits in later" Gregory thought.

Gregory slipped out of the restaurant to follow the man with the money. The young man hailed a cab that took him to a large gated Villa in the hills above town, with Gregory following in the rented Fiat. He passed the Villa, continuing up the road until he found a spot where he could see the Villa's grounds. MI6 provided him with the latest generation "Starlight Scope". The "Starlight Scope" enhances starlight or moonlight by 100,000 times giving the shooter a clear view in very low light situations.

Gregory could see the man clearly bathed in the green glow from the scope. The young man gave the brief case to a man on the lawn of the Villa. Zooming in on them, Gregory thought "Just as I thought, you lying bastard" the man who received the package of money was Drago himself.

There were two other men with Drago, Tito was one, and the other had his back to Gregory. The young man got back into the cab and left. Drago, Tito and the third man were talking on the lawn. The third man was very animated while talking, waving his hands about and gesturing to Drago. Gregory was a bit shocked, but not really, when the third man turned to leave and he saw who it was, "Romano".

"I knew that oily little son of a bitch couldn't be trusted. We need to get the skinny on that little worm fast. I'll bet he set up Holloway and the Mossad team, and he sure as hell's trying to sell me to Drago. He's working for Drago against the Don. Ok, he's only met me once and thinks I'm a writer researching a book. The rest of the team is under cover and we can assume he knows nothing about Zussman, or he'd be dead already. I'm sure Drago has given him orders to check me out, find out who I really am and report back to him. It's time to end this little game of theirs." He was thinking.

Gregory parked about a block from his hotel and walked in the shadows, watching for Drago's informants on the way back. He phoned Hill and Baines and left a coded message for Guy Zussman to meet on "Contessa" at 0500 Friday morning".

Aboard "Contessa" the team sipped hot black coffee and listened while Gregory laid out the operation to eliminate Drago, Tito, Boris, Alexei and Romano in one quick move. MI6 confirmed that Romano is working both sides of the fence, pretends to be loyal to the Don, then sells him out to Drago, collecting Euros from both.

Guy Zussman said "I've heard whispers that Drago's handing a large amount of cash to Boris and Alexei Saturday night, and that they'll be moving against the Don on Sunday as he leaves for church. Tito will be with all of them in the casino for the exchange. Drago is paranoid about getting ripped off, and needs his enforcer close by."

Gregory said, "Guy you told me that Tito drinks Negronis. Handing Zussman a small vile, he told him, this contains Ethylene Glycol; put a few drops in his drinks. Negronis are sweet so it won't be detected in the drink. The Ethylene Glycol will crystallize in his kidneys and bladder; it will give him the uncontrollable need to urinate. When he heads for the john, Guy, you be waiting and take him out. After he's eliminated, go out through the kitchen to your car and drive to the airfield via route number one, handing him the directions he scouted out earlier. A plane will be waiting to fly you to Rome, then on to Tel Aviv.

Gregory continued, "I'll make an anonymous phone call at 10:45 p.m. to Romano, tipping him off that the Don has found out about the cheating, and is sending two shooters to the casino to hit Drago at 11 p.m. That little shit Romano will head straight for Drago with the information, then out the door to his car to get the hell out of there before the shooting starts. Drago, Boris and Alexei will go straight to Drago's Alfa and head for the Villa with the money".

"Connell, here's a specially prepared silenced Walther PPK 9mm, with no serial number, and a custom grips that won't show finger prints, just in case it's found. The rounds are specially packed, full metal jackets, with a one third the powder charge. As you all know, a large amount of the noise a shot makes is a sonic boom made by the bullet breaking the speed of sound. With these rounds, the speed at the muzzle is only 500 ft. per second, or roughly a third the speed of sound, so there will be no boom. Together with this mini Brausch silencer, it would sound like a small fart, not a gun shot. The full metal jacketed rounds will enter the scull but won't have the power to exit; they'll just rattle around awhile and make strawberry jam out of the victim's brain. Very quiet, instantly fatal. When that little prick Romano heads for his car, he'll be moving fast and be very nervous. Connell, take him out silently, two shots to the head, and then go straight to the airfield via route two. Take the 11:30 flight on BOAC to London, here's the ticket", Gregory said.

"Byron, Drago has his beloved Alfa detailed Monday, Wednesday and Friday every week in his parking space at the casino. You'll be working at the garage this Friday so you can have access to the car." Gregory said.

"That works for me boss, but how I do get a job there. Also, would a Mob boss allow a new face to work on his car?" Byron asked.

"Mobius contacted Don Marcos, and the Don said he would give the man who usually details Drago's car time off to go to Sicily to see his mother who's been ill. You'll be replacing him. Everyone knows the Don is a family man, and letting the detailer go to visit his ill mother would be right in character. Since you'll be assigned by the Don, no one will question anything you do." Gregory explained.

"Got it boss, in just a few minutes I can attach a rope of "C-4" under the rear seat and both front seats, plus a Thermite secondary charge. When the right rear door is opened and closed, an electronic trip is activated. When Drago puts it in reverses, then puts it in drive, the "C-4" will detonate liquidating everyone inside. The explosion will trigger the Thermite which burns at four thousand degrees, and can't be extinguished till it's burned out, keeping the Polizia and fire brigade busy."

"Holy shit! Byron "C-4"; that'll blow up the whole goddamn parking lot and half the casino. We want these bastards dead, but we don't want to kill everyone there. And what if Drago uses the car before were ready" Gregory exclaimed.

"Not to worry boss, not to worry. I'll rig a remote activating trigger that will let me activate the explosive sequence whenever I want. The "C-4" ropes are very, very small, just enough to liquidate everyone sitting in the car. It won't even blow the doors off." Byron said with a grin.

Gregory looked closely at Byron then said, "You're the explosives expert. Let's get it done. Just don't blow me up in the process. We'll meet back at Vauxhall Cross"

"Guy, I'll see you back at the casino, and I'll have your back until you're on your way to the airfield."

Gregory checked out of the hotel and drove to the casino around nine. Carefully parking where his car could not be blocked in, he went into the poker room and took a seat at the ten thousand Euros buy-in table. The beautiful waitress in her golden gown, brought him a glass of Glenlivet 18 year old single malt, and he settled in to play and watch.

Drago and Tito were at their usual table watching the action on the casino floor, when Alexei and Boris arrived with a large brief case. They joined Drago and Tito, ordering two large glasses of Vodka. Gregory noticed that Tito was on his second "*Negroni*" so things should be going to plan there. Drago, Alexei and Boris were in close conversation, with Tito keeping an eye on the immediate area around them, instead of the casino floor as he usually did. Gregory had no doubt that all four were armed. Tito excused himself and headed for the john. On his way back he ordered another round for the table. "His next trip to the john will be his last" Gregory thought.

Gregory knew that the Ethylene Glycol was working and Tito would head for the john within ten minutes. A few minutes later he noticed that Zussman was not at the bar. Tito got up to head for the john saying "I'll be right back boss, got to take a piss again". "Hurry up goddamn it, I need you here" Drago said.

When Tito entered the john, he paused, scanning the room as usual to make sure he was alone. Guy Zussman was in the third stall, with his feet up on the door, so the stalls all looked empty. Tito went to the urinal and unzipped his trousers, Zussman waited for about ten seconds, thinking "I don't want this guy's piss on these expensive shoes" then he slipped silently up behind Tito with a razor sharp Special Forces boot knife in his right hand. With his left hand he grabbed Tito by the hair and plunged the knife into his neck one inch from the base of his skull, severing the spinal cord at the 3rd and 4thcervical vertebrae, cutting off all motor response and breathing. Tito was dead instantly with all but no blood loss and collapsed into Zussman's arms without a sound.

Zussman dragged the limp Tito into the open stall, put him on the toilet, locked the door and climbed over the top.

Guy Zussman causally walked out of the john, turning left and out the kitchen door, got in his car and drove to the airfield as agreed, thinking, "The killing of the vicious enforcer Tito, who had inflicted so much pain and misery, took less than five seconds, job done"

At precisely 10:45, using the house phone in the casino lobby, Gregory phoned Romano. He did not identify himself but said, "The Don knows about Drago's plans and the rip off, he's sending two shooters to the casino now, they should be there in minutes" then hung up without another word. Gregory signaled Byron to activate the explosive trigger in Drago's Alfa, then took his seat back at the poker table and waited.

Romano came in looking very anxious walking straight to Drago, and whispering in his ear that the shooters were on the way, and then walked very quickly out of the casinos front door. He was heading for his small Lancia in near panic. Just as he opened the car's door, Connell Baines stepped out from behind a van and put two 9mm bullets in Romano's scull. The special Walther PPK made all but no sound. Romano's lifeless body fell into his car, and then Baines pushed the body the rest of the way into the car, rolling it on the floor, and closed the door. Walking calmly to his car, he drove to the airfield as planned tossing the gun in the river as he drove over the bridge. "Damn clean kill, done without any noise, no one even turned around." he thought.

Drago's face was hard when he heard the news from Romano. He said to Alexei and Boris "We must go now." Standing up and moving quickly, with the two Russians in tow, he headed for the men room to get Tito. Drago burst in to the men's room and seeing Tito's feet in the stall shouted, "Get your ass out of there, we're leaving right now". When Tito didn't respond Drago kicked the stall door open. Tito's face was dead white, mouth agog, dead eyes staring straight ahead, pants around his ankles. "Fuck!" Drago exclaimed, and headed fast for the door with a shocked Alexei and Boris right on his tail. All three drew their pistols and moved like a flying wedge through the crowded casino, out the front door to Drago's Alfa. Drago got in the driver's side, Alexei on the passenger's side and Boris in back. Both Alexei and Boris were ready to shoot their way out of the parking lot while Drago drove. Drago slammed the car in reverse spinning the wheels out of the parking space, and then jammed it into drive.

The "C-4" detonated with a heavy thump, liquidating all three killers in an instant and igniting the Thermite charge. The Thermite lit up the interior of the car in a white hot fire ball. Within three seconds the interior was burning at four thousand degrees, blowing out the windows, the tires burst into flames and the gas tank exploded with a tremendous boom.

People poured out of the casino and surrounding shops and restaurants to see what the hell had happened. The Polizia and Fire Brigade sirens could be heard screaming towards the inferno that was Drago's Alfa. Gregory rushed out of the casino with at least fifty other people, then turned right and walked to his car while all eyes were on the now melting Alfa. He drove to the executive terminal and boarded the special MI6 aircraft with its engines running. Within minutes the plane was airborne, making a sweeping right turn passing over the chaotic scene at the casino. The fire brigade could do nothing to extinguish the Thermite. All they could do was keep the crowd away, and let it burn itself out. By this time the car was reduced to a puddle of molten steel. The Polizia would be busy with the explosion and the body of Tito in the men's room.

"Welcome to hell Signore Drago, you and your merry band of killers. You've caused much death, pain and sorrow in your time, now that time is over." Gregory thought as he looked down from the plane.

As the plane headed back to London Heathrow, Gregory drifted off into a sound sleep, thinking "The mission was a complete success, all the opposition eliminated, no losses, no collateral damage, and a chance to meet with the stunning Sophia Gambini in Rome in a week.

CHAPTER THREE

Moscow

L ike many of the old guard Soviet officers; Major General Nikolay Vistin came from a family of politically powerful party members. They enjoyed a fine home in Moscow as well as a large Dacha in the country, where Nikolay would relax and go fishing with friends. He felt that these privileges were his due, but he wanted more, much more. Though he had an almost pathological hatred for the capitalistic exploiters of the West, he wanted to enjoy all the things that the wealthy in the West enjoyed, the Mansions, Yachts, Private Jets, Exotic cars, all of it. This was what he wanted, and he saw no reason that he should not enjoy the same things. He decided he would find a way to make it happen. With the breakup of many of the Soviet States, Nikolay realized that with his newly promoted position as a Major General, working in the Kremlin, he could get access to weapons of almost any type and sell them for extraordinary prices. He set up a top secret organization he named "*Ophidian.*" The ophidian can move silently, unseen, and then strike with blinding speed and deadly result. Vistin liked the symbolism. The organization was made up of many small operatives, through whom, he would broker these arms deals without anyone within the Russian military or political system being aware he was in any way involved. He established private numbered accounts in Switzerland and the Caribbean island of Aruba where such accounts were common place for drug dealers and other scoundrels. Ophidian recruited many of its operatives from government employees who wanted more than their positions would ever allow them to have. The prospect of this kind of wealth made them forget the negatives, and greedily focus only on what they would be able to buy with the money they were promised. Ophidian is a dedicated fraternity, and once these men became operatives and completed their tasks, they would pay with their lives and the lives of their families if they tried to leave or betray the organization. Nikolay made tens of millions of Euros brokering these illegal arms deals, but he knew that the really big money would come from nuclear weapons. Even as lax as security was in many of the breakaway republics, he could see no way to broker a nuclear weapon and not be found out. He would have to find another way, but he was determined to find it.

CHAPTER FOUR

Vauxhall Cross London

Gregory met with Mobius at Vauxhall Cross early Sunday morning, for a debrief of the Italian mission to eliminate the Russians attempting to sell weapons to terrorist organizations on Isola di Pantelleria.

"I've read your report Gregory, and the reports from Mossad, and it looks like you and your team did an outstanding job. In and out clean with no MI6 or Mossad involvement discovered. It looks to the island law enforcement that it was done by the Conti Copa or some other family, so they are just writing it off." Mobius said.

"Thank you sir, the operation did run very smoothly. Agents Baines and Hill did excellent work, and we couldn't have asked for better man on our team than Guy Zussman, he's a true professional". Gregory explained.

Mobius continued, "MI6, Mossad and the American CIA all feel this may be just the tip of the Iceberg. With the continued instability in Belarus, Ukraine and other break away Soviet Republics, the security of weapons of mass destruction is abysmal at best. Petrov and Kozlov certainly aren't the only ex-officers looking to make a big score with these weapons. There are others, but the elimination of Petrov and Kozlov should reduce their aspirations for a bit, and give us time to find out who the hell else is in this game. Right now we're very low on leads."

Gregory said, "Two of the parties in the cheating scheme were a Miss Sophia Gambini, upcoming star of the Italian cinema, and another man whose name I haven't discovered yet, early thirties, Italian. I can't believe that Sophia knows anything about what Drago was using the money for, and I suspect he was forcing her in some way to go along. She's quite successful now, and getting more famous every day, so why would she be involved in this. I arranged to meet her in Rome next week for dinner. She thinks I'm an author, and I'll try to find out how she got involved with Drago, who the other man was, and see if there are any connections to others."

"Ok Gregory, see what this Gambini woman knows, and if she has any connection to this business other than cheating the casino for Drago. We know there are other ex-officers attempting to acquire weapons, there's simply too much money to be made for Petrov and Kozlov to have been a one off. We don't have any solid intelligence on who they might be at this time, so be careful. Follow any trail and move quickly. Check in with Gianni Russo at MI6 Station "R" Rome. Russo is very well connected, knows everything going on, if there's a Russian connection he'll know."

Mobius's assistant Miss Trent booked Gregory on Alitalia's morning flight to Rome's Leonardo da Vinci airport, "Lucky fellow, I've never been to Rome. I don't suppose you could use some company?" She asked with a pout.

"That sounds like a great idea, and we'll have to do it someday. Unfortunately, this is company business, and with you along Kim, it would simply have to be a pleasure trip" Gregory said.

CHAPTER FIVE

ROME

Arriving just after noon, Gregory took a cab to the Hotel Magnificent Roma. Cabs in Rome always made him nervous. Riding in the back of the old Mercedes diesel, that seemed on its last legs, he was thinking "They drive like absolute maniacs, road signs and traffic lanes are just so much decoration to them. Traffic lanes mean nothing to these people, motorcycles, scooters and cars all trying to take the same piece of road at the same time. Christ Almighty, the most dangerous part of this mission may well be this cab ride to the hotel".

"For God sake watch where you're going man", he shouted as the driver swerved past a large truck almost crashing head on into a small Fiat.

Of course the driver paid no attention at all to his passenger.

"I hate Roman drivers" he thought. Only by the grace of God they finally made it to the Hotel Magnificent Roma's front entrance. He got out of the cab sweating bullets. Paying the driver he was thinking "I'd like to strangle this asshole rather than pay him".

The doorman greeted him and escorted him to the reservations desk. The peace and elegance of the lobby had a calming effect, and he soon started to relax a bit.

"My name is MacNee, Gregory MacNee, checking in", he said to the manager at the front desk.

"Ah yes Mr. MacNee, welcome to the Hotel Magnificent Roma, we have a lovely corner suite for you sir. Front, the manager called out, and a bell man appeared at once. "Take Mr. MacNee to suite number 8103."

The bellman showed Gregory to his suite and explained all of its amenities. Giving him his key and turning to depart, the bellman said "Welcome to our hotel sir, please enjoy your stay with us. If there is anything you require, just touch five on your telephone."

Settling in, he had a short Black Label from the bar in the room to slow his heart rate, and then a hot shower to wash off the cab ride. Then he ordered a light lunch of a Caprese salad, made with fresh local Buffalo mozzarella cheese, ripe local heirloom tomatoes, basil and a sweet balsamic reduction, plus lots of fresh cracked black pepper, along with a Birra Moretti. After lunch he phone the head of MI6 station "R" Rome, Mr. Gianni Russo and arranged to meet in an hour.

Gregory took the short walk down the Via Vittorio to MI6 Station "R" Rome, with hundreds of people who seemed to be in a great hurry to get to wherever they were going. Horns blared, as cars and scooters darted in and out of the traffic that was buzzing by like so many angry hornets. He thought to himself, "Rome's a strange place; beautiful yes, but the traffic is horrendous, and with cab drivers who seem intent on killing themselves, and their passengers. I couldn't live here; it's no place for an Englishman". He felt safer on the sidewalk then in that bloody traffic. Arriving at MI6 station "R" he was met by Gianni Russo who greeted him warmly.

"Mr. MacNee, a pleasure to meet you", I hope you had a pleasant flight. By the way, I believe congratulations are in order for an excellent job on the island". Russo said

"Thank you Mr. Russo, the team did a great job".

"London informs me that you met Miss Sophia Gambini, who was involved in the cheating scheme with Drago" Russo continued.

"Yes, we want to find out why she did it and who the other man was. Also we need to find out if they have any further connection to the Russian agents. We're sure there are more ex-officers out there looking for these lucrative arms deals, but we need some fresh leads in order to put a stop to this." Gregory said.

"As I'm sure you're aware, Sophia's an actress, and becoming a star quickly.

My people have asked around, and were told, that she was having an affair with her makeup artist, Tony Bianchi, and that he got into trouble with Drago. Seems Drago was holding markers for gambling debits to the tune of thirty thousand Euros, and the debit was overdue. One afternoon Drago's enforcer Tito, broke into Bianchi's apartment when Bianchi and Sophia were making love and threatened to kill the both of them if he couldn't pay. Drago knew Bianchi didn't have the money, so he offered them a deal to say alive.

The deal was to play 21 at the Casino Degli Dei and turn the winnings over to him. They were instructed how to bet and told if they asked any questions or mentioned the plan to anyone they would be killed. To say the least, it was an offer neither could refuse". Russo explained.

"I see, does this Bianchi have any connections to Russians looking to acquire weapons that your people are aware of?" Gregory asked.

"No, none that we know of. I've had him followed and checked out. Just seems to have a gambling problem. We also found out that Sophia ended the affair and wants nothing to do with Bianchi anymore; in fact she fired him as her makeup artist. Can't blame her really; when your lover puts you into a situation like that, it's time to find a new lover. And from what I've seen of her, that will be not be a problem at all. She's"Assolutamente bellissima molto sexy" Russo said.

"Thank you for your time this afternoon Mr. Russo. Hopefully I'll be meeting Sophia for dinner and I'll see if I can discover any other leads from her into the Russian weapons operation. If I come up with anything I'll let you know". Gregory said.

Walking back to the Hotel Magnificent Roma, Gregory was thinking, "Thank God Sophia doesn't seem to be involved with the Russian deal. I want to get to know her much better. I'll have to be careful when I bring up Tony so she doesn't get suspicious as to why I'm asking." Arriving back at the hotel he went to the concierges desk and arranged for a limousine for the next few days, "No more taxis on this trip" he thought. Going up to his suite he phoned the number on the card Sophia had given him back on the island.

The phone was answered by a woman saying "Gambini residence"

"May I speak with Miss Gambini please, Gregory MacNee calling."

"Please hold Mr. MacNee, I'll see if she is free"

Gregory was thinking, "Damn, her home number, I was expecting an office or service. This is promising".

"Buon Pomeriggio Sophia, this is Gregory MacNee, we met at Casino Degli Dei last week, I hope you remember me. I said I'd give you a call when I got to Rome".

"Buon Pomeriggio Gregory, yes of course I remember you. I'm so glad you called. Are you here in Rome now"? She asked.

"Yes, I just arrived this morning. I'm staying at the Hotel Magnificent Roma. I'll be here for a couple days and was hoping we could get together tonight for dinner at Restorante La Pergola around eight.

"That would be lovely." she said. "My address is 712 Via Sante Maria Penthouse #1."

"Great, I have a car and driver during my stay so I'll pick you up at eight." Gregory said.

Gregory showered and dressed a dark blue three piece suit from his tailors on Savile Row in Mayfair, and his new bespoked lamb skin loafers. He wanted to look his best for a dinner date with such a beautiful young actress.

Pulling up to her apartment building, in a very fashionable area, Gregory thought "She certainly lives well; a beauty like her should live in a place like this".

He was announced by the doorman and greeted by the maid.

"Please have a seat Mr. MacNee; Miss Gambini will be with you shortly. May I offer you a drink sir?"

"No, thank you, I'm fine."

Gregory was looking at some of the photos around the elegant room thinking "beautiful, simply beautiful". Suddenly he detected the unmistakable fragrance of Herme's 24 perfume. Turning he saw Sophia, looking radiant in a tight fitting low cut silk dress, in a deep forest green, standing with her left foot slightly ahead of her right and her hands together in front of her. An elegant stance, enhancing her fabulous figure.

"Buonasera Gregory, it's lovely to see you again" she said.

"Buonasera Sophia, you look lovely. Tell me, how did you know that Herme's 24 was my favorite perfume"?

"Because I was sure you're a gentleman with exquisite taste, also it's my favorite too" she said with a playful grin.

"This is a beautiful home you have, have you lived here long?"

"Well yes and no actually. You see my grandfather owned the property so I was a frequent guest, then moved here about two years ago when he passed away and I inherited the building".

"It's quite elegant and suits you perfectly. If you're ready we should probably go, I don't want them to give away our table. I'm told that Restorante La Pergola is very popular" Gregory said.

"Oh I, doubt that they would give Mr. Gregory MacNee's table away. They would never treat an important British executive with All Empire International that way." She said with a knowing smile.

The doorman at Restorante La Pergola met Gregory's limousine immediately, and escorted them inside to the Maître d' hotel, who greeted them warmly. "Mr. MacNee, Miss Gambini, welcome to Restorante La Pergola, my name is Angelo, please follow me, your table is ready." As they walked through the elegant dining room, Gregory noticed all eyes; both male and female were on Sophia. The men watched her with longing, the women with envy and hatred. "Who can blame them; this woman has style, beauty and sex appeal in abundance. I can't keep my eyes off her myself. It must happen to her all the time" he thought.

Gregory ordered them a bottle of Dom Perignon Rose and the Normandy Blue Lobster, grilled simply, and served with drawn butter and lemon to start.

Sophia said, "Blue Lobster, I've never had it, oh I've heard of it of course, but never had it".

"It's wonderful, only comes from the cold waters off the Normandy Coast.

I think it's best flame grilled quickly and simply, brings out all the sweetness of the lobster, and paired with Dom Rose, well it's a marriage made in heaven, or at least in Normandy." Gregory said. As they enjoyed their lobster and chatted he found that he was totally captivated by this beautiful young woman. It wasn't just her figure and sex appeal, or her remarkable deep brown eyes with flecks of gold, no; she has what the French refer to a "Joie de vivre" or a zest for life that can't be put on. "She's simply one of the most charming women I've ever met" He was thinking.

Taking a sip of champagne Gregory asked, "I don't remember mentioning All Empire International, how did you know about that?"

"When we met on the island I thought you looked familiar. I thought back a few years and remembered an article I read in International Business Daily that had your photo in it. When you phoned, I looked up the old article and sure enough, it was you." Sophia told him.

"Do you follow International Business closely?" He asked somewhat surprised. "I wouldn't have thought that someone in such an exciting profession as yours would care much for the sometimes rather dry corporate world".

"Well, I don't follow it as much now, but before I became an actress I studied at Wharton School of Business at University of Pennsylvania in America and planned to go into the corporate world. While I was there I was asked to do a commercial for Alitalia.

I thought it would be fun and my friends encouraged me to try, so I did. It was fun and exciting, and I found I enjoyed all the attention. After graduation I came back to Rome and a director who knew my family asked if I would like to try being in a film here. I said why not, so now I'm an actress and loving it" Sophia explained.

"Ah, that explains it. Well yes, All Empire International was started by my great, great grandfather shipping goods of all kinds throughout the British Empire, including trading with Shanghai in the early days of what are known as the Old China Traders. Since then of course we've expanded many businesses all over the world including international banking. Though running the company is a rewarding career, I always wanted to be a writer so I decided to take the time and work on my book about corruption".

"Tell me more about Gregory MacNee, who he is, other than

the great, great grandson of the founder of All Empire Industries?" she said leaning in close to him.

"Well the short story of my life, I was born in Belgravia London, my father was Sir Gregory William MacNee III, Chairman of All Empire International and British Ambassador to China, based in Hong Kong. My mother, Claire Marie MacNee, was the only daughter of a very large producer of fine champagne and patroness of the arts. My parents were killed in an automobile accident on Victoria Peak in Hong Kong when I was only ten years old. I was raised, principally, by Steppings, whose family has been with the MacNee family for over three generations. I took my degree in chemical engineering at Oxford, and then served in the Royal Navy Submarine Service, retiring as a Lieutenant Commander. At the moment I'm writing a book and dining with one of the most beautiful and exciting women I've ever met" he said.

"Thank you Gregory she said with a modest look. You've had quite an interesting life. It must have been exciting being on a submarine."

"It was exciting, very much an adventure I'll never forget. But after seven years it was time for a new challenge."

Changing the subject suddenly, Gregory said "Oh by the way, did you read that Valerio Drago, and his right hand man, were killed back at the casino just after we left in what was explained as a gang land murder?"Gregory told her watching for her reaction at the news about Drago.

At this question Sophia flushed with anger saying, "The man was a pig, he deserved to have been killed, but slowly not just blown up. He threatened so many people and forced them to do things they would never do. I'm glad he's dead."

Gregory was slightly taken aback by how passionately she reacted to hearing Valerio Drago's name.

Sophia had a look of great despair in her beautiful deep brown eyes and her mood darkened. She wrapped her fingers around the base of her champagne glass, stared blankly into the streams of rising bubbles softly saying, "I'm sorry for my outburst Gregory". After a moment or two she raised her eyes to look into his and said, "I was having an affair with my makeup artist Tony Bianchi, and he had problems with gambling. Apparently he owed large gambling debits to Valerio Drago. One afternoon one of Drago's henchmen threatened both our lives if we didn't go along with a cheating scam at the twenty one tables at the casino back on the island. I had no choice but to go along. It ended my relationship with Tony and made me feel unclean, like a liar and a cheat. I don't really know why I'm telling you this; it was a terrible time for me and I suppose I just needed to get it off my chest."Shaking off the dark mood and quickly regaining her composure, she reached across the table and took Gregory's hand in hers and said "Let's not talk about that anymore. That's all in the past; this is an evening of pleasure".

"I'm sorry Sophia; I didn't mean to upset you so. It just popped into my head when I was thinking about when I first met you back on the island. I won't mention it again. Let's order" he said signaling the waiter.

They both ordered the Seared Scottish Salmon Fillet with Sant Erasmo Island Artichokes and red beets, with a balsamic reduction, paired with a fine Gaja Sori San Lorenzo.

Gregory said, "Tell me about your latest film project"

"Well after the success of "*Love on the rocks*" my agent started to receive many offers. This film is titled "*Dreams of Gold*" and it's about the Italian downhill ski team leading up to the Olympic Games. Their top skier is their best chance for a gold medal at the games, but he has problems with drinking and women. I'm one of those problems" she said with that sexy smile he found so attractive.

"I can't wait to see it." Gregory said.

They had finished their meal and were ordering espresso, both choosing to pass on desert, when Angelo the Maître d'hôtel came hurrying to the table and said "Forgive me Mr. MacNee, there is a phone call for you, they said it's most urgent"

Excusing himself, Gregory followed Angelo to his office and took the call. It was short and sweet.

Mobius said "Gregory, your presence is needed in London at once. I have a jet waiting at the airport now.

"Yes sir, I'm on my way". Looking back at the gorgeous Sophia he thought, "Oh for God sake couldn't it have waited till morning."

He said "Angelo, Miss Gambini and I must be leaving immediately, handing him his Platinum card to settle the bill. And please add thirty five percent for the staff".

He walked back to their table and Sophia asked "Bad news?"

"Yes, very bad news, I must return to London immediately. Seems to be a big flap at the office that requires my personal attention"

They drove back to Sophia's apartment and he walked her to her door.

"Sophia, I'm so terribly sorry about this, but it can't be helped. I've been looking forward to this evening with you since we met. Perhaps I can come to Cortina and see you again?"

"Don't worry about it, I understand." she said looking very disappointed. "Yes, if you can come to Cortina that would be wonderful, we can snuggle by the fire. I'll be staying at the Hotel Cristallo"

They kissed, and her body felt hot against his and her lips even hotter. The kiss was a promise of exciting times to come.

CHAPTER SIX

MOSCOW

General Vistin heard about a young physicist in England, by the name of John Patterson, who had developed a revolutionary new method of producing extremely small nuclear weapons. The actual destructive power was much less than conventional nuclear weapons, but the fallout it produces was highly radioactive. Such a small dirty device could have many uses to the Middle East factions constantly struggling against the Israel and the United States. Since his organization was unable get a nuclear device from any of the sources they had, he devised a plan to get the physicist, and sell him. He knew the Middle East was the market for such a sale and put his agents in the field to make the contacts. He found that Patterson was sympathetic to the communist cause so he had his man Paval Orlov find an operative to coerce young Patterson, with promises of helping the communist cause and freeing the working man from the yoke of the elite.

Paval Orlov found a disgraced Ex-Russian Army Captain, Anatoly Garin who began working on Patterson and convinced him to give him small technical secrets that the British National Atomic Program was developing. Nothing large mind you, just small things that would help his communist brothers break free. Patterson was a willing helper, and was later set up to move over to the Soviet Union. Under the guise of helping Patterson come to the Soviet Union, Pavol Orlove, under secret orders from General Vistin, arranged to have Patterson kidnapped and sold to a Mid-East terror group for a huge sum.

CHAPTER SEVEN

VAUXHALL CROSS LONDON

Gregory arrived at Vauxhall Cross just after dawn feeling tired, and more than just a little angry. This meeting cost him a night of passion with one of the most beautiful and exciting women he'd ever met. Waiting for Mobius, he was thinking of an old quote made by an American, whose name escaped him at the moment, "I slept and dreamed that life was beauty, awoke to find that life is duty." how true, how bloody true. He thought bitterly.

Mobius greeted him saying "Sorry for ruining your night Gregory, but such is life when we're in the service of the crown. We have a big problem with this one. It seems that one of our top nuclear physicists, Dr. John Patterson, was abducted on the road during a ski trip to Zurs in Austria. The car was found at the bottom of a ravine. His two companions had been shot at close range; one survived and is in the Hartmannspital in Vienna, and is expected to pull through.

He told the police that two men took Patterson, they tried to stop them and one of the men shot them both. The Police didn't have much of a description of the men, but said they thought they may be Russian."

"This can't be a coincidence that Russians are involved again so soon. Do we have any intelligence on official Russian covert operation or any criminal organizations within Russia that may be working with terrorists?" Gregory asked.

"We very much doubt that this is any kind of official Russian operation, so it must be an as yet unknown criminal organization." Mobius said.

"The American CIA believes that an Islamic Jihadist group Hezbollah, or The Islamic Brotherhood for Jihad, or possibly both, may be behind this kidnapping. They think terrorist organizations are working on a new plan to create economic chaos in the American and the West. The terroist know that the U.S. military is simply too powerful, even if they have an atomic device, so they plan to disrupt the economy with such weapons. The killing of tens of thousands of infidels is simply a bonus to them. What the CIA thinks they're planning, is to attack the economy of America and Western Europe by detonating small nuclear devices in major financial centers such as New York and London. That would basically bringing the capital markets and the economy of the US and Western Europe to a standstill. What the CIA believes, and we tend to agree, is that someone has kidnapped Dr. Patterson for this reason and will force him to develop the small weapons they require. Patterson is one of the U.K.s foremost experts on small nuclear devices, so with him working for them, all they have to do is get a relatively small amount of enriched plutonium. This can be done through the Russian agents. It's doubtful that this is any kind of official Russian government operation, so we must assume a underground criminal organization operating somewhere within Russia. If the KGB was aware of this organization they would shut them down. Moscow knows this could lead to nuclear war and they don't want that. We suspect that it's someone within the Russian military system running their own organization without the knowledge of mother Russia. At first it seemed that it was just Petrov and Kozlov working with Drago. Having removed those three and having other Russians involved with the kidnapping of Dr. Patterson so soon, indicates there is much more behind this. Ex-officers wouldn't have the connections to acquire atomic weapons or arrange to sell Patterson to The Islamic Brotherhood for Jihad or Hezbollah on their own". Mobius explained.

"Do we have any idea where they've taken Patterson or who is running this operation?" Gregory asked.

"No, right now we don't have any leads on who the kidnappers are, or where they may have taken Patterson. I need you to get to Vienna and talk to the survivor, David Cohan, and see if you can get a lead on these men. Get together with Tobias Fuchs, our man in Austria, he can help co-ordinate whatever you may need. Find the good Doctor and bring him back undamaged. When you think you've found him, tell us what support and equipment you'll need to get him home, and I'll sent it to you within eight hours. Move quickly Gregory, we need to find Dr. Patterson. The CIA is also investigating this kidnapping and will do all they can to bring him out safely. However, they said the U.S. cannot allow him to fall into the hands of terrorist organizations" Mobius said

"Are they suggesting that if they can't get him out they would kill him?"

"You can draw your own conclusions from that, but it would seem that's what they mean. We can't let that happen. Patterson is too important to our nuclear program and he's a citizen of the United Kingdom, it's our duty to bring him home alive. I have several agents working with their contacts in Moscow to try to get a line on this Russian organization and find out who the top man is". Mobius told him.

CHAPTER EIGHT

VIENNA AUSTRIA

G regory was on the seven A.M. British Airlines flight from London Heathrow to Vienna International, reading over the full report on Dr. John Patterson. Patterson is thirty four years old, five foot eight, black hair, dark brown eyes, currently has a beard. Graduated Kings College Oxford with a degree in mathematics at the tender age of nineteen, then received his PhD in nuclear physics from MIT at twenty one. He could see why this particular physicist was so important. Patterson had a genius for developing small atomic weapons with very high yields and light weight. This type of weapon could be placed just about anywhere. If one were placed in or near the New York Stock Exchange or other major global financial center, the economic devastation is obvious. They could be used all over the country and with no specific enemy to attack, the military would be helpless to stop it. The terrorist would get a real chance to destroy what they consider the "Great Satin" and wreck the economy in Western Europe as well.

Tobias Fuchs met Gregory at the British Airlines counter and they drove to see Cohan together.

"Good to meet you MacNee, Tobias said. Mobius told us to hold off questioning Cohan until you arrived. The man's in bad shape but should survive. Mobius felt that we should only question him once then let him try to recover a bit".

"Who is this Cohan, and what's his connection with Patterson? " Gregory asked.

"David Cohan's an American. He and Patterson were old friends from his days at MIT. Patterson and Cohan got together a little ski holiday. Cohan works with Jet Propulsion Laboratories in California on satellite tracking systems, and has no connection to Patterson's research program that we can discover".

"What about the man that was killed, who was he?"

"His name was Hans Schmitt, local ski instructor who was hired by Patterson as a driver and ski tour guide during their trip. Looks like the poor bastard was just in the wrong place and got killed." Fuchs explained.

They arrived at the Hartmannspital on Nikolsdorfer Gasse Vienna just blocks from MI6 station "V". Fuchs showed the police guard his I.D. and they were let into the room.

"I thought this was a low visibility case, doesn't having a police guard make it rather high profile to the staff?" Gregory asked

"Here in Vienna it's standard procedure in an unknown shooting situation, so no, the staff wouldn't be curious" Fuchs explained.

"Mr. Cohan, my name is Gregory MacNee; I'm with the British Government and was asked by your government to ask you what happened to you and Dr. Patterson. Do you feel strong enough to answer a few questions sir?"

"I suppose so, Cohan said in a very weak voice"

"As briefly as you can, tell us what happened"

"Well we had dinner at the Thurnhers Alpenhof, sort of a last night splurge, and were heading for the train station at Langen Am Arlberg to go back to Lichtenstein, when we saw a car broken down in the middle of the road. Our driver, Hans, pulled over and we all got out too see if we could help them move the car out of the road. They thanked us for stopping saying their car just stopped. Their English was rather poor; I think they were Russians, so we weren't able to really communicate. We offered to help push the car to the side of the road. John was on the right, I was on the left and the two Russians were in between us with our driver at the wheel. Suddenly the two attacked us. John was knocked out with a sap or something; I was hit hard in the face and went down on my knees. Hans jumped out of the car and we both tried to help John but one of the men drew a pistol and shot Hans in the face and shot me in the right side. That's all I remember until I woke up here in the hospital. The police told me Hans was killed. They said they don't know anything about John, his body was not found" Cohan told them.

"Mr. Cohan, we suspect that your friend Dr. Patterson was the target of a terrorist kidnapping. We're trying to get a lead on who might be responsible and rescue him. Can you tell us anything more that might help us find him? Did you notice the type car, color, registration plate number anything of that nature and can you describe the two men?" Gregory asked.

"The car was an older Mercedes; I remember the emblem on the trunk lid when we started to push it. I think it was white or yellow, some light color, it was very dark. The men are hard to describe, they were about six feet, husky, but they were wearing ski jackets and hats. One had very blond almost white hair sticking out from his hat, I remember thinking his hair was very light for Russian. It all happened so fast and unexpectedly I really didn't notice that much" Cohan said.

"Mr. Cohan, I understand you work for Jet Propulsion Laboratory in the United States, have you ever worked with Dr. Patterson on any projects"?

"No, we never worked together; we were just at MIT together and became close friends. We haven't seen each other in several years and I don't really know what he's working on in England. John's specialty was Nuclear Physics and I'm an Aeronautical Engineer so there should be no connection to our work or at least none that I'm aware of".

"Thank you for your help Mr. Cohan. If you think of anything else that may help us find Dr. Patterson, please contact Mr. Fuchs. Get well soon." Gregory said.

They left the hospital and walking back to station "V" Gregory said, "That's not much to go on. I'm going to head over to Zurs and ask around, see if I can get a handle on these two Russians. Please phone the chief of the local police and ask him to assist in the questioning around the village, and the Thurnhers Alpenhof restaurant. I'll meet you back here in a few days".

Gregory rented a car and drove to Zurs checking into the Thurnhers Alpenhof Hotel. He headed down to the restaurant bar and ordered a Guinness Extra Stout. When the barman, named Curt, brought his drink Gregory said, "Curt were you on duty last Wednesday night?"

"Yes Sir, I was here from five to eleven"

"Some friends of mine were here last Wednesday evening and were involved in a rather nasty accident after they left. One was Hans Schmitt, a local ski instructor. Do you know Hans?

"Yes, everyone in the village knew Hans. It's hard to believe he was killed in a shooting. Things like that don't happen here".

"Curt, it appears that one of the other men with Hans, a Dr. Patterson, was the target of a kidnapping and Hans was killed during that kidnapping. I'm investigating this incident for the British Government. Do you remember the group with Hans?"

"Yes I do. Hans introduced me to the other two men, one was John and the other David, and both were guest of the hotel."

"David survived the incident and said one of the men who attacked them was a heavy set man with very blond or white hair who spoke with a Russian accent. Do you recall seeing anyone in the bar area or restaurant at the time Hans was here that fit that description?

"Let me see, last Wednesday, it was kind of slow, you know I do remember two men who I think could have been Russian, drinking at the table in that far corner. They didn't talk to anyone and seemed a bit out of place. Most of our customers are society people here on ski holidays; these two looked more working class, and did not look like skiers, if you know what I mean. They were both heavy set, kind of bulky, didn't look like sportsman. And yes, one of them had almost white hair, looked odd since he didn't seem more that thirty."

"Do you have any idea what their names were?

"No, they paid their bill through their dinner check. Hanna was their waitress. Let me go get her, she would know" Curt said.

Curt returned a few minutes later with a young woman in her early twenties. "Sir, this is Hanna, she was the waitress who served the two men you're asking about the night Hans was killed". Curt said.

"Good Afternoon Hanna, we're trying to locate the two men Curt mentioned to you. Can you tell me anything about them that may help us contact them?

"Yes sir, I remember them. The reservation was under the name of Anatoly Garin, not staying with us, he was staying at the Hoffenburg Haus just outside the village. Mr. Garin addressed the other man as Gregor but I don't know his last name. They weren't very friendly; barely looked at me when I took their order, then they stiffed me on the check. Hanna said.

"Where they here for a long time"? Gregory asked.

"Longer than I'd have like them to stay, a couple hours. They seemed to be watching someone else in the dining room but I never saw who. They paid in cash and left rather abruptly. And like I said, no tip." Hanna said with a disgusted look.

"Thank you Hanna. Thank you Curt, you've both been very helpful." Gregory said.

"I hope you nail those bastards if they had anything to do with Hans's death. It just wasn't right shooting him like that" Curt said shaking his head looking at the floor.

Gregory drove out of the village to the Hoffenburg Haus and spoke with the manager on duty who said, "Both men had stayed here and had not returned since Wednesday or checked out. They had two rooms under the names of Anatoly Garin and Gregor Delov. They paid cash when they checked in but they still have an outstanding bill for room service. The maid said that the rooms were empty, no luggage or personal items left. Looks like they skipped out on me".

"I don't believe you'll be seeing either of them again. You said the last time you saw them was Wednesday? Was there anything unusual about them or anyone that came to see them?" Gregory asked.

"No, they seemed a bit out of place in a ski area, but no, other than that nothing. No one came to see them. Oh, one odd thing that did happen when they were here, though I don't know if they had anything to do with it; was that we had a car stolen from our parking area Wednesday, an old yellow Mercedes. That type of thing doesn't happen here much; in fact I think it's the first stolen car we've ever had." the manager told him.

"Well, thank you for taking the time to speak with me." Gregory said.

Gregory headed back to the hotel and phoned Miss Trent in London asking her to find out all available information on Anatoly

Garin and Gregor Delov and get the information, and any photos, to him as soon as possible. Then he called Tobis at station "V" and told him what he had discovered asking him to check with the local police and see if they have come across the stolen Mercedes. He also asked him to contact Interpol and see if they had any information on Garin and Delov saying he would return to Vienna in the morning. In less than two hours Miss Trent phoned and said that Anatoly Garin is thirty seven years old, six feet, heavy set with black hair. Gregor Delov is thirty one, five ten, heavy set with whitish blond hair and tattoo on left arm of Red Star. Both were Russian officers kicked out two years ago for stealing and other crimes against the State. Delov did one year at Novocherkassk military prison released last June. Their current whereabouts were unknown. She told him that she would FAX photos of both from their military file to MI6 station "V" Vienna.

Arriving at MI6 station"V" Vienna at ten, he was giving the photos of Garin and Delov that came from London.

Tobis said "Interpol had very little on the two, but were keeping an eye on them when they were in Berlin two weeks ago because of their criminal records. They said that Garin had been seen with two men from Palestine that where in Berlin on student visas, but they weren't causing any problems they had no reason to question them. They said both Garin and Delov have not been seen in over a week. They weren't tracking them so they don't know where they went".

While they were talking, Tobis received a call from the train station security at Langen Am Alberg saying that they have found what they thought was the stolen Mercedes in their car park. They sent the number plate information to the Zurs police and confirmed that it was the stolen car. They said it had damage to the front end and blood on the back seat. The parking ticket in the car was from nine thirty five Wednesday evening.

"Let's head over to the rail station at Langen Am Alberg and see where the trail leads" Gregory said.

Tobis's assistant came in with a message for Gregory from Mobius.

The message said, "Gregory; the American CIA has two agents investigating the abduction of Dr. Patterson, and they'll be making contact with you two days. See what they've discovered and let them know what you have. We could use the help and so can they. The agents are John Waxman and Mathew West. Both are experienced agents. West is the senior man; ex-U.S. Marine Special Expeditionary Force; tough and reliable, counterinsurgency expert, speaks German, Russian, French and Vietnamese. He's got a chest full of medals he earned the hard way. Waxman is electronics engineer recruited from Cal Tech, speaks seven languages with no accent. West's, thirty three, six foot, built like a linebacker, broad shouldered, muscular with dark thinning hair and brown eyes. Waxman's, thirty five, five foot ten, slight build, thick black hair just beginning to grey, dark brown eyes, heavy beard trimmed close, wears glasses with steel rims, looks like an Iranian and could pass for an accountant."

"Tell Mobius I'll let them know where I'll be. I'm heading back to the rail station, then wherever the trail leads" Gregory said to the assistant.

Arriving at the rail station Gregory said to the security chief, "Let's have a look at the security camera films from last Wednesday night. We're looking for three men, two stout one with very light hair and one possibly in a wheel chair. We're hoping to see where they went. Let's start with the first class section, if Patterson was unconscious he would be in a wheel chair and they wouldn't have put him in a standard seat, they would have bought a sleeping compartment so not to have attracted undue attention." After scanning the tapes closely for an hour or so, they saw two large men, one with whitish hair pushing a man in a wheel chair wearing a large hat, and with his legs covered with a blanket heading for platform 375 for the number 1593 train to Berlin.

"Ah, I think those are our boys. Looks like Berlin is my next port of call". Gregory said. Using the station security phone Gregory phoned Miss Trent telling her he was headed to Berlin on the next train, and that the CIA men should meet him at the Berlin Central station.

The train to Berlin Central only had a few second class seats available for the fourteen hour trip. Second class travel was about what Gregory had expected, the usual mix of screaming baby's and college students on holiday. Finding his seat, he was thinking, "Thank God, at least I have an empty seat next to me". Of course this didn't last long. He noticed a very heavy set man in his late fifties carrying a bag of groceries with a large sandwich sticking out of it coming his way. Watching with some apprehension, he noticed the man had very tiny feet for his massive bulk. The way he seemed to float down the aisle, bouncing off the seats, reminded Gregory of the helium balloons on string that he had as a boy. Unfortunately, the man floated right into the seat next to him and for the next fourteen hours they were literally pressed together as the man ate his garlicky sandwich and drank beer. There was no dining car so Gregory bought a box meal of a dry ham and cheese sandwich and cheap white wine then drifted, with some difficulty, into a light sleep.

CHAPTER NINE

BERLIN

The security chief at Berlin Central station had been alerted that Gregory would be arriving on the 1593 train and was there to meet him. He had been asked to have the security tapes for Thursday's a.m. arrival from Lang Am Alberg Austria available. He was also met by the two CIA agents, Matt West and John Waxman.

West and Waxman showed Gregory their identification and West said "Greg, I'm Matt West, and this is John Waxman. Your boss at MI6 gave us your description and arrival time."

Gregory was always somewhat put off with the American's enthusiasm for shortening everyone's Christian name, but shook hands with West and Waxman saying "Nice to be working with you both, oh by the way, it's Gregory".

"Oh yeah, sorry, you limeys are kind a ticklish about formality aren't you" West said.

"No, not particularly, just many of us limeys prefer to be called by our given names" Gregory said.

"Ok, that's fair enough I suppose. I didn't mean to offend. We're just less formal in the states. Gregory it is then". West said shaking Gregory's hand warmly.

"There's no offense taken Matt. Let's go look at the security tapes and see if we can get a handle on our two Russians friends, they've got a big lead on us". Gregory said as the followed the security chief to his office.

Gregory gave the CIA men the official description of Anatoly and Gregor and showed them the photos London had sent him, and told them what he had seen on the security camera tapes in Langen Am Arlberg. He also gave them the report he had received from both Interpol and Mobius.

West told him, "CIA has been tracking several Russians, but not these two. Ours have been in contact with Muslim fundamentalist groups we suspect are tied to The Islamic Brotherhood for Jihad and Hezbolla, among other terrorist organizations. The intelligence is light on these groups at the moment, many of them meet in Mosques, and it's been tough to get someone on the inside to gather information on them. We have a few people, but we're not sure how reliable they are."

"We just had a run in with some rouge Russians working in Italy. You have Russians working with The Islamic Brotherhood for Jihad and Hezbolla, and now we have suspected Russians involved in kidnapping Dr. Patterson. This must be being run through a bigger organization. Has CIA had heard anything about a new criminal organization in Russia in the past few months? Gregory asked him.

"No, nothing new, just the usual suspects. As you know, there's been a lot of criminal activity all over Russia since the wall came down." West said.

"That's true of course, but this smells of something bigger than Russian gang bosses vying to control territory. This group is working outside the country. MI6 is looking for a connection to whatever group is running this." Gregory said as they reached the security chief's office. There was a bank of monitors on the back wall of the office showing the entire station platform by platform as well as the parking area outside.

"Gentlemen, I have the tapes for Thursday morning and afternoon set up on the monitors just over here. Please take a seat and use this control to pause, fast forward or rewind. I'll have coffee and sandwiches brought up for you." The security chief said.

"Thanks chief, this may take some time." Gregory said.

"If these are the men we're looking for, I saw them board the train in Austria. Patterson looked unconscious, they had him in a wheel chair with a large brown fedora on his head hiding his face and a blanket covering his legs so I couldn't make a positive ID, but I'm sure it's him." All three agents scanned the tapes on three large high definition monitors, closely inspecting the hundreds of people pouring off the train. After what seemed like hours they spotted two men fitting the description of Anatoly and Gregor with a man in a wheel chair wearing a hat and with his legs covered by a blanket heading for exit thirty five.

"There go the bastards West said. Let's check the other cameras and see if we can get a handle on where they went from here."

They followed Anatoly and Gregor from camera to camera out the door where they got into a small white Ford Transit van. The van could be seen exiting the train station and taking B-96 towards Tempelhof. They couldn't read the faded lettering on the side, but they could read the number plate. Gregory phoned Miss Trent and told her that he had linked up with CIA, and asked her to get the registered address for the van giving her the plate number. He asked her to phone him as soon as possible and told her they would be on the move shortly. Gregory rented an Audi A8L sedan at the Hertz desk for the trip to Berlin, then went back to the security office. Miss Trent phoned him there and said the van was registered to a company known as Berlin Sea Food Emporium at 7397 Am Strom in Tempelhof. The owner was one Ismail Aziz, 52 years old Palestinian ex-pat living in Germany for eight years. Aziz's wife passed away last year, no children. He has a nephew named Imaad, who has been living with him in Germany since his wife died. She also told him she reserved rooms for them at the Grand Hotel just a few blocks from the Seafood Emporium.

"Thanks Kim, as efficient as always" Gregory said.

They drove to the Tempelhof area of Berlin and checked out the town, as well as the Seafood Emporium, before heading for the hotel. Gregory took a large suite with sweeping views of the harbor to act as a meeting room for the team. West and Waxman took one room with twin beds and a view of the parking lot.

"You do like to live well don't you" West said with more than a bit of sarcasm after they'd checked in.

"I see no reason to be uncomfortable" Gregory said with equal sarcasm raising an eyebrow. "Let's get some sleep; we've all been on the move for almost twenty hours. Tomorrow we'll find out more about Mr. Aziz, and what part he's playing. Hopefully it will lead us to Patterson and whatever group is behind this".

Rising just before dawn, Gregory walked around the quiet streets and down Am Strom along the river to pier thirteen and the Sea Food Emporium. The Emporium was closed, as were all the shops in the area so early in the morning. Peering through the dirty windows, he thought "That's strange, everything's in place but they can't have been open for months". That evening Gregory and the CIA men went to the Bahnhof Haus for drinks. Ordering three pints of Weizenbock, Gregory asked the barman, named Fritz, "Do you know the owner of the Sea Food Emporium up the street? I believe his name is Aziz"

"I know who you mean, but I can't say that I know him. The old man was always a bit stand offish, but he's really tended to avoid people since his wife died. You can't really blame him I suppose, I heard he took it very hard" Fritz said.

Gregory asked, "Do you happen to know his nephew? I believe his name is Imaad"

"I know of Imaad, but I didn't know the relationship. We were never introduced. Imaad came here from the Middle East shortly after Mrs. Aziz's death to help out I guess. He acted as if he was really uncomfortable with Germans or anyone not from the Middle East. He made a point of avoiding us. I thought this was a strange place for him to come. He would only order tea and talk with a few men from the Mosque, then leave. Why do you ask? " Fritz said.

"My car was hit in a parking lot in Berlin and the security camera showed a white Ford Transit van with number plates registered to the Sea Food Emporium. I thought while I was here I would speak to Mr. Aziz about it. I went to the store to see him, but it was closed and seems like it's been closed for some time. Have you seen Mr. Aziz lately?" Gregory said.

"No I haven't seen him for some time. Imaad was around quite a bit, but like I said, he never even spoke to any of the other shop owners or people in the area and was never open for business. He met here in the dining room last weekend with a couple of Russians, and another Mid-Eastern guy. Maybe he sold the store to them".

"You say he met with two Russians? Did one have very light, almost white hair" Gregory asked.

"Yes, as a matter of fact one of them did look like that" Fritz told them.

"I think I know the man with light hair and if it's the same man, I believe I heard him say he was looking to buy a business in this area. Do you know where he is staying? Gregory asked.

"I'm sorry no, I don't have any idea. They had quite a bit to drink that night and left by taxi. Ask Max in the Templehof cab out front. He was working that night and probably got the fair". Fritz told him.

"You wouldn't happen to know where Aziz lives would you. I'd really like to get the damage to my car fixed without going through my insurance, so I need to speak with the owner of the van" Gregory said.

"No idea I'm afraid. Both of them used to go to the Mosque just a few blocks away by the State Park. Someone there may be able to help you with that" Fritz told him.

"Thanks for your help Fritz" Gregory said sliding a twenty Euro note across the bar.

Gregory said to West, "I'm going out and talk to Max if he's there. Maybe we can find Delov.

After some gentle persuasion and another twenty Euro note, Max looked at his records and said he took a drunken Russian to 1374 Leonardyweg by the park.

Back with West and Waxman he told them what Max had said.

"Well, what do you think Gregory asked West and Waxman?"

"I think it'll be tough getting the boys at the Mosque to tell us anything" West said.

"So do I" said Gregory. Matt you head over to Leonardyweg and see if you can find out anything from the people in the area. See if they've seen Aziz about, and ask about Delov or Garin. I'm going back to the hotel and contact London.

"I'll go over to the Mosque in the morning and see if I can speak to the Imam, and ask him about Mr. Aziz. I speak Arabic and understand the Lavantine Arabic dialect they speak in Palestine. I'll tell them I'm a friend from the old country on holiday in Germany and would like to say hello and offer my prayers for his dear departed wife." Waxman said.

"Sounds like a plan John, be careful though, these boys are

always a bit suspicious and if their playing with any of these terror groups it could be dangerous". West said.

Back at the hotel Gregory phone Miss Trent in London.

"Kim I need you to find out all there is available on this Ismail Aziz. I need to know his wife's name, family, when she died, as much as you can. Also, the nephew, Imaad. We need complete information by morning if not sooner. Also, please get in touch with the German Secret Service Head Quarters in Berlin and let them know I'll be calling; we could use some local help here. Sorry for the rush job but things are moving here". Gregory said.

"I'll get right on it Gregory. Call you back as soon as possible". Miss Trent said.

About two hours later Kimberly Trent phoned back saying "Ok Gregory here's all we have on Ismail Aziz and family. They lived in a large apartment block on Olderstabe Tempelhof just three miles from the Seafood Emporium. His wife's name was Bashera Aziz formerly Bashera Kassab, she was forty nine and died of breast cancer on the fifth of November this year. She had one sister, Aliya Kassab-Abbasi living in the neighborhood of Moussly in Damascus Syria. Aliya's husband was killed in the attack at the U.S. Marine barracks in 83' leaving Aliya and their son, Imaad Abbasi. Imaad is twenty two years old, five foot seven, medium build, black hair, dark brown eyes, beard and mustache; I'll send a passport photo to you. Records show he's always been difficult and in trouble with the law. He has an intense hatred for the US since his father was killed working at the Marine base. He's a devout Muslim Fundamentalist. Though there is no evidence that he's been actively involved with any terror organizations, he is believed to be sympathetic towards those he refers to as "Allah's Holy Warriors" and believes that the Jihad against the U.S.A., "The Great Satin" is a Holy cause". She told him.

"He sounds like he may be our connection in this kidnapping, along with the two Russians and Middle East terror organizations. Thanks Kim, I'll be in touch". Gregory said.

Later that afternoon West returned to the suite and told them, "I talked to the neighbors and people working in the shops in the area, and they said they saw Aziz a day or two ago. They said he was always quiet, but didn't talk to anybody since his wife died. I asked if them if they ever saw men fitting the description of Garin and Delov, and told them we served together years ago. They told me they had seen Delov last week, but not for the past few days. They said many of the flats where rented short term, and that Delov was staying in one at the end of the fourth building in the complex. I think if we keep an eye on the place, one or both may turn up, and if one does show, we should grab him."

"I agree with you Matt. We need to work on a plan to do just that."

Gregory said.

"I'll get with Langley and see if they have anything more on Imaad Kassab" West said.

"John, be damn careful when you go to the Mosque tomorrow. It looks to me that they could be aware of Imaad's activity and may be involved. This could get ugly real fast" Gregory told Waxman.

Meeting the Imam, Abd al Bari, the next morning at the Mosque, Waxman said "My name is Adnan Ahmed, I'm looking for Mr. Ismail Aziz, my family knew his family back in Palestine, and I was hoping to say hello and convey my family's condolences for the death of his wife. I went to his shop but it was closed and I don't have a home address, I was hoping perhaps someone here at the Mosque could help me get in touch with him".

"Mr. Aziz has not come to prayers for some time. After Mrs. Aziz passed away, Ismail became somewhat of a recluse, praying more from home than coming to the Mosque; but he did come at least once a week. As I said, I have not seen him for some time. He may have returned to Palestine to be closer to the family. As to his home address, I believe they live in Tempelhof, but I don't know the exact address" Abd al Bari said.

"Yes, I understand. I was told that his nephew Imaad came out after Mrs. Aziz passed away and was helping with the business. Since this is the only Mosque in the area, I thought he must have come here to pray. Do you know him or were I may find him?" Waxman said.

"I'm sorry, I know of no nephew of Mr. Aziz or any other gentleman named Imaad who worships in this Mosque. Perhaps you have the name wrong" Abd al Bari said, with the beginnings of annoyance.

"That's possible I suppose. Well thank you for taking the time to speak with me". Said Waxman

After Waxman had gone, Yosef Mohammed, one of The Islamic Brotherhood for Jihad's leading killers, came out of the small office where he had been listening to the Imam's conversation with Waxman. Western Intelligence believed Yosef was working for The Islamic Brotherhood for Jihad and thought to be responsible for at least five brutal murders in the Gaza Strip over the past few years, as well as several bombings in Ramallah in the West Bank. Yosef had taken Imaad Abbasi's identity so he could operate freely in Tempelhof, and coordinate the acquiring of the English physicist Patterson. Imaam Abbasi believed he was helping the cause of the fight against the hated Americans and Israelis by agreeing to go into hiding while Yosef assumed in identity. Yosef said to one of the men who were kneeling nearby "Amir, check out this Ahmed, he sounded like an American. If he is, he's most likely an American spy. One of our people said that men were asking questions about me at the Bahnof Haus last night and one fits the general description of the man calling himself Ahmed.

If he is an American spy we may need to kill him. Also, I think Ismail Aziz has out lived his usefulness. Have Jamal take care of him at once. We've come too far to have our plans disrupted. I'll be at the safe house with Patterson. Let me know what you find out immediately".

Waxman met the team back in Gregory's suite and told them about the meeting at the Mosque.

"It sounds like Ismail Aziz's nephew Imaad's our third prime candidate in this kidnapping operation. He hates the U.S.A. and Israel, all infidels and is a big supporter of their Holy War. It can't be coincidence that he is, or was, here when Garin and Delov grabbed Patterson and came here" Gregory said.

"This guy's got to be lying or this Imaad is a bad Muslim. If he's as devout as London says, he would go to prayers wherever he was". West said.

"Yeah, I got the idea the Imam was lying. There were several other men kneeling close by and they seemed to be doing more listening than praying. I think the Mosque is a meeting place for these guys just like back in the States". Waxman said.

"Well, I guess the next move is to head over to Aziz's apartment and see what we can find there. John, you go check out the apartment and talk to the neighbors. Matt, go to the Mosque and keep an eye on it, see if Imaad comes in and when he leaves follow him. I need to find out where Garin and Delov have gone. They must have Patterson stashed somewhere near by their flat. He's worth a bundle to them so they won't want to let him out of their sight. "Gregory said.

Gregory phoned the German Secret Service, code name CASCOP, Head Quarters in Berlin and requested an urgent meeting with the head of station. He was told he could meet him in one hour. Meeting with the CASCOP head of section, Hans Schumacher, Gregory explained the situation.

"Thanks for seeing me on such short notice Mr. Schumacher. I'm Gregory MacNee with British Intelligence.

"It's nice to meet you Mr. MacNee. How can the German Secret Service assist Her Majesty's Government?" Schumacher asked.

"I'm working with two CIA agents here in Berlin; we're searching for two ex- Russian military officers, Anatoly Garin and Gregor Delov, who we believe kidnapped Dr. John Patterson, an English nuclear physicist. Patterson was taken while on the road in Zurs Austria several days ago. We've tracked them to Berlin, and think we have a lead on a third man who may be working with them here in Berlin, a Syrian by the name of Imaad Abbasi". Gregory explained

"So I understand. I've spoken to your chief, Mobius, in London and he's asked for our assistance in finding these men. Do you have a location fix on any of them at this time?" Hans asked.

"We saw the van the kidnappers drove when they arrived in Berlin on a security camera at the Central rail station. It's regis-tered to the Berlin Seafood Emporium in Tempelhof. The regis-tered owner of the van is a Palestinian named Ismail Aziz. Aziz has not been seen for some time. His nephew Imaad Abbasi, is the Syrian I mentioned. We believe he may be involved with the Islamic terrorist groups, The Islamic Brotherhood for Jihad or Hezbollah, and that he's is using the Mosque in Templehof as a meeting point and information drop, but we don't have proof of that yet. One of the CIA men is watching the Mosque to see if Imaad shows. We also have a possible location for the Russian, Gregor Delov at 1374 Leonardyweg in Templehof. We got the address from a cab driver who took Delov there last weekend. One of the CIA men spoke to the neighbors and they say the flat was a short term rental, and they remember Delov staying there, but said they have not seen Garin or anyone fitting the description of Patterson. What we need is a man to keep an eye on the flat to see if Delov or Garin show up. "Gregory said.

"I'll assign someone to the flat right away and have some officers from the local police anti-terrorism unit to ask around the area for information on all these men and report back to me." Schumacher said.

Gregory gave him the photos of all three men saying, "We're sure about these three, but there are probably others working with Imaad that we don't know. The additional manpower would be of enormous help in finding where they went and who else may be involved. If any of your men see Delov, Garin or Imaad, please have them follow them and contact me right away. Tell them not to make contact, just find out where they are. I think when we find Garin or Delov we'll find Patterson. They won't let him out of their sight until they've been paid for the job, so one will be with him all the time". Gregory said.

"Always glad to help MI6 and CIA. If there is a terrorist cell operating here in Berlin, we need to get a fix on them". Schumacher said.

"Thank you Mr. Schumacher. With your local knowledge and local assets in the area hopefully we can nail them down quickly. Wherever they have Dr. Patterson I think they'll be moving him to the Middle East as soon as possible. We need to find him before that happens". Gregory said shaking hands with Schumacher.

***

Gregory went back to his suite, and contacted Mobius in London,attaching the portable scrambling devise to the phone. "We have the Germans helping us and may have a possible location on one or both of the Russians. If we can isolate Garin or Delov, we need to grab one so we can sweat them for information on Patterson's location and who is running this Russian operation. If we can grab one of them, I'll need to fly him back to London quickly and have our guys squeeze all he knows out of him fast. Please have the base commander at Gatow have an aircraft ready". Gregory said.

"I'll arrange everything for transport and with an interrogation team here.

Move fast and be careful. If you grab one of the Russians and the others find out, they may well kill Patterson and run. Good luck". Mobius said.

Waxman and West returned to the suite and told Gregory what they had discovered. "The German special branch guys are watching the Mosque and will let us know if Imaad shows up. They'll tail him if he leaves and contact us. I didn't see him come or go, but I'm sure that place is dirty" West told him.

Waxman said "The bartender at the Tempelhof Bar said Delov had been drinking there two nights ago. Templelhof Bar is a cheap beer joint just half a mile from the rented flat. The bartender said Delov got pretty drunk and was pawing the waitress until she threatened to quit. They had to cut him off and Delov got pretty ugly about it, but stopped short of starting a fight. He said Delov left and was driving an old green Opel coupe. They thought about calling the police because he was quite drunk and shouldn't have been driving, but decided not to because police would say that they should have cut him off sooner, and they might get fined. They said he's been in before and his drinking was never a problem, but he seems to be drinking more each time. He comes in about every other day".

Gregory phoned Hans Schumacher and asked him to send two special agents to watch the bar tonight and let him know if Delov shows.

"Of course Gregory, I'll see to it right away. By the way, the local police found a body floating in the river that fits the general description of the man Ismail Aziz. They're running a forensic identification check on the body now. He didn't drown Gregory; he had a 9mm bullet hole in side of his head, and hasn't been dead long. We don't know if it was murder or if he committed suicide due to the loss of his wife. They haven't found the gun yet, but it's probably gone down river." Schumacher told him.

"Where are they holding the body Hans, I'd like to check it out and see if it is Aziz." Gregory said.

"He's in the morgue at the Tempelhof Sisters of Mercy hospital down town. I'll phone the administrator and tell him to give you whatever assistance you require."Schumacher told him.

"Thanks Hans. I'll go check it out and let you know what I find."

"Matt, they just fished a body out of the river with a bullet hole in its head that fits the description of Ismail Aziz. Let's go over to the hospital and see if he's our man." Gregory told West.

Arriving at the hospital they met with the administrator, Kurt Weinburg, who escorted them to the morgue. "I was contacted by Mr. Schumacher of the Special Branch, and told to give you everything we had on this man. He was spotted by a couple kids playing on the bridge. They called the police and he was brought here. The man didn't have any kind of identification on him but, it may have been washed away by the river. The police forensic teams took some samples and are working on identification as we speak.

I'm sorry gentleman but that's really all I can tell you." Weinburg told them.

Gregory looked at the body and took a photo to send to MI 6 for identification.

"It looks a hell of a lot like Aziz to me; based on the description London gave me. If this guy turns out to be Aziz, the big question is, did he kill himself or did someone eliminate him since we've been asking questions about his whereabouts." Gregory said to West.

"It's easy to make murder seem like suicide, particularly if the victim was despondent over a great loss. It sounds to me like someone didn't want us talking to him" West said.

"That's my guess as well. If so we're getting close and someone is getting nervous." Gregory said.

Phoning Kimberly Trent Gregory said, "Kim I just emailed you a photo on the secure server of a man the German police fished out of the river for identification. We think it may be Ismail Aziz. Have the identification section check our records against Interpol to see if it's a match".

"I see it now Gregory. I'll forward it to Smyth down in the identification lab and he'll get you an answer right away." Kimberly said.

"Thanks Kim. Let me speak with Mobius please".

When Mobius came on the line Gregory told him about the body of the man they suspect to be Ismail Aziz.

"If this man turns out to be Aziz, and if they killed him to keep him from falling into our hands, we'd better step up our pace in finding and rescuing Patterson. If they feel were closing in, they may move him or kill him if they can't get him out quickly enough." Mobius told Gregory.

"I quite agree sir. We have a solid lead on one of the Russians. It seems that Delov goes to a local bar every other day and gets drunk and makes a play for the waitress. I need a young woman agent to come here right away to act as bait for Delov the next time he goes to the bar. We'll wait until he's drunk then have her come on to him and make sure he keeps drinking. When they leave together well grab him off the road. We'll need to make sure they don't know we have him or we'll blow the whole operation.

"Ok Gregory, I'll have an agent on a plane within the hour and she'll contact you at your hotel. Her name is Susan Jamison, twenty eight, thick natural platinum blond hair cut in a short bob style, eyes of deep green, five foot six, trim athletic body of a professional ice skater, very attractive, looks very Scandinavian, she's also a very capable agent". Mobius said.

"Great, she sounds perfect. Delov won't want to pass on a chance with a woman with her looks." Gregory said.

Talking with West and Waxman, Gregory said "The bartender said Delov comes in about every other day. If he goes drinking after Garin takes over watching Patterson, and he was there the day before yesterday, he should come in tomorrow. I have a young woman agent coming from London to act as bait.

Tomorrow night I'll head over to the Tempelhof Bar early with our agent and see if Delov shows. Matt you and John go rent two non-descript cars. If Delov shows I'll give you a call and I want you to come to the bar separately, and park one car around each corner. We have to assume were being watched, either by the Russians or Imaad's men, so don't be seen together. The weather is getting worse and that could help us since there won't be many people on the street when we take him."

Amir phoned Yosef on a secure mobile phone and told him "I've used all my sources at the airport and within the government, but could find no one by the name of Adnan Ahmed that came in from Palestine or any other place. It seems that he gave us a false name, because Adnan Ahmed does not exist".

"I thought as much. This Adnan was seen in the area of The Grand Hotel several times. I want the mysterious Adnan Ahmed taken care of so he can't interfere with our plans in any way". Yosef told Amir.

"Right away, I'll see to it personally. There will be no mistakes" Amir said.

"First, eliminate Aziz's nephew. He's becoming a liability. If the CIA are sniffing around they may find him, and my cover will be blown. That would disrupt the whole operation and the brotherhood would be very angry at all of us, and you know what that means. I don't want the body found, is that understood" Yosef told him.

"Yes, I understand perfectly, and I'll see to it that the body disappears without a trace." Amir told him.

Gregory met with MI6 agent Susan Jamison at the suite, and the description Mobius gave him was no exaggeration, "What a knock out, no way any man wouldn't take a chance to get to know her better" Gregory thought.

After checking her ID, Gregory said "Susan, I'm Gregory MacNee, I'm glad you could make it on such short notice. How much of the operation did Mobius go over with you?"

"It's good to be working with you Gregory. Actually Mobius just told me that it was important that I get here right away and report to you". Susan said.

"Ok, here is what we have going on. We have a British physicist, Dr. John Patterson, who was kidnapped in Austria a few days ago by two Russians. We don't know where they're holding him but it is imperative that we find him and extract him quickly. We believe he'll be taken to the Middle East and forced to work for a radical Islamic terror group". Gregory said.

"I see, so where do I come in?" Susan asked

"We have a lead on one of the Russians, Gregor Delov, and have information that he drinks at a local bar here in Tempelhof. He shows up every other night or so, we think it's after his partner takes over watching Patterson.

CIA agents Matt West and John Waxman will be here in a few minutes and we'll go over the plan".

West and Waxman returned to the suite. "Susan, these gentlemen are CIA agents Matt West and John Waxman. Gentlemen, this is our agent Susan Jamison. She'll be assisting us with the plan to grab Delov." Gregory said.

"It's good to meet you Susan" Both of them said.

"So Susan, here is what we're planning. It seems that Delov goes drinking at the Tempelhof Bar about every other night. We're told Delov's drinking is increasing more and more and after he gets drunk he makes a play for the waitress. She doesn't like it at all and threatened to quit the last time. If he goes to the Tempelhof Bar tonight or tomorrow night and gets drunk, which seems to be his pattern, once he's drunk, you come on to him and invite him to come to your hotel. Matt and John will be in two separate cars parked at each end of the street and I'll be sitting at the back of the bar. Delov will think it's his lucky day. When you head for the hotel in his car they'll box him in and bang into the back of his car. Once he's stopped, jam him with this, it's a Ketamine derivative, and with the alcohol in his system he'll be unconscious instantly. Once he's out, we'll toss him into my Audi and you'll drive to Gatow Air Base. They'll have a plane ready to fly him back to London for an emergency de-brief. I'll get rid of his car and meet Matt and John back at the suite. Do you have any questions" Gregory asked.

"No, it sounds pretty straight forward to me, but what if he's not interested in me?" Susan asked with a grin.

"I'd say there's no bloody chance of that Susan" Gregory said.

About nine thirty, Gregory received a call from one of the German Special Section agent, named Ralph Weisman, who was working undercover at the Tempelhof Bar to say that Delov had just shown up.

"It's show time folks" Gregory said. "Matt, you and John head over and take up positions that can't be blocked with a clear view of the parking area, and Delov's Opel. Susan and I'll head over shortly and go in separately. The weather is getting really bad but that should play in our favor. It's raining so hard Delov won't be in a hurry to leave, also very few people, if any will be out in it, so no one will see when we move on him.

The rain was coming down in sheets now, with strong wind gusts as they were driving to the Tempelhof Bar. The River had turned into a torrent of muddy water,with large waves churning into brown foaming spray against the legs of the bridge. Gregory said to Susan "This could be the answer we're looking for, making it look like Delov crashed and was swept away. We can't let them know we have him or the games up."

They arrived at the Tempelhof Bar a bit after ten and Gregory went in through the kitchen's back door. The cooks gave him an unwelcoming look so he said "Sorry gentlemen, it's raining so hard I'd have been soaked running from the parking lot to the front". They just went back to work, so Gregory made his way through the kitchen door into the back of the bar, taking a seat in the far corner with an unobstructed view of the room unseen by Delov. In a few minutes the German agent Weisman, dressed as a waiter, came over to take his order.

"Our boy's at the table on the far right with his back to the wall, I suppose so no one can come up behind him. He's on his third large vodka now. He came in alone, but there was a dark skinned guy, could be Middle Eastern, who came in, looked around for a minute then left without sitting down. He didn't match the photo of your man Imaad, but he could be keeping an eye on Delov." Weisman said.

"We have an agent, Susan Jamison, coming in to pick up on Delov and get him to take her back to her hotel. When they leave we'll pick him up on the road.

We're not expecting any trouble with this operation, but I assume you're armed just in case things turn ugly" Gregory said.

"No problem, the bartender is one of our men, as well as one of the cooks.

We wanted the place covered on all sides, not knowing how many of the opposition are about" Weisman said.

Susan Jamison arrived twenty minutes later and took a seat at the bar, where she ordered a glass of the local Riesling. Dressed in a form fitting dark blue business suit, even windblown from the storm, she managed to look very attractive indeed. Delov took notice as soon as she removed her rain coat. He made short work of his third vodka and came to the bar next to Susan and ordered another.

Smiling at her he said, "Nasty night to be out and about"

"It sure is. I wish I was back at my hotel warm and dry" Susan said.

"What brings you out in such awful weather? Delov asked

"I was at a business meeting next door and my ride's late,so I thought I'd duck in here and have a drink while I wait. I hope she gets here soon, I'm really tired" Susan said with an exasperated look.

"I'm Gregor," he said extending his hand, "and you are?"

"My name is Susan; it's nice to meet you Gregor"

"It's nice to meet you as well Susan. So what business brings you to Templehof?" Delov asked.

"I'm a structural engineer working for The Finland Maritime Commission based in Helsinki. I'm here to look over the plans for a new pier and warehouse they're planning at the Port of Tempelhof."

"Ah, so you're Finnish then" he said with a look of surprise. "You sounded more British" Delov said with a smile

"Yes I'm Finnish. I was born in the village of Vantaa, but was educated in England, and went to graduate school in St. Petersburg."

"What a small world. I attended the N.G. Kuznetsov Naval Academy in St. Petersburg, and then did six years with the Northern Fleet." Delov explained.

"Interesting, are you still in the Navy?"

"No, I left a couple years ago. The Soviet Navy is downsizing, and the prospects for promotion were getting rather small. I decided to move into the commercial shipping business. More money and better hours" Delov said with a laugh.

"So what brings you to Templehof?" Susan asked.

"One of our bulk container ships is making its first visit here in a few days and the company wanted one of their executives here when she arrives. I'm only here for a few days." Delov said, lying smoothly.

Signaling the bartender, Delov ordered vodka and asked "would you like another Susan?"

"Why yes I would. That's very kind of you".

"Bring us another round he told the bartender"

"So, are you staying in Templehof long Susan?"

"About another week then I'll go back to Helsinki." Their drinks came and Susan said. "Thank you Gregor, after I've finished this, I really need to get back to my hotel and have some dinner. I haven't eaten since breakfast, and the food here is awful. I suppose I'll have to walk if my friend doesn't show up."

"After we finish our drinks, I can drive you to your hotel if your ride hasn't arrived, and perhaps we could have dinner together. I haven't eaten all day either, and I agree with you about the food here. It's bad even by German standards" He said with a laugh.

"That sounds fine. The food at my hotel is somewhat basic, but good quality and generous portions" Susan said with a smile.

They finished their drinks, and after buttoning up their rain coats tightly they headed for the door.

"They're on their way" Gregory told West and Waxman by a small radio he had concealed in his coat.

West and Waxman started their engines keeping their headlights off and peered through the driving rain at Delov's Opel.

Gregory went quickly through the kitchen and moved the Audi into position to come along side Delov's car when West and Waxman made their move.

Running through the pouring rain Susan and Delov jumped into his Opel. Moments later they were on the move towards the bridge.

"Man, this weather's a bitch to drive through. I can just barely see where I'm going. You'd have been soaked to the skin trying to walk back to your hotel in this". Delov said.

"That's the truth. I really do appreciate the lift Gregor."Susan said feeling for the syringe with the Ketamine.

West pulled out driving very slowly with his lights out in front of Delov with Waxman coming up from behind.

Delov, in his haste to get back to Susan's hotel, didn't see West's car through the driving rain with no lights until he was too close to stop on the slick roadway. He jammed on the brakes but skidded into the back of West. Waxman came within inches of Delov's car with his horn blaring, boxing him in tight.

"Stupid son of a bitch!" Delov roared as his car hit West.

"Delov shoved the car into reverse but Waxman was already too close behind him to move. Delov put the car in park and was about to open the door when Susan jammed the syringe into his neck. He never got the chance to turn his head to look at her before he passed out.

West jumped out of his car and ran to the driver's side of Delov's car just as Gregory's Audi arrived next to him. Waxman reversed his car and parked on the side of the road then hopped into West's car driving it away. Gregory and West muscled Delov's unconscious bulk into the back of the Audi where Susan was at the wheel. West climbed in the back with Delov and they headed for Gatow air base as fast as the weather would allow.

Gregory drove Delov's Opel to the end of the road. He got out with the car in neutral, and put a weight on the accelerator. With the engine roaring Gregory pushed the gear selector into drive. The car lurched forward picking up speed fast as it crashed through the barricade at the end of the road into the fast moving river. The car was gone in an instant, tumbling along with the torrent the river had become, bouncing off the rocky shore, then simply disappearing beneath the muddy brown water.

Gregory ran back to Waxman's car and drove back to the underground car park at his hotel. Arriving at the suite from the garage elevator, dripping wet, he immediately phoned the base commander at Gatow and asked him to please let the special RAF transport pilots know their passenger would be arriving momentarily and to give them immediate clearance to take off.

The Gatow main gate had been alerted that a large black Audi with Susan at the wheel would be arriving, and to send them to executive terminal number one without delay. The Special Air Services Lockheed C130 Hercules had its engines running and Susan drove right up to the rear ramp. Two large SAS men carried the still unconscious Delov up the ramp like he weighed nothing, and strapped him onto one of the hard aluminum benches in the cavernous interior. The rear loading ramp was closing as Susan strapped into one of the officers seats up forward. Within moments the giant transport was airborne and on the way to RAF Waddington, where the MI6 interrogation team was waiting. West drove back to the hotel through the driving rain and met the rest of the team in the suite where Gregory was on the phone with Schumacher explaining what they needed next.

"Han's, please have the local news report that Delov was involved in an accident and was washed down river with little chance of survival. Make sure the print and TV news have the story so Garin, Imaad and whoever else in involved in this think it was a traffic accident and that Delov is dead." Gregory told Schumacher.

"Consider it done. I'll make sure the major papers and news channels get the story right away. So Delov is on his way to London?" Schumacher asked.

"Yeah, our team will have him in less than two hours. Please make sure your guys keep watch on that Mosque. Your agents at the Templeof Bar said there was a Middle Eastern guy who came in, looked around and left after Delov came in and may have been keeping an eye on Delov. If Imaad is using the Mosque, he'll be back and we can track him. Also, please assemble a heavily armed special opps team to assist in extracting Patterson when we find him. If things get nasty, we'll need the support". Gregory said.

"I'll get on to the Commander of the KSK 3rd Commando Company to put together a special team, and alert the elite

64th Helicopter Wing that their services may be required."
Schumacher told him.

"That sounds good Hans. Thanks for all the help" Gregory said.

Hanging up the phone and turning to West and Waxman, Gregory said, "Nice work tonight guys, went like clockwork. Let's try to get a few hours shuteye while the team in London does their thing."

The next morning'sTempelhof Tribune carried the following story, as requested by the German Secret Service and Templehof Police Special Branch.

"Late last night during the worst part of the storm, a Russian citizen, believed to be Mr. Gregor Delov, of St. Petersburg was involved in a traffic accident, crashing through the barricade at the river end of Colditzstrabe and into the river. Mr. Delov is reported to have left the Tempelhof Bar about midnight with an as yet unidentified female tourist from Finland, and apparently lost control of the vehicle and crashed through the barricade just a few minutes later. The vehicle was swept away in the fast moving river coming to rest against the Templehof bridge pilings. It appears that alcohol may have been a contributing factor in the crash. No attempt can be made to recover what remains of the vehicle or search for bodies until the river subsides. Any hope that the vehicles occupants survived is slim".

That afternoon Imaam came to the safe house furious. "That stupid drunken son of a bitch partner of yours killed himself with some whore from a God cursed bar last night. What the hell are you two asshole Russians thinking, going drinking and whoring when you're involved in such a project as this. Even for Russians, this is beyond stupid and irresponsible." Imaam raged at Garin waving the newspaper in his face.

Garin stood toe to toe with Imaam, his fists bunched, shaking with rage and said, "You take it easy and watch your goddamn mouth Imaam. Talk to me like that again and I'll kill you where you stand, and sell this Limey asshole to another shithead terrorist group. Any of your psycho brothers will pay just as much for him. So you just settle down".

Realizing he had gone too far Imaam took an apologetic attitude saying,

"You have a most explosive temper Garin, but you're right and I apologize for my outburst. I was just very upset. It's unfortunate that Delov was killed, but you have to admit it showed very poor judgment on his part doing what he did in light of the importance of this project and that amount of money you both were going to make"

Calming down as fast as he was enraged, Garin said "Gregor was an ass to go drinking just before the completion of this project. I know he wouldn't have said anything to anyone about it, so we're still on track. It's just more money for me at the end of the day. I never really thought he had the guts for this type of work, but he had some good connections. I'll need to get on to Moscow right away with the news and see if they want to make any changes."

"My superiors will accept no changes at this late date. The plan will go ahead just as we planned". Imaam said.

CHAPTER TEN

Moscow

Major General Nikolay Vitsin arrived at his third floor office in the Kremlin late this morning and now stood staring at the brown waters of the Moskva River, feeling unusually nervous and ill at ease. Watching the flowing water of the Moskva always helped him think. He usually moved with a straight forwardness and command that was obvious to anyone seeing him. This morning however he felt that his world could come crashing down in an instant. Early this morning he had received a coded message from his deep cover operative, Anatoly Garin, through his covert contact at the Council of Ministers, Paval Orlov , that Gregor Delov had apparently been killed in a traffic accident with an unidentified Finnish woman the previous night. General Vitsin had spent a decade building his secret organization, and it was about to pay off in a very big way. His Ophidian operation to kidnap and sell a nuclear physicist to a Middle Eastern terror group, code name Narusheniye, (disruption) would make Vitsin very rich and cause continued chaos in the West. If the KGB or GRU had even a hint that he was involved in an operation of this sort, without the Kremlin's knowledge and approval, he would be disgraced and executed in very short order. He knew however, that if Narusheniye was successful, the Chairman of the Presidium of the Supreme Soviet would officially chastise him, but privately congratulate him on his ingenuity and for the chaos Narusheniye would cause in Western Europe and the USA. With the financial markets in the West in utter chaos, Russia's economic problems would be solved in one quick stroke. The Presidium would overlook the money General Vistin would have from the project, and he would be free to enjoy all he had ever wanted. Narusheniye must not fail.

General Vistin was thinking, "Now I'm working in the Kremlin. The Kremlin is the most profoundly paranoid place to work on earth. The KGB and GRU are organizations imbued with a siege mentality born of decades of propaganda, secrecy and fear. Even though we're told the KGB is a mere shadow of its former self since the wall came down, only a fool would believe it. Then there's Directorate "K", they take paranoia to a whole new level. They suspect everyone of being a traitor and enemy of the state. I must be very careful". He knew every office was bugged and the KGB watchers were always near.

Because of the risk of discovery, and the catastrophic results to him personally if he were discovered, he had over the years developed an elaborate escape plan that could be put into operation within hours, but it was a last resort and would be final. Once executed, there would be no coming back to Russia. Ophidian had covertly supplied the Crescent Moon Shipping Line enough money to keep an Iranian flagged tanker in operation, and used its influence to get the company lucrative deals transporting oil from ports in Saudi Arabia to Guangzhou China and ports along the Baltic. This arrangement made the shipping company's owner Farzad Ahmadi, very wealthy, and he owed everything to Ophidian. If the day came that Vistin needed to escape, he would contact Farzad Ahmadi and tell him a favor was needed. He would tell Ahmadi that Ophidian would be sending an agent in two days to his office in Bandar-e Abbas to let him know what was required. The agent would tell

Ahmadi that Ophidian had an agent that needed to disappear for a year or so, and that they wanted this agent to be made procurement officer on their tanker, *Emperor of the East,* which Ophidian had paid for. The agent would work aboard the ship for the next eight months to a year, and that the ship's captain Bijan Shah, was to treat him as he would any officer aboard his ship and ask no questions. The Ophidian agent would rendezvous with the *Emperor of the East* at the port of Ystad in Sweden. Vistin would board the ship and sail the oceans under an assumed name, letting his beard grow, trimming it in the Iranian style for the next eight months to a year, then leave the ship in Guangzhou and fly to France with false papers. Vistin already spoke English and Farsi so he would fit in. The plan was as good as it could get, and knowing he had an escape plan ready to activate helped him settle down and carry on.

Taking his scrambler with him he walked to Saint Basil's church in Red Square and phoned his secret operative, Paval Orlov, and told him to be at the usual meeting place at twelve forty five.

Paval Orlov arrived at the small café on the promenade along the Moskva at twelve thirty and took a table in the back. The lunch crowd was thinning out, and General Vistin walked in at precisely twelve forty five and took a seat at Orlov's table saying in a low voice, "Paval what the hell is happening. First your two operatives are killed in Italy, by what is being reported as a Mafia hit, costing us the casino financing operation that we've worked hard to acquire.

Luckily our man went to Dragos villa and secured the money Drago was supposed to turn over to us, so that was not a total loss. But now I'm informed that we're having issues in Berlin with another of your choice of operatives, Delov".

Orlov said "Nikolay, Garin reported that Delov was apparently killed in a car crash late last night. Delov was an ass to be drinking and womanizing with so much at stake, but Garin is certain that he would not have discussed any part of the mission with any-one. They're saying that he was apparently killed, due to the severe storm the river is far too rough to recover the bodies, but there seems to be no chance anyone could have survived the crash".

Still speaking in low conspiratorial tones, General Vitsin said, "I want you to find out who the woman was. Was she really just a tourist picked up in a bar or could she be a spy. If she was an agent there to spy on the ass Delov, then someone knows about Narusheniye and we need to complete it and get out fast. If the KGB or GRU get any ideas about this we're finished".

"You're right of course Nikolay, I'll get some people to check it out right away. Can we move up the time table if needed"? Paval asked.

"I don't know, three hundred million Euros is difficult to raise and move even for these groups. Things are moving about a fast as its safe. If that much cash moves to quickly someone's bound to notice it". Vitsin said.

Paval Orlov stood hanging on to the strap in the crowded carriage of the Moscow Metro Central line returning to his office thinking, "I should have never gotten involved with Ophidian and Vistin's crazy plans. I'd only seen the wealth I would attain and the power and privilege that wealth would give me". His father had been a good party member and served with distinction during the war, but those things did not lead to wealth and luxury in the Soviet Union. Life at home with four brothers and two sisters had been hard. Both his mother and father had worked twelve hour days at the Volga factory in order to feed their family. When he was fourteen his father died of lung cancer so Paval had to work days and complete his education at night. After graduation he had used his father's contacts from his Army days to help secure a minor position on the Council of Ministers. Through hard work and dedication to the party he had moved up to his middle executive level. The job was considered to be a good one in the Soviet Union and came with some nice benefits, however he wanted more than a job at the Council would ever provide.

He wanted the fast cars, big homes and beautiful women that the wealthy men enjoyed, so when he was approached by one of General Vistin's agents he jumped at the chance. Now he realized what a foolish thing it is to be motivated by wealth alone, never giving the consequences a second thought. If the General's hair brained scheme went wrong, the KGB would take him away before he could run and his life would be over. Not just professionally but literally over, he would be shot.

Arriving back in his office Orlov sent a coded message to Borya Sokolov, one of the Generals top assassins, telling him to go at once to Tempelhof and back up Garin on the transfer of Petterson to The Islamic Brotherhood for Jihad group. Borya had been with the General when they were fighting in Afghanistan and was his top sniper. Since those days Borya had removed targets for Vistin from time to time making a nice living doing so.

The coded message said, "Borya, the Boss said you're needed in Templehof as soon as you can get there. Get close to Garin at the warehouse by the Templehof Cemetery. Find a vantage point so you can observe the warehouse, but don't let Garin know you're there. Contact our usual supplier for equipment in Berlin and await further instructions."

Borya responded to the message saying "I'll be on my way within the hour and will contact our man in Berlin for any additional supplies I may need"

General Vistin stood looking at the Moskva, but not seeing it. He was going over in his mind the escape plan he had worked out before Narusheniye had begun. He had worked out a plan to get out of Russia and away from the KGB if things did go wrong and his association with Ophidian was discovered. Over the past ten years he had secretly moved millions of Euros into numbered Swiss accounts owned by multiple shell corporations, as well as numbered accounts in Aruba that were ultimately owned by Ophidian and Vistin. Recently he had been buying rare artworks using agents to move some of the cash into other untraceable assets that were easily moved and hidden in case things went wrong and he had to flee Russia quickly.

What he would make from Narusheniye, would increase his wealth by at least twenty times setting him up for the life of luxury he wanted. He felt that it would still work if the fool Delov hadn't said anything to the woman. The General decided then and there that once the operation was completed, Garin would die screaming for his choice of Delov whether the operation was successful or not. The man had put Nikolay's entire future a risk because of his stupidity and for that he would pay dearly.

CHAPTER ELEVEN

Berlin

Dr. John Patterson was the classic wunderkind. School was a breeze, with acceptance to Oxford University with full scholarships assured at an early age. Patterson's father was of the lower class, a delivery driver who worked sometimes, drank far too much and was terminally short of money. His mother, Kate Patterson, having had enough of her husband's drinking, womanizing and the endless financial problems ran away with a rich American oil man never to be heard from again. Growing up poor, Patterson always resented the upper classes and felt that they made a point of keeping his type in their place. During his time at Oxford he made friends easily but still held his disdain for their wealth and position. He had never had much luck with the young women he met at school; they all seemed to know where he came from and wanted little to do with him. John Patterson was the perfect candidate for the communist movement popular at Universities in those days. He hated and resented those of the upper class and felt that working men must bind together to end the injustice of the upper classes.

After graduation he attended The Massachusetts Institute of Technology, known just as MIT, in America on a scholarship to complete his Doctorate in Nuclear Physics and found that the same class system existed in the Ivy League colleges and political system in America as in Briton.

Life was easy for the wealthy and connected while the rest of the working class struggled just too put food on the table. He felt that somehow he could effect change in this corrupt and unfair system. Harboring these feelings he was easily recruited by Anatoly Garin. Garin had promised that the Communist workers party could use his genius to help the working man take control and assure a better world for all. Patterson had bought into the whole dream of the communist utopia. He had been in secret contact with Garinfor years giving him new technological secrets to help the cause he so deeply believed in while keeping his involvement with the Communist a total secret from all his friends and working associates.

Though this double life was sometimes difficult, he also found it exciting at times feeling like a secret agent in the cinema. Several months ago Garin had convinced Patterson to move over to the Soviet Union permanently.

"Anatoly, the British Government will never grant me permission to relocate to the Soviet Union due to the nature of my work for them." Patterson had told Garin.

"Not to worry my friend, we have already considered this and have devised a plan that you would appear to have been kidnapped while on vacation. We would move you into a nice Moscow suburb where you will continue your work for the cause". Garin told him.

Patterson went along willingly, but during what he thought was a staged kidnapping by his fraternal communist brothers, his friends had been shot and he now found himself manacled to a steel frame bed, in a filthy dark room, drugged gagged and being sold like a slave to Mid-Eastern Terrorist where his genius would be exploited and used to kill hundreds of thousands of innocent hard working people around the world for a cause he did not believe in.

"My God what a fool I've been. The Communist dream I was

sold was just a lie, easily thrown away by Garin and others to make
themselves rich and allow them to become part of the hated upper
class at the cost of thousands of lives. If I can find a way to escape
and get back to Briton, I'm sure I can negotiate a way to stay out of
prison for treason, they need what I know. But for the first time, I
feel totally helpless and can see no way to escape, but somehow I
must find a way, and soon".

Less than twenty six hours had passed before Mobius contacted
Gregory through a secured line at MI6 station "B" Berlin.

"Gregory, the interrogation team has been sweating Delov
nonstop since he got here and he's singing like a bird. He was
recruited into an organization called Ophidian when he was released from prison. Said he was desperate for money and when
they offered him a sizeable amount for a simple job he jumped on
it. He told us that Patterson is being held in an old abandon warehouse on Gradestrabe, at the far North East end of the Templehof
Cemetery on the second floor. It seems that Patterson's to be delivered to the terrorist group, he thinks is The Islamic Brotherhood
for Jihad, early this Monday once the funds are confirmed in an
account in Aurba. Garin is in control of the operation so Delov's
not really sure who is buying Patterson, but he's heard The Islamic
Brotherhood for Jihad mentioned in discussions between Garin
and Imaam. The mosque is a meeting place and information drop
for the terrorist as you suspected. Also, Imaam suspects one of
your team of being a spy. Delov's not sure which one of the team,
but the description Delov overheard fits the CIA man Waxman"
Mobius told him.

"Shit, I was afraid that he might have been compromised by
asking questions at the mosque. We'll have to watch our backs very
closely" Gregory said.

Mobius continued, "Also, as we suspected, Delov said the

operation is being run by a Mr. Big but doesn't know who he is. He continues to tell us he's just a little fish, hired muscle, just signed on for the money because he was broke after getting out of prison. Claims he had no idea that the kidnapping was related to terrorist and was drinking to calm his nerves. He said he wanted out, but there was no way to get out. He said that he suspects the man at the top of Ophidian is a heavy weight in the Russian military machine and will kill anyone trying to defect from his organization. I'm having some of our people in Moscow see if they can get more information on this Ophidian organization.

"I thought this was too big for these two, and this Ophidian had to have been running the Russians in Italy as well. I'm working with the German Secret Service to put an assault team together to rescue Patterson. We'll be ready in 36 hours. Gregory told Mobius.

"Ok Gregory, you'll have overall command of this operation and make sure the Germans are well briefed. Let me know soon if you need any specialist to add to your team. It's bound to be tricky and we want to get Patterson out alive and well. Good Luck" Mobius said.

Disconnecting the encryption machine, making the phone line secure, Gregory briefed the CIA men on what Mobius had told him.

"First of all John, Delov told the interrogators that Imaam suspects you of being a spy. He was listening to your conversation at the mosque and didn't buy your cover of a friend from the old country. He has one of his men looking into who you are. You'll need to watch your back very closely.

"I had a feeling that the guys pretending to be praying were part of this deal. I'll watch my back and stay in the shadows so we don't blow the whole operation." Waxman said.

"Good, now Delov has been singing and said that they're

holding Patterson on the second floor of an old warehouse at the North East end of the Templefhof Cemetery. Their planning to deliver him to The Islamic Brotherhood for Jihad this Monday morning so we need to move quickly. Let's get together with the Germans and put a plan of action together this afternoon". Gregory told West and Waxman.

"Langley wants to have a special strike team in on the recovery to back us up. They said we could have a team here in the morning from the Special Forces Clandestine Warfare Operations unit stationed just outside Berlin". West said.

"I understand what CIA wants Matt, MI6 wanted to put a SAS team in as well, but I've decided to keep this a tight operation with just the three of us and the Germans. This is their back yard; they know every street and ally. If we have teams from CIA and MI6 as well, we'll lose logistical control, too many cooks as it were. Also, we don't have time for the CIA, SAS teams and the Germans to train together. No, let's keep the tight team that we have here now." Gregory said.

West said, "I agree Gregory. Langley won't like it but, with too many guys coming in it's bound to go wrong."

Gregory phoned Schumacher and set up the meeting with his men and the German Special Forces commander for just after noon.

Schumacher and Lt. Colonel Markos Weir met with Gregory and the CIA men in Schumacher's private conference room at the Chausseestrabe HQ.Gregory explained what was reported to Mobius by the interrogation team and laid out the situation to both Schumacher and Colonel Wier.

"Gentlemen, we need a team to begin round the clock surveillance of the warehouse immediately. We need to know who's there as well as whose coming and going, also we'll need complete surveillance of the mosque. Since they're using the mosque as a meeting place and information drop for The Islamic Brotherhood for Jihad people, we need to know everything going on there. Delov said that they're holding Patterson at the warehouse but we don't know how many terrorist fighters they may have there now or how many their planning to bring in for the transfer Monday. We also don't how heavily armed they are. We have to make our move no later than very early Sunday morning which doesn't give us much time to prepare. I think we need to find a way to isolate that mosque. It's too difficult to watch the mosque and the warehouse at the same time. There is no way for us to go in and search the place, the media and public wouldn't stand for a raid on a house of God, no matter what we think is going on there. We'll need to find a legal way to close it down for a time at least". Gregory said.

"I have two agents watching the mosque now and they said there has been increased activity over the past few days. They haven't seen your man Imaam coming in or going out the front or back. We'll work with Colonel Weir's men and bring in special equipment at both locations beginning this evening. Colonel Weir is an expert in counter terrorism and his teams have handled this type operation many times. Colonel, what do you suggest should be done immediately?" Schumacher said.

Colonel Wier said, "For now we'll need to put men in the adjacent buildings and in vehicles around the warehouse and the mosque with a clear view of both. I'll have all the specialized surveillance equipment in place by two A.M. tomorrow morning. Han's can you secure court orders allowing us access to the buildings and permission for communications surveillance and wire taps by this evening?

"That's not a problem sir. I've spoken to the Prime Minister and explained the situation, due to the importance of this operation and her policy on terrorism she said she'll have the permissions we need in less than twenty minutes."

"Good, we'll put a tap on call communications. We'll also use listening devices and a new infrared camera system that can see heat signatures through most walls to see what's going on in the warehouse and mosque. I'll get together with my deputy commander and work out the logistics of the assault and the extraction plan for Patterson using Helios from the 64th." Weir told them.

Gregory said, "Colonel, we'll be working on the overall plan here all afternoon and will work out the details when we meet with you and your assault team first thing in the morning when your surveillance teams have collected some useful data. After we take the warehouse, neutralize Garin and whoever else is in the building and secure Patterson, we'll need a chopper to carry him to Gatow Air Base. We'll need a small fast chopper that could operate in the tight area around the warehouse.

Discussing their plan later in the day, Schumacher said, "I'll arrange an EC665 Tiger attack helicopter from the 64th. They're experts at this type flying and the EC665 Tiger is armored in case they take any small arms fire".

Gregory said, "After looking at this situation from all sides, I think we'll need a plan to take Patterson and neutralize the mosque at the same time. If we take the mosque first they may be able to alert Garin and they'll move Patterson at once. I'm sure they must have an escape route incase they're found out. If we take Patterson first the bad guys at the mosque will scatter to the four winds and you'll have terrorist lose in Berlin."

"I agree with you Gregory. We need to round up these guys or we could face a retaliatory strike later on." Schumacher said.

"Ok, we'll go back to the hotel and devise a plan to deal with both locations at once and meet back here in the morning" Gregory said.

"Gregory, you and Matt head back to the hotel and I'll drive over and check with the surveillance team watching the mosque to see if there've been any changes" Waxman said.

"Alright, see you in a bit" West said.

John Waxman was driving the black Audi a few blocks from the mosque when a bullet pierced the windscreen hitting him in the left shoulder. The car careened across the street crashing through the guard railing and sliding down an embankment. He pushed the door open and fell into the cold muddy water in the ditch badly hurt wondering what the hell had happened.

As he was dragging himself up the embankment Amir El Farhad walked slowly towards him. Waxman thought he was someone who saw the crash and was there to help. As he tried to speak to Amir, he saw him pull a gun from his pocket and point it at him. Rolling over slightly trying to get some cover, Waxman drew his Colt .45 automatic with his right hand taking Amir by surprise. Waxman fired an upward shot; the bullet entered Amir's throat an inch or so behind his chin and proceeded upward. The top of Amir's head exploded upward in a volcano of blood and bone. His body jerked backward and his finger on the trigger of his own gun pulled, firing the weapon striking Waxman in the leg. Amir's corpse fell forward crashing over Waxman covering him in blood and dirt on the way to the bottom of the ravine. Waxman was totally disoriented from his wounds and the impact of Amir's body but was still trying to crawl up the muddy embankment. The last thing he heard was people shouting and the scream of sirens.

Back in the suite Gregory and West discussed what would be the best course of action to deal with both the mosque and the warehouse.

"We could just hit both locations with assault teams and take them all at once. We'll work our way into the warehouse when they're sleeping and just take them before they can react. Once in position, when the guys watching with infrared cameras give us the go we move in." West said.

"That may work on the warehouse, in fact I think it's the only way to get Patterson, but we need something more subtle on the mosque. We have the problem of the public opinion on raiding places of worship to consider.

I've been thinking of something along the lines of an emergency evacuations and search for health and safety reasons. That would get us inside alone but not look like law enforcement is involved except to protect the people." Gregory said.

"Ok, but what type emergency could we use. These guys are harboring terrorist so they won't be receptive to anything like water main breakage or electrical issues. In fact, I can't think of anything that would persuade them to open up except if the place was on fire, and I don't think we could get away with torching it." West said.

"A few years ago we needed to get into the Russian embassy in Istanbul and have a look around and there was no way the Russians would let that happen. Our team came up with a device that would emit foul smelling odor that could be introduced through the ventilation system and gave everyone a very bad headache and stomach problems.

The embassy was closed for three days and we sent in HAZMAT teams to check for bio hazards before certifying the building safe. It worked very well. It was a simple device and I can have Mobius get some to me by tonight.

We can add a non-lethal nerve agent to simulate something serious. This stuff will cause difficulty breathing and extreme headache and nausea and body aches. The nerve agent takes effect almost instantly and the effects will last twenty four hours or

longer so everyone there would be hospitalized and held for observation. There's no long term ill effect to the nerve agent but they'll
think their dying."Gregory explained.

"Right, that should handle the mosque. Now, as to the warehouse, we can put a team together with the Germans and quietly
infiltrate the building. Once the surveillance team gives us the green
light, we'll toss in some flash bang grenades and using night vision
equipment we'll take out the bad guys and bring the good Doctor
home. We can get some of the new silenced SMG9-SC 9mm from
our station in Berlin. Are you familiar with the SMG9 ?" West asked.

"Yes, I've done some training with that weapon and can handle it well. It's a fine weapon for close in fighting" Gregory said.

"Good, both John and I have extensive training with the SMG9
so that's set. We'll work out the final details with Schumacher and
Wier in the morning and go over the plans with John when he gets
back." Gregory said.

Later that night Gregory received a call from Schumacher
who told him "I've just received a phone call from the local police telling me the CIA man Waxman has been in a crash. They
said he's apparently been shot and is in Templeof General Hospital
Intensive Care Unit."

"What's his condition?" Gregory asked.

"Stable at the moment though he's lost a lot of blood and
one of the bullets shattered his right femur just above the knee".
Schumacher told him.

"I'll get West and we'll meet you at the hospital" Gregory said.

"I've ordered a car to pick you up; they should be down stairs
now. I'll see you at the hospital" Schumacher told him

"Gregory went to West's room and told him, "Schumacher just
phoned and said John's been shot and is in the Templeof Hospital
ICU. There's a car waiting down stairs, let's go".

"Son of a Bitch", West said grabbing his jacket and heading out the door. I knew it was a bad idea for him to go to that damn mosque as an old friend.

When they arrived at Templehof Hospital, the doctor on duty told them "One bullet entered Waxman's left shoulder striking the Glenohumeral joint fracturing it and ricocheted upward cracking the left Clavicle before exiting just missing his head. The second bullet moved downward shattering his left femur just above the knee. He's lost a lot of blood and has a mild concussion from an impact to the left side of his head; probably hit the door frame on the car during the crash. His condition is serious but not life threatening."

West asked, "Is he awake and can we talk to him"?

"He's groggy and on medication for the pain, but you can speak to him for just a few minutes then he's going to surgery".

Showing the doctor his I.D. Schumacher said, "Doctor, this is a security matter and cannot be discussed with anyone, particularly the press. Is that clearly understood?

"Yes sir, I understand and I'll instruct the staff not to discuss it or allow anyone in the room."

They went into the room and West said, "John, it's Matt, you're going to be alright. You're a little shot up but nothing that won't heal. We'll be sending you home as soon as you're able. That was a nice bit of shooting, an amazing shot, killed the bastard before he knew what hit him. Did you recognize the guy?"

In a weak voice Waxman told him "I didn't get a real good look at his face, it all happened so fast, but I'm sure he was one of the men pretending to pray at the mosque the other day when I was talking to the Imam."

"That's what we figured John. You rest now; we'll be working with the Germans to take care of these assholes so I won't be able to see you until we're back in the States. Take care buddy" West said.

When they had left the ICU, Gregory asked, "Do we have any ID on the shooter Hans?"

"The ID found on the body is for Amir El Farhad. We ran him through our computer and Interpol's, Farhad is thirty five years old, a lorry driver, moved to Germany from Iran with his family ten years ago. Minor scrapes with the law but nothing major. Speeding tickets, a few fights nothing more. No record of criminal activity with Interpol or known contact with any terrorist group". Schumacher said.

"Has he left Germany recently or in the past few years?"

"Yes, his wife's mother died two months ago, and they went back to Iran with his two kids for the funeral. He came back to Germany but his wife and kids stayed there. Seems she hated it in Germany so she left him. At this point that's all we have been able to find out."

"Alright, we'll check with MI6 and CIA to see what other connections he may have. For now we need to get back and meet with Colonel Wier.

"Ok, sounds good. Waxman is in good hands and I'm having a guard posted on the door to make sure no one gets in. See you back at the office in a couple hours." Schumacher said.

Gregory returned to the suite and hooked up the encryption devise and phoned Mobius. "The CIA man Waxman has been shot and is in the hospital in ICU. It appears one of the men from the mosque; Amir El Farhad, fingered him as an agent and shot him through the windscreen of the car he was driving. Waxman killed El Farhad but he's heading back to the U.S. due to his injuries. I'll need replacements fast. Are Connell Baines and Byron Hill available"? Gregory asked.

"I'll get them on a plane within two hours and they'll be there by mid-morning. Do they need to bring any special equipment with them" Mobius asked.

"Yes, have them bring some of the ZX4M gas projectiles, the kind that we used in Istanbul a couple years ago on the Russian Embassy and some R42 nerve agent to use on the mosque. Also, we'll be using SMG9-SC 9mms and the new M84 flash bang grenades in the extraction, plus anything else they feel may come in handy. With Waxman getting shot we have to assume Garin and his teams have been warned that agents are here in Templehof. We need to move quickly so they don't move Patterson. If they're handing him over to The Islamic Brotherhood for Jihad Sunday we would have a damn hard time finding him again and grabbing him before the hand off. We might have to take him on the move and odds are good they'd kill him."

"We'll get moving straight away. Let me know if you need anything else.

Keep me informed and watch your back" Mobius said

Gregory contacted the surveillance team watching the warehouse and gave them an update on the Waxman shooting. "Have you noticed any unusual activity in the warehouse in the last few hours"?

"No sir, things seem to be much the same as they have been, three people moving about and the forth still in the room apparently manacled to the bed." Captain Weidig said.

"Very well, keep a very sharp eye on them and the area, if there are any changes in routine contact me instantly" Gregory told him.

"Will do sir".

Not ten minutes after Gregory got back to his suite, he got another phone call from Schumacher who said, "I just received a report from the team watching the mosque. They had the infrared cameras looking through the walls at the mosque and activity has increased quite a bit. Boxes have been brought in from a rear door showing metallic signatures and there are five individuals there now in the middle of the night".

"Got it, things seem to be heating up a bit. See you in a couple hours."" Gregory said.

During the night Borya Sokolov had moved into an abandoned fourth floor apartment with a good view of the warehouse and surrounding area where Garin was holding Patterson. Contacting Paval Orlov, Borya said "I'm in a good position to watch both the warehouse and the surrounding area. I visited our man in Berlin and picked up the tools I'll need."

"Very well Orlov said, I'll contact you when the funds have been received. When that happens you know what the General wants you to do."

Borya had picked up a Dragunov SVDS Sniper Rifle with a 1 PN58 Night Vision Scope and some 7N1 steel jacketed sniper rounds just in case any of the targets were using body armor. His mission was to back up Garin until the transfer then bring him back to the General. General Vistin wanted to watch Garin die slowly and painfully for his stupidly; however, if it looked as though Garin would escape, he was to kill him. "Nothing to do now but watch and wait" Borya thought.

At the morning meeting in the conference room in Chausseestrabe, they went over the plans with Schumacher and Colonel Wier.

Gregory said, "This is what we're thinking will work at the mosque so we could inspect inside and seal it up so nobody can get in and not have a public outcry. We have a device that we can run through the gas pipe that will block the flow of gas and then crack the pipe without making a spark once it's inside the mosque. The gas will be blocked to make sure the danger of fire is removed but the device will emit a strong odor of gas that will fill all the rooms. There's a non-lethal nerve agent we'll add to make the people inside the mosque quite ill, severe headache, muscle spasms, difficulty breathing, all simulating a real gas leak but won't have any lasting effect.

Then we can use the local police and fire department to immediately evacuate the mosque and seal it off until the leak can be found and repaired. We'd be moving fast and they would have no time to move their equipment out or go back inside to get it. Once they're evacuated and taken to hospital, we can have the mosque sealed until repairs have been made and it's been declared safe. This should essentially take them out of the game".

"I'll get on to the Police Chief, Fire Chief and Gas Company to set it up. Could we use the same scenario on the warehouse? "Schumacher asked.

"I don't think so Hans, they may have gas masks in the warehouse because they may be ready for an assault from the police using gas. The attempt on John's life proves that, at lease the terrorist think they've been discovered. No, we've worked another angle on the warehouse." Gregory said.

"I agree Gregory; our surveillance team is set up in an adjacent building and has been watching with infrared cameras. There are four individuals in the warehouse, three are moving about and the forth seems isolated in a small room. We're assuming that would be your man Patterson. We have seen weapons on the three men moving about and several metallic signatures in the rooms indicating additional weapons. There's also a chemical signature that we assume are explosives." Colonel Weir explained.

"Colonel, we feel that Matt West of the CIA, me and two of my team from London, Connell Baines and Byron Hill, who'll replace John Waxman, along with a team of your best men can infiltrate the warehouse quietly and wait for the green light from your surveillance team. The bad guys must be sleeping in shift with at least one man on guard. When the others are sleeping we'll hit the room with flash bang grenades and using silenced SMG9s take out the heavies. I'd like to take Garin alive if possible so we could question him on the head of the organization running this thing." Gregory said.

"Ok, when are your men Baines and Hill arriving and how long will you need to bring them up to speed on the operation?" Weir asked

"They'll be here by 0730 this morning. We'll be going over the plan and checking all the equipment they've brought. I've worked with Baines and Hill on several operations and they're the best we have, it won't take long for them to be on point." Gregory said.

"Very well, I'll brief my men and be ready to move as soon as you give the word." Weir told him.

Gregory and West met Connell Baines and Byron Hill as they arrived on a special SAS transport at 0730 at Gatow Special Operations Center. "Connell, Byron this is Matt West with the CIA. Matt is a very experienced agent and USMC trained so he's a great guy to have on this extraction. We've been working this case together since the beginning and we're ready to move as soon as you're ready. Did you bring all the toys?" Gregory said.

"Got everything on your shopping list boss, plus a few extras Byron said. I brought a couple mini Uzi's with special heavy hitting rounds in case things get tight and we need some additional stopping power. I also have some C-4 just in case we need it, a few silhouette charges to help us with locked doors and night vision goggles. Do we need any heavy explosives on this job?" Byron asked.

"We don't think so; from what we've seen of the warehouse.

There don't appear to be any hardened doors or rooms and we want to take Patterson alive and un-harmed. Let's get moving, we'll bring you up to speed on the way and swing by the warehouse so you can get a bearing on the area of operation." Gregory told him.

Using a back stairwell unseen from the street, they when up to check in with Captain Weidig of surveillance team.

"Good morning gentleman, Gregory said, any new developments"?

"Glad you stopped by sir, we were about to give you a call. Three more men have taken up station on the floor below and forward of the targets. Their all armed and have been walking a patrols every forty minutes or so. Each man has a side arm and they have some heavy stuff in the room." Weidig told him.

"Have you seen them in the daylight, what do they look like?" West asked.

"Dark skinned and bearded sir, from the Mid-East I'd say. Could possibly be Italian, but look more Mid-Eastern."

"If they follow their recent movements they should make a patrol in about ten minutes sir." Weidig told them.

"I'm not really surprised. Since John was shot we know they're aware the law's looking for them. We'll stay here until they move and try to get a good look at them." Gregory said.

Right on time two of the men left the building leaving the third man to guard the staircase up to the next floor. Walking in different directions, both were dressed in dark gray and wore dark jackets which would hide their side arms. They were keeping a sharp eye on everything in the area and checking all the shadows. There was no doubt what they were there for.

"Yeah, I'd put them from Iran or Syria. I wonder how many more of these punks are somewhere close by." West said.

"We'll keep a close watch and get the routine down before your extraction and keep you well informed sir" Weidig told them.

***

Driving back to the hotel West said, "We'll take the new guys out as quietly as possible first but may have to move on both rooms at once".

"I think we should have a one of Wier's teams take the new guards at and at the same moment we'll take Garin and his playmates so we don't lose Patterson. Let's face it, even taking the guards quietly in an old building like that will make one hell of a racket and you know Garin will hear the action and be ready for trouble" Gregory said.

"Right, that works. We'll all move together." West, Hill and Baines agreed.

Arriving back at the suite, Gregory used the secure line to phone Mobius in London to give him an update on their situation.

"Connell and Byron are here with our equipment and we're ready to make our move at 0230 this morning. It looks like The Islamic Brotherhood for Jihad boys have brought reinforcements. They have at least three more fighters on station on the floor below Garin. We've decided to have the German Special Services guys deal with the new comers at the same moment we hit Garin's room. Take them all at once." Gregory told Mobius

"It sounds like your moving in the right direction and your method of isolating the mosque and the men inside is brilliant and should work well. Take them out and keep the press off our backs. Also, I wanted to tell you that we've heard from our people in Moscow and they said there are whispers about a criminal organization called Ophidian but there are not a lot of details at this time. We have some people inside the Kremlin trying to find out about it. I'm sure it's not an official Russian military organization, so someone is running a clandestine organization from within the military. He would have to be someone high up in their structure to operate without detection. We'll discuss it when you get back to London." Mobius said.

Disconnecting the secure line, Gregory told West, Hill and Baines, "London says they may have a line on this Ophidian. Matt, get on to Langley and see if the CIA has anybody inside the Kremlin who can verify what our spies are telling us about Ophidian and see if they know who the main man could be.

"Right, I'll go back to my room and shoot a message on the secure line right away. We must have someone in the Kremlin but I'm sure whoever is running this Ophidian has covered his tracks carefully or the KGB would've nailed him. I'll also have our people in Aruba check the bank computers for large transfers. These numbered accounts are supposed to be private but the current administration has a link to the banking systems computer to look for drug money." West said with a sarcastic grin.

An hour later, West returned and said "Langley says there's a private investment bank known as Banco de Aruba that's rumored to take large cash amounts from drug lords and the likes. They're checking to see if any large cash deals have come from Eastern Europe or Mother Russia. They also said one of our operatives has heard of Ophidian and said it was rumored to be headed by a Russian General, though they don't have a name.

"Good, that's a start on tracking down whoever is running this. For now let's get Patterson back." Gregory said.

That afternoon the surveillance team watching the mosque reported that there had been no further activity during the night but there were now six persons inside.

"Got it, we begin the operation at 0200 this morning. We'll be

moving so let us know instantly via radio if there is any change."
West told them.

"Roger that sir."

At 0200 Sunday morning Gregory's team, moving under the cover
of darkness, inserted the ZX4M gas projectiles loaded with the R42
nerve agent into the gas main on the street side of the mosque then
slipped away undetected and headed for the warehouse to join up
with Colonel Weir's teams. Ten minutes later the police and fire
department arrived in force surrounding the mosque banging on
the door until someone answered.

"We have a very dangerous gas leak in the area, possibly toxic
and everyone must evacuate the building immediately the Fire
Chief said pulling the man out of the door. How many others are
inside" he demanded,

The man looked pale and coughing said "There are five others
inside; at least one was overcome by the gas".

"You two men put on your gas masks and follow me. We have
others inside. Jon, get some ambulances down here. We have one
man unconscious and there may be more." The Chief shouted.

Within minutes all six men were outside with two unconscious and the others on the ground coughing and retching.

The Chief shouted to the police, "I want this area sealed off.
Move anyone well back and seal the building. No one goes near
this building until we have the gas shut off and cleared."

The German Special Branch team wearing gas masks, simply for cover, moved through the mosques. They went through
the large worship area with many prayer rugs spread out on the
floor and past the Minbar where the Imam delivers his sermon
and found a secret door leading to a small room. The door was
locked so they picked the lock. The team leader radioed "We've
found a large cache of weapons in a hidden back room and

boxes that may contain explosives. Send for the explosive removal team at once."

"Roger that lead"

The scream of ambulance sirens echoed through the quiet of the early morning. The emergency medical service teams stabilized the six men with oxygen and loaded them into on to stretchers to be transported to the hospital. Everyone was too sick to put up a fight so the area was secured with thirty minutes. The German Special Forces men disguised as firemen wearing gas masks went into the mosques to make sure no one was still inside and to have a closer look at the heavy boxes that the lead team had found.

At the hospital the six men were treated and their identification taken and sent to Schumacher's office for a check to see if any were wanted either by the German Authorities, Interpol or other governments. Checking with the German Immigration Authorities it was discovered that there was no record of five of the men entering Germany by air or sea and no known home address were listed. They had Palestinian passports but were not registered in the country. These men would be questioned by the local police as well as the Special Branch and held for additional questioning by the German Federal Police. One of the sick men was the Imam of the mosque; Abd al Bari, forty seven years old, originally from Syria, had been living in Germany for fifteen years and Imam of the mosque for over eight years. Abd al Bari had no criminal record and was not wanted by Interpol but since he was harboring those who had entered Germany illegally, he too would be held.

At the mosque the Explosive Disposal Teams used sophisticated portable X-Ray machines to examine the boxes found in a secret room they discovered. The X-Rays showed that the boxes contained plastic explosives. After checking for booby traps they opened the boxes and found AK47 assault rifles and a sizable amount of C-4 plastic explosive. The teams reported back to Schumacher and he ordered a special armored trailer to pick up the boxes and bring them to headquarters for disposal. He also contacted the officer in charge at the hospital ordered all six men be taken into custody upon suspicion of terrorist activity and turned over to the Special Branch when they were fit enough. He ordered guards posted on their rooms.

Schumacher radioed Gregory, "We made a nice haul at the mosque this morning. Five of them seem to be here illegally and all six are being held on being in possession of illegal weapons and suspected terrorist activity. Good call on that one".

"Great, at least we've taken that lot out and you can follow a trail to where they came from. It also gives us an idea of what to expect when we hit the warehouse."

Gregory and his team linked up with Colonel Weir and his men at the far end of the warehouse complex dressed in black camouflage with black balaclavas to keep their identity secret. All were armed with the SMG9 and full combat gear wearing micro radios with a tiny microphone attached to their throats.

Gregory said, "The surveillance team reports all quiet. One man seems to be sleeping in target one with two men active and armed. The three men in target two seem to be playing cards. All sitting at a table all armed.

"Communications check all operators" Col. Weir ordered.

"Loud and clear, all working sir"

"Colonel, you and your Red team move into position to take target two on the lower floor. Green team and I will move up the back stairs to target one and signal when we're in position". Gregory said into his mic.

"Roger that Green. Red team, lock and load and follow me"

Both teams moved silently up the stairs and were ready to move on the final signal from Gregory.

Byron Hill applied a silhouette charge to the door of target one while Gregory and Connell Baines prepared to toss the M84 flash bang grenades as soon as the door was blown.

"Now, now, now" Gregory said into his mic.

Red team burst through the door of target two, weapons leveled on the three men who were playing cards. Taken totally by surprise, they jumped to their feet and stood wide eyed in momentary shock. "Drop your weapons and get on the floor now" Weir ordered. Two of the men started to comply when the third, the leader it seemed, tried for his gun with the other two following his lead. Weir's team fired three quick bursts of 9mm rounds killing all three before any could even reach their weapons. The team swept the rooms and all closets. All clear team leader the operators said. The whole operation took less than thirty seconds.

At the same moment Byron detonated the silhouette charge opening a hole in the door big enough for men to pass through. Gregory and Connell immediately tossed there M84 stun grenades into the room and took cover behind the wall. The concussion and flash were immediate and powerful disorienting everyone inside. The team moved in quickly through the hole in the door taking up a three prong position, weapons level on all three men. Garin, Imaad and a third man stood wide eyed with their hands in the air.

"Take your guns out with your left hand and drop them on the floor" Gregory shouted.

Garin did as ordered. Imaad; glaring at them with hatred burning in his eyes began to remove his gun as ordered, but as fast as lighting spun the weapon around to fire. He was fast, but West was faster. West put two 9mm rounds through Imaad's neck severing the spinal cord. The gun clattered to the floor and Imaad crumpled straight down to the floor without a sound. The third man already had his weapon out as if to follow Gregory's order, but when Imaad made his move the other man fired a shot hitting Gregory in the chest knocking him to the floor. The man bolted over him for the door knocking Byron off balance. West fired at the man as he went through the door but only winged him. He stumbled but kept running. Byron Hill was up and charging after him taking the stairs two at a time. The man turned to kill him but Byron was already in firing position and fired a short burst hitting him at point blank range.

Garin stood completely still with his hands high, quite happy to obey orders and survive the encounter seeing the carnage around him. West helped Gregory up saying "Damn good thing he hit you in the armor". The bullet had knocked the wind out of Gregory so all he could manage was "No shit".

"Red team has target secured. All three enemies neutralized. We're moving to secure your hallway now Green". Colonel Weir reported on radio.

Taking a moment to catch his breath Gregory said. "Roger that Red. "Matt, Connell, watch him, Byron let's get Patterson".

"Get on your knees with your fingers laced behind your head. If you even twitch you won't have a head" West told Garin keeping his SMG aimed at Garin's face.

The door was locked so Byron fixed a small shaped charge to the door blowing off the area around the door knob and both men rushed inside crouching low ready to fire. The room was dimly lit and wreaked of sweat, urine and fear from the man imprisoned there for days. Patterson lay chained to the bed with his mouth open with fear trying to speak but no words would come out.

"Dr. Patterson, we're British Intelligence; here to bring you home." Gregory said.

"Byron, get those manacles off him and see if he can walk"

Gregory said while sweeping the room for anyone that may be hiding in the shadows.

"I'm on it Boss" Byron said moving swiftly to unlock Patterson.

Getting Patterson slowly to his feet Gregory asked "Doctor, can you walk?"

"Give me a minute, but yes I think I can" Patterson said in a weak voice.

Moving back into the main room where West had tied Garin's hands secured behind him with plastic double cuffs, Patterson stood in shocked silence at the carnage he saw.

Gregory said "Ok, Doctor Patterson, we need to move now gently pushing towards the door. Matt you take Garin, Byron, help the Doctor, let's move out"

"Red team, Green team has the room secured, hostiles eliminated. We have the Doctor and are moving out into the hall now" Gregory said into the mic.

"Roger that Green, Red team has the hall".

Both teams moved as one down the stairs and out of the building coming around the building into the street heading for the extraction point.

"Surveillance one to all teams, we have a shooter in the building down the block up high, take cover".

A moment later a shot rang out missing Gregory's chest and hitting one of the Wier's men in the hip putting him down. A second shot hit the block wall beside them, pieces of the shattered wall where the bullet hit exploded outward hitting both Gregory and Patterson in the face. Gregory grabbed Patterson and dove behind a large steel dumpster just as another round sliced through the steel just missing them both. Everyone took what cover they could find and began to fire randomly where they thought the shots were coming from.

"Son of a bitch is using steel jacketed rounds, one just cut through this dumpster like butter." Wier said.

"Surveillance one, we're under fire. Where the hell are the rounds coming from?" Weir shouted into his mic.

"Down the block straight ahead on the fourth floor. We can see him but can't get the angle to take a shot.

Garin took this as an opportunity to try to escape and ran for the alley on the other side of the street.

Borya saw him and sighted him down and fired. The steel jacked round took Garin's left leg off just below the knee.

Garin screamed in pain and tried to crawl to the alley. Another shot rang out, and the steel jacketed round ripped through Garin's hip, ricocheting off the pavement shattering a window in the building across the street.

No one could get to Garin, who just lay there screaming in pain.

Everyone fired at the window but it was no good. They were all unable to get the angle to take the target down. Borya continued to fire at them trying to drive them out of cover.

"Angel one here, all teams hold your fire we have the target, stand by" came over the radio.

The EC665 Tiger attack helicopter from the 64th was hovering in the extraction zone just a mile away. They moved in to help and dropped straight down between the buildings. Aiming their forty million candle power night sun search light at the apartment. The beam lit the apartment up many time brighter than daylight, Borya had no place to hide. He was squinting against intense light trying to get a shot at the Tiger when the choppers weapons officer opened fire with his 7.62mm mini gun firing three thousand rounds per minute. The apartment wall was shredded along with Borya in the room behind it. The fight was over in seconds.

"Bloody hell," Gregory shouted to Wier over the scream of the helicopters twin turbines, "nobody would've survived that."

"Angel one here, you're clear, target has been neutralized. Proceed to extraction point." Said the calm voice.

"Roger that, thanks Angel one". Wier said.

"Surveillance one, Green team leader, we have wounded here, get an ambulance on the double." Gregory said into his mic.

"On the way now Green" reported surveillance one.

While Colonel Wier helped stop the bleeding for his injured man, West and Gregory ran crouching to get Garin.

"West provided cover for them both. Gregory said, "Garin, who's behind this. The shooter was here to kill you so you've been betrayed by your organization. An ambulance is on the way, but it doesn't look good, tell me, who are you working for?"

Garin was bleeding out fast, and just semi-conscious, at this point he knew he was dying. "Paval Orlov brought me into Ophidian. They're working with a group known as The Islamic Brotherhood for Jihad in Syria."

"We took the mosque and the fighters there; did they have a backup plan?" Gregory asked.

"If we were found out we were to move to a boat call *Storm Cloud* parked on dock six. They said they would take Patterson for pick up from there. But it was strictly a backup." Garin told him.

"Hang on, the ambulance will be here soon" Gregory told him.

"Surveillance one, where's that ambulance, we have a dying man here?" Gregory said into the mic.

"Two minutes out Green one"

"Garin, they're two minutes out, hang on. Tell me, who's running this Ophidian organization?" Gregory said.

Garin was going fast and tried to speak but his words were slurred and he died before he could repeat them but it sounded to Gregory like Ophidian and Vistin.

"Ok Matt, he's gone, leave him, let's get to the extraction area" Gregory said.

Dr. Patterson was more than a little shaken with his face

bleeding from the shards of wall that hit him and Gregory, but kept moving with the team.

The team moved through the streets keeping tight to the walls to the extraction point where the EC665 Tiger was waiting to take off for Gatow airbase.

In the small building in the staging area Gregory said, "Matt, I'm going with Patterson back to London. Check with your people at Langley and tell them that Garin tried to say the name of the man on top of Ophidian, It sounded like Vistin. Check it out and I'll call you from London."

"Right, I'll head back to the hotel then back to Langley and talk to our operatives in the Kremlin and our bank guys at the Justice Department to get more information about the money transferred to Aruba and see if the name Vistin rings any bells." Matt said.

"Thanks for all the help Matt. Talk to you soon" Gregory said.

Gregory walked Dr. Patterson out to the waiting chopper and helped him strap in and took a moment to talk to Colonel Wier.

"Colonel, before he died, Garin said they had a backup plan to move Patterson to a boat named *Storm Cloud* parked at dock six. They're part of The Islamic Brotherhood for Jihad group so be damn careful when you take the boat."

"We'll have the port authority inspect the boat at first light and be in position to take them down." Wier told him.

"Thanks for all the help Colonel. Your team's reputation for professionalism and efficiency is well deserved. Will your man be ok?"

"The bullet past right through and punched a hole in his hip, but missed the main artery, he'll be ok."

"Glad to hear it, your men are true pros. Thanks again." Gregory said shaking Wier's hand warmly"

"No problem, we're always ready to give our British brothers a hand when they run into a little spot of bother" Wier said affecting his best British accent.

The helicopter touched down at Gatow airbase five minutes after leaving the extraction point and Gregory and his team helped Patterson into one of the officer's seats in the front of the waiting SAS special C141 aircraft for the flight back to London.

During the short flight Patterson began to sweat and shake apparently going into shock. He started to babble "I should have never gotten involved with these people, they're evil, evil; I should never have believed them".

Gregory said, "Dr. what are you saying, you were working for Garin?"

Patterson did not answer; he just kept repeating "They're evil, evil."

The special SAS aircraft touched down at London Heathrow and was met by an ambulance with MI6 security escort. They took Patterson to the hospital for medical examination and observation.

CHAPTER TWELVE

MOSCOW

Paval Orlov sat on the side of his bed, sweat streaming down his face, his heart hammering inside is chest. He had just received word that both the warehouse and mosque were raided. Patterson had been taken by German Special Forces and that Borya was killed during the raid. Garin was seriously injured but it was unknown whether he survived or not.

Phoning the private number for General Vistin he said to the General's aid, "This is Comrade Orlov, I must speak to the General at once".

"I'm sorry sir; the General is on his way to Morocco for the North African Trade meeting. If it's important I can put a call through to him once he lands in about two hours".

"Yes, please get a message to him to call me as soon as he lands"

CHAPTER THIRTEEN

HIGH ABOVE THE TYRRENIAN SEA

G eneral Vistin sat comfortably in the plush leather seat sipping a steaming cup of his favorite Jamaican Blue Mountain coffee onboard the special executive military transport jet flying at thirty six thousand feet over the Tyrrenian Sea on his way to Morocco. The North African Trade Meeting was just his excuse to be in Morocco at the same time as a very exclusive art auction being held at the Museum of Fine Art in Casablanca. For the next several days he would pretend to listen to a gaggle of whining politicians from all over the North African continent. It would be well worth it when in two days he would attend the art auction.

Some of the rarest works of the Old Masters and Impressionist would be auctioned and he intended for his agent to purchase a Botticelli, two Monet's and a Degas. This would add to his already substantial secret collection stored in a vault in Switzerland. With the money just transferred into his account in Aruba from The Islamic Brotherhood for Jihad group he knew he could out bid most of the other buyers. He decided to go to the auction, out of uniform and unknown to his agent to see the works himself. At this moment he felt calm and sure his grand scheme had worked and all had gone well. He knew that now he was the very wealthy man he always aspired to be.

CHAPTER FOURTEEN

VAUXHALL CROSS LONDON

"Nice work Gregory, did all go to plan with the extraction?" Mobius asked.

"It all when to plan except for an assassin sent to kill Garin. Shot one of Colonel Wier's men, and damn near killed me. The assassin killed Garin before the 64ths hilo took him out. Garin told me before he died that they had a backup plan to move Patterson to a boat named *Storm Cloud*. Colonel Wier and his men are going to take the boat at first light. Garin also said he was hired by a Paval Orlov and was working for an organization known as Ophidian. I asked him who the top man was and he tried to tell me but he was dying. It sounded like Vistin." Gregory told him.

"Vistin?, there's a General Nikolay Vistin working with their Ministry of Defense in the Kremlin. Vistin was a Colonel during the worst of the fighting in Afghanistan and was known as a tough commander and loyal to the party. It's also known that Vistin is a man who'll do whatever it takes to achieve his objectives without regard to normal human emotions and sympathies. He was known for his malicious disregard for humanity and wouldn't hesitate to order an entire village wiped out if he suspected any of the enemy were in the area, men, women and children it made no difference to Vistin. He was promoted to General just last year and moved into an office at the Kremlin. It's hard to believe Vistin would be involved with this Ophidian organization. His family has always been tough hard line communist and well connected within the party. Some say his rapid rise to the top was because of his family connections and not his military service, but things like that are often said by those passed over." Mobius said.

"Matt West is checking with CIA on Ophidian and Vistin to see if their operatives in Russia and the Kremlin can uncover any connection. Hopefully we can find out if this Vistin is our man soon. Since thing went bad in Berlin and The Islamic Brotherhood for Jihad people didn't get what they paid for and if this General Vistin is the man, The Islamic Brotherhood for Jihad will be out to settle accounts with him." Gregory told him.

"As to Paval Orlov, we know of him, he's a minor on their Consul of Ministers. He's been with the Consul for years and does work with different departments in the Kremlin. We'll see if he's had any dealings with General Vistin in the past six months or so. If so, we may be able to get information from him on Ophidian and Vistin. People in his governmental position are easily scared by the threat of the FSB and the KGB and worse, Directorate "K". That lot at Directorate "K" have a reputation for brutality equal to the German Gestapo during the war" Mobius said.

The next afternoon, Mobius told Gregory "German Intelligence identified the remains of the assassin, and there wasn't much left after the mini gun got done with him, as one Borya Sokolov. Ex-Russian army sniper who served with then Colonel Nikolay Vistin in Afghanistan. They say Sokolov just arrived in Berlin two days before your teams fire fight."

"It's beginning to look like this General Vistin could be out man. True, a lot of solders served in Afghanistan, but it would have to be more that co-incidence that the shooter in Berlin served with Vistin and there's no connection to Ophidian." Gregory said.

"How's Dr. Patterson doing?" Gregory asked.

"He's pretty shaken up of course but overall seems physically ok, considering what he's been through." Mobius said.

"This is rather unusual sir, during the flight to Heathrow; Patterson started to babble uncontrollably that he should've never gotten involved with these evil people. I couldn't get him to explain what he meant, but it could be that he was in liege with Garin and Vistin and they sold him out." Gregory explained.

"Christ, we never had any clue that Patterson may have been working with the people that snatched him". Mobius said with a shocked look.

Gregory phoned Matt West at CIA Langley and asked what information he had found on the Ophidian organization and if they had any connection with General Vistin.

"There've been rumors of a fairly new criminal organization called Ophidian, operating out of an Eastern Bloc country but there's very little intelligence on them in our files. We found two numbered accounts with a total of about one hundred sixty million Euros at The Swiss Private Capital Bank in Zurich and two more accounts with more than sixty five million Euros at the Banko De Aruba in the Caribbean.

There's been a substantial amount of funds coming in from a Russian OOO, that stands for Obschestovo S Ogranichennoi Otvetstvennost'yu which is a Russian LLC, called All Russia Oil and Gas Trading OOO with a home office in Lobokovichi on the border of Belarus. We believe that this is a shell and there's a good odds that if we dig deep enough we'll find Ourobors and Vistin at the bottom. We're looking for a link to Vistin and our Justice Department is leaning on the banks to find out the owner of these accounts. There was three hundred million Euros transferred from a private bank in Egypt this morning into one of the accounts at

Banko De Aruba. We think its payment for Patterson. I'm heading for Aruba tomorrow morning to meet with our people and the
bank President to get more information." West told him.

"Good work Matt, since they didn't get what they paid for the
boys from The Islamic Brotherhood for Jihad will definitely be on
the war path for anyone involved. Pavol Orlov is known and is definitely a target. If Vistin is the man at the top of Ophidian they'll
be after him as well. Those chaps in The Islamic Brotherhood for
Jihad don't rest until vengeance is properly metered out according
to their law." Talk to you soon. Gregory said with a grin.

"Yeh, they'll barbeque Vistin's ass for sure" West said laughing.

Gregory disconnected the secure line and told Mobius what
West had told him.

"Agent West said, the CIA working with their Justice
Department to pressure the Banko De Aruba to give the name of
the owner of the suspected accounts and put a lock on the account
they suspect belong to General Vistin so no funds can move out.
Vistin wouldn't know that yet so he thinks he has the money and
will try to run with it." Gregory explained to Mobius.

"That's good work; CIA also said one of their operatives
in Moscow has heard rumors that General Vistin has been buying rare works of art and valuable collector cars through agents.
They're having their bank people cross check works that have sold
against funds transferred from the accounts they suspect belong to
Vistins". Mobius told Gregory.

"Is Vistin in Moscow now sir?" Gregory asked.

"No we're told he is heading to Morocco, officially for the
North African Trade meeting. Coincidentally, there is a major art
auction going on in Casablanca in four days. I want you to go to
the auction too. With your position as Chairman of All Empire
International we'll be able to get you a VIP invitation.

Since your status with MI6 is a complete secret, you'll be

accepted as just another wealthy art collector and you can keep an eye out for Vistin" Mobius said.

"But sir, I don't have any knowledge of fine art, and couldn't tell a fake from the real article". Gregory said.

"Don't worry about that Gregory, we have an art expert from the National Gallery, Sir Jonathan Vandeveer, that will go with you. He'll coach you so you fit in and won't draw unwanted attention to yourself. You'll be leaving on a private Gulf Stream tomorrow morning. Miss Trent will book you a suite at the Royal Casablanca and arrange for a driver. I want you to just observe Vistin, assuming that he shows up at the auction, don't make any attempt to contact him or pick him up. We need to simply follow him and see if there is a link to Ophidian. We can't risk your connection with MI6 being found out". Mobius said.

"Yes sir, I understand. If he's at the auction, we'll see what he does, then I'll track him once he leaves. If he shows up at the auction we can assume that he'll be buying through an agent. Vistin's agent will be the high bidder since he'll want to move that cash so we can also track the agent and see where that leads us. Are Connell Baines and Susan Jamison available?" Gregory asked.

"Yes, we'll have them meet you at the airport. Susan will be traveling as your Personal Executive Secretary and Baines will be your Personal Security Advisor". Mobius said.

"Do we have any idea what art works the General plans to bid on?" Gregory asked.

"We can assume he will be buying the most valuable works at the auction. There are works from Botticelli, Raphael, Degas, Pissarro and two Monet's to be auctioned so those are most likely what Vistin will be buying." Mobius said.

CHAPTER FIFTEEN

MOROCCO

General Vistin's plane touched down and taxied to the executive terminal at Mohammed V International Airport where a special State limousine met him and his security detail and drove them to the Royal Casablanca Hotel. Arriving at his suite, General Vistin found a message requesting him to call Paval Orlov as soon as possible.

General Vistin dismissed his aids and attached his private security scrambler to the hotel phone. He had this scrambler custom made for him so the KGB or Western Intelligence would not be able to listen in on his phone calls.

"Paval, this is General Vistin, I take it all went to plan in Berlin?"

"No, Nikolay things did not go to plan at all. In fact they went completely wrong. Both the warehouse and the mosque were raided by the German Special Branch and they took Patterson. Borya is dead and Garin was badly injured and may be dead, we haven't gotten confirmation on that yet. Because there was a gun battle both in the warehouse and in the street, the German Police, Western Intelligence and Interpol are all over this due to the connection with Mid-Eastern terror groups picked up at the mosque. Four of the men killed at the warehouse have been identified as from Syria, and the *Storm Cloud* was taken, and the crew arrested on suspicion of terrorist activity. It's also being reported by the International Press that Borya and Garin were both Russian citizens so they're saying there may be a Russian connection to the terrorist. The KGB has sent three agents to look into the deaths and they're also looking into whether Delov was involved since he was killed in the same area within a week of the raid. Directorate "K" has assigned several agents to look into Delov and Garin's activity here at home. What should we do Nikolay, when Patterson starts talking were done?" Orlov said in a near panic.

General Vistin sat staring at the wall trying to process all the information.

"Stay calm Paval, we knew some things could go wrong. You had better put your escape plan into action soon, but not right away. Borla's dead and Garin; if Garin survived; he is most likely unable to tell them anything yet. It will take days for the KGB to uncover any connection with Garin and Delov. Patterson will not want the British to find out about his involvement with us so he'll tell lies about his abduction. That should give us a week at least. Don't panic; just move forward with your plan to visit the Kazakhstan Transportation Minister to discuss the light rail system Russia will help them build." General Vistin told him.

Disconnecting the scrambler, General Vistin poured himself a large glass of vodka and sat considering what his next move should be.

Aboard the MI6 Gulfstream, Gregory met with Susan Jamison and Connell Baines to go over the upcoming mission to locate and track General Nikolay Vistin while Sir Jonathan Vandeveer of the National Gallery took a nap in the rear of the plane. "I'm going as myself no cover, just there to bid on some of the works to be auctioned. Susan, you're going as Ms. Cynthia O'Brian, my Personal Executive Secretary. By the way, I love the auburn hair, very becoming on such a lovely Irish lass Miss O'Brian" Gregory said.

"Why thank you kindly sir. I rather like it too." Susan said with a smile

"Connell, you're my personal Security Advisor Max Ross." Gregory said.

"The money from The Islamic Brotherhood for Jihad was transferred into and account in Aruba Monday morning and since we rescued Patterson Sunday The Islamic Brotherhood for Jihad group paid three hundred million Euros for nothing. As you can imagine, they'll be a bit piqued and be out for blood. Vistin's heading for Casablanca to buy rare works of art and stash them in a vault somewhere, perhaps Switzerland thus putting the funds into easily hidden assets and then go into hiding before the KGB or The Islamic Brotherhood for Jihad catch up to him. What we need to do is identify who's doing the buying for Vistin and find out where the art works are being stored. Once we know that, we have a plan to inform the KGB through contacts that Vistin has been working outside the government and against Russia. That is if The Islamic Brotherhood for Jihad doesn't find him first.

General Vistin is in his early forties, just less than six feet tall, solidly built, thick black hair just starting to grey at the temples and heavy eye brows. Here are photos of him from his official military file and some of his official security detail as well as photos of him in civilian dress.

The auction is formal so we'll be looking for him in black tie and likely without his military aids. I'm sure he'll have his private security people moving about the auction and we don't know what they look like, so be careful not to draw attention to yourselves". Gregory explained.

"How will we spot the agent bidding for Vistin?" Connell asked.

"We'll be watching Vistin for clues as to which items we think he's looking to bid on. When those item come up for sale we'll watch the bidders. If it looks as though the bidding is all through, I'll up the bid. We're sure Vistin's willing to outbid anyone so the bidder will be his agent." Gregory said.

"What if they don't continue bidding after you've raised the bid?" Susan asked.

"Then I'll be starting my own art collection" Gregory said with a laugh.

"I'm hoping it doesn't go that way of course. We feel that Vistin wants these works to add to what we're told is a growing private collection. He needs to shift his money from cash to less traceable assets so we're assuming he won't be out bid. Of course, I'll make sure to make the increases small enough that he won't give up". Gregory said.

"So when we spot the agent, I'm to follow him?" Connell asked.

"Yes, once the auction breaks up you follow the agent at a good distance and make sure you're not detected. You'll track the agent then find out where the art he bought is being sent. Because of the amount of money involved, Vistin's personal security will be watching everyone closely." Gregory said.

"So you and I will stick with Vistin?" Susan asked.

"Right, that's the plan at the moment but we may have to improvise as we go along." Gregory explained.

The Gulfstream touched down at Mohammed V International and as it taxied to the executive terminal, Gregory notice a Russian military Tupolev executive jet parked at the east side of the building. "It looks like General Vistin beat us here" Gregory said. Gregory, Susan and Connell with Sir Jonathan Vandeveer in tow walked out the main doors of the terminal where a black Rolls Royce Phantom was waiting with Byron Hill acting as diver.

"Good morning sir, my name is Charles Smyth, I'll be your driver during your stay here in Morocco." Hill said with a grin.

"Byron Hill you old fraud; no one told me you'd be joining the party, but it's good to have you along." Gregory said with a look of surprise.

"Kimberly thought it would be a good idea to have me close at hand in case things get dicey." Byron told him.

"We can always count on Miss Trent to look to all the details. A very efficient young woman our Miss Trent." Connell said.

Gregory, Susan and Connell climbed in the back of the Rolls and Sir Jonathan Vandeveer got in front with Byron, separated by the sound proof partition.

They arrived at the Royal Casablanca's main entrance where they were ushered through the plush lobby. Susan Jamison checked them in at the front desk.

"Ms. O'Bryan, Mr Gregory MacNee's Personal Executive Secretary, checking in for Mr. MacNee and party." she told the desk manager.

"Ah yes, Ms. O'Bryan, we have the Presidential Suite for Mr. MacNee, and two adjoining suites for you and Mr. Ross" the manager said.

"Thank you that will be quite satisfactory. See that the luggage is brought up at once please." Susan said putting on an air of indifference.

Meeting in the Presidential Suite, Connell swept it for any listening devises. Once the room was cleared, Byron said "Our man General Vistin arrived about an hour ago and is staying at the Royal as well. He has a suite one floor below you and at the end of the hall. I'll try to get a bug in the room so we can hear what's going on."

"What a fantastic stroke of luck. It'll be much easier to track his movements and see who his security people are." Gregory said.

General Vistin decided to continue as planned with the auction but would be looking at several additional works. Since The Islamic Brotherhood for Jihad's money was already in his Aurba accounts, he wanted to put a good portion into art from this auction. He also would have his agent purchase a few classic Ferraris that were coming up for auction at Christie's in Paris two weeks from now. These assets were easily moved and hidden. He also knew that since Patterson was taken and the funds had already been paid that The Islamic Brotherhood for Jihad group would be livid and out to get him by any means.

Paval Orlov phoned Vistin the next day and said, "Nikolay I've arranged a meeting with the Transportation Minister in Kazakhstan in a few days to discuss Russian assistance in with their proposed light rail system. I'll be flying to Almaty International in two days. Listen Nikolay, things are getting hot here. The KGB is all over this shooting in Berlin and I've had two Directorate "K" agents here at the Counsel asking questions about Sokolov. They know he served with you in Afghanistan and are looking for a connection to what happened in Berlin. They've also been asking if I've had recent contact with you or Sokolov. I was able to put them off for the moment but they'll be back. They have requested that I meet in their offices in Lubyanka on Monday but I was able to put them off with this upcoming mission in Kazakhstan; but they'll be on me as soon as I get back. Nikolay, I need that money transferred into my Swiss account now".

"Be calm Paval. I'll arrange for the funds transfer Monday morning when the bank opens in Zurich. I'll also arrange to get you away from Russia and out of the reach of the KGB and Directorate

"K". Just stay loose and go to Kazakhstan, but watch your back, The Islamic Brotherhood for Jihad will not be happy about this. Contact me when you're there and be sure to secure the line." Vistin told him.

Hanging up the phone General Vistin stood watching the traffic out the window on the street below thinking, "I may have to deal with Paval sooner than I'd planned. If he cracks I've got big problems."

CHAPTER SIXTEEN

MOSCOW

P aval Orlov was very nervous over the next few days waiting to get out of Moscow and head for Kazakhstan. He felt that every eye in Moscow was watching him. The FSB seemed to be everywhere he went, and he felt it was only a matter of time before they picked him up for official questioning. Once they took him to the Lubyanka Building he felt he would never see the outside again. When he used the phone he thought he heard a buzzing sound on the line and assumed the FSB or KGB had tapped the line, so he only used pay phones and attached the scrambler Vistin had given him. Orlov wanted to put some distance between him and the FSB agents that kept coming to his office asking questions. He felt that they suspected him, and knew he was involved with General Vistin and the shooting in Berlin.Finally, boarding a commercial flight from Moscow to Almaty Kazakhstan, he began to relax for the first time since the shooting in Berlin. He enjoyed several glasses of Vodka and took a long nap, sleeping better than he had in days. He felt that once the five million Euros promised to him by General Vistin was in his numbered Swiss account, he would take on a new identity and disappear to some remote island living like a king for the rest of his life, away from General Vistin, Moscow, the KGB and FSB. All he needed was to get through the next few days of official business and he'd be off and gone forever.

CHAPTER SEVENTEEN

DAMSCUS SYRIA

The leadership of Islamic Brotherhood for Jihad met in their headquarters on the outskirts of Damascus to discuss the loss of the English physicist, the loss of the mosque contacts in Berlin, and the capture or death of eleven of their Jihadist brothers as well as the loss of three hundred million Euros paid to the head of the Russian Ophidian organization.

Their leader, Adnan Mohammed Wasen, addressed the assembled fighters saying "Brothers; the loss of the English physicist Dr. Patterson, is a major disruption in our Jihad against the Infidels in the West. Brother Yosef Mohammed and four of our loyal fighters were killed by the Germans trying to bring Dr. Patterson to us. Our mosque was raided under false pretenses and our fighters were taken prisoners. The leadership is convinced that we were betrayed by the Russian Orlov, and the head of the Ophidian organization, who have stolen three hundred million Euros donated by the faithful in Egypt. This cannot be tolerated. The money is unrecoverable, and though it's a huge loss to our cause, can be replaced. However, this betrayal by the Russians must be avenged."

At this statement the room exploded in angry approval.

After letting the brothers anger grow to a fever pitch, Adnan Mohammed Wasen said, "I'm ordering our fighters to go and

avenge our lost brothers and kill the Russian betrayers wherever
they try to hide."

This was met with cheers of agreement and men standing to
volunteer to hunt down Orlov, and discover and capture the head
of Ophidian. "They will be found and beheaded for this betrayal
the men shouted." The entire group was now standing, pumping their fists in the air shouting, "Death to America, death to the
Russians, death to the Infidels, death, death, death".

CHAPTER EIGHTEEN

CASABLANCA MOROCCO

T he gleaming black Rolls Royce arrived at Grand entrance of the Casablanca Museum of Fine Art at seven thirty in the evening, with Gregory, Susan and Sir Jonathan Vandeveer stepping out onto the red carpet into a sea of paparazzi. Connell Baines was following just behind in a grey Mercedes S-Class. Gregory was dressed in his Savile Row tuxedo, in a deep midnight blue. Susan looked stunning, and every bit the Executive Assistant, in a beautifully tailored Versace gown in forest green. Each of them had a micro transceiver in their ear so they could alert each other when Vistin and his bidding agent were spotted. They each accepted a flute of Cristal champagne, as they walked past the string quartet into the main room of the gallery. The works of art were on display under bullet proof glass among discreetly located, heavy security.

"It looks like the who's who of the European business community and the heavy weight art collectors are all on hand tonight. I recognize some of them and would rather avoid them so we don't get bogged down in conversations. We have about forty minutes to view the paintings before the auctions starts. The Monet's' are over in the section by the reflecting pool. We'll inspect the paintings and watch for Vistin and his security people". Gregory said.

Sir Jonathan explained the details and history of the different works to Gregory, as well as what he felt they may sell for, while Susan casually scanned the room.

"The most valuable of the Impressionist works here are "Water Lilly Pond" by Claude Monet 1899 and "Nympheas" 1908 being sold individually. They should bring in the neighborhood of twenty to twenty five million Euros each. These two, by Camille Pissarro, are "Le Boulevard Montmartre de matine'e de Printemps" 1897 and "Le Boulevard Montmartre de effet de nuit" also 1897, depicting the view the artist observed from his room at the Hotel de Russie. Being sold as a pair they should bring between thirty and forty million Euros plus" Sir Jonathan explained.

He continued to explain the other works from Botticelli, Raphael and Degas while Gregory listened and watched for General Vistin to arrive. Scanning the room while listening to Sir Jonathan, Gregory saw two men enter the room watching all directions. Both were powerfully built and look out of place in such an elegant affair. It was obvious that they were security men but with all the wealthy people at the auction that was not surprising. He continued to watch to see who followed these men, and in a few minutes General Vistin arrived alone. He moved with confidence through the room to look at the Monet's. He looked just like his file photo, except a few pounds heavier. Susan moved closer to Gregory and said, "Vistin just arrived and is heading for the Monet's. He has two men following close behind, the one by the fountain with the blond hair, and the other standing by the statue of Venus."

"I see them. Connell did you copy?" Gregory said into the tiny microphone.

"Roger that, I see them all" Connell replied.

Gregory and Susan, with their champagne in hand, walked around the room looking at the other works to be auctioned. Gregory noticed that many of the eyes seemed to be looking at Susan, rather than the art, as she passed. He felt that this was just as well since no one would have notice him. They saw General Vistin looking at the Degas, so Susan walked over to look at it as well.

Susan, with a lovely smile, said to Vistin, "It's beautiful isn't it. Are you here to bid on this?"

General Vistin looked up from the painting gruffly, irritated by the interruption, then seeing what a lovely young woman was speaking to him softened and said, "Oh no, I'm just in town on business and was able to get a pass to attend the auction. Are you planning to bid, Miss?"

"Cynthia O'Brian, no I'm Mr. MacNee's Personal Executive Secretary accompanying Mr. MacNee. He's here to participate in the auction, and hoping to buy one or more paintings, Mr.? "

"Vladimir Romanoff," Vistin said extending his hand and lying smoothly.

"No, I'm just here for the North African Trade Meeting."

"Have you ever been to Casablanca before?" Susan asked.

"Yes, many times over the years Miss O'Brian" Vistin said

"Will you be staying on after the trade meeting? Susan asked.

"Unfortunately no, I have to get back to Finland." Vistin told her.

"Oh, it's too bad you have to leave so soon. This is my first trip here and I'll have a free day or two after the auction to go sightseeing. It would be nice to have a guide" Susan said looking a bit disappointed.

"Well, I'd love to show you around if my schedule will permit it Miss O'Brian. Oh, it looks like they're going to start the auction now. I'll be at the Royal for the next two days." Vistin told her, hoping he could spend some time with this lovely young woman.

"We're at the Royal as well. If you have the time to sightsee, have the desk call the Presidential Suite to reach me. Now, if you'll please excuse me, I have to join Mr. MacNee now. Delightful to have met you Mr. Romanoff," she said extending her hand.

Vistin kissed her hand gallantly and said, "It was my great pleasure meeting you Miss O'Brian. If I can get away, I will contact you; perhaps we could have lunch and visit some of the sights."

"That would be wonderful; I look forward to hearing from you. Enjoy the auction." Susan said as she moved away back to Gregory.

"So what did you two talk about?" Gregory asked her.

"Just making a bit of close contact. Came on to him a little and he suggested that we might meet for lunch. He said his name is Vladimir Romanoff here for the North African Trade Meeting. For a man on the run from the KGB and The Islamic Brotherhood for Jihad, he certainly seems calm and at ease." She told him.

"Well, when you think you've just got an extra three hundred million Euros in your account I suppose you feel you can hide in style and buy whatever protection you need. And he's right about that, except we blocked the money." Gregory said with a grin.

A page walked through the room ringing a small bell saying,

"Ladies and Gentlemen, the auction will begin in ten minutes. Would you please take your seats."

General Vistin sat to the right side of the isle towards the rear of the room but with a good view of the auction stage and a good view of Susan. His security men sat behind him on the right and left.

"We're in the second row ahead and to the right of Vistin. Connell is behind Vistin to the left so he can keep an eye on him. Byron is standing by the doors and can see the whole auction floor. From there he can watch our backs and keep an eye on Vistin while looking for the man who's bidding for him." Gregory told Susan.

"Ladies and Gentlemen, welcome to the Casablanca Museum of Fine Art. This evening, we are privileged to be auctioning some of the finest works of art from the finest artists throughout history. We will begin with *"Dangeuse au repos"* 1879 pastel and gouache on joined paper by Edgar Degas. May I have an opening bid of ten million Euros?"

The bidding continued and Vistin didn't seem to be particularly on edge, so Gregory felt he was not bidding on this piece. The works continued until the first of the Monet's was announced.

"Ladies and Gentlemen, next we have *"Water Lilly Pond"* *1899* oil on canvas by Claude Monet. May I have an opening bid of fifteen million Euros?"

The tension in the room jumped considerably with this introduction. Byron said into his mic, "Vistin's watching with intensity he hadn't displayed before, so I think his man is bidding."

The bidding moved swiftly to eighteen million Euros, then began to slow. A middle aged man with thick grey hair in the front row elegantly dressed with a red bow tie and cummerbund continued to top each bid moving the price to twenty one million Euros. When the bidding was about to be closed Gregory upped the bid to twenty two million. The man with the red tie waited a few minutes then raised the bid to twenty three million. Gregory raised the bid each time by one million Euros drawing gasps from the audience. Finally after several more rises Gregory raised the bid to twenty eight million Euros. After a long pause the auctioneer called twenty eight million once, twice and was just about to say sold when the man with the red tie raised the bid to thirty million Euros. The audience held its breath and the auctioneer looked to Gregory who after a prolonged pause for dramatic effect, signaled no more.

"Sold to the gentlemen in the first row for thirty million Euros" the auctioneer said.

Connell Baines was watching General Vistin. Connell said into his mic, I thought he was going to have a stroke during that one".

The man in the red tie looked greatly relieved to have won the bid, but was more on edge as the next item came up.

This act was repeated with the next Monet, "Nympheas", finally selling to the same man for twenty nine million Euros. General Vistin's agent had purchased both Monet's, as well as the Pissarro's, sold as a set for forty seven million and a pair of Botticelli's for another twenty six million. As the agent was leaving the crowded room, Susan brushed up against him and planted a tiny transmitter on his collar. "I'm so sorry sir, the rooms jammed isn't it?" She said with an embarrassed smile.

"That's quite alright my dear, the room is packed." He said.

"Sir Jonathan, thank you for all your help. We'll get together at my club for dinner when I get back to London." Gregory said as he moved towards the exit.

"Well, the General just unloaded one hundred thirty two million Euros of The Islamic Brotherhood for Jihads money, or so he thinks. He won't be happy to find his account locked and he'll have to scramble and use his other accounts to pay for the art he just purchased." Gregory said to Susan.

"Connell, stay with the agent and see where he goes and don't lose him". Gregory said.

"Byron's bring the car up now. We want to be inside before Vistin gets to his car so we can use the traffic to fall in behind him without being noticed." Gregory said into the tiny mic.

Byron was waiting at the entrance holding the rear door of the Rolls open for Gregory and Susan when they came out. They got in and Byron got behind the wheel driving just slowly enough to be in position to be two cars behind General Vistin's Mercedes limousine when he departed the auction. They followed the limo through the traffic, but instead of getting on the N1 back towards the Royal Hotel, the General headed down Avenue Hassan II towards the port.

***

"Gregory, Connell here, the agent just turned onto the N1 south. Where the hell's this guy going"? Connell said.

"I don't know, just stick with him. We're heading down Avenue Hassan II toward the port away from the hotel" Gregory told him.

"Looks like my guy might be heading in the same direction" Connell told him.

Twenty minutes later Connell said, "Gregory, he just parked near the Place des Nations Unies, and is walking towards it.

"Ok Connell, we're almost at the same spot. We see him." Susan said.

The traffic was typical for this time of night in Casablanca, in other words, grinding slowly. General Vistin's Mercedes pulled over to the curb and the agent got inside. They immediately pulled back into the traffic with the Rolls just one car behind.

"Careful Byron, we're too close. The driver is no doubt one of Vistin's security men and he may spot us." Gregory said.

"Ok boss, I'll fall back a bit and stay behind this minivan. That should shield us but let us see where he goes." Byron said.

The microphone Susan had placed on the agents jacket was working perfectly, and they listened to the conversation in Vistin's limo.

"Excellent work Theo, though I did pay more than I would have liked, I'm still pleased that we got the works I wanted." Vistin said.

"Do you want them moved to the vault in Zurich as usual?" Theo asked.

"Yes, that's fine. When will the paintings be delivered?

"They'll be crated and shipped by air Tuesday morning and should arrive at the Private Client Bank by one o' clock Wednesday afternoon general." Theo said.

"That's acceptable. I'll have my security people at the bank by noon for the delivery." Vistin said.

Gregory said to Susan and Connell, "We need to have someone at the Private Client Bank Wednesday to see what vault is being used. We were told that Vistin has been buying art, so he probably has it stored there as well. I'll contact Mobius and see if we can pressure the bank for information on the vault. Byron, we got what we needed, let's head for the hotel."

Back at in their suite at the Royal, Gregory attached the encryption device to the phone and called Mobius saying, "Susan chatted up General Vistin at the auction and he's hoping to meet her for lunch. He bought two Monet's, a pair of Pissarro's and two Botticelli's for one hundred thirty two million Euros. I bid him up so he paid about fifteen million too much but he's still happy. Susan put a bug on the agent doing the bidding for Vistin, and Connell got his name from a woman working at the auction registration desk.

His name is Theo Accola, Swiss and probably living in or around Zurich. Ask Miss Trent to find out about him. We tailed Vistin's limo and listened in on a conversation Vistin had with Accola. Vistin told him to move the paintings to a vault at the Private Client Bank in Zurich so we believe the other paintings he's purchased would be in that vault as well." Gregory told Mobius.

Mobius said, "Try to keep tabs on where Vistin goes from there. Our people in Moscow reported that Paval Orlov is heading for Almaty Kazakhstan for a meeting with their Transportation Minister ostensibly to discuss Russian help building a light rail system in the industrial hub in Almaty. We think he may be getting ready to bolt. The KGB is investigating the shooting in Berlin. Also the FSB and Directorate "K" have been seen going to Orlov's office twice though we don't know what their looking for.

"Do we have anybody in Kazakhstan that can follow Orlov's movements? Gregory asked.

"We have several assets in that area, but we're flying Neville Johnston out this afternoon so he'll be there when Orlov arrives." Mobius said.

"Do you think we should pick up Orlov and sweat him for all the details about Vistin's organization? Gregory asked.

"I don't think so, he is a Russian government official with their Consul of Ministers on official business. If MI6 was found to have abducted him, it would have serious political ramifications. No, we just track him for the moment." Mobius said.

"Now that we know or think we know where the art works are going, I'll call West at CIA and see if their people in the Justice Department can lean on the Private Client Bank and get them to open the vault to see what's inside. If they can claim the works are stolen, they may be able to get inside." Gregory said.

"It's worth a try, but these Swiss banks are notoriously tough about giving any information on their accounts, so I doubt they would allow any agency into their vaults without a heavy weight court order." Mobius said.

"Well possibly not, but it's worth a try. I'll be in touch" Gregory said.

Hanging up the phone Gregory said to Susan, "Give Vistin a call tomorrow and try to arrange lunch with him. I know he's interested, and if he hasn't heard about the loss of his money, he will take you up on it."

"Sure, no problem, he'll go" Susan said.

"Byron, were you able to get a bug inside Vistin's suite?" Gregory asked.

"Easy peasy boss, I was chatting up one of the chamber maids and slipped a bug in the flower arrangement she was bringing to the suite." Byron said with a grin.

"Well done. I want one of you to monitor the bug round the clock for the next day or two and record everything". Gregory told them.

"You got it boss. The bug is sound activated and has a range of over a mile so we'll hear anything going on in the living room. Assuming they don't use an electronic jammer or find it." Byron said.

Early the next morning Miss Trent contacted Gregory and told him what she had found out about Theo Accola.

"Good morning Kimberly. Thanks for getting back to me so soon. It's only six A.M. in London, don't you ever sleep?" Gregory said playfully.

"Never when there's work to be done dear" She said."I ran Theo Accola through our computer and Interpol's and he's more or less clean. Fifty one years old, last reported address in Zurich Switzerland, Swiss citizen and longtime art dealer, married once but divorced years ago, no children. Accola's reported to have been involved in some shady art deals and is suspected of selling forgeries as genuine but that was never proven. He's working with an art dealer in Moscow, Vladimir Chekov, and has traveled to Moscow every month or so. There are no known ties to General Vistin, but obviously one exists since he's doing the buying for Vistin. His bank account receives sizable deposits but it seems to go quickly, my guess is he's over extended. That's about all for the moment" She told him.

"Thanks Kim, great work as always. I owe you dinner when I get home" Gregory said.

Over a breakfast of steak and eggs, with a tray of special Moroccan pastries and a pot of steaming Moroccan coffee, Gregory said,

"Susan; give Vistin a call in about an hour and tell him I've given you the afternoon off. If he accepts the lunch date try to get as much information about him as you can without being obvious. We want information, but don't want him to suspect you of being more than a beautiful young woman interested in an older man."

"I'll charm the pants off him." Susan said.

Gregory looked at her with the left eyebrow raised, but said nothing.

"Of course not literally" She said laughing

"Thank God for that" He said light heartedly.

Gregory asked Byron, "Any action on the bug last night?"

"No, nothing just watched some TV and went to bed. Got up this morning around five and ordered breakfast and just chit chat with his security detail about the Trade meeting." Byron told him.

Susan phoned Vistin asking if he could make it for lunch today. He said "I'm sure I can slide out of this afternoons meeting. I'll meet you in the lobby at one."

"Will you have time to show me around the town a bit? I'd love to learn about this city from a man with your experience." She said.

"I would be delighted to show you around. Until one then." Vistin said hanging up and thinking his day just got brighter.

CHAPTER NINETEEN

ALMATY KAZAKHSTAN

T he flight arrived on time with no drama and Olrlov was met by the driver the Consul arranged for his use during his trip. They drove to his hotel through heavy traffic and he was somewhat surprised at how beautiful the snowcapped mountains surrounding the city were, even in the heavy smog. His room was on the twenty fifth floor, had a nice view of the city, and he sat in the big leather chair sipping a glass of Vodka, staring out at the view thinking, "It's just about over, soon I'll be free and wealthy".

The meetings over the next three days went along the lines he had expected with the Transportation Minister, basically wanting Russia to build the light rail system as a gift to his beleaguered people. This was to be expected and Paval Orlov was feeling more in his element negotiating with the man. After several hours of meetings with the Transportation Minister, Paval Orlov was walking to his car feeling drained and weak from the strain of the past week. He couldn't shake the feeling he was being followed and was thinking "Am I just being paranoid thinking I'm being followed so soon? Because of what happened with The Islamic Brotherhood for Jihad there's bound to be some repercussions but it's too soon. The KGB probably wouldn't be following me here, but The Islamic Brotherhood for Jihad just might if they found out I was coming.

It's easy to spot a Syrian in Moscow, but anybody could be with The Islamic Brotherhood for Jihad here. I just can't tell."

Orlov was sitting in the back of the car as his driver headed for his hotel through the grindingly slow Almaty traffic. They stopped behind a large truck when two armed men appeared, one on either side of his car. One man got in the passenger side and the other in the back with Orlov, holding a large caliber pistol to the side of Orlov's head. "Tell him to drive or we will kill you both right here" the man in back said. Orlov did as they ordered, and they drove for several miles out of the city onto a dirt road into the hills to a small building in the middle of nowhere.

Getting out of the car, the man in front shot the driver in the head without saying a word. Orlov thought he might be sick. The man with the gun to Orlov's head said, "Get out and walk straight inside. If you try to run you won't make two steps before your dead."

As the wind whipped down from the higher snowcapped mountains, Orlov was surprised how much colder it was here than in the city, as he walked into the freezing cold room. It was cold, but he was sweating profusely and shaking from fear. The building looked as if the wind would topple it at any time. Orlov felt a boot in his back and fell face down on the dirt floor. The room smelled damp and musty and of the animals that took refuge from the cold outside. As his eyes adjusted to the darkness he saw the room had only a kerosene lantern hanging from a rope, a dirt floor and nothing but a rickety wooden chair in the middle. There was also a chain hanging from the ceiling. He tried to stand but three men grabbed him roughly, and he was thrown to the floor, where they kicked and punched him. He felt a searing pain shoot through his left side when several of his ribs cracked. They dragged him to his feet, and a very large man smashed him in the face with a club of a fist, he felt one of his front teeth go down his throat and his nose break. The room was spinning as he became sick either from fear or pain, probably both. He dropped to his knees and vomited all over himself as blood was streaming from his broken nose and his world went black.

CHAPTER TWENTY

CASABLANCA MOROCCO

G eneral Vistin left the Trade Meeting at the midday break and headed back to the Royal Hotel, looking forward to his afternoon with the beautiful Miss O'Brian. He told his military security detail, "I won't need you any more today. I'm meeting a young lady for lunch and wish to be alone."

"As you order General, but shouldn't we say close?" The Major in charge of security asked.

"No Major. I'll be fine and prefer to be alone when I'm entertaining a young woman." Vistin said with finality.

"Yes Sir. Men you're dismissed until twenty one hundred hours." The Major said.

Vistin took a long hot shower and dressed casually. He poured himself a glass vodka, and standing by the window, enjoyed the view from his suite. He felt happy. The idea of an afternoon rendezvous, with a beautiful young woman he just met was more exciting than he would have thought. "This is going to be memorable" he said to himself.

Entering the lobby, General Vistin saw Susan waiting for him looking extremely sexy, wearing skin tight cream colored jeans with a soft blue silk blouse that displayed her lovely figure perfectly. His heart started to beat a little faster as he walked towards her. He was thinking "You're a very lucky man Nicolay. This is what being rich is all about".

Walking up to her he said, "Miss O'Brian, it so nice to see you again so soon. You look lovely."

"Why thank you Vladimir. I'm so glad you could get away today. Please call me Cynthia." Susan said with a beaming smile.

"Would you like to have lunch first or tour the galleries" He asked.

"Why don't we see some of the sights on the way to lunch? It is just about that hour after all". She said.

"Fine, there are two contemporary art galleries on the way to the waterfront where there's an excellent sea food restaurant. It's a delightful day for a stroll." He told her.

"Great, let's go then" She said letting him take her arm.

They walked along the main road down to the crowded waterfront with many trendy restaurants, galleries and shops, and Vistin told her about the historical parts of that area of Casablanca, completely captivated by her charm.

For lunch they enjoyed fresh seafood Kebabs seasoned with Saffron, Paprika and Ginger, on bed of freshly made couscous.

Vistin said, "Though Morocco is predominately Muslim, and alcohol is prohibited to them, this restaurant does have an excellent Volubilia Gris, named for the Roman ruins in that region of Mekens, that pairs well with the local seafood. They're allowed to sell a limited amount to foreigners."

"Sounds interesting, let sample a bottle" Susan said.

During lunch Susan asked, "So tell me Vladimir, what business are you in that brings you to Morocco?"

"I'm with the Russian Government. We're working with North African countries to expand their trade in Eastern Europe." he told her.

"That sounds like interesting and rewarding work that would help this part of Africa quite a bit." she said.

"We feel it will help the region, and the people here."Vistin told her.

"So tell me about yourself Cynthia."Vistin said

"Not really so much to tell. When I was young I always wanted to dance for the ballet and was training from the age of eight. When I was thirteen my body started to change, and I became a bit too top heavy, so that was it for ballet". She said with a blush.

"I'm sure you were very disappointed, but the change looks well worth it from here."Vistin said with a smile.

Susan blushed again and continued, "So, I decided I should put all that effort into my education. I was accepted to Queens College at Cambridge, and took a first in foreign languages with emphasis on Asian languages. After graduation, I was hoping to get a position at the United Nations as a translator but nothing was available. I met Mr. MacNee through a friend when I was visiting Paris and we started chatting about what I wanted to do. He offered me a job as his Private Executive Secretary since his company does a good deal of business in Asia, and it sounded good. The pay is excellent and I get to travel a great deal, stay at the finest places, and meet interesting people; like you Vladimir."

At this Vistin pretended to look embarrassed at the complement. "Well thank you for that Cynthia. Travel is a bonus in both of our positions I suppose." Vistin said, feeling things were going quite well with this beautiful young woman.

"Do you live in Moscow now Vladimir?" Susan asked.

"My family has had a home on Mokhovaya Street for decades and it's just a short walk to my office in the Kremlin. Traffic in that part of Moscow is dreadful all the time, so it's good to be able to walk to the office. We also have a nice Dacha in Rublevka so I can get away from the city from time to time." He told her.

"And you Cynthia, do you live in Central London?" Vistin asked.

"Well, yes. Central London is extremely expensive, and I don't think it's worth paying that much rent since I'm traveling so much. Luckily for me, Mr. MacNee owns a very large home in Highgate, and lets me live in the guest house on the property rent free. Bit of a job perk I suppose." She said.

"Are you and Mr. MacNee close friends?" He asked watching her reaction to the question.

"Well yes, we have become good friends over the past few years. Not intimate friends of course, he's a brilliant man and a great boss and I consider him a good friend. Do you have anyone special at home?" She asked looking at him quizzically.

"No, not really. I never married and I'm working so much, either in Moscow or traveling, I just don't seem to find the time to spend with anyone long enough to build any kind of meaningful relationship, as I'm sure you understand as a traveler yourself." he told her.

"I do understand indeed. I'm never home more than a few days a month. I see my family at Christmas and that's been about all for the past few years. I do miss them, and not having really close friends, but the travel is exciting at my age. There is plenty of time for a relationship in the future." she said.

Feeling the subject was going off the reason for this lunch, and getting to personal, Susan abruptly changed the subject.

"Your knowledge of art is quite extensive. Have you been interested in art for long?" She asked.

Vistin realized that he had moved the conversation into intimate territory to quickly and said, "Yes, I've been interested in art for many years, and if some investments I have working pay off, I'd like to start a small collection of my own. Nothing like the works we saw the other evening of course, but some nice things I've seen in my travels." He explained with sincerity that seem real but of course was a lie.

They continued to discuss art and more general subjects and were discussing perhaps meeting for dinner, when Susan's phone buzzed.

Looking at her phone she said, "Excuse me Vladimir, I'm dreadfully sorry, but Mr. MacNee needs me back at the hotel right away."

"How disappointing. We were having such a lovely afternoon. But I'll walk you back. I wouldn't want you to get in hot water with your boss." He said truly disappointed.

They walked back to the Royal Hotel and he escorted up to the Presidential Suite.

"Thank you for joining me for lunch Cynthia. I enjoyed our time together this afternoon very much."Vistin told her.

"If I'm free, perhaps we can meet for an early dinner tomorrow evening. It's been a delightful afternoon, thank you Vladimir." she said giving him a quick kiss on the cheek.

Vistin felt the heat of her lips on his cheek as he walked to the lift. His pulse was racing and his breath was coming in short bursts. "What an extraordinary young woman. It's been a long time since I felt like this. I've never had a woman half my age before, it's intoxicating". He was thinking.

Susan came into the living room of the suite and Gregory said, "So did you have nice time? What did you find out about our General Vistin."

"He's charming" she told him. "He's a bold face liar of course, but a charming one. Claims to be with the Russian government here to help the West African Countries increase trade with Eastern Europe, just a man of the people. As far as the art, he said he hopes to start a small collection with money from investments. Investments like selling a nuclear physicist to terrorist. He's not married and has no children, lives on Mokhovaya Street in Moscow close to his office at the Kremlin. Not much more than what we already knew." She said.

Gregory received a phone call from Mobius on the secure line.

"Gregory, I just got word from Johnston in Almaty, that Paval Orlov was kidnapped in broad daylight while being driven back to his hotel. Johnson was about four cars behind Orlov when two armed men got in his car and they left. He was unable to clear the traffic to follow, and didn't intervene since it would have resulted in a fire fight in the street and MI6 involvement would have been discovered. So now it looks like The Islamic Brotherhood for Jihad has Orlov, and I'm sure they'll sweat him for everything he knows. I think there's no chance in hell they won't kill him, so we need to stick to Vistin."Mobius told him.

"Christ, they're moving faster than I expected. I was hoping we could question Orlov for details on how extensive Vistin's organization is, and whether he has other operations going at this time." Gregory said.

"Was Susan able to get any useful information during her rendezvous with Vistin this afternoon?" Mobius asked.

"Rather difficult to say really. Since he's lying about his name and claims to be employed by the Russian government to assist countries in North Africa increase trade with Eastern Europe, who knows what's true. He did tell her he was never married and lives on Mokhovaya Street near the Kremlin. He may have been telling the truth on that hoping to get Susan to visit him and take her to his home. Ask Miss Trent to see if she can find out if he lives there, and if he really has no wife or children to tie him to Moscow. If he's telling the truth about no wife, ex-wife, or children, he would be more apt to leave the country quickly to stay ahead of the KGB. He's very interested in getting to know Susan better and suggested dinner in the next day or two, so we might be able to stay with him and get more out of him" Gregory said.

"Sounds good, but Gregory, make sure she doesn't get too involved with Vistin. He is charming, and she is young, if you take my point. Make sure it's purely professional."

"Yes Sir, I understand completely" Gregory said.

Mobius continued, I'm sending two agents, Marcus and Wilson to pick up Theo Accola in Zurich and track him while we think of a way to squeeze information out of him regarding his current and past dealings with Vistin."

"Ok, we should wrap up here in Casablanca in a few days, then we can head to Zurich to work on Accola, and try to find a way to recover the art works in Vistin's vault". Gregory told him.

Gregory phoned Matt West in Aruba and told him about Orlov.

"Matt, it seems that Paval Orlov was picked up by The Islamic Brotherhood for Jihad in Kazakhstan. I'm sure they'll get everything from him before he dies and they may have people heading to Aruba to try to recover their money. You'd better watch your back damn closely while you're down there." Gregory said.

"I'll definitely do that Gregory. You know, even though Orlov's involved in this shit, I pity the poor bastard. He'll die hard in their hands; that's for damn sure. "West said.

"Do you think your Justice Department can pressure the Private Client Bank in Zurich to let you take a look inside Vistin's safety deposit box in their vault?" Gregory asked him.

"I'll ask them, but I doubt a Swiss Bank would do that without an order from their government. And then it would take some arguing. It seems you have a line on the art works."

"We bugged his buyer's agent at the auction and found out his name is Theo Accola, art dealer in Zurich. We followed him to a meeting in Vistin's limo. Vistin told him to put the new paintings in with the others in his vault at the Private Client Bank in Zurich. They're scheduled to arrive on Wednesday. We have two agents heading up there to keep an eye on Accola until the works have arrives. By the way, how is John doing?" Gregory asked.

"He's still in the hospital but out of ICU. He's able to eat solid food again but can't walk yet. He'll be ok." West told him.

"Glad to hear it. I think Vistin may be heading your way soon. Since his account was locked in Aruba he'll need to use other accounts to pay for the art he just bought at the auction, that will take over one hundred thirty two million Euros from his Swiss account and he couldn't have planned for that. I'm betting he'll be down to see his banker in short order. I'll let you know if he heads that way". Gregory said.

General Vistin returned to his suite after the Trade Meeting feeling light hearted. He had phoned Susan at the noon break and she accepted his invitation to dine with him that evening at seven thirty. He poured himself a small glass of vodka and put some light classical music on the sound system and relaxed in the large leather chair by the window.

Byron said to Gregory, "You'll want to hear this boss" and put the bug in Vistin's suite on speaker.

They heard the phone ring and he answered in a jovial mood. "Hello Theo my good friend. What can I do for you on this lovely evening?"

Listening to what Accola told him, Vistin began to shake with rage and bellowed into his phone, "What the hell are you talking about the funds were unavailable. Before the auction I checked them myself".

After a pause he said, "My Swiss account as a backup, who the

hell authorized you to use my Swiss account. That much would almost clean those accounts dry".

"You're Goddamn right I'll contact the President. I'll do better
than call the bastard, I'll be in the bastard's office by nine A.M. and
he better find my money in one Goddamn hurry". Visting growled.

Slamming the phone down, Vistin called his aid and said. "I
have official State business in Aurba first thing in the morning.
Have my plane prepared to take off immediately. This is a secret
mission so tell the pilot just get the plane ready with clearances
to Aurba".

"Yes general, right away. Will you be coming back here or
should we check you out of the hotel?" The aid asked.

"Just get the damn plane ready and pack my things, I'll have
Fedor take care of the rest of my things and check out. I'll only
take you and Gregor with me on this mission, we don't need the
rest. Tell them to check out and take a commercial flight back to
Moscow. They are not to speak to anyone regarding this mission,
is that perfectly clear Major". Vistin told him.

"Yes General, perfectly clear" The Major said.

"Ok, that's what we've been waiting for." Gregory said. "Connell
tell my pilot we're on the way. I had him fuel the Gulfstream for the
flight so we're ready to go now. We're faster than Vistin's Tupolev
and have longer range. Vistin will need to refuel in Newfoundland.
We have extra fuel tanks and can go nonstop. Also, we're ready to
leave now, so we'll be there at least six hours ahead of him. Susan,
you stay here tonight then head back to London. I'll keep the suite
because once Vistin has met with the bank he will have to come
back to finish the Trade Conference. I'd love to have you along but
if Vistin spots you he'll know I'm involved and work out an MI6
connection and the game would be up".

"No problem Gregory, we've come too far to blow the operation by having him see me where I'm not supposed to be. At least this gets me out of dinner with him. I wasn't looking forward to that. I know he'd make a move on me and I'm not going that far for the service" Susan said with a grin.

"Thanks for understanding Susan. Ok guys let's move out". Gregory said.

"See you back in London Sue" Byron told her.

CHAPTER TWENTY ONE

KAZAKHSTAN

Paval Orlov was in a freezing world of pain. His couldn't feel his feet or arms and his shoulders felt as though they were on fire. He tried to open his eyes, but they seemed to be swollen closed. As he slowly regained consciousness, he managed to force his eyes open to a cold dark world.

"He's coming around sir." Orlov heard someone say.

"So, the betraying infidel's back with us" a man's voice said

Orlov had trouble focusing his eyes, and his ears where ringing. He had been stripped naked; his arms were stretched upward by the chain in the ceiling with his hands in manacles and his feet just touching the ground. The skin on his wrists was torn and dried blood caked his numb arms. He began to shiver uncontrollably.

"What I'm I doing here, who are you people, what do you want?" He asked, his swollen tongue making it hard to speak.

The man standing in front of him said nothing, just smashed him in the face again and again.

Two of Orlov's teeth fell in a pool of blood on the floor, and he swallowed three more from the last blow. He was unconscious again.

The leader of the group Sami Mohammad Assouli said "Rouse the dog"

One of the men took a bucket of cold water and through it in Orlov's face.

Sami Mohammad Assouli's lieutenant, Junaid Mohammad, took Orlov by the hair and shook in back to semi-consciousness.

"You betrayed the brotherhood to the German infidels you pig. They killed four of our brothers, and you stole our money. Tell me who the head of Ophidian is, and where do we find him. Assouli hissed.

Orlov thought that only by denying he knew who the head of Ophidian was, he may survive.

"I don't know who he is or where to find him. I work through contacts on the phone. I was ordered to find agents to kidnap the physicist Patterson and to have them hold him for you to pick up. I had nothing to do with the money you paid Ophidian." Orlov told them.

"Liar!" Assouli shouted. "I want his name".

"I swear I don't know. I'm contacted by phone and given an instruction, that's all." Orlov said.

"You know you have someone in the organization to contact. I want his name and contact number now, or Junaid will slit your throat right here." Assouli told him.

"My contact is Nikolay and his number is in my wallet. I don't have an address only the contact number" Orlov said.

"Junaid, find the number and locate this Nikolay immediately". Report to me personally the moment you find him." Assouli ordered.

"It will be done sir" Junaid said.

All of the men except one guard left the room, leaving Paval Orlov hanging there freezing and bleeding. He prayed they would let him live if they found Vistin. He had no idea how long he'd been hanging there, he'd passed out many times from the pain and could no longer feel his arms. After what seemed like an eternity a light and wind swept through the dim room as Sami Mohammed Assoulin and Junaid returned.

"We've discovered the identity of your contact within the Ophidian organization; General Nikolay Vistin, and we believe he is the head of that organization. Tell us where we can find him now" Assoulin said.

"I had no idea that General Vistin was the contact Nikolay, or that he had anything to do with Ophidian, I swear it" Orlov cried.

"Tell us where to find this General Vistin." Assoulin said.

Orlov felt he had to tell them since they had found out about General Vistin somehow, or he would be killed.

"I only know General Vistin through official Government Business. I heard he was going to Casablanca yesterday on Government business, but may be headed back to Moscow; I really don't know." Orlov told him.

Assoulin said to one of the brothers, "Kazim, contact our brothers in Aurba and have them keep watch for General Vistin. Since that's where the money was sent he may show up. Also get some fighters to Casablanca right away to see if he's still there. The order for both teams is, kidnap General Vistin if possible, if they can't, kill him."

Turning back on Orlov he said "Where is Vistin's office in Russia?"

"In the Kremlin, you'll never be able to reach him there, security is far too tight" Orlov said.

"Then were does he live? Tell me or we'll kill you right now"

Thinking it was his only chance of survival, and that it was Vistin's stupidity that put him in this situation, Orlov said, "He lives on Mokovaya Street in Moscow near the Kremlin".

"How many guards at his home?" the man asked

"Only one at the front of the building I think. But I've never been to his home. One guard is standard for high ranking officials." Orlov told him.

"That's all we need to know. Junaid, show this infidel what happens to those who betray the faithful" the leader said.

Junaid Mohammed, drew a twelve inch long combat knife from its scabbard and walked up to the shaking Orlov. He grabbed Orlov by the hair and pulled his head back and up.Orlov was in a state of object panic. He was shaking uncontrollably as the knife touched his throat.

CHAPTER TWENTY TWO

THE ISLAND OF ARUBA

D uring the long flight to Aurba, Gregory phoned Matt West and told him that they were en-route to the island and that General Vistin would arrives about six to eight hours later.

"He found out that the bank made his money unavailable and went nuts, dropped everything, and ordered his plane fueled for the trip immediately." Gregory told West.

"Well, we figured he'd be a bit miffed when he found out. How did he pay for the art?" West asked laughing.

"His buyer's agent, Theo Accola, told him that the auction used his Swiss accounts as a backup and that the paintings had been paid for from those accounts. Vistin told Accola that he had not been given permission to use the Swiss accounts, and that he would deal with him once he had straightened out things with the President of Banko de Aruba. He was seriously pissed Matt." Gregory said.

"Well, it should be an interesting fireworks display at the bank when they meet. We'll have to get there early". West said.

"I'll want to hear it but I can't let Vistin see me. I'll have to stay in the shadows. I never actually met him at the auction, but he knows that Susan works for me and might have noticed me since I was bidding against him. He'll know something's afoot if he sees me in Aruba as well, and we can't afford a connection with me and

MI6 exposed. I have Connell and Byron with me so they can be on hand at the bank." Gregory told him.

"I'm at the Costa Aruba on Renaissances Beach just north of Oranjestad. Give me a call when you're in and we can talk in more detail about what to do about Vistin". West said.

The MI6 Gulfstream landed at Queen Beatrix International Airport in Oranjestad, well ahead of General Vistin's Tupolev. Miss Trent, had arranged a car and driver for Gregory and his group. Stepping out of air conditioned comfort of the Gulfstream onto the tarmac; Gregory was hit by the hot humid air.

"Bloody hell, were you expecting this kind of heat in February" Connell asked Gregory.

"I knew it was generally warm down here most of the year, but no, this is a bit much." Gregory said.

"Christ we've only been here five minutes and I'm sweating bullets." Connell said pulling off his jacket and wiping his brow.

They got into the Mercedes S Class sedan; and were thankful for the cars excellent air conditioning system. The driver headed North on Route One to LG Smith Road then on to the hotel just twenty minutes away from the airport. The driver had no idea who they were or what their business in Aruba was, so as they drove to the Hotel Costa Aruba he continued to point out different places of interest along the way. Miss Trent reserved a large corner suite for Gregory and two adjoining rooms for Connell and Byron.

Arriving at his suite Gregory poured a glass of the local Coecoei on ice and phoned West, while enjoying the hotels excellent view and air conditioning.

"Hello Matt, we're here, I'm in suite number one on the fourth floor. Give me about twenty minutes to get settled in then come up." Gregory said.

***

They all met in the suite, and Gregory told West about what had happened back in Casablanca at the auction, and the overheard conversation with Theo Accola.

"Well, if that much money was taken from his accounts in Switzerland, he'll damn sure be on his way here, and madder than hell to try to get his money unstuck from the accounts here. Do you think we could just pick him up and squeeze the information about his organization out of him?" Matt asked.

"We'd love to do just that, but no way. We can't abduct a Russian Military Official. We have no proof that would stand up in court that he has any organization, or had anything to do with what happened in Italy or Patterson's kidnapping. It would be a huge International incident and could actually lead to war. No, we need to find a more subtle way get what we need to know." Gregory told him.

"Yeah, I suppose that's true. But it's too damn bad. We could have him in less than twenty four hours". West said.

"If your Justice Department can put enough pressure on the banks here in Aruba to get them to lock up Vistin's accounts, why can't they get us a look inside his safe boxes in Switzerland?" Gregory asked West.

"Aruba's long been a clearing house for drug money and smuggled goods pirates and the like. The Kingdom of the Netherlands is trying hard to clean things up but as you can imagine, it's not an easy job. Aruba is one of four autonomous constituents of the Kingdom of the Netherlands. They have their own constitution and make their own rules. Because of this, the government has looked aside when banks took accounts with known drug dealers and other criminal organizations. The local government is working with the Kingdom of the Netherlands to help fight terrorist and the big drug cartels. They're trying to close up this loophole, so they agreed to work with the U.S. Justice Department on banking issues like this. They won't be able to keep Vistin's money locked up for long without positive proof that the funds came from terrorist, so we need to gather that proof quickly. Switzerland is quite another matter. They've always been neutral and don't yield to pressure from anyone." West told him.

"I understand. We'll just need to find the proof they need before they release the funds to Vistin. If he gets hold of the money he'll definitely leg it out of Russia for some safe haven, that's for damn sure." Gregory said.

General Vistin's Tupolev landed late in the evening and was met by a driver from the Russian embassy, who flew in from Venezuela to meet him. He arranged for a rental car for the General's security men as well. The General got into the Mercedes with Major Alexie Dragomirov, an ex Russian Spetsnaz group commander, and one of General Vistin's most trusted security men. Sergeant Gregor Petrovich, drove the chase car as they headed for hotel Koninklijk Baai.

Gregory and West were waiting at the airport, and followed Vistin at a discreet distance to his hotel.

"Welcome to the island paradise of Aruba General Vistin. We hope you have a pleasant stay" Gregory said joking to West.

After finding out where Vistin was staying, Gregory and West headed back to the Hotel Costa Aruba deciding to tail Vistin to the bank in the morning since they were not sure which branch he would be headed for.

Back in his suite, Gregory phoned room service, ordering a late dinner of Tropical Bouillabaisse, mixed seafood with coconut cream and saffron to start and Blackened Mahi Mahi with Ajo blanco puree. West opted for the slow cooked short ribs, and both decided on the local Balashi Pilsner.

" Gregory, everything has got to be fancy with you Englishmen. Fancy suites, private jet, fancy food, everything" West joked.

"We simply like what we like Matt" Gregory said, accepting the good natured jibe.

After dinner Gregory phone Mobius on the secured line and let him know what has happening.

"General Vistin arrived a little while ago and we tracked him to his hotel. We'll trail him to the bank and listen in to the blowing up he's bound to give the bank President and let you know if the bank releases the funds. However it goes at the bank, I'll head to Zurich and grind Accola about the paintings just as soon as possible." Gregory told Mobius.

"Ok Gregory, I'll tell Marcus and Wilson to contact you when you arrive in Zurich. They've been tracking Theo Accola since he returned to Zurich and found his home. He is going to his gallery as normal so he should be easy to isolate and question." Mobius told him.

The next morning Gregory, West and the team were waiting in a non-descript white rented Ford sedan half a block from the front of the Koninklijk Baai's main entrance so the Vistin's security men wouldn't pick them up. They followed Vistin down Route One and were lucky not too loose him in the heavy traffic in the round-about at Las Americas then up Stadionwed to the main branch of the Banko de Aruba and parked in the car park at the side of the building.

General Vistin's driver parked right outside the front doors of the bank in the no parking zone. The General, and his two security men, strode purposely into the bank and Vistin said to the Presidents secretary, " I'm Nikolay Vistin, here to see Jayden Visser, now."

The President's secretary said, "I'm sorry sir, Mr. Visser is in a meeting at the moment. If you would please take a seat, I'll tell him you're here."

"That's unacceptable young woman. You tell him I'm here, and want to see him immediately." Vistin said glaring at the secretary.

"Let me see if he can see you sir" the secretary said, raising and knocking on the Presidents door.

"That's not necessary" Vistin said, striding past her and walking in.

"I'm sorry Mr. Visser sir, this gentleman just refused to wait" the secretary told Jayden Visser as he was rising from his desk.

"It's quite all right Miss Stone, quite all right." Visser told her.

"Mr. Vistin, it's a pleasure to meet you. Won't you please have a seat? Miss Stone, please bring some coffee for Mr. Vistin." Jayden Visser said soothingly.

Miss Stone hurried back with coffee in bone china cups, and a plate of fresh croissants, setting them on the table between Jayden Visser and General Vistin.

"Thank you, that will be all Miss Stone" Visser said calmly.

"General Vistin said to his security men, "Alexei, you and Gregor, wait outside, this won't take long."

"Yes sir," Major Dragomiroff said, as he and Gregor closed the door to Visser's office.

"Now what the hell is all this about my money not being available? We checked when the funds arrived prior to the art auction, and we were told they were available. After the auction Theo Accola, my man in Switzerland, called me and told me the bank said the funds are unavailable. I had to take one hundred thirty two million Euros from my other accounts to cover the purchase. Where the hell is my three hundred million Euros Mr. Visser?" General Vistin bellowed.

"Sir, it seems there was a miss communication between what

was told to your man in Switzerland, Mr. Accola, and what was told to you. The Kingdom of the Netherlands, with the co-operation of our Government here on Aurba, is working to stem the flow of funds through Aurba to terrorist and drug cartels. When funds come from curtain areas they have mandated that the funds must be held for seven business days so an investigation can be made as to the source of those funds. Since the three hundred million Euros transferred into your account came from a source in Saudi Arabia the hold was automatic." Jayden Vasser explained calmly.

General Vistin was purple with rage, "No one ever disclosed that your Government ordered a hold on funds in a private numbered account. Why the hell do you think your clients use these accounts, because they want the Government to know about what's in them and who they belong to?"

"Of course not Mr. Vistin, the bank does all it can to keep that information confidential, but this is a new program that we cannot do anything about. If you would like to have the Russian Government contact the Kingdom of The Netherlands with a formal protest, perhaps the Government would remove this requirement. Barring that, there is simply nothing the bank can do." Visser explained in an offhand manner.

General Vistin sat glaring at Jayden Visser. "That's bullshit, I'm not interested in what your Government wants, and Moscow has nothing to do with this. You have my money and I want it now." He stood up and walked around the desk, grabbed Visser by the tie, jerking to his feet. He drew his pistol from its shoulder holster and jammed it against Visser's temple. "You'll transfer all the money in my accounts, including my three hundred million Euros, today to my accounts at the Private Client Bank is Zurich or you won't see your family again. I have men watching them and they'll be picked up on my order. You'll watch them die, before I kill you. Do you understand me?" Vistin hissed in Vasser's ear.

Vasser stood shaking, weak in the knees, and pleaded with Vistin. "It's not my fault sir, please don't hurt my family, I'll get the money transferred today somehow, I swear. Please just don't hurt my family."

General Vistin shoved Visser back into his chair and put his pistol back in his holster. Pointing at Visser he said, "Today. If my people find the funds are not there you won't see the sunrise. I guarantee it."

General Vistin walked to the door, turning and pointing at Visser again "Today, not a moment later." he strode out slamming the door.

Gregory and Connell were standing at the small desk holding the account withdrawal slips, and watched Vistin stride towards the door with Gregor walking in front of him, and Major Dragomiroff just behind.

"That was a hell of a noisy private conference. Vistin looks pissed" Gregory said to Connell.

"He is pissed. Of course we knew he would be. Looks like the folks at U.S. Justice Department have some serious clout in the world banking community." Connell said.

Matt West went into Jayden Visser's office and was shocked to see Visser white and sweating with fear.

"What happened here Mr. Visser?" West asked, closing the door.

"I did what was agreed to with your Justice Department, but Vistin threatened to kill my family before my eyes if the funds didn't transfer today." Visser said in a voice choked with emotion.

West poured Visser a brandy from the decanter on the sideboard, and handing to him said, "Here, drink this, it'll help settle you down. Can we delay the transfer at all" West asked.

"No Mr. West. I'm having all his funds transferred at once and closing his accounts. I was willing to help the U.S. Justice Department, but not risk my family's life or my own. There is no legal basis for holding the funds and even if there were it's not worth my family.

"We completely understand Mr. Visser. Thank you for the delay you made, and your understanding and cooperation with the U.S. Government." West said.

Gregory was waiting by the desk when West came out of Visser's office, and joined him on the way to the front doors of the bank.

"So, what happened in there? Is Visser going to hold Vistin's funds for a few more days?" Gregory asked him.

"That was indeed an interesting meeting Vistin had with Visser. He threatened to kill Visser, and his family, if the funds weren't transferred today. He told Visser if the funds weren't transferred to his Swiss accounts by the end of business today, he would kill Visser's family before his eyes, then kill him." West told Gregory as they walked toward their car.

"Well, we knew he would be pissed but I really didn't think he would threaten to kill both Visser and his family" Gregory said.

"Three hundred million Euros is a lot of cash, and Vistin is a violent man, who won't hesitate to kill to achieve his ends, but CIA really didn't think he would react like that or we wouldn't have asked Visser to get involved. We wanted to disrupt the cash flow, but not get an innocent banker and his family killed." West told Gregory

"Of course not Matt. Well, let's see where Vistin heads from here. He should go back to Casablanca since the North African Trade meeting won't be over for a few days, and that's why Moscow sent him. Ask your people to check with the tower and see where Vistin's pilot files his flight plan to." Gregory said.

***

General Vistin and his men drove back to their hotel, and Vistin found a message tucked under the door, addressed to Nikolay Vistin. Vistin walked into his bedroom and read the message.

"You've stolen our money, and caused the death of our brothers. We will have our vengeance for this betrayal."

Vistin sat on the end of the bed and lit a cigarette, inhaling the smoke deeply, and considered what to do next. He was surprised how quickly The Islamic Brotherhood for Jihad had found him.

"Major, have my pilot get the plane fueled and cleared for Morocco at once. I need to get back to the conference." Vistin said.

"At once General. Major Dragomiroff said.

Arriving back the Hotel Costa Aruba, they met in Gregory's suite, and Matt West phoned the control tower at Queen Beatrix International, asking to speak the Director of Flight Operations. West identified himself, and asked the director to please let him know when the Russian Tupolev files its flight plan.

"Yes sir, actually we just had a flight plan submitted for Tupolev RA-87641 from Queen Beatrix International to Mohammed V International Casablanca, with fuel stop at Generalissimo Francisco de Miranda Air Base in Venezuela, departing at fourteen hundred hours today. "The director told him.

"Thank you Mr. Director. The United States Government appreciates your cooperation and assistance in this matter. Please keep in mind that this in a National Security matter, and must not be discussed." West told him.

"Yes, of course I understand, agent West. It's our pleasure to assist you in any way we can." The director said.

Hanging up, West said to Gregory. "Looks like Vistin's heading back to the trade conference this afternoon. His pilot filed a flight plan to Casablanca via Venezuela leaving at fourteen hundred today.

"Well guys, get your gear together, looks like we're going back to Casablanca. I'll call our pilot and have him fuel up and file our flight plan, then I need to report to Mobius, so we'll be ready to go in about two hours." Gregory told his team.

"In that case, I'll head back to Langley tonight. CIA is digging into the Syrian's working with Vistin, to see if they're The Islamic Brotherhood for Jihad and how deep they are with Vistin's Ophidian organization. We need to track them. Those bastards are dangerous to everyone. Oh, by the way, any further word on Paval Orlov?" West asked Gregory.

"No, nothing so far, but I think the outcome of his kidnapping is obvious. It's a damn shame they got to him, before we could get any information on Vistin's organization from him" Gregory said.

"He'd much rather be in our hands than the Syrian's, that's for damn sure" Connell said.

Gregory connected the scrambler and phoned Mobius. "We're heading back to Casablanca this afternoon. Vistin's leaving at fourteen hundred and stopping in Venezuela for fuel, so well beat him there by six hours. He threatened to kill the President of the Banko de Aruba and his entire family, if the three hundred million Euros was not transferred to his bank in Switzerland this afternoon. It was no idle threat. The bank President, Jayden Visser, was really shaken up. He said Vistin was a mad man and had pressed a gun to his head as he told him his men would pick up his family and they would be killed while he watched, and then he would die. To say the least, the money is being transferred as we speak.

"We knew Vistin was dangerous, but I'm a bit surprised he threatened Visser and his family. Before you leave, contact the police chief and ask them to put some officers on Visser and his family until Vistin is gone." Mobius said.

"Will do sir. We'll watch Vistin until he leaves the conference in Casablanca, then I'll let you know where I'm headed next. Please ask Kim to get my suite back at the Royal." Gregory said.

CHAPTER TWENTY THREE

DAMASCUS SYRIA

T he leaders of The Islamic Brotherhood for Jihad, met at their
headquarters at the large mosque on Aal Al Bait, near the east
end of the Bab el Saghir Cemetery in Damascus to discuss
what to do about this Russian infidel that betrayed them. Andnan
Mohammed Wasen, stood and addressed the assembled men.

"Our brothers, Kawa Deknish and Zakwan Jabili, flew to the
island of Aurba to abduct this General Vistin, and bring him to
us so we could mete out the justice of Allah. Due to flight delays
they arrived too late, and he has slipped through our fingers. Kawa
and Zakwan questioned the Aruba air traffic controller, and after applying the required pressure; they were told Vistin's plane
filed a flight plan back to Casablanca so they have gone there to
intercept him".

Turning to the men on his right, Mohammed Wasen addressed
the two fighters he had specifically called to attend the meeting.

"Brother Rasha Adjim, Brother Fathi Halir; you are to go
to Casablanca at once to back up Kawa and Deknish in binging
General Vistin here to us. When you arrive you will go to this address on Avenue Khalifa Ben Ismail, in the Hay Al Falah district,
and meet with Ranim Alfia. Ranim will supply you with whatever
weapons or tools you need in order to abduct Vistin or to kill him
if you're are unable to abduct him. Either way, he must not be

allowed to return to Moscow. The equipment available will include weapons to destroy his aircraft if it becomes necessary. We will have our vengeance on this infidel before he can reach Moscow."

"If Vistin does manage to escape us, and gets back to Moscow, we have fighters in the Georgian Republic and we will enlist their assistance in this Holy cause. There will be no failure. Either Vistin is captured or killed, or you will die in the attempt. Go now my brothers and do Allah's biding, Adhhab Mae Allah".

All the men in the room stood joined in repeating "Allah Akbar, Allah Akbar" over and over.

CHAPTER TWENTY FOUR

CASABLANCA MOROCCO

G regory arrived back in Casablanca late that day and checked back into the same suite.

Checking in, he asked the young woman at the reception desk, "Excuse me miss, could you tell me if General Vistin and party have checked out yet?"

"Let me check. No sir their still registered in suite three eighteen" The young woman said.

"Thank you Miss. General Vistin is a friend, and I was hoping to get to Casablanca before he headed home." Gregory said with a smile.

Since they knew that Vistin was still on his way back from Aruba, Byron went down to Vistin's suite and knocked. No one answered so he picked the lock and went inside. After quickly checking to make sure the suite was empty, he put one bug in the living room, one in the bedroom and attached a special newly developed micro bug inside both the living room and bedroom phones where they could not be detected. Then slipped out, relocking the door behind him.

Back in their suite Byron said, "Ok boss, we have him tapped on the phone and in both rooms."

"Nice work Byron. He'll most likely have a scrambler on the phone, but at least we can pick up conversations on our side. The Trade Conference is scheduled to end in two days, so we'll have to see where Vistin goes from there. I want to get to Zurich and work on Theo Accola, and try to get the art works away from Vistin as soon as possible." Gregory said.

"Since Vistin owns the art and it's been paid for, how would you get Accola to turn them over to you?" Byron asked.

"I'm not sure yet, but I'm working on a plan. Since Accola was actually the buyer, even though he was secretly buying them for Vistin, he's the owner of record. If I can think of a way to force him to release the art to us, Vistin's screwed." Gregory told him.

"Yeah, Vistin is screwed, and Accola's dead." Byron said.

"You're probably right about that, but I'll need to think of something to get that art work. We're working with CIA, to have the funds just transferred from Aruba, confiscated by Her Majesty's Government, stating that the money was to fund terrorist activity in Switzerland and England. If we can pull that off and get a hold of the art as well, Vistin's organization would be broke." Gregory said.

CHAPTER TWENTY FIVE

HAY AL FALAH CASABLANCA

R asha Adjim and Fathi Halir met with Ranjm Alfia, at the address given to them by Andnan Mohammed Wasen.

"What equipment do you need my brothers, to complete your task" Ranjm asked them.

"We'll need two Uzi 9mm machine pistols, and what do you have that would bring down a large jet?" Rasha asked.

"We were able to secure three of the new FIM 92A Infrared Stinger handheld missiles. They have a maximum effective range of five miles in good weather, and if you hit an engine, it would bring the plane down" Ranjm told him.

"Excellent. What have you given Brothers Kawa and Zakwan to complete their task?" Rasha asked.

"They took two 9mm pistols and two American magnetic Claymore mines. They didn't tell me what they would need the Claymores for, but they are powerful weapons, and should do whatever job they have planned." Ranjm said.

"Adhhab Mae Allah my brothers". Ranjm said as they were leaving.

CHAPTER TWENTY SIX

CASABLANCA

General Vistin's Tupolev landed at Mohammad V International Casablanca late in the evening, and he was picked up an official Russian State Mercedes with an embassy driver. He had ordered another car for Gregor, providing extra cover since he had received the note from The Islamic Brotherhood for Jihad. They drove back to the Royal and he went directly up to his suite.

"Major, I want one of you on guard in the living room, and Gregor in the hall all night."

"Yes General. Should we be expecting trouble sir?" Dragomiroff asked him.

"Possibly, as you know The Islamic Brotherhood for Jihad has made threats, and since they won't be able to get close to me at the conference, if they're here in Casablanca, they might make a move here at the hotel. So be alert Major. Anyone who looks like they may be from the Middle East, keep a damn close eye on them."

"Yes sir, we will sir."

General Vistin poured a large glass of vodka, and relaxed in one of the overstuffed chairs, looking out at the view feeling relaxed, and in control of the situation once again. He bought the art works he was hoping to, got his money back from Banko de Aruba, and would finish his official business, then return to Moscow without any of the Presidium knowing anything about the real reason for his coming to Casablanca.

The following morning he checked with the reception desk on the way to the conference and asked the young woman behind the desk, "Can you tell me if Miss Cynthia O'Brian was still in residence?"

Checking her log she said, "I'm sorry sir, we don't seem to have a Cynthia O'Brian registered here. I looked back for the past week and don't see her name. Could she be registered under a different name?"

"Yes, I'm sorry; I believe she's Mr. MacNee's Executive Secretary, so perhaps she was staying under the name of her boss."

Checking again she said, "Ah yes sir, Mr. MacNee had three suites and one was for Miss O'Brian. Unfortunately Mr. MacNee and party checked out several days ago."

"Oh, that is most unfortunate; I was hoping to get back to Casablanca before they left. Oh well, it's of no real importance. Thank you for checking."

General Vistin was quite disappointed to hear that the lovely Miss O'Brian had checked out. He was looking forward to getting to know her on a more intimate level, and now that would have to wait until he could look her up in London when all this was over. The next two days of the conference would be tedious but it had to be done. Nikolay was looking forward to being back at his office in the Kremlin, where he knew The Islamic Brotherhood for Jihad men could not reach him. Moscow was not at all friendly towards anyone from the Middle East at this time, so he felt safe.

Major Dragomiroff said " Sir, there have been two dark skinned men hanging around outside the hotel the past two days, but they have made no move to enter the hotel or follow us on the drive to the conference. It's difficult to spot The Islamic Brotherhood for

Jihad men here in Casablanca, since there are so many people that look like Syrians, but I have seen these two several times. We need to watch our backs until we leave."

"Agreed, but if they haven't moved on us while we were walking to and from the conference, and to the hotel, they're probably just looking for a handout when the opportunity presents itself." Vistin told him.

General Vistin and Major Dragomiroff were half dozing in the back of the Embassy Mercedes grinding along in the heavy afternoon traffic on Rue Barathon, heading back to the Hotel Royal on the final day of the conference. The traffic would move a few feet and stop again, while the drivers blasted their horns in frustration. Motorcycles, scooters and bicycles continued to weave past on both sides towards the roundabout. Kawa Deknish and Zakwan Jabili rode two small motorcycles that were passing on either side of the Embassy Mercedes as the car moved slowly. Major Dragomiroff heard a metallic thud sound, on both sides of the car, as if both motorcycles had hit the car at the same time, then the motorcycles pulled away quickly.

"Bomb!" Dragomiroff shouted and he pushed General Vistin out the rear door of the slowly moving car and he jumped out the other side.

General Vistin hit the road hard, fracturing his right shoulder, as the car continued to move away. The explosion from the two contact mines Kawa and Zakwan attached to the car was massive, blowing the top of the car straight up like an open tin can. The Embassy driver was killed instantly from the impact of two directional contact mines at once, as the burning car careened across the intersection crashing into a parked van, setting it on fire as well. Seeing that Vistin had jumped clear of the car, Kawa and Zakwan turned around with pistols drawn to finish him off. Major

Dragomiroff, rolled clear of the car, and came up with his pistol drawn and fired at Zakwan bearing down on the General. His first shot missed but his second shot hit Zakwan in the chest and the third in the face. Zakwan we went down hard as his lifeless body slid into a storm drain on the side of the road. Seeing his partner shot down, Kawa tried to turn and get away but Gregor; following in the trail car, slammed on the brakes and jumped out with his Markov 9mm machine pistol and opened fire. Kawa weaved around one of the cars in the line but was hit more than once by Gregor's shots, and swerved into the oncoming traffic running head on into a large cement mixer going in the opposite direction. His body was thrown into the air landing on the trunk of a taxi.

Gregor and Dragomiroff picked up General Vistin and hustled him into the back of Gregor's car. Driving over the sidewalk, and through the gathering crowd to clear the traffic, Gregor sped away from the chaos at the intersection.

"How bad is it?" Gregor asked Dragomiroff, as he examined the General. Should I head for the nearest hospital?"

"Yes, head for the hospital" Dragomiroff said, as he checked the General to see if he was shot or hit by the flying debris from the destroyed car.

"No, I'm all right. Get to the airport at once." The General ordered.

"Major, call my pilot and tell him to get fueled and cleared for Moscow without delay. Tell him to get emergency diplomatic clearance. " Vistin ordered.

"But sir, I think your shoulder may be broken, shouldn't we get you looked at by the hospital?"

"No Major. Do as I tell you" Vistin snapped.

"Yes General"

Vistin realized that the attack was from The Islamic Brotherhood for Jihad, in retaliation for the loss of the three hundred million Euros. He was shocked that they would have come at him so soon, and knew that Paval Orlov must have told them were to find him. Now the only safe place from the terrorist was back at the Kremlin.

Gregory and West were trailing Vistin from the conference several cars behind, when the attack happened. Gregory was thinking that now that the conference was over, he could go to Zurich and put pressure on Theo Accola to recover the art works Vistin had purchased with terrorist money. They were shocked by the sudden attack on Vistin's Mercedes, but they were too far back to do anything to help, so they just watched things un-fold like the scene from a movie.

"What the hell just happened?" West shouted.

"Looks like the boys from The Islamic Brotherhood for Jihad are on the job sooner than any of us predicted. There's nothing to do here, let's just head back to the hotel and report." Gregory said.

General Vistin and his security team drove right up to the waiting Tupolev, and the pilot began taxiing as soon as they were aboard and the door was closed. They took their seats and buckled in.

"There's been a terrorist attack, and attempt on my life. Get us the hell out of here and watch for other threats. We don't know how many of them there are or where they are." Vistin told the pilot over the intercom.

"Roger that sir. Hold tight everyone were rolling" The pilot said.

They were airborne within twenty seconds, when the co-pilot shouted, "Man with launcher to the right, break left".

The big Tupolev banked forty five degrees hard left, as the stinger missile streaked past, just missing the right wing tip. The pilot immediately banked hard right pitching the nose down, when a second stinger shot past the wind screen. Before the terrorist could fire a third missile the pilot put a stand of tall trees, from the Bouskoura Forest, between them and the terrorist line of fire, as they quickly accelerated moving out of missile range.

"We're clear of the threat General." the pilot called over the intercom system. "That was goddamn close sir."

"Well done Marco, very well done" General Vistin told his pilot.

"Thank you sir, this old gal doesn't exactly handle like a MIG, but she came through when we needed her." The pilot said, with a grin.

It took over one hour to get back to their hotel through the traffic jam that ensued after the bombing attack, and seeing that Vistin had not returned to the hotel, Gregory phoned the control tower at Mohammad V International and asked if the Russian Tupolev was still there.

"No sir, they took off an hour ago, and someone shot a couple missiles at the jet as she took off, but missed. Moroccan Special Security Services, the local police and the airport police are all over the area searching for the terrorists and the airport is closed until further notice. All flights are being diverted to Mellil Airport for now." The controller told Gregory.

"Holy shit Matt, someone shot missiles at Vistin's plane as it took off, but missed. The Islamic Brotherhood for Jihad is really pissed off. I'm phoning Mobius now and you need to get this to Langley." Gregory said.

Gregory attached the scrambler and phoned Mobuis.

"Sir, we were tailing Vistin back from the conference when his vehicle was attacked with explosives, attached to it by two passing motorcyclists. The Embassy driver was killed, but Vistin's security detail saved his life and killed the assassins. It was a bloody big explosion sir, and quite a mess in the street. It has to be The Islamic Brotherhood for Jihad. They're really playing for keeps. We lost Vistin in the chaos after the bombing, but I just phoned the airport control tower and they said someone shot missiles at his plane as it took off, but missed. He got away and is headed back to Moscow."

"Jesus Christ Gregory; these are really some crazy bastards. Bomb attacks on busy streets in the middle of the day, and shooting missiles at his plane. I don't think Vistin will be leaving the safety of the Kremlin anytime soon." Mobius said.

"Well sir; there's no reason to stay here any longer, so I'll see you back in London tomorrow. I want to go over a possible plan with you that I've been thinking about to recover the art that Vistin bought." Gregory said.

"Ok Gregory. Have agent West thank CIA, and their Treasury Department for their help in Aruba. See you tomorrow" Mobis told him.

CHAPTER TWENTY SEVEN

VAUXHALL CROSS LONDON

Gregory met with Mobius to give him a report on what had happened in Aruba and Casablanca.

"General Vistin threatened the life of the president of the Banko de Aruba if he didn't transfer all the funds in his accounts to the Private Client Bank in Zurich immediately, so of course he did. The paintings are in a vault at that same bank, but the vault is under the name of Theo Accola. I've been thinking, if we can apply enough pressure on Accola, we may be able to recover the paintings, since they were purchased with money supplied by terrorist." Gregory said.

"If Accola gave the art to us, Vistin would have Ophidian assassins kill him without hesitation, and he knows it. You know that by what Vistin threatened to do the banks president and his family for holding his funds for just a few days. What kind of pressure would we be able to put on Theo Accola to make him essentially, commit suicide?" Mobius asked.

"Sir, the situation has changed somewhat. With the kidnapping of Paval Orlov by The Islamic Brotherhood for Jihad, and let's face it, if they haven't killed Orlov by now they surely will soon, and two attempts to kill Vistin with explosives and missiles, we have a powerful weapon to convince Accola that turning over the art to us may be the only way for him to stay alive." Gregory said.

"How do you plan to neutralize Vistin? He's back in Moscow now, and I'm sure he had doubled his security since the two attempts on his life by The Islamic Brotherhood for Jihad. Even if he wasn't' in Moscow, Her Majesty's Government, forbids the assassination of foreign Government officials. So how do you propose to accomplish this?" Mobius asked.

"I haven't worked out all the details yet, but we could have our people inside the Kremlin let us know what happened when Vistin reported the attempts against him, and see where we can go from there." Gregory said.

"Ok, since we won't have any useful intelligence from our people in Moscow for a few days at least, why don't you take a few days to rest up. You've been on the go for days." Mobius said.

"Thank you sir, I think I will. Once I've rested up a bit I'll work on a plan to end Vistin, and perhaps recover the art and the money. Call if we get anything from Moscow that we can use." Gregory said.

The next day after breakfast Gregory decided to phone the Hotel Cristallo in Cortina d' Ampezzo. "Buongiono Signorina, could you tell me if Signoria Sophia Gambini is still staying with you?"

"Let me check Signore. Si Signore, Signorina Gambini is still here with the movie company." The clerk told him.

"Grazie Mille, Signorina. May I please be connected to her suite?" Gregory asked.

"Ovviamente solo un momento Signore, I'll ring" the clerk said.

Gregory got Sophia's voicemail, and left a message saying "Buongiono Sophia, this is Gregory MacNee. I have few days off, and will be heading to Cortina tonight to do a bit of skiing. I'd love to see you again, and finish our disrupted dinner date in Rome. I'll be staying at the Miramonti Majestic, and will give you a call when I arrive. I hope you can take a little time from working. See you soon"

CHAPTER TWENTY EIGHT

MOSCOW

General Vistin's Tupoliv landed safely at Chakalovsky Military Airport after the six hour flight from Casablanca. He was met by an armored ZiL limousine, and driven directly back to the Kremlin. Ill at ease because he knew there would be many questions by his superiors regarding the two attempts on his life, and particularly the one that took the life of the embassy driver and the missile attack, that caused a major incident at Mohammad V International. Every Moroccan security agency and police force was investigating the incident and hunting the terror suspects.

Arriving at his office, his secretary, Katrina Volga, said "Welcome home General, I'm so glad you were unhurt in the attacks".

Looking somewhat shocked Vistin said, "Thank you Kartina, it's good to be home. How did you know about the attacks?"

"Sir, everyone in the building has heard about it. No one knows the details of what happened of course, just that you had been caught in a terror attack that killed an embassy man and that you managed to escape un-harmed."

"Well yes, it was a terrible thing to lose our driver to those maniacs. We were not expecting trouble at a meeting that was to assist the people of all North African countries, so we had a very limited security detail. I guess we must be on alert at all times in the world today." Vistin said pretending great sorrow.

"When you've settled in sir, General Pushkin at the First Directorate would like you to go up to his office for a meeting." Katrina said.

"Very well, call him and tell him I'll be up in half an hour. I haven't had breakfast so would you please bring me some coffee and pastry?" Vistin said.

General Vistin walked across his fine office to stare at the muddy brown water of the Moskva River, and tried to think of what to tell Genera Pushkin about the attacks.

Miss Volga brought a steaming pot of coffee and a tray of pastries, setting them down on the table in the sitting area of General Vistin's spacious office.

"Will that be all sir?" she asked.

"Yes, thank you Miss Volga. Just be sure to tell General Pushkin I'll be up shortly".

Sipping the strong hot coffee and staring at the muddy water for several minutes he thought, "I'll just seem as shocked as everyone expects me to be. Only I know what the purposes of the attacks were, so I'll just play the victim".

He finished his coffee and felt more comfortable. He took the stairs to General Pushkin's office.

General Vistin was ushered into General Pushkin's office by his aid. Rising from his desk and walking to greet General Vistin with a bear hug, General Pushkin said, "Nikolay, Thank God you're all right."

Vistin flinched and stiffened as pain shot through his shoulder.

Surprised at this, General Pushkin pulled back and said "Nikolay, were you injured?"

"Not really sir, just a very sore shoulder where I hit the pavement rolling out of the car in Aruba."

"Damn shame about the driver, but at lease you'll be alright. Please sit and tell me what the hell happened over there."

"I don't really know what happened sir. The last day of the conference we were driving back to the hotel and were stuck in heavy afternoon traffic. Two motorcycles passed on either side of the car, slowed momentarily and attached two magnetic contact mines to both sides of the car. Major Dragomiroff recognized the threat and we both bailed out. Tragically, the driver was unable to jump and he was killed instantly when the mines detonated. I hit the pavement hard and thought I broke my shoulder. Major Dragomiroff hit and rolled, coming up firing at the men as they tried to come back to finish me off. He killed the lead man, and Gregor Petrovitch, who was following in the chase car immediately stopped and open fire killing the second." Vistin told him.

"Was there any threatening note or call that would have given you any indication who the assailants were, or why they attacked?" General Pushkin asked.

"No Sir, nothing. We were quite out in the open, so Gregor drove over the sidewalk to get free of the traffic and get me to safety. We headed straight for the airport as a precaution instead of going back to the hotel. Gregor radioed my pilot, Captain Marco Chekhov, that we were on our way, and to be prepared for immediate take off."

"Yes, we were informed that the terrorist tried to bring the plane down with shoulder fired surface to air missiles." General Pushkin said.

"Yes sir, if it had not been some very aggressive flying by Captain Chekhov, they would have blown us out of the sky." Vistin said.

"This is a very serious situation Nikolay. While you were away one of our Ministers, Paval Orlov, was kidnapped in Kazakhstan right off the street, again in broad daylight. We don't know why, no demands have been made. We don't know who these people are or what they want."

"Have there been any demands or claims of responsibility for the attack on me in Casablanca sir?" Vistin asked feigning ignorance.

"No nothing. I have two KGB teams working on this. One is in Kazakhstan, trying to find out where they've taken Orlov. I've ordered a team of Special Forces Spetsnez men to extract Orlov once the KGB locate him. The other team is heading down to Casablanca to investigate the attack on you.

"Do you think Orlov is still alive sir?" Vistin asked

"We don't know but there seems no reason to kidnap him just to kill him. There must be something they want. This is what we need to find out, and fast.

Whoever these people are, I will not allow attacks on our Government officials."

"I understand sir. If this continues, no one in Government will be safe".

"That's exactly right Nikolay. We will find and prosecute these individuals or whatever group they belong to, in the strictest terms. I will not allow these outrages to continue. I want you to meet with the anti-terrorist team leader and tell him everything that happened to you. I mean every detail, even details that may seem inconsequential to you. These men are expert at this type of situation and may see a lead that you yourself may not have seen. "

"Yes sir. I'll arrange the meeting at once."

"Also Nikolay, I've ordered round the clock security for you, and have increased the security detail at your residence, including men stationed inside your home."

"Thank you sir. I truly appreciate your concern, but I should be fine with just Major Dragomiroff." Vistin said.

"No Nikolay, that's not good enough I'm afraid. I know it's

inconvenient to have men posted inside and outside, but the threat is too real. These lunatics attacked with contact mines and missiles. No, the men are to stay round the clock." General Pushkin told him with finality.

"Yes sir. Thank you sir." Vistin said

Leaving General Pushkin's office, Vistin was thinking, "How the hell am I supposed to get my money and leave the country for a safe haven with round the clock security? With the KGB all over this I'm sure to be found out, and then it's all over. I must find a way to misdirect the KGB so I can escape and enjoy my wealth. But first, I need to eliminate everyone who has had any association with Ophidian, or they will lead the KGB back to me"

When General Vistin arrived back in his office he called Major Dragomiroff on his private secure line. "Major I want you and Gregor, to find and eliminate, everyone who has been associated with Ophidian in Italy, Belarus, and Lithuania. Time is of the essence in this, the KGB is investigating the attacks and we must be sure no one can give them any information that may lead back to us. Begin immediately, and leave none of them alive."

"Yes General. We will find their current locations and eliminate them. This may take some time though. Some of these people have not been used for some time."

"Time is something we don't have much of Major. Find them where ever they are, and don't leave a trail of bodies that could let to us. Misdirect law enforcement where ever these people are, but leave none alive to talk." Vistin ordered.

CHAPTER TWENTY NINE

CORTINA D'AMPEZZO ITALY

G regory flew into Canova di Treviso airport, and picked up a service Range Rover that the ever efficient Kimberly Trent had ordered delivered for his use. He checked to be sure the standard kit was in the secret compartment, which contained a Sig 9mm automatic pistol with two spare clips, emergency medical kit, and a portable satellite phone. He enjoyed the two hour drive up the A27 to Cortina d' Ampezzo. He was feeling light hearted at the thought of enjoying a peaceful ski holiday, and seeing the beautiful Sophia Gambini again. As he drove through the beautiful Italian country side, he was thinking, "I need this. No killing or plotting, just relaxation, and romance, with Sophia. "

He made good time despite the snow. The Range Rovers five hundred ten horsepower supercharged V8 engine and its excellent all-wheel drive system handled the snow with ease. Checking into the Hotel Miramonti Majestic in just over two hours, he settled into his luxurious suite and phoned room service. He ordered Petto d' Anatra, breast of duck braised in a sweet red wine and shallots, with fresh vegetables and a dry red Chianti. The room service waiter arrived within ten minutes, and Gregory ate while enjoying the magnificent view of the snowy Tofane mountains and the charming village. After his lunch, Gregory phoned the Hotel

Cristallo and left a voicemail for Sophia, saying he had arrived and for her to please give him a call when she was free.

About an hour later he received a call, "Buon Pomeriggio Gregory" came Sophia's lovely voice. "It's wonderful to hear from you. You are here in Cortina yes?" She said.

"I arrived about two hours ago. I've only got a couple of days, but was hoping we could get together." Gregory said.

"Oh, I would love that. I'm tired of working all the time. Unfortunately we're shooting at night for the next few weeks, but it does give me the whole day."

"Great. Why don't I meet you at your hotel and we could do a bit of skiing, then have lunch together." Gregory said.

"That sounds like fun. Let's get an early start so we'll have more time together before I have to go to work. I'm enjoying the work, but it is getting a bit tedious. Skiing and lunch with you sounds like just the right cure." She said laughing.

"In that case, I'll see you at eight. I'm truly looking forward to seeing you again Sophia." Gregory said.

"I'm looking forward to seeing you as well Gregory. See you in the morning" She said.

Hanging up he sat looking at the view thinking, "This will be a wonderful few days, with nothing to do but enjoy life".

CHAPTER TWENTY THIRTY

VAUXHALL CROSS LONDON

I t was six thirty in the morning and Mobuis sat at his desk sipping coffee and reading the multitude of intelligence reports that came to him each morning.

He received reports of all crimes that might have security implications, such as assassinations, killings, and suicides in specific areas that may indicate a security risk to the United Kingdom. He noticed that three suspected anti-Russian activists, had died in three separate auto accidents, within hours of each other in Belarus. His intelligence assets in the area suspected that the Ophidian organization had worked with anti-Russian factions in Belarus, though the names of the operatives were unknown. He put the report aside with the intent of having inquires made as to who the three were, to see if they had any possible connection with Ophidian.

Miss Trent came into the office and said, "Sir, I have Gianni Russo on hold from station R. He said it's urgent that he speaks to you."

"Very well Miss Trent, put him through"

"Good morning Gianni, what's the trouble so early in the day?" Mobius asked.

"Good morning Mobius. I just read a report from the Rome Metro Police, that a young man was found dead in his Rome apartment yesterday from an apparent over dose of heroin."

"That's unfortunate Gianni, but what does it have to do with MI6 operations?"

"The man's name was Tony Bianchi, the former makeup artist and lover of Sophia Gambini, the woman that Gregory was investigating in the Casino Degli Dei operation."

"I see. Was he known for drug use? Many in the film industry are they say"

"No Mobius, quite the reverse. Bianchi was known as a health freak. A vegetarian who only eats organic vegetables, works out at a health club daily, the lot. It's possible of course, but highly unlikely. With the deaths in Belarus and now this, it's possible that Vistin is cleaning up any loose ends associated with Ophidian that may lead back to him."

"That would make sense. Our man in Moscow reported that the KGB and FSB are fully involved in investigating the terror attacks in Morocco, the kidnapping of Paval Orlov in Kazakhstan, and the shooting in Berlin. He said they've increased security around Vistin and the Kremlin."

"Gregory might want to contact Miss Gambini and get some security around her. If they did kill Bianchi, she would be on their hit list as well. I understand she is currently shooting a film in Cortina d' Ampezzo." Gianni said.

"Actually, Gregory's in Cortina as we speak, and I'm sure part of the reason for his trip was to be with Miss Gambini, though not for security reasons. I'll get word to him right away that she is likely a target. Thanks for phoning this in Gianni. We had better move fast or they'll kill her and possibly Gregory if he's with her." Mobius said.

Hanging up, Mobius touched the intercom and said, "Miss Trent, get in touch with Gregory, and have him contact me a once. It's most urgent."

"Right away sir." Miss Trent said.

Phoning the Hotel Miramonte she was informed that Mr. MacNee was not in his room at this time. "Please ask him to phone his office the minute he returns. It's most urgent."

CHAPTER THIRTY ONE

THE KREMLIN MOSCOW

Geneeral Vistin arrived at his office at seven in the morning, with his enhanced security detail in tow.

"General, please go to the conference room on level one immediately. General Pushkin and the senior staff are waiting." Miss Volga said, without the usual conviviality's and with a concerned look on her face.

Walking down the hall to the top security conference room, General Vistin was wondering what the hell happened now? Security in the building had been increased many times, with heavily armed teams of two on each floor. He had been challenged by guards several times, even though he was in uniform with his ID badge in view. His ID was checked again before he was allowed to enter the conference room. Entering the room he saw the entire senior staff sitting around the long table, with a box in the center, and grim faces to a man.

General Pushkin stood and pointed to the box saying, "General Vistin, this box was delivered at the reception desk addressed to you. Please look inside."

Vistin lifted the lid on the box and stepped back with a gasp, "Holy Shit!" he exclaimed.

From inside the box, the decaying face on the severed head of Paval Orlov, stared at him with dead eyes wide open.

"The man who delivered this now in custody, and being questioned by the FSB officer in charge of internal security. He claims he was paid only to deliver the package and knows nothing about where it came from. We will find out who paid him and track them down". Pushkin said.

Recovering his composure, General Vistin said, "Were there any demands or anything else that came with the box?"

"No, just a blood stained note that read, "Death to all betrayers of The Islamic Brotherhood of Jihad. "

CHAPTER THIRTY TWO

CORTINA d' AMPEZZO ITALY

Gregory and Sophia had a sumptuous breakfast in the beautiful La Veranda dining room at the Hotel Cristallo, while catching up on the past month or so, and enjoying the sweeping views of the village and Tofane Mountains. After breakfast, they took a stroll through the village to walk off breakfast before hitting the slopes. They admired the work of the artists in Cortina's International Snow Sculpture Festival, which was always a favorite of Gregory's. The sculpture of Saint George slaying the dragon was truly amazing. In an hour or so they headed for the black diamond runs through the cliffs on Faloria-Cristallo, then the less taxing runs of Pasuo Falzarego, taking in the vast view that run provided. After a wonderful afternoon of skiing, they headed back to the Hotel Cristallo.

"Gregory, this has been the best day I've had since I arrived in Cortina." Sophia told him.

"It was great. The ski conditions were perfect, and the company much more so. It's a shame the day needs to end now. Can we get together again tomorrow?" Gregory asked.

"I have a little surprise for you. When we were at lunch, I phoned the director and told him I hurt my ankle and wouldn't be able to come in tonight. He wasn't happy, but they'll manage one day without me. So we have all night together." She said taking him by hand and leading him into her suite.

***

Gregory sat in the huge Jacuzzi tub, sipping a flute of perfectly chilled Mumms. Sophia came in wearing only a dark blue silk robe, looking sexier than ever. As she let the robe slip to the floor, Gregory was looking at Sophia's beautiful body thinking, "What an exquisitely beautiful woman she is, perfect in every detail. Her slim waist, muscular yet feminine legs, full firm breasts, perfectly tanned olive skin, shiny jet black flowing hair and eyes so dark brown they almost looked black. She was even more exciting to him now than she was when he'd first met her. This will be night I'll remember for a lifetime." He thought.

She slipped into the tub and took a sip from his champagne. Looking deeply into each other's eyes, they kissed. Gregory took her in his arms and they made love passionately, in the hot swirling water of the Jaccuzi. Sophia made love with the fiery passion that Gregory had heard Roman women were famous for. By six thirty they had made love two more times, each time with more intensity than the time before. They lay exhausted in each other's arms watching the crackling fire, and drinking the last of the forgotten bottle of Mumms.

"Let's order some dinner. Suddenly I'm famished." Gregory said.

"Must be the cold weather" She said, rolling on top of him."

An hour later they phoned room service, ordering steaming bowls Cioppino, that the Hotel Cristallo had become known for, followed by pasta with porcini mushrooms, scallops and shrimp in a rich cream, white wine saffron sauce. They ended their meal with double espresso and Grand Marnier.

Walking together to their soft warm bed, Gregory was thinking how lucky he was to have met this extraordinary woman. All the violence was gone from his world, at least for the time being.

CHAPTER THIRTY THREE

THE KREMLIN MOSCOW

General Pushkin was outraged by the attacks on his men and the kidnapping, and brutal murder of a State official. Sitting back down at the head of the conference table, he controlled his rage, and said in a dangerously calm voice, "General Vistin, I order you to go to Lubyanka Prison and meet with Colonel Krymov of the Spetsgruppa "A" known as Alpha Group, immediately after this meeting adjourns. Alfa Group is an elite anti-terrorist group of the FSB, and Major Remizov of the Spetsnaz Special Unit attached to the GRU. Follow up on what our interrogators have learned from the man who delivered this package. You will find whoever is responsible for these attacks, and eliminate them, with extreme prejudice. Since the end of the Cold War, attacks against Russian citizens and State Officials have become more frequent, and bold. We will send a strong message to anyone who is contemplating an attack on Russians, at home or abroad, that we will find them and send them straight to Hell, no matter where they try to hide."

Entering Lubyanka Prison through the heavily guarded main entrance, General Vistin met with Colonel Krymov and Major Remizov, in the commandant's office. The three men took the stairs down to interrogation cells, three floors under the ground level.

General Vistin said to the burly guard at the desk, "We're

here to question the man who delivered the box to the Kremlin this morning"

The three officers were led into the interrogation cell. The cell was a dimly lit cold steel box, fifteen feet by fifteen feet, with a steel floor and a steel chair bolted to the floor with thick leather straps for the arms and legs. An ominous drain was located beneath the chair, where the man who delivered the box had been interrogated.

"Where is he? You had orders to have him here for questioning by me." General Vistin snapped at the interrogator.

"Sir, the prisoner was unconscious, and had to be moved back to his cell. We had to use some, rather extreme measures, to get information from him." The lead interrogator said.

Glaring at the interrogation team of two men, General Vistin said, "You had better have gotten some useful information out of him. If he dies before we can use the information to find the people behind this, you'll take his place in that chair."

"Sir, his name is Omar Kaseem, originally from Damascus Syria, who recently moved to a slum in East Moscow. He told us, after much persuasion, that two members of a group he believes could be linked to the terrorist organization known as, The Islamic Brotherhood for Jihad, pressured him to deliver the box. He said that they meet regularly at a mosque on Tverskaya Street in the south of the Tverskoy District. The mosque has many members who are Islamic fundamentalist; though he says they are not terrorists. The two who pressured him into delivering the package are only know to him by their first names, Rasha and Fathi Halir, and they are also from Damascus. They work as maintenance men at the Olimpiyskiy Stadium near the mosque, but he has no idea where they live. They told him to deliver the package and not to ask any questions. He said he was told if he didn't do just as they told him, things would go badly for his family still in Syria. So he did as they asked. That was all he knew." The lead interrogator told Vistin.

Turning to Colonel Krymov, Vistin said. "Colonel put a team together, and locate both of these men. I want them alive and brought here. I will interrogate them myself. Check with the Olimpiyskiy Stadium to get their addresses and descriptions. Call me at once when they are located and in custody."

"Yes sir. I'll put three of my men, who served undercover in Afghanistan, at the mosque. Captain Vasily Loginov and I will go the Olimpiyskiy Stadium. I have a squad of Special Services Police to surround both buildings. If they're in Moscow, we'll bring them in." Colonel Krymov said.

Colonel Krymov questioned the manager of the Olimpiyskiy Stadium, and was told that both men, Rasha Adjim and Fathi Halir, were at work somewhere in the facility. The Colonel and his men moved so quickly, that they arrested both men without any gun fire. Both were taken immediately to the interrogation cell at Lubyanka Prison. Driving back to Lubyanka, Colonel Krymov phoned General Vistin to let him know they had both men in custody and were heading back to Lubyanka.

"Good work Colonel, take both men to interrogation cell number one. I will be there shortly." General Vistin told him.

General Vistin was shown into interrogation cell one, by the officer in charge, and was met by Colonel Krymov.

"Sir, their names are Rasha Adjim and Fathi Halir. Their papers show that both are originally from Damascus Syria, and have lived in Moscow for less than one year. Of course they claim not to know why they've been brought here, and swear they have done nothing. We checked their passports and both were reported to have left Russian territory, destination Damascus Syria, two weeks ago. And this should interest you sir, they returned to Russia from Casablanca just three days ago." Colonel Krymov told the General.

"So, these two were most likely the ones who attempted to shoot down of my plane, or they coordinated it." General Vistin said, staring at Rasha Adjim and Fathi Halir coldly.

"That would seem likely sir." Colonel Krymov said.

"Thank you Colonel, I will question them myself. Please wait outside."

"Yes sir. Simply press the button on this panel when you need me."

Standing before Rasha Adjim and Fathi Halir General Vistin said,

"You two know why you've been brought here, so don't waste my time pretending you don't."

"Please Comrade General, we have done nothing. There is no reason that we should have been arrested while doing our jobs at the Olimpiyskiy Stadium." Rasha Adjim said.

"If you call me Comrade again, I'll have your tongue cut out. You're both Syrian, not Russian." General Vistin said with a murderous look in his eyes.

"But general, we have done nothing"

"I won't waste time with your lies. We know that you were responsible for the attempted destruction of my plane in Casablanca three days ago. We also know that you used coercion to get this man Kaseem to deliver a package to the Kremlin this morning, with threats to his family still in Syria."

"But general" Rasha Adjim began to say, but Vistin backhanded him across the face.

"No more lies. I know you're responsible. What I want from you is the name and location of the man who sent you." Vistin said.

Rahsa Adjim and Fathi Halir looked at General Vistin with a renewed strength and sense of purpose and said, "We will never betray the brotherhood of Islam. We will tell you nothing."

"I rather think you will tell me his name, and where to find him. You'll tell me things I don't even want to know before you leave here, I assure you." General Vistin told them.

Pressing the button on the control panel he said, "Colonel, please come in."

"Colonel, take these men to special interrogation cell six in the sub-basement and prepare them for a more, in-depth, interrogation."

CHAPTER THIRTY FOUR

CORTINA d' AMPEZZO ITALY

When morning came, Gregory awoke with Sophia's head on his chest under a thick eiderdown comforter. He was lying there looking at the beautiful view of the snow covered Tofane Mountains, and stroking her smooth back when she reached over and pulled him on top of her, and they made love again. It was well past noon before Gregory finally got up and showered.

"I've got to head over to the Miramonte and get some fresh cloths, shave and make a few calls. Do you think you can get out of work tonight as well?" Gregory asked.

"Believe me, I'd love to, but I can't. I could pull off one day because of a sore ankle, but not two. I should be finished before mid-night, let's meet back here." She told him.

"Done. It's going to be the longest night I can remember. Why don't I pick you up at the location?"

"Great, we're filming at the Olympic Ice Stadium. I'll be counting the hours. She said.

They held each other tightly, and then he kissed her and had to go.

Walking slowly back to the Range Rover through the lightly falling snow, feeling a bit light headed, he was thinking "What and extraordinary woman. It was a great idea to come to Cortina during the lull in the Ophidian storm".

***

Gregory arrived back at his suite, still in the somewhat light headed euphoria one feels after spending the night making love to such an extraordinary woman. The first thing he noticed was the message light on the phone was flashing. Phoning the desk he was told that it was urgent he contact his office without delay.

As he attached the scrambler to the hotel phone, Gregory was thinking,

"Christ All Mighty! What now? I can't even take a few days without a new emergency."

Mobius answered on the second ring. "Gregory we have a dangerous situation building. Over the last forty eight hours there have been six people killed in what at first glance looked to be accidents. Looking more closely, they seem to be in the areas we believe Ophidian has been operating. It looks to us as though Ophidian might be cleaning house and eliminating anyone who has had any contact with them or their operatives. One of the people that turned up dead was in Rome. That person was Tony Bianchi, Miss Gambini's ex-lover and make-up artist."

"Do they have anyone in custody or suspects?" Gregory asked

"At the moment they have no suspects and no witnesses. The Rome Metro Police are reporting it as a heroin over dose. Station "R" has looked into his death and all reports show Bianchi was health maniac who, according to friends and associates, claim he would never touch drugs. If Ophidian is killing anyone who has had any association with them, either directly or indirectly, as this Tony Bianchi and Miss Gambini had in their dealings with Drago, we feel Miss Gambini could be a target. It's no secret that she's filming in Cortina, and we feel she could be in extreme danger. You could get caught in the cross fire if you're with her." Mobius said.

"I just left her and she'll be filming tonight on location at the

Olympic Ice Stadium. Do we have a lead on who the killers might be?" Gregory asked.

"Interpol reported that General Vistin's security men, Major Alexie Dragomiroff and Gregor Petrovich, arrived at Leonardo da Vinci Fiumicino International Airport in Rome thirty eight hours ago on diplomatic passes. They had no reason to follow them, so they don't know where they are at the moment. Bianchi's time of death was estimated just four hours after their arrival in Rome." Mobius told him.

"If Dragomiroff and Petrovich killed Bianchi, and are planning to kill Sophia, they could be in Cortina now. Sir, I'm going to talk to the local police and get additional security around the Ice Stadium right away. Then I'll get on to the Italian Special Services and see if we can put a tight security ring around Sophia. I don't want to raise an alarm at the filming location, but will get under cover security around the area. As soon as she is done for the night, I'll get her out of Cortina and back to a safe house in London where we can protect her." Gregory said.

"Ok Gregory, get moving. I'll contact Italian Special Services and get some people up there as fast as possible. Watch your back, or you could become a casualty as well." Mobius told him.

Gregory shaved and dressed quickly then drove to the Polizia Di Stato Cortina and asked for the Senior Captain in charge. He was shown to Capt. Mario Guiliano's office, were Gregory showed the Captain his MI6 I.D. and explained the situation.

"Captain Guiliano, we have intelligence that two Russian officers, Major Alexie Dragomiroff and Gregor Petrovich, may have been involved in a murder in Rome. The Rome Metro Police are reporting the death as an accidental over dose of heroin, but our department has every reason to believe that the man was murdered by Dragomiroff and Petrovich, and that they may be headed to Cortina, if they're not already here. We believe that Miss Sophia Gambini may be in great danger from these two men." Gregory explained.

"Miss Gambini the film star? Why would these Russian wish to harm such a beautiful young woman?" Captain Guiliano asked.

"I'm sorry Captain, I can't go into all the details for security reasons, but it's imperative that we get additional police protection immediately for her and everyone filming at the Olympic Ice Stadium tonight, while we try to locate Dragomiroff and Petrovich. We feel these men are extremely dangerous." Gregory told him.

"We are not a large force Mr. MacNee, but I'll pull three uniformed officers off their regular duties and assign them to the Ice Stadium for Miss Gambini's security." Captain Guiliano said.

"Please have your men in plain clothes Captain. We need to keep a low profile on this. Because of Miss Gambini's status as a movie star, the press will always be close at hand, as well as fans, and the ever present paparazzi. " Gregory said.

"I understand Mr. MacNee. Can you describe these men?

"No, note really, I've only seen them twice, and with heavy winter clothing they'll be hard to identify. In a few minutes my department will be scanning Dragomiroff and Petrovich's official Russian Army photos, as well as their passport photos. Please make sure all your man get a copy and memorize their faces. I'll be taking Miss Gambini to a safe location as soon they have completed shooting this evening.

CHAPTER THIRTY FIVE

LUBYANKA PRISON MOSCOW

Rasha Adjim and Fathi Halir were taken to the special interrogation cell six, and stripped naked. They were strapped into two cold steel chairs that faced each other. A series of electrodes were attached to their genitals, feet, and to the base of their sculls. Though it was very cold in the cell, they sat strapped in, with the sweat of pure fear dripping from them as they waited for General Vistin

General Vistin arrived and dismissed both Colonel Krymov, and the technician in the control booth, that operated the electrical equipment attached to the two suspects.

"You're dismissed Colonel. Please take the technician with you. I'm quite familiar with how to operate this equipment." General Vistin told him.

"Yes Sir. Shall I wait outside?"

"No, that won't be necessary Colonel."

"Very well Sir." Colonel Krymov said, saluting the General and both men withdrew from the cell.

General Vistin walked slowly and took a chair from the control room, placing it were both men could see him. Sitting down he stared at the Rasha Adjim and Fathi Halir, with a frighteningly calm look on his face, but with furious hatred burning in his eyes.

"General, we can tell you nothing. We will never betray our bothers in Islam." Rasha Adjim told him trying to look strong.

"You coerced this man Kaseem into delivering a box to the Kremlin this morning, and you tried to shoot down my plane. Who do you work for and where can we find this man?" General Vistin asked calmly.

"We will tell you nothing" Rasha Adjim said.

General Vistin stood up and put one hand in his pocket and waved the other hand around the chairs and control room. "This is a most advanced, and ingenious devise for getting the truth from anyone. Science was never my strong suit, but the principle is easy enough to comprehend. It taps directly into the skin's thermal pain receptors, and the central nervous system, and sends the impulses directly to the parietal lobe in the brain. It sends impulses to individual nerves clusters in one location or all over the body at once. With a series of impulses, it feels as though the subject area is on fire. It can't be blocked out, and even though the subject feels as if they are burning, there is no permanent damage. The subject won't lose consciousness no matter how long the treatment. Since there is no damage caused to the nerves what so ever, the subject can be subjected to these impulses for hours with no lessening of the effects. Ah, better yet, let me show you how it works".

Both men were struggling to get free, but it was useless, they were securely strapped in and could not move or twist the electrodes free.

"I think since Mr. Adjim seems to be the spokesmen, we'll let him experience this first. I'll just apply a bit of the power. We don't want to spoil the rest of the experience for you." Vistin said

Vistin went into the control room and adjusted the machine to its lowest power setting, and advanced the control for the electrode attached to Rasha Adjim's genitals.

Adjim let out a blood curdling scream and twisted trying to get free while a horrified Fathi Halir looked on.

After less than fifteen seconds Vistin reduced the power to off, and strode out and took his seat again.

"As you see, this is a unique experience. The pain is beyond what could be normally tolerated without permanent damage to the body, but with a difference. Now that the power is off, aside from a slight throbbing, there is no damage what so ever. I can keep the power on for hours and the sensation would not diminish. And by increasing the power and applying it to all the electrodes at once the subject's body feels as if it's in a raging fire but they will not die.

Though the mind feels like it will explode, the subject can't even pass out, because the nerves affecting that area of the brain are not receiving the impulses. A truly ingenious devise, wouldn't you agree Mr. Rasha Adjim." Vistin explained calmly, as though addressing a university class on electrical engineering.

Sweat was pouring from Rasha's body, and he was shaking violently, as the effects began to dissipate and his mind began to refocus on the room. He had never felt anything like that before. It felt as though someone had held a burning torch to his genitals.

Fathi Halir was sweating and shaking in panic as he prayed to Allah to save him.

"Now Mr Rasha Adjim, will you give me the name of the man who sent you and where to find him?"

"General, we were only acting under orders when we shot missiles at your plane in Casablanca. We were following the orders of our supreme commander. I can tell you no more than that." Adjim said in a weak voice.

"Ah, so you two were the ones who tried to blow my plane out of the sky. I didn't realize it was you. I'm glad to know it wasn't personal, just orders." Vistin said with a sarcastic sneer. "However, that is not why you're here, but it is a bonus. You sent the severed head of a Soviet Government official to me in a box this morning"

"General please, we knew nothing of the box's contents. We were told to find someone to deliver it and not to ask questions". Rasha Adjim whimpered.

"You say you were acting under orders from your supreme commander. What is the organization, and where do I find him?" General Vistin asked calmly.

"We were also pressured by threats to our families in Damascus." Rasha Adjim told him.

"I ask you again. What organization, and who issued the orders." Vistin said.

"The Islamic Brotherhood for Jihad. I don't know the supreme commanders name, or where to find him. We were simply given orders."

"Liar!" Vistin said.

"I swear to Allah, I'm telling you the truth General."

"Well, unfortunately I don't believe you. I think a bit more persuasion may help you remember more clearly." Vistin said walking towards the control room.

Setting the controls, Vistin began adding power to the electrode attached to Rasha Adjim's genitals which brought out the same horrific scream. Then he advanced the settings on the other electrodes.

Rasha Adjim's genitals were on fire and he thought he couldn't stand it any longer. Then his entire world exploded. He shrieked until no sound came out of his mouth. His eyes bulged out to the point that a horrified Fathi Halir, strapped to the opposite chair, thought they may pop out of his head. It seemed an eternity until Vistin reduced the power. Rasha Adjim's trembling body sagged, dripping sweat and his bowels emptied.

General Vistin walked slowly and calmly back into the cell.

It was rank with the stink of fear, sweat, and feces. Vistin, in the same calm voice said. "What organization and where do I find this man?"

"The organization is The Islamic Brotherhood for Jihad, and the supreme commander is Adnan Mohammad Wasen." Fathi Halir said in an almost hysterical voice.

"And where can I find this Adnan Mohammad Wasen?"

"I don't know where his headquarters are, I swear it. We meet at the large Mosque on Aal Al Bait, near the east end of the Bab el Sagir cemetery in Damascus." Fathi Halir said.

Looking straight into Rasha Adjim's eyes, Vistin said. "Is this the truth or do I increase the power and leave it on for twenty minutes?"

"No more, no more, for the love of Allah, no more; he speaks the truth." Rasha Adjim said, raising his head weakly.

"We shall see" Vistin said.

Walking slowly around behind Rasha Adjim, Vistin drew his Makarov pistol and shot Rasha Adjim in the back of the head at point blank range, covering

Fathi Halir, strapped to the chair facing him, in his brother's blood and brains.

General Vistin left the cell and phoned Major Remizov at GRU Headquarters.

"Major Remizov, put a team together for a special operation into Damascus immediately. I have the name of the supreme commander of The Islamic Brotherhood for Jihad, and the location to find him. I will join you in two hours." General Vistin said.

"Yes General. I'll have my men gear up and we'll be ready to depart when you arrive." Major Remizov said.

Pressing the intercom button Visting told the technician from cell six, "Take the prisoner back to a holding cell. Don't clean him or allow him to dress. We'll let his condition loosen his tongue further. And get a cleaning crew to clean up the mess."

General Vistin met Major Remizov and his team at GRU headquarters, and told them what he wanted done.

"Major, what's the best way for us to get a small force into Damascus, to pick up The Islamic Brotherhood for Jihad supreme commander and get him out alive?"

"Well sir, Syria is a tough place to move around in these days. They have endless military check points and roaming patrols. We can fly into a dirt strip at the base of Mt. Hermon in Lebanon, and travel overland to Damascus. I'll contact a group of anti-Syrian fighters that have worked with us before, and they can arrange to help us slip across the border and guide us to the target." Major Remizov told him.

"Very well, major. I'll move some agents into place to watch the mosque, keep track of our targets movements, and follow him to see where he lives and where he goes for a few days. I want to pick him up on the road if possible, with no gun fire if we can avoid it. As supreme commander of this Islamic Brotherhood for Jihad group, he's bound to travel with heavily armed fighters. We need to identify them, and learn their routine. I want this to be a quick snatch and run operation, in and out fast. We want him alive for questioning, and starting a gun battle in the streets of Damascus, would be very dangerous" Vistin said.

"It may take several days to plan a route in and out with minimal contact. We'll most likely have to travel over land in the desert not to be detected. If you can give me the target area we need to reach, I'll get in touch with my contact at once. My men are ready to go now." Major Remizov said.

"We'll go over it with your contact when I arrive. Tell them to plot a route to south Damascus. I would prefer not to reveal the exact location until we arrive, in the area in case there are informants within this group. If the man we're after gets wind that he has been compromised, he'll disappear and we'll never find him in Syria. We must get in and out with him. and have no contact with Syrian fighters, or things could get very sticky. You and your men fly into the airstrip at

Mt. Hermon tonight and arrange things with your contacts, including any equipment we'll need to travel off roads through the desert."

"Yes sir general, I understand. Our man would find allies everywhere in Syria.

I'll send word we'll be there in approximately nine hours." Major Remizov said.

"Once my agents get back to me with some solid intelligence on our man's movements; I'll contact you and be on my way" General Vistin told him.

Leaving Major Remizov, General Vistin used a special satellite phone to call Major Dragomiroff.

"What is the situation with our previous associates Major?" Vistin asked when Dragomiroff answered.

"All associations have been neutralized except one. She's in Cortina d' Ampezzo working on a film. Gregor and I are taking the next train and should arrive there in about nine hours, assuming these Italian trains can ever run on time. I'll signal when she's been naturalized." Dragomiroff told him.

"It's a shame to waist such a beauty, there are so many other things she could be used for, but she must go." Vistin said.

"Yes sir. We're on our way."

General Vistin locked the satellite phone in his brief case and sat thinking,

"Just a few more people to eliminate and I'll be safe.

Dragomiroff and Gegor, will have to be eliminated of course, and then Ophidian will be history. It's a shame it has to end so soon, Ophidian was a great money making venture, but at least I'll live to enjoy the fruits of my labors."

CHAPTER THIRTY SIX

CORTINA d' AMPEZZO ITALY

G regory left Captain Guiliani's office and drove to the Hotel Cristallo, hoping to catch Sophia before she left, but was too late. He decided to go back to the Miramonte to get his spare Sig 9mm, and some heavy clothing in case they had to move fast to get out of Cortina. He phoned the set, and was told by a surly woman, that Miss Gambini was unable to take any calls and suggested that he call back another time, or better still, to make an appointment to speak to her.

"Bloody Hell, all I need is to have to run the gamut of studio functionaries just to get to her. Well, that could help if I'm not the only one trying reach her, and give me the few extra minutes I may need to get her safely away from Vistin's men."

He put his gear in the Range Rover with the spare Sig and ammo in a secret compartment in the center console for quick access. Driving to the front entrance of the Olympic Ice Stadium, he walked up to the guard shack and told the guard he was a personal friend of Miss Gambini's, and that they were to meet this evening.

"I haven't been told of anyone meeting Miss Gambini tonight. I'll tell you, what I told the other two men wanting to meet with Miss Gambini, if I don't have advanced word that you have permission to enter, I'll have to send a runner to the set for permission to

allow you in. There are no phone calls allowed when they're filming so you'll just have to wait." The disinterested guard told him.

"You said two other men where here to see Miss Gambini, how
long ago was that?" Gregory asked.

"Maybe half an hour ago, I guess."

"Can you tell me what they looked like, tall, short, what they
were wearing, it's really quite important."

"I think they wore dark blue or black parkas and knitted caps,
medium height I think. Look I can't remember, it really doesn't
matter anyway, if they aren't on the approved list, we just tell them
to get lost. We always have people trying to get into the filming.
Those pain in the ass paparazzi, are always trying to get candid
photos to sell to the rag press." The guard told him.

Seeing this was getting nowhere Gregory said, "Alright, please
send a runner right away. She'll approve my entrance. I'll be back
in twenty minutes."

Driving around the right side of the stadium he parked the
Range Rover where it couldn't be seen by the guard, and looked
for an entrance on foot. He found a gap in the fencing that he
could just fit through, and went looking for the trailer Sophia was
using as a dressing room. He found it in a brightly lit area where
the caterers had laid out food and hot coffee for the crew, under
a large tent with outdoor heaters burning brightly to keep the
chill at bay. Gregory asked one of the crew for directions to the
set and was shown the way. He knew that Vistin's men would be
able to find her the same way, if that's who the other two men
asking to see her were, which seemed likely. If they were already
in Cortina, they would want to get this done quickly and be out
of the country fast. He went into the staging area on the sets far
left side unnoticed by the crew. There were at least twenty people there with large cameras set in a semi-circle, the bright stage
lights illuminating the actual shot. He stood in the dark but could

not see Sophia. Causally he asked one of the young women standing close by, where Sophia was. "She's in the green room over to the right, and not due on set for another twenty minutes". He quickly made his way over to the green room and found Sophia inside. When he walked in Sophia looked up surprised, but delighted to see him.

"Gregory, what a delightful surprise. You couldn't wait for tonight yes?" She said with a devilish smile coming to him and holding him close.

"Sophia, something has come up and I need to get you away from Cortina right now."

"Gregory I can't leave, I'm due on the set in twenty minutes. But that does give us a little time to play"

"This is very serious Sophia; your life is in danger and I have to get you away from Cortina. Get a warm coat, gloves and a hat if you have one. We have to leave now, I'll explain on the way."

"But I can't leave now, and what do I tell the director? What do you mean my life is in danger?" She said quite confused.

"Don't tell him anything, we don't want anyone to know you've left. There are two men after you that I believe are here in Cortina now. The guard at the gate said two men already tried to get in but he turned them away at the gate, because he had no pass for them. I can assure you they will be back, or at the very least be waiting for you when you leave."

She put on heavy coat and a knitted cap, and Gregory hustled her quietly out where he came in without any of the crew noticing.

Walking quickly through the falling snow Sophia said, "Why would two men be trying to harm me? Who are they?"

"We believe their Russian agents."

"Russian agents, why would Russian agents be interested in me? And just who are we?"

They got in the Range Rover and Gregory headed away from

the Olympic Ice Stadium on Via Alberto Bonacossa, driving carefully in the increasing snow while keeping an eye out for danger.

"Sophia, I'm afraid I haven't been completely honest with you about who I am, and what I do."

"You mean you're not Gregory MacNee of All Empire International?" She asked looking very confused.

"Yes Sophia, I am Gregory MacNee, and my family does own All Empire International, but I'm also a British agent. Unfortunately, I can't tell you everything. I was sent to Isola di Pantelleria to investigate the murder of one of our agents, as well as the disappearance of two Mossad agents from the island. That's when we met. During the course of my investigation I discovered a group of rouge Russian agents working with Valerio Drago, who was planning to kill Don Marco Conti, and take over the Conti Cosca. As it turned out these Russians were not working for the Russian government, but a criminal organization known as Ophidian, secretly run by a high official in the Russian military system. They were planning to use the Casino Degli Dei and the Conti Cosca, run through Drago, as a source of covert funds to purchase weapons from breakaway Russian Republics and sell them to Middle East terrorist groups."

"But what do they want to hurt me for? I was forced to go along with a cheating scam at the casino because of Tony's gambling debts."

"It seems that there have been several attempts to kill the head of this criminal organization in the past few weeks, and before he is found out by the KGB, he has given orders that anyone associated with any of their operations be eliminated. There have already been several killings disguised to look like accidents in the past forty eight hours, and we think you are on their list."

"What would make your people think I'm on the list?"

"I'm sorry to have to tell you this Sophia, but Tony Bianchi was found dead yesterday of what the police are calling a heroin overdose. But we believe he was killed by Ophidian's agents"

"Tony dead, Oh my god." She gasped.

"Yes, again I'm sorry to have to tell you this way, but we think he was killed by the men who are looking for you, and they made it look like an overdose to cover their tracks."

"There is no way Tony used drugs. He was a confirmed health freak".

"That's what our people were told by those who knew him. That's why we think this organization is killing anyone who had worked for them whether those people were aware of it or not. They're eliminating any loose ends, and because you were associated with Bianchi in the cheating scheme, I'm afraid you're a loose end and therefore in great danger until we can stop this group."

Sophia sat stunned and confused staring out into the darkness through the heavily falling snow, and began to weep, thinking that her whole world was falling apart. "I can't believe this is happening to me. I have an affair with Tony and wind up being forced to cheat a casino run by Drago, a mafia killer. He got blown up and I break up with Tony, then meet you and feel things are getting back to normal. There's a wonderful new man in my life. Now it turns out that man is a British spy, and now Russian spies are out to kill me. So where are we going now?" She said in a numb voice.

"We're heading for the Mestre train station in Calalzo di Cadore. From there we'll head for Marco Polo airport in Venice, and fly to London where I can keep you safe until this is all over."

CHAPTER THIRTY SEVEN

DAMASCUS SYRIA

After the long drive through the desert from Mt. Hermon in Lebonon, General Vistin and his men waited in a van with, Damascus Plumbing Service, written on the side, around the corner from the mosque on Aal Al Bait.

Vistin asked one of the Lebanese fighters named Rashid, "Why are we in a plumbers van?"

"Plumbers can go anywhere, anytime, without having to answer too many questions. If you go into a building with heavy security and tell the guards that the toilets on the second floor are clogged, and shit's everywhere, no one really questions it, they just let you pass." Rashid told him with a grin.

"Come to think of it, I suppose you're right. Very clever, I'll have to remember that." Vistin said.

Major Remizov had two men with communication gear watching the mosque from both the front and back, and would alert Vistin when Adnan Mohammad Wasen left. They had found out from their Lebanese fighters, where Wasen lived and had arranged an ambush to take him on the way.

It was well past nine when one of the watchers radioed that Wasen just got in his black Mercedes, with a driver and two guards, heading east with no follow car.

"We need to make this quick, and take him on the road before he reaches his walled compound in the Mazanet Ash-Sham district. If he gets there, we won't have a chance at taking him, there are fighters all over the compound. With all the fighting and unrest in Damascus these days, the Syrian army has imposed a curfew from ten P.M to six A.M. They have road blocks and patrols all over the city, and the last thing we need is to be stopped by the army." Major Remizov told his men.

Vistin and his team in the plumbing van, fell in behind Wasen's Mercedes heading north on Aal Al Bait. Major Remizov and Rashid drove onto Badawi road well ahead of him. Slowing the car, Remizov put on his emergency flashers, to make it look like he had a mechanical problem, as he approached a road construction site narrowing the road to one lane. The car came to a jerking stop in a cloud of dust blocking most of the road, giving Wasen's big Mercedes no room to pass. Remizov and Rashid dressed in dirty coveralls, common to construction laborers, got out of the car cursing and started to try to push the car out of the way on the soft gravel road. Wasen didn't see this as a trap and told his guards to go help the men move the car. Vistin and his team had pulled the van over just around the bend behind Wasen's Mercedes, so they were not seen by his driver. Vistin's men got out moving quickly into ambush position on either side of the darkened road.

"Move that goddamn piece of shit off the road now!" Wasen's men told Remizov in Arabic, with an angry wave pointing towards the side of the road.

Rashid said to them in Arabic, "The god cursed car is old and its transmission is locked in gear. We can't get into neutral to move it."

"Get out of the way" one of the guards told Rashid shoving him aside, "I'll get this fucking thing moving."

The guard handed his AK47 to his partner and got into the car.

Ramizov stepped to the side and drew his Makarov .380 pistol and shot the guard standing outside the car through the right eye, then shot the other guard twice while he tried to get the car into neutral. One of Vistin's team shot the driver of Wasen's Mercedes through the wind screen with his AK47 rifle, the bullet entered the man's forehead and he collapsed in the front seat. Shocked by the sudden attack, Adnan Mohammad Wasen sat staring at his dead driver. Before Wasen could react, Major Remizov and his men wrenched open the back door of the Mercedes, knocked Wasen unconscious with a rifle butt, secured his hands behind his back with plastic wrist securers, put duct tape over his mouth and a burlap sack over him. Vistin and Major Remizov hustled Wasen into the van, while the two Lebanese fighters shoved one of the bodies onto the cars floor then put the other dead guard in the trunk. They drove both cars a short distance then pushed them into a deep ravine where they wouldn't be found for days.

Both Lebanese fighters got into the van and the group drove quickly, but carefully, through the darkened city out into the desert to make their way back to their extraction point in Lebanon, giving them their best chance of not encountering any road blocks or patrols.

General Vistin stared at the unconscious form of Wasen in the sack, knowing that he could not let Wasen speak to anyone. He must find a way to kill him without it looking as though he did so. If they got him back to Moscow; Wasen would expose Vistin in the plan to buy the physicist Patterson.

He would just wait for an opportunity to kill Wasen to arrive.

CHAPTER THIRTY EIGHT

CORTINA d' AMPEZZO ITALY

Driving the thirty five kilometers to Calalzo di Cadore on the dark snowy road through the forest, Gregory knew they were vulnerable to attack and continued to scan ahead and behind for any vehicles.

Still staring out into the night, Sophia said bitterly, "So you're a British spy and you make love to me hoping to find out more about these Russian. Is that about it Gregory? If you're name really is Gregory."

"No Sophia, that's not at all true. Until the mission to Isola di Pantelleria all I knew of you was that you were a gorgeous and talented film star. I never thought I would meet you and my department had no connection between you and Drago. We met by pure chance. When I came to Cortina, it was to take a holiday and to get to know you better. It had nothing to do with my mission. Ophidian started eliminating people just forty eight hours ago and my office contacted me so I could protect you and get you to safety."

Gregory noticed headlights behind them as he entered bends in the road and they seemed to be coming on faster than one would drive under these conditions.

"I think we may have company Sophia. Hang on this could get little dicey."

The car came on fast, and was soon just a bend or so behind

them. The driver moved quickly and passed on Gregory's left. Pulling in front of the Range Rover the driver began to brake swerving back and forth trying to force Gregory to stop. Gregory moved right then quickly left and over took the car. The car's driver then tried to come along side, and tried to force them off the road, but as they came to the next bend Gregory used the bulk of the big Range Rover and hit the front of the car causing it to spin out of control into some trees lining the road. Unfortunately, the force of the collision caused the Range Rover to skid on the frozen road into a heavy snow bank, then slide off the road becoming stuck in a ditch.

"Are you ok Sophia?"

"I'm ok." She answered, just as a bullet pinged off the Rovers body work, and another hit the service special bullet resistant glass of the back window.

"Stay in the car and stay down" Gregory said grabbing the Sig 9mm as he rolled out the driver's side scrambling into the trees. He saw Gregor low down behind the driver's door firing at the Rover's passenger's side window. Gregory fired two shots and saw Gregor go down, while Dragomirov continued to fire.

Having bullets pelting the back of the Range Rover, Sophia panicked and got out of the car. She ran for the trees on the opposite side of the dark road.

"No Sophia, stay in the car" Gregory shouted but she was already crossing the road. Using the Rover for cover, Gregory moved around the front and tried to catch Sophia. Dragomirov fired and hit Gregory in the right leg spinning him around; he fell but rolled and returned fire. Dragomirov fired a volley at Gregory then raced across the road in pursuit of Sophia. Gregory reloaded and ran forward quickly checking to make sure Gregor was out of the fight. Gregor was lying on his back with an expanding circle of blood red snow beneath him, and his dead eyes staring at the sky. Staying low and moving as fast as he could in the deep snow with a bullet in his leg, Gregory headed towards the direction Sophia had run. He was about twenty or thirty meters behind her when he saw Dragomirov in the tree line off to her right.

"Sophia get down he shouted" and fired two rounds at Dragomirov, to try to draw his fire. Dragomirov fired and Gregory saw Sophia's body thrown forward landing face down in the snow.

Dragomirov spun and fired again. Gregory felt searing heat rip through his left side and stumbled to his knees. He was momentarily dazed but saw Dragomirov move out of the line of the trees he was hiding behind. Ignoring the intense pain in his side, he fired three shots. He saw Dragomirov spin wildly as the gun flew from his hands and he fell into a clump of snow covered branches. Running on pure adrenalin, Gregory got to his feet and moved, in a combat crouch, to Dragomirov with his Sig ready to fire. Dragomirov lay sprawled out in a tangle of branches. Moving closer, Gregory saw that most of Dragomirov's neck just above the left shoulder was blown away. Another shot had caught him in the chest just above his heart. He was very dead. Gregory immediately ran to Sophia. Grabbing his side as he ran, he could feel blood pumping out. He was beginning to lose all feeling in his arm, with the numbness moving into his shoulder.

His head was spinning as the adrenalin began to wear off and he was growing faint. As he approached Sophia, his worst fears became reality. The beautiful young woman laid motionless face down, her long black hair covering her face and a log where she fell, with wide pool of red snow beneath her head.

"Christ, I failed her" he thought falling to his knees beside her still body.

The snow increased and fog began to hide the carnage as he knelt next to her.

"I was sent to protect her and failed" was his last thought as unconsciousness swept over him from the loss of blood.

CHAPTER THIRTY NINE

MOUNT HERMON LEBANON

The plumbing van bounced across the desert frontier crossing the Syrian border into Lebanon, without encountering any paroling aircraft. They had to take a circuitous route out of Damascus, being careful to avoid ambushes from all the factions fighting in the city, as well as government patrols. After several spine jarring hours in the desert they finally arrived at the extraction point at the base of Mt. Hermon. The Antonov An12 sat waiting to take the team home. General Vistin and Major Ramizov, pulled Adnan Mohammed Wasen out of the van, took the burlap bag off him, and ripped the tape from his mouth.

As his eyes adjusted, Wasen saw eight armed men surrounding him "Who the hell are you people, and what do you want with me." Wasen said through swollen lips.

Vistin told the Lebanese fighters "You men guard the perimeter while I question Wasen". The fighters immediately moved off.

Wasen again said, "Who are you, and why have taken me and killed my men? What the hell do you want with me?"

"I wanted to have a little chat with the man who sent men to kill me in Aruba, and try to blow my aircraft out of the sky in Casablanca." Vistin said with his face an inch away from Wasen's.

Wasen's eyes widened realizing who he was talking to. He was shocked that this Russian had come to Damascus through a war torn area personally to take him.

"Oh yes, there's also questions about the head of a Russian minister you had sent to the Kremlin, you vicious bastard. We have much to discuss when I get you back to Russia." Vistin told him with a look of pure evil.

"Tell the pilot to prepare to get the hell out of here" Vistin shouted to Ramizov.

Moments later the four big turbo props began to spin, building power, as Vistin's team boarded the aircraft through the rear cargo door.

Wasen knew that he was finished, and had only one card left to play. He was in Lebanon surrounded by men that hated him, and would kill him without a second though. Once he boarded the plane, he would be tortured and forced to divulge information that would hurt The Islamic Brotherhood for Jihad, and slow the holy cause they were fighting for. He knew that any man can be broken, so he had to find a way to martyr himself for the cause, before that could happen.

"Put him aboard" Vistin told one of his men and watched triumphantly as Wasen was led to the rear cargo door.

Wasen pretended to stumble then kicked out viscously at the man's knee who was leading him. With lighting speed he began to run but was tackled by one of the Lebanese fighters. They rolled on the ground and Wasen kicked the man in the face stunning him. With the speed and agility of a much younger man, he got to his feet and ran straight into the spinning props of the Antonov. Vistin and his men stood shocked as Wasen was chopped to bits by the big props. Vistin was shocked, but was inwardly thrilled by this turn of events. All the Russians were shocked by what had happened, but the Lebanese were not surprised at all. They were just upset because they didn't have a chance to sweat

Wasen for information and watch him die the slow death they felt he deserved.

Strapped into the officers section of the Antonov An12 heading back to Moscow, they flew on in silence until Vistin said to Ramizov, "This has been a disaster. The counsel wanted to question Wasen. We were given instructions to take him alive and bring him back to be questioned, and executed at their convenience. There's going to be hell to pay when we get back to Moscow."

"We did the best we could sir. Who would have thought the man would deliberately run into the props?" Ramizov said looking at the floor.

Outwardly Vistin appeared upset and distraught, but inwardly he was thrilled, and thought "This solves all my problems even though the Senior Party Members lost their prize."

CHAPTER FORTY

THE KREMLIN MOSCOW

Ggeneral Pushkin sat at the head of the long table in the top security conference room with the other senior party members. He was furious, red in the face, his fist bunched, puffing strongly on his Cuban cigar. Surrounded by a cloud of smoke like a steam locomotive, he listening to General Vistin's report about the mission into Syria to bring Adnan Mohammad Wasen to Moscow for questioning.

"General Vistin, you were instructed to bring his man, Adnan Mohammad Wasen, here to be interrogated about the activities of The Islamic Brotherhood for Jihad. You had the best men available, and you let him kill himself while he was restrained with cuffs. How the hell do you explain this General?" Pushkin growled, staring intently at General Vistin, who was still standing at attention.

"Sir, Major Ramizov and his men performed brilliantly, and everything went to plan. It never occurred to us that the man would run into the spinning props of the plane." Vistin said.

"Never occurred to you, you should have anticipated something like this from one of these people. They're extremists in every sense of the word."

Vistin knew that trying to make any excuse, whether valid or not would only infuriate General Pushkin further, so he simply said, "You're right of course General Pushkin. I make no excuses and take full responsibly for my failure."

Calming a bit but saying nothing, General Pushkin looked at the other senior party members, then back at Vistin, who stood sweating at attention awaiting his fate. Finally after what seemed like hours to Vistin, General Pushkin said, "It's too risky at this time to try to go into Syria and find another member of The Islamic Brotherhood for Jihad to question. Once they've found the guards bodies and discovered that Wasen was abducted, they'll be on high alert and we would lose both men and intelligence assets in any further covert operations. So, do you have any other suggestions General, on how we are to collect intelligence on The Islamic Brotherhood for Jihad?"

"Yes sir. We have one other suspect in custody that we believe had been involved with The Islamic Brotherhood for Jihad operations here in Moscow. We will interrogate him to acquire further leads to this group."

Again looking slowly from one party member to the other General Pushkin said, "The council wants some solid intelligence on The Islamic Brotherhood for Jihad in Russia, and any planned operations within three days General. If we don't have it, and any other attacks happen on our soil or to our comrades in the field, you will be held personally responsible. Do I make myself clear General Vistin?"

"Yes sir, very clear General Pushkin sir."

"Dismissed General" General Pushkin said.

General Vistin went back to his office and poured a large glass of vodka, then dropped heavily into his chair staring out the window at the Moskva River thinking, "That didn't go well at all". He knew that Pushkin hated him, and always resented his rise through ranks to his current status. Pushkin would love to smack him down hard to show him that his current position was completely undeserved and at Pushkin's convenience. The other members that made up the senior committee were old and fat. They were useless as far as he was concerned, but their offices held great power over anyone, and they would follow Pushkin's lead. "I need to sweat Fathi Halir, and get something to give Pushkin and the counsel in one big hurry. Once they have solid intelligence on The Islamic Brotherhood for Jihad, things will calm down and the council will have other things to interest them."

After taking a few minutes to calm down and reorganize his thoughts, Vistin phoned warden Petrovich at Lubyanka prison and told him to get Fathi Halir ready for questioning.

"I'm sorry General Vistin that will not be possible sir. The prisoner Fathi Halir is dead sir.

"What the hell happened, Petrovich" Vistin exploded into the phone.

"The prisoner was found dead in his cell two days ago sir. We kept him stripped down as you ordered and he was given nothing sharp with his meals. He apparently drowned himself in his own toilet sir. We attempted to inform you, but you could not be reached."

Vistin slammed the phone down, and closing his eyes thought, "Holy shit, I'd better think of something to feed Pushkin and give the senior committee members fast. Give them something else for them to play with and in one big goddamn hurry. If necessary, I could have Dagomirov assassinate Pushkin and put the blame on The Islamic Brotherhood for Jihad. If I did that, the membership would have all security people hunting them down, and my experience with these terrorist would be a useful asset, taking me out of the fire and putting me back in their good graces.

This is a very big move, but I'm playing for very high stakes, yes, Pushkin must die."

CHAPTER FORTY ONE

PIEVE DI CADORE ITALY

Gregory felt a blinding pain in his side and couldn't move his leg. He slowly became aware that he was in a hospital bed with his leg immobilized and a bag of blood plasma, along with other bags of fluids hanging next to the bed, with various tubes in his arms and monitors attached to his chest. The nurse at her station noticed on her monitor that he had regained consciousness and pressed the button on her desk saying, "Doctor Clamenza, the patient in room four is awake."

Doctor Vitorio Clamenza came into the room and said, "I'm Doctor Clamenza, how are you feeling Mr. MacNee? You had a pretty close call".

"I feel like hell Doctor. Where am I?'

"You're in the Hospital Giovanni Paolo II, in Pieve di Cadore. You were in pretty bad shape when they brought you in. You've been shot twice, and had lost a lot of blood. The bullets didn't do any serious damage, but you had a large laceration in your right leg which has been cleaned and stitched up. It was quite deep but thankfully missed your femoral artery. The other bullet glanced off the fourth rib in your left side fracturing it, and took a chip out of the costal cartilage as well as nicking your liver. It will be painful for a while but will heal completely in a few weeks."

"How did I get here?"

"You were brought in by officers of the Polizia di Stato in Cortina. I've been told this is a security matter and instructed by the Italian Special Services in Milan not to discuss this with anyone" Doctor Clamenza said, looking a bit disgusted.

"Was anyone else brought in with me?" Gregory asked.

"Captain Mario Guiliano, of the Polizia de Stato is waiting outside to talk with you if you feel strong enough."

"I'll see him now, thank you Doctor."

Captain Guiliano came into Gregory's room looking somber. "How are you doing Mr. MacNee?'

"I'm alive, so it could have been worse."

"What's the last thing you remember?"

"I remember shooting Dragomirov just after he shot and killed Sophia Gambini. I went to her but it was too late. I remember thinking I was dying, numbness moving from my side up my neck. My legs were freezing cold then I collapsed, then nothing until I just woke up."

"Well Mr. MacNee, first of all, Sophia Gambini is not dead."

"Sophia's not dead? Oh thank God." But I saw Dragomirov shoot her just before I shot him. When I got to her, her head was in a pool of frozen blood and I couldn't feel a pulse."

"She wasn't shot Mr. MacNee. The way it looks to us is that Dragomirov shot at her but missed. She must have tripped at the same moment on the branches covered in snow and hit her head on a log when she fell, knocking herself out. She has a concussion and had a bad laceration on her forehead extending down to the side of her right eye. That's where all the blood came from.

"Thank God for that. Is she still in the hospital?"

"Yes, she'll be here for several days. There're bringing in the best plastic surgeon in Italy from Rome to stitch her up, so there should be no scaring."

"Can I see her Captain?"

"Let's wait till you can walk first. I have quite a few questions that need to be answered Mr. MacNee. There are the two dead men in the morgue that you shot in the forest. There's was a badly beaten guard at the Olympic Ice Stadium, and one of the catering staff has a broken arm. Please tell me what happened."

"Well, the two men in the morgue are Major Dragomirov and Gregor Petrovich, the men I warned you about. I went to the Olympic Ice Stadium to find Sophia, and the guard told me that two men tried to get in to see her but he turned them away. I got in from the side and went to her dressing room and told her she was in danger and we had to leave. We were headed for the Mestre train station in Calazode di Cadore. Dragomirov and Gregor caught up to us and tried to force us off the road. Ultimately we both crashed and they tried to shoot Sophia through the rear window of my Range Rover. Sophia panicked and ran for the woods. I killed Gregor, and was shot in the leg by Dragomirov, and then he went after her. I followed them and he shot me again in the side, then shot, or I thought he shot, Sophia before I killed him. As to the guard and caterer back at the Ice Stadium, they were fine when we left. I suppose Dragomirov and Gregor returned and beat them for information about where Sophia went and that's how they got to us so fast."

"Mr. MacNee, my department is always willing to cooperate with the British Secret Service, but an incident like this can have a terrible impact on a luxury ski resort like Cortina d' Ampezzo. We've had to impose special restraints on the media using the power of the President in Rome to keep a lid on this. We had to say that Miss Gambini was in a car crash and she'll be fine. Because of her star status, it's a media circus out there. We can't allow them to get wind of the killings or it would be a disaster for Cortina."

"I understand Captain, and my department appreciates all your help. How are the guard and caterer doing?"

"They'll both be ok, but it's cost a considerable sum to keep them quite. We'll be billing your department for this of course."

"We understand, and again, thank you for your help. We both would have died in the snow if your men hadn't found us."

"Prego Mr. MacNee. Get well soon" Captain Guiliano said, as he was leaving.

"Thank God that Sophia is alive and will be as beautiful as ever. I hope she'll talk to me again." Gregory thought as he drifted back to sleep.

It was several days before Gregory was able to be wheeled to Sophia's room, with a guard on the door to keep the press away. When he entered the room she was sitting in a chair with a huge bandage covering the right side of her face, and she had burses on her arms and what he could see of her shoulder.

"Sophia, Thank God you'll be alright. I thought they killed you."

"I don't remember that much of what happened after we crashed. I remember someone shooting at the car. I was terrified and just ran. That's all I remember. They tell me I hit my head on a log. It still feels like someone's beating my scull with a hammer. You don't look so good either." She said with a painful grin.

"When I got to you, I thought you were dead, and my heart turned to water. I can't begin to tell you how I felt when they told me you were alive and going to be alright. The killers that were after you are dead, and you're safe for the moment. My department has arranged to move you secretly into a private villa at a very exclusive private clinic on the shores of Lake Como to recover while we deal with Ophidian. Once they know their agents failed to eliminate you, they may send others, you're still a threat in their eyes."

"What do these people think that I know, that they're willing to keep trying to kill me to keep me from revealing?

"We think the main man in this organization is high up in the

Russian military and running Ophidian without the knowledge of the Russian Government. He knows if government finds out about his activities, he would be tried and shot, so he is trying to eliminate anyone who may have any link, no matter how slight, between him and Ophidian before the KGB finds out.

"My God Gregory, this is incredible! I have no idea who is running this Ophidian and I don't care. I'd never even heard of it until just now. Jesus, I meet and fall for a wonderful man, and then I'm being hunted down and almost killed by the Mafia and Russian spies. In the movies the whole spy vs. spy thing sounds exciting and exotic. In real life though, the experience has been pure hell."

"You're right of course. These people are not exciting; they're just vicious cold blooded killers. They're willing to kill thousands for money and power without a second thought."

"So you and your people move me to Lake Como, and I just wait for the spies to find me?

"MI6 will have round the clock protection for you while you're there, nobody will be able to get to you. We should have this business with Ophidian wrapped up soon, but need to keep you safe while we finish them off."

"Alright, when do I go to Como?"

"We'll move you out tonight. Since you're so recognizable, they'll wrap your face in bandages and move you on a stretcher in ambulance. You'll have a cover name and story, that you were burned in an accident, and that you have your own private nurse so the staff at the clinic won't be interacting with you. Your private nurse will be one of our best agents, Susan Jamison. I've worked with Susan on several assignments and she is the best of the best."

Taking her hand tenderly in his, and looking into her beautiful dark brown eyes, Gregory said, "I hope when this business is finished, we can get together again and take up where we left off."

"Gregory, honestly, I think I was falling in love with you, and still could, but your world is too violent for me. It may not happen soon, but some day someone else would be trying to kill me or you would wind up dead. I'm just not up to that, so I don't think we will be able to get together again, as much as I would love too." She said with a tear running down her cheek.

"Of course Sophia you're right. This is a nasty business. But there must be people who rise up and fight those that are willing to kill the innocent, and for now at least, I'm one of those people. I'll miss you more than I'm able to express in words Sophia, we could have had something beautiful. Someday maybe things will be different. Take care of yourself Sophia; I'll see you in the movies kid." Gregory said, kissing her cheek gently.

CHAPTER FORTY TWO

VAUXHALL CROSS LONDON

One week later, Gregory had recovered sufficiently from his gunshot wounds to meet with Mobius and work out a strategy to deal with Vistin and Ophidian.

"Doctor says you're fit enough for field work again. Do you really feel up to it, or did you just con her into putting you back on active duty?" Mobius asked watching Gregory carefully.

"I'm still a bit sore but can handle whatever I have to, sir."

"Good. Let's get down to business then. Our people in Moscow report that Vistin went after the head man at The Islamic Brotherhood for Jihad in Syria; a man named Adnan Mohammed Wasen. His orders were to bring the man back to Moscow to be questioned at Lubyanka prison by senior party officials only. We heard that the man managed to kill himself, or allegedly kill himself, by running into the spinning propellers of the Antonov An12 sent there to bring him out. Of course I'm not so sure Vistin didn't throw him into the props. We know Vistin didn't want him questioned by the senior party members, or his involvement with Ophidian and The Islamic Brotherhood for Jihad would have been discovered." Mobius told him.

"I'd imagine Vistin's superiors were just thrilled when they got the report that this Wasen killed himself." Gregory said.

"Yes, that's putting it mildly. His direct superior, Deputy

Chief of the GRU First Directorate, General Pushkin, was livid. Our people in the Kremlin found out that Pushkin has always hated, and resented Vistin, for his easy rise to General using Vistin's family connections. They think that Pushkin would love to use Vistin's failure to bring Wasen to them for questioning, to convince the senior party members that Vistin is incompetent and should be forced to retire. We may be able to use this information to stop Ophidian and put Vistin out of business entirely." Mobius said.

"I think I see where you're going with that sir. If we can get credible information linking Vistin to The Islamic Brotherhood for Jihad, and Ophidian, to Pushkin, he would begin an immediate investigations. The KGB and GRU would also launch an investigation. If the evidence is compelling enough, they would order Vistin's arrest pending the outcome of the investigations. Of course they would find what trails we leave and Vistin would be put on trial for high crimes against the State." Gregory said.

"That's exactly what I've been thinking. Vistin would be out of the picture for good and the KGB, GRU and FSB would smash his Ophidian organization for us. I want you to get to work on plan to get the GRU and KGB onto Vistin, without leaving any MI6 finger prints on the information." Mobius said.

"Sir, do the Italian police still have the bodies of Dragomirov and Gegor on ice, and do you know if they have they contacted anyone in Russia about them?"

"They still have them in the morgue in Calazo di Cadore. I asked the Italian Special branch to keep them without contacting the Russian Embassy until we finished our investigation into the incident, and they agreed."

"Good, perhaps we can help two dead men atone for their sins, and help bring down Ophidian and Vistin. I'll get to work on a plan straight away." Gregory said.

***

Gregory went to his home in Highgate London, to work on the plan. Sitting at the huge oak desk in his study, with a crackling fire, sipped a fine eighteen year old Glenlivet, while a hard rain beat against the windows; his mind kept drifting back to what might have been with Sophia. Returning to the present issue, he thought, "It was a beautiful time, and who can tell what the future holds, but it's over and it's time to get back to work." Forcing her from his mind, he began to write down all the details of his recent encounters with General Vistin's operatives from the Ophidian organization. He needed to concoct a way to get this information to General Pushkin. It would have to be done with a little information here, and there, with trails that would connect them all, including his suspicions that the Russians working with Valero Drago were in fact Ophidian agents. There would have to be trails linking the activities in Berlin, Casablanca and Aruba to Ophidian and The Islamic Brotherhood for Jihad. Though it was well past midnight in London, he hoped that Matt West would still be at his office at CIA Headquarters in Langley Virginia. Phoning CIA, he wasn't surprised that West answered on the second ring.

"Matt, this is Gregory MacNee in London. I need some of the information you have on Ophidian and General Vistin. But first, how's John doing?"

"Gregory, it's good to hear from you buddy. John is doing better, but still not working. He's recovering from home now and the director will tie him to a desk until he's completely well. So, what can CIA do for the leading light of MI6?"

"I'm glad to hear John's doing better Matt, and hope to see him when I come to the conference next month. I don't know if you've kept up with Ophidian, and our good friend General Vistin, but we think we've worked out a way to close the books on him."

"I've heard that The Islamic Brotherhood for Jihad tried to

shoot Vistin's plane down in Casablanca, and that he tried to snatch a bigwig with The Islamic Brotherhood for Jihad in Damascus; but the guy killed himself before they could get him back to mother Russia. The details were a bit sketchy." West told him.

"All true. The Islamic Brotherhood for Jihad guy was Adnan Mohammed Wasen, a heavy weight in that organization, and Vistin did snatch him. We're told that Wasen ran into the spinning props of an Antonov An12 before they could get him onboard. Not that It would have made much difference; Vistin had to kill him before they got to Lubyanka for questioning."

"I suppose that's true. But damn; running into the aircrafts spinning propellers is a nasty way to go. Of course those people are crazy anyway. So what do you guys need to put Vistin away that CIA can help with?"

"MI6 has operators inside the Krimlin that have discovered that General Pushkin hates Vistin, and would love to ruin him. Using his failure to bring Wasen back to the senior party members for questioning as a spring board, we'll get information to Pushkin with trails that will lead to connections between Vistin, Ophidian and The Islamic Brotherhood for Jihad. We need the banking records your Justice Department collected on Vistin's accounts in Aruba and Switzerland. With the bank information, combined with further trails from our investigation, the KGB and GRU will discover connections between Vistin and Ophidian, that will connect Vistin and the death of Pavol Orlov at the hands of The Islamic Brotherhood for Jihad."

"Christ All Mighty, when the KGB and GRU gets hold of that information the party will skin Visitn alive. But will they believe it if it comes from CIA and MI6?"

"They may be doubtful, and Vistin may be able to spin his story making it look like Western Intelligence is trying to discredit him with the Russian military and the party. That's why we're setting a trail for the KGB and GRU to follow that won't lead back to MI6 or CIA. The information will appear to have been stolen by Russian agents. We'll have our people in the Kremlin start a rumor regarding Ophidian having ties with someone high up in the Russian military machine.

The trail will have to be vague but mention General Vistin. Pushkin will jump at the chance to crush Vistin, and will put the KGB on the trail. We'll make the information hard to find, but not impossible, and make it tantalizing enough that Pushkin and the KGB will keep digging until they find it. The difficult part will be our man getting the information to Pushkin, without being discovered, and found out to be foreign spy, which would be fatal. But we'll find a way to get it done."

"Sounds like a hell of a plan, and it just might work. Let me call my guys at the DOJ and get copies of those bank account statements to you. It'll probably take them a day or so, DOJ is notoriously slow to do anything."

"Great, thanks Matt. Please tell John I wish him a speedy recovery."

"Will do Gregory. Let me know if you need anything else from us."

Gregory was in his study till dawn working on a rough plan to let Pushkin know that General Vistin was bent. It would be complicated, but it should work.

Two days later after receiving the banking records from Matt West at CIA, Gregory made arrangements for a clandestine meeting with the MI6 operator in Moscow. The operator, known only as Max, said Gregory would be contacted and given instructions where to be for their meeting. Max was a deep cover agent, and Gregory was not given any description of him, just told to follow whatever instructions Max gave him.

Gregory woke early, and phoned police headquarters in Cortina asking to speak to Captain Guiliano.

"Buongiorno Captain, this is Gregory MacNee in London."

"Buongiorno Signor MacNee, How can we assist you this morning?"

"Captain, I understand that the bodies and papers of the two Russian agents that were killed last week attempting to kill Ms. Gambini, are being held at the police headquarters in Calazo di Cadore".

"Si' Mr. MacNee, the Italian Special Services said they're identities were not to be disclosed, and the Russians weren't to be contacted until we heard from your government."

"Yes Captain, that's correct. Her Majesties Government, and my department, deeply appreciates all your help and understanding in this matter. What we need is for you to send a message to the Russian Embassy, saying that two men were killed in an apparent kidnapping attempt of an Italian film star outside of Cortina de Ampezzo a little over a week ago. They had no identifying papers but their finger prints were run through Interpol, and they were identified as Alexie Dragomirov and Gregor Petrovich, both Russian citizens and both officers in the Russian Military. Tell them that Interpol is looking into any connection between the two Russian killed in Cortina, and the two that were killed in a bombing in Isola di Pantelleria with a well known Mafia boss. The Italian government will be filing an official complaint with the Russian Embassy regarding these two incidents. Since there is an ongoing investigation into the attempted kidnapping by foreign nationals on Italian soil, the bodies will not be released until Interpol has completed its investigation."

"I understand Mr. MacNee, we'll send the message this morning." Captain Guiliano said.

"Excellent. Again, many thanks Captain." Gregory said.

***

All the information from CIA had been encoded onto a micro dot, that Gregory carried as he boarded the eight A.M. Aeroflot Russian Airlines flight from London Heathrow non-stop to Sheremetyevo International airport outside Moscow.

CHAPTER FORTY THREE

MOSCOW

Security inside Russian was less stringent than in the dark days of the Cold War, but there was still a general paranoia by the Russian Internal Security people know as the FSB, who still saw enemies behind every tree. Gregory felt he may not be watched quite as closely arriving on the Russian National Airline as he would on British Airways. The flight was bumpy but otherwise uneventful. Clearing customs and security went much quicker than he'd expected. Miss Trent had arranged for transportation to his hotel, and a large black BMW was waiting at the curbside, with the driver holding a sign for Mr. MacNee. They ground through the slow morning traffic in silence, for the twenty eight kilometer drive to the Russian Imperial Hotel Moscow, located in central Moscow on Ulitsa Okhotnyy Ryad, just a few blocks from the Kremlin. He checked into a plush suite with a lovely view of the city towards Red Square. After settling in, he ordered a light lunch from the Spa café, of crab and salmon sushi with green tea. Enjoying his lunch looking out over the city, Gregory was thinking how much Moscow had changed, and yet not changed. The city looked much as he remembered, but the vibe was much more western. The hotel and surrounding area seemed to breathe money. There were expensive cars everywhere, with men and women wearing the latest designs from top European designers. Eating some of the best sushi he had ever tasted, while sitting in Moscow would have been unheard of not many years before. After lunch, he took a walk towards Red Square and the Kremlin to get a feel for the area. Returning to the hotel, he decided to wait to hear from Max. Gregory was growing somewhat impatient when he had no word from Max all day. It was past eleven when he decided to call it a day and retire for the evening. Rising early, he found an envelope tucked under the front door of his suite with a single ticket for the famous Russian Ballet "La Bayadere" at the Bolshoi Theater that evening at seven. The Bolshoi Theater was on Theater Square, across from Revolution Square, just a short walk from his hotel. There were no other instructions.

Gregory dressed in a charcoal grey cashmere suit with a navy blue silk tie, so he would fit in without standing out in the formal environment of the Bolshoi Theater. The driver of the hotels BMW dropped him off in front of the theater at just past six. As he approached the doors, he scanned the heavy crowd trying to guess who Max was, and looked for any security men or woman paying particular attention to him, or anyone else in the crowd, but he could not spot any.

Taking his seat on the isle, just left of center in the first circle, he had an excellent view of the stage as well as the crowd. As everyone began to take their seats, a strikingly beautiful young woman with long blonde hair, elegantly dressed for a formal night at the ballet, scooted past him taking a seat four over from his left. The theater darkened, and the curtain rose. He decided to just enjoy the ballet and wait for Max to make the next move. There were several bars set up in the lobby, so at intermission, Gregory when out for a glass of wine. The lines were long at each bar, and as he waited, he noticed the blond from his row of seats waiting two lines over. It occurred to him that it seemed rather odd that such a beautiful woman would come to the ballet alone. Arriving at the bar he thought again how much Moscow had changed. The bar had an outstanding wine list that just a few years earlier would be unheard of in the finest restaurants in the city. He ordered a Chateau Mouton Rothschild and moved to a quiet corner to watch for Max. He was standing near a large pole sipping his wine and scanning the well healed crowd when he heard a voice ask, "Enjoying the show?"

A bit startled he said. "Absolutely. This is my first time here, but I certainly see why the Bolshoi has the reputation for excellence it has."

Turning around he saw that it was the beautiful blond from his row of seats who had asked the question.

"You move very stealthy. I never heard you and can't believe I didn't see you, Miss?"

"Funny you should say that, I have a friend in London who seems startled every time we meet." She said flashing him a thousand watt smile.

"I can certainly believe it, Miss?"

"Mika, Mika Khabalov" she said, holding out her hand.

"It's a pleasure to meet you Mika. My name is Gregory, Gregory MacNee." he said taking her had gently. Mika means "God's Child" in Russian I believe."

"It's nice to meet you as well Gregory. Yes it does. Do you speak Russian?"

"Well no, not really. I'm familiar with a few phrases and I've always been interested in the meaning of words and names."

"You are English yes?" She asked. Her voice was as smooth as his glass of Mouton Rothschild's and very sexy, with a charming Russian accent.

"Yes, I'm English. You mentioned a friend in London, have you been there?"

"Oh yes, many times. I studied at Cambridge for two years. Are you just visiting Moscow?"

"No, I'm in the aviation business and my company is working with the Russian aircraft manufacture Tupolev, on a new avionics package for their latest airliner."

"Sounds like interesting work. Oh, the show will be starting again in a minute; we need to return to our seats." She said.

"You're right. Would you like to get together for a cocktail after the show?"

"I'm afraid I can't tonight Gregory. Here's my card. Give me a call and perhaps we can meet tomorrow evening, I get off work at six." She said.

"That would be wonderful. I may have to re-arrange a meeting or two but I'll be available." Gregory said.

Walking back to their seats he asked, "What type of work do you do Mika?"

"I work for the government at the Kremlin as a computer programmer." She told him.

"That sounds interesting as well." he said as they reached their isle. "Enjoy the rest of the show Mika and I'll phone tomorrow."

After the show ended, Mika left without another word.

Riding in the back of the BMW on his way to the hotel he was thinking, "Why the hell didn't Max make contact. Perhaps something spooked him and he'll try again. Well the evening wasn't a total loss. The Ballet was beautiful and so was Mika. She's something pleasant to look forward to at any rate."

Back in his suite at the Russian Imperial he was thinking, "Max never showed up, but somehow this woman must be connected to Max. Both work at the Kremlin, so maybe she was sent as a first contact in case he was being watched by the FSB or KGB. He took out her card and was looking at her full name, Mika Anastasia

Khabalov, that's when it hit him. In Russian, the capital letter for K is X, so her initials are MAX. He had met Max and didn't even realize it. "Damn, he thought, she's very smooth that one. Very smooth, and very beautiful indeed."

The next evening at seven he phoned the number on her card and decided to play the game of asking for a date in case her phone was bugged. She answered on the third ring.

"Good Evening Mika, this is Gregory MacNee. We met at the Bolshoi last evening."

"Ah yes, good evening Gregory."

"I was wondering if you're free to have that cocktail we talked about, and if you haven't eaten, perhaps we could have dinner."

"As a matter of fact I just got home and haven't had dinner. I know a fine Thai restaurant in the Tverskaya district only a few blocks from the theater. Would eight thirty be good?"

"That sounds great. Would you like me to have the hotel driver pick you up or should we meet at the restaurant?"

"I live quite close, so I'll meet you at the bar at eight thirty."

"I look forward to it." He said.

Hanging up the phone he thought, "She is being very careful, she must feel that they're watching or at least listening. In that regard Moscow has not changed at all, someone is always watching and listening."

Gregory arrived at eight fifteen and took a seat at the crowded bar so he could watch for any surveillance teams, that may have listened to their conversation and staked out the restaurant. At precisely eight thirty Max walked in, and every eye turned her way. She was looking fabulous in a pale pink cashmere sweater and white slacks that were just tight enough to show her off tiny waist and ample curves, while still look elegant and sophisticated.

He stood when she approached the bar. "Mika, I'm so glad you could make it this evening. What can I get you?"

"Good evening Gregory. I'm glad our schedules worked out as well. I'll have a very dry vodka martini, up with a twist."

Gregory said to the barman, "We'll have two Beluga Gold Line martinis, very dry with a twist, and please have them sent to our table. I asked for a quiet table in the back" he said, as he gently took her arm and guided her through the crowded restaurant. Keeping up the appearance that this was a date, Gregory held her chair out for her and said, "You look fabulous this evening Mika. You certainly don't look like you've had a long day at the office."

"Why thank you Gregory, that's nice of you to say" she said looking shyly at the table.

Their drinks arrived and Gregory said, "Would you care to order now or wait a bit and enjoy our drinks?"

"Oh, I think we should order. They're always busy here and we'll probably have time for this drink and another before the food gets here. It takes a while, but the food is excellent."

Gregory said to the waiter, "We'll order in just a moment. I've never been here and would like a moment to look over the menu".

"Of course sir, I'll be right back but please take your time." The waiter said with a slight bow.

They investigated the menu and wine list waiting for the waiter to return. Mika said, "I've had their Red Duck Curry and it's excellent. Why don't you order for both of us."

"I'd be happy to Mika. I enjoy Thai food in London quite often."

The waiter returned and Gregory said, we'll have the Goong hom pa for two to start, followed by the Coconut Prawn Soup with Lemon grass and lime leaves. The lady will have the Red Duck Curry, and I'll have the Chicken Penang Curry, spicy"

"Excellent choice sir. And to drink?"

"We'll have a bottle of the Domaine Zind Humbrecht Pinot Gris from Alsace. And please make sure it's properly chilled."

"Of course sir. Thank you."

Gregory said to Mika, "The Alsace region is not particularly fashionable in the wine community at this time, but the Domaine Zind Humbreacht Piont Gris is excellent and pairs quite well with spicy food. I think you'll enjoy it."

"I'm quite sure I will. What is Goong hom pa?" I've never had it she asked.

"Marinated King Prawns wrapped in crispy pastry. It's really quite tasty" He told her"

When they were alone Gregory said "I was noticing your card and your initials in Russian. M.A.X. if I'm not mistaken."

"Yes, that's right Gregory. I knew you'd figure it out." She said with that fantastic smile. "Mobius was somewhat vague about what needs to be done. Can you fill me in?"

"Do you feel safe discussing this here, or is there somewhere else you'd prefer?" Gregory asked.

"Here would probably be best. The place is public and generally noisy, so I doubt were being listened to. I check my place for listening devises regularly, but here is probably best for now."

They leaned in towards each other and Gregory took her hands so they looked like lovers having an intimate conversation and said, "We've discovered that a Russian General, Nicolay Vistin, is operating a clandestine organization known as Ophidian. This organization has brokered deals with terrorist organizations and organized crime, to sell those stolen Russian weapons as well as kidnappings and murder for hire. These deals included the kidnapping and attempted sale, of an English physicist to The Islamic Brotherhood for Jihad. His specialty is the development of extremely small nuclear devises. If they used these devices against Israel and the West the result would be catastrophic."

Mika listened intently and said "I understand Gregory, what do you need me to do to help stop this madman?"

"We need you to put an information trail in the Russian security computer system so that systems algorithm will pick it up, and lead the KGB and GRU to people and secret bank accounts that belong to Ophidian. The trail has to be set up in such a way that the KGB will think that they have uncovered those links using intercepted CIA reports."

"Where will I acquire this information?" Mika asked.

"I'll bring it to you tomorrow morning. Meet me at Saint Basil's Cathedral on your way to your office. I'll be waiting with a bouquet of roses for you. There will be a special, undetectable, micro dot on the inside petals of the rose in the center of the bouquet with the information we want put in the Russian system on it." Gregory said.

"Roses first thing in the morning? How romantic of you." She said leaning in close and flashing that fantastic smile. He could smell her perfume as she took his hands in hers. Gregory felt like he'd just touched a live wire. A flush of heat shot through him from head to foot just looking into her beautiful ice blue eyes, and he thought to himself, "Steady on son, keep your mind on business. Your objective is to get the KGB onto Vistin's trail. There may be time for getting to know Mika better once the job is done."

Getting his mind back on business, with more than a little difficulty, Gregory said, "The Italian embassy is filing an official protest with the Russian embassy, regarding an attempted kidnapping of an Italian film star by Russians in Cortina d' Ampezzo last week. The men involved were killed, and the Italian Special Branch and Interpol discovered that they were both officers in the Russian Army. They were in fact, clandestine agents working with Ophidian, and were there on General Vistin's specific orders."

"Are they really Russian Army, or was that just a cover?" Mika asked.

"Yes, they were active duty Russian Army, and served with Vistin in Afghanistan. They were currently assigned to his personal security detail and supposed to be here in Moscow. But they were killed in Cortina trying to kidnap and kill the Italian film star, because she had inadvertent contact with Ophidian. We think Vistin's cleaning house and eliminating all loose ends. One of the trails should be, the CIA is investigating activity in Berlin related to The Islamic Brotherhood for Jihad. Several of their brothers were arrested at a mosque hiding weapons, and six others were killed in a shootout in Templehoff. One of the men killed was a Russian named Borya Sokolov. Sokolov served with Vistin in Afganistan. Another trail should show Interpol and the Italian Special Branch investigating the bombing of a Mafia strong man, Valerio Drago, where two un-identified Russians were also killed. Large amounts of cash were transferred into the shell corporation accounts in Switzerland and Aruba belonging to Ophidian." Gregory told her.

"Imputing the date trails should be easy enough. Once we receive the complaint from the Italian embassy, mentioning the Russian Army officers, I'm required to forward a copy to General Pushkin's office at the GRU First Directorate and the KGB. It will be easy to add a side bar that the two men served with General Vistin. They will initiate an investigation immediately." She said.

The waiter returned with their meals and opened the wine pouring Gregory a small amount for his approval. Gregory gave the waiter a nod of approval then the waiter poured a glass for Mika and served their Goong hom pa.

"The Goong hom pa is wonderful, and the wine is an excellent choice for this spicy food. I'll have to remember it for next time.

I hadn't realized how hungry I was, I haven't eaten since breakfast." She said.

"For now let's just enjoy the rest of our evening" Gregory said.

The next morning at seven Gregory was waiting for Mika with a large bouquet of red roses, at the entrance to St. Basil's Cathedral. He drew some looks of curiosity from passersby, since it was odd to see a man waiting with flowers at that hour of the morning. The odd looks changed to envious looks once Mika arrived looking stunning in a blue business suit that fit her perfectly. He gave her the flowers and a kiss on the cheek saying, "The micro dot's on the inside petal of the center flower. Contact me once you completed the transfer of data to the Russian system."

"Thank you so much for the flowers darling, they're beautiful" She said kissing him softly and saying, "It should be done by noon."

Mika left him and walked to the Kremlin. She was joined by two young women who were all questions about the handsome gentleman who gave her flowers first thing in the morning. She passed through the security check with smiles from the guards and no problems. Once at her office, after taking care of the important communications from the Embassies, she imputed the coded data with CIA trails into the KGB searchable data base, as well as the Directorate "K" data base. Directorate "K" was the division responsible for internal counterintelligence. They would handle the bugging of offices, phones and homes, as well as kidnappings and possible assassinations; of those they deemed enemies of the state. They were the ultimate in dangerous paranoids who saw everyone as a traitor that must be exorcised for the good of the state. After she had completed the data input, she saw the report from the Italian embassy, with the official complaint about the attempted kidnapping and shooting. Per regulations, she forwarded the report to the KGB duty officer's desk and to General Pushkin's office at the GRU.

She ran into General Pushkin in the lift later that evening.

"Good evening General" She said, with her unforgettable smile.

"Ah, good evening Mika. Are you working late this evening?" General Pushkin, like most of the men working in the Kremlin, was captivated by Mika's beauty, extraordinary figure and her outgoing personality.

"Yes, just a bit sir. We had a few late embassy messages that needed to be sent to the appropriate offices. In fact, there was one from the Italian embassy forwarded to your office."

"I've been in meetings all day Mika and I'm done for the night, but I'll look for it first thing in the morning." Pushkin told her.

The lift arrived at street level, and as they walked to the exit, Pushkin said, "Do you need a ride home Mika? My driver's waiting, and it would be no inconvenience to drop you off"

"Oh, thank you so much sir, but I'm meeting some friends out front"

"Very well then. Have fun tonight Mika" General Pushkin said, feeling disappointed that he couldn't spend more time getting to know this beautiful young woman.

CHAPTER FORTY FOUR

THE KREMLIN MOSCOW

G eneral Vistin paced around his office, with his hands clasped tightly behind his back, trying to think of what his next move should be. It seemed that with one set back after another, and the failure of the sale of Dr. Patterson, his plan of looking like a hero to the Chairman of the Presidium of the Supreme Soviet Party was all but gone. He knew now that he would have to escape Russia, and soon. After trying to reach Major Dragomiroff for over a day, he intercepted a communication from the Italian Embassy in Rome to the Russian Embassy in Moscow. The gist of the message was that that two Russian citizens who had been identified as Alexie Dragomiroff and Gregor Petrovich, had been involved in what was being investigated as a kidnapping attempt of an Italian film star, outside the alpine village of Cortina d' Ampezzo several days before. The report said that the attempt had failed, and both men had been killed in a gun battle. Furthermore, the men were now identified as officers in the Russian Army. The Italian Special Branch, and Interpol, was now investigating to see if the Russian military or the KGB was involved conducting illegal operations on Italian soil. The Italian Government is demanding an immediate answer and apology. Vistin assumed the police had killed both Dragomiroff and Petrovich, but the report was unspecific as to that point. Regardless of who killed them, he would have to act quickly.

This incident would take several days to filter through the bureaucrats in the embassy. Since Russian military personnel were involved, the report would be sent to General Pushkin's office at the GRU First Directorate as well as the KGB Director. They would find that Dragomiroff and Petrovich both served with Vistin and were attached to his security detail. He would have to move very quickly to eliminate Pushkin, and get the KGB looking for the terrorist assassins, that would take the heat off him long enough for him to make his escape.

Vistin arranged transport to a Russian airbase at Alakurtti, on the Finnish boarder, under the guise of meeting with the base commander to discuss supplies the Special Forces detachment at the base needed. Once he arrived at Alakutti, he would make his way over the Finnish boarder, pick up forged identity papers he had arranged for and put his escape plan into action. Vistin left his office and walked along the bank of the Moskva to a phone box. He attached his portable scrambler to the phone and contacted one of Ophidian's top assassins in Vilnius Lithuania, named Borodin.

Vistin dialed a special number that only he had. The phone rang three times when a gruff voice answered saying, "Taip, Kas tai yra?" (Yeah, what is it)

"Borodin, Vistin said, I have a job that requires your immediate attention. Meet me by the fountain in Gorky Park at six tomorrow morning. Don't be late." He hung up without another word.

Borodin was originally from Syria where he was a professor of chemistry at one of the top universities in Damascus. Several years ago he began drinking. At first his bosses at the university overlooked it, but as it picked up they ultimately had to discharge him. Nearly broke, and with all but no chance of securing a job in a strongly Muslim city, he became an easy target for Ophidian agents, who were always looking for men and women who were experts in their fields but had fallen from grace for various reasons. Borodin was a small man in his early sixties, with thinning grey hair and a drooping grey mustache. His appearance was totally unremarkable, and his demeanor would allow him to move about completely un-noticed by anyone. He was a shadow of a man, that if you asked someone to describe him, they wouldn't be able to do so with any accuracy. This obscurity worked in the killers favor. Borodin was master assassins whose favorite methods included poisons, knifes and booby traps, which would be very difficult to detect due to their exotic nature. He abhorred the use of guns; any unsophisticated cretin could pull a trigger. He considered himself an artist, and his work required flair and imagination before he could be satisfied.

Packing just one bag with the basic tools of his trade, he rushed to catch the train to Moscow via Minsk which left in two hours. Sitting in the main train station in Vilnius, waiting to board his train, Borodin was thinking "Why would General Vistin himself be meeting me in Gorky Park? The job must be very important and dangerous. No matter, the more dangerous the job the better the payday would be."

Arriving at five minutes before six, as the sun was just beginning to lighten the sky, Borodin took a seat next to the large fountain and waited, hunching his small shoulders and turning up his collar against the cold morning breeze.

General Vistin arrived precisely at six, wearing and old stained overcoat, thick gloves and an old hat with a tattered scarf around his neck. He looked like any of the down and out people on the street in Moscow these days.

Vistin made eye contact with Borodin, then dropped a wine bottle in a paper bag on the grass next to the fountain. Walking slowly up to Borodin he said, "Your instructions and target are in the bag. You'll be working as a custodian at the Kremlin starting today. Your identification is in the bag. Do the job quickly."

"A rush job will cost double, two hundred thousand Euros" Borodin said.

"The funds will be transferred to your Swiss account this afternoon. Get it done." Vistin told him.

Borodin nodded his head in acknowledgment.

Vistin kept walking and was gone in moments. He took a circuitous route through the rubbish filled alleys, where the down and outs slept against walls, covering themselves with cardboard against the cold. He kept his eyes peeled for watchers in case the KGB was watching or following him. The plan was a good one. He had planted incriminating evidence in the apartment that Borodin would be using. There were forged documents showing that Borodin had arrived in Moscow from Syria just days before, and a note claiming responsibility for Pushkin's killing in the name of The Islamic Brotherhood for Jihad. Borodin would of course be killed as soon as his work was completed so he wouldn't be able to tell the KGB anything when they found him. Before going to meet Borodin in Gorky Park, Vistin rigged the apartment that Borodin would use to explode after Pushkin had been killed. He had put a copper tube, with special heat activated foam inside, in the heater of the one room apartment, along the gas line to the pilot light. Vistin had a radio trigger that would heat the tube allowing the foam to expand out the end, extinguishing the pilot light releasing a steady stream of gas into the closed room. He also put a small flint striker inside the telephone. Borodin was an alcoholic, and Vistin knew he would get very drunk while he waited in the apartment to leave on the evening train, and not feel that room getting colder. When sufficient time had passed, Vistin would trigger the devise and put an end to Borodin. Then he would make his escape.

The KGB would find the charred body of the suspected assassin and assume he had been eliminated by the Brotherhood. He was sure that the KGB and GRU would focus all their energies towards eliminating this Islamic threat that was growing in Russia.

Borodin walked over to the lawn, picked up the bag and pretended to drink. He walked slowly to the Park Kultury Metro Station on the red line. Sitting on a bench in the far corner of the station, he looked in the bag. Inside the bag he found the key to an apartment on Ulitsa Shchepkina, in an area close to a large mosque and just a mile or so from the Kremlin. He was instructed to eliminate General Puskin very quickly. The instructions gave the location of General Pushkin's office, his home, and his morning habits.

Arriving at the apartment, Borodin sat on an old sofa in the dreary one room apartment that smelled of dust and mold. He played a tape of his favorite Tchaikovsky piece, "The Seasons", and drank vodka from a water glass. He was considering the best way to complete this latest commission for Ophidian, and get away alive. It was an audacious plan to be sure. To kill a Russian General inside the Kremlin and get out alive would be the biggest challenge of his life. He knew with his creativity and talent, it could and would be done. He thought, "Explosives and knives are out of the question due to the security checks coming in or out of the building, as well as the security on each floor. No, poison would be required. It would have to be something fast acting and very difficult to trace. Perhaps a derivative of Thallium in sufficient dosage would do, or perhaps a concentrated dose of Fentanyl. No, that's not that answer. Both would be difficult to acquire and prepare on such short notice and away from my usual suppliers, and both would take too long to finish Pushkin off." He continued to brood on the problem while drinking and letting the music free his mind. Then in a flash, the answer came to him. "Takifugu, yes of course, Takifugu or Puffer fish as it's known in the west. There's a sushi restaurant just a block from here. The current sushi crowd is mad for the most exotic fish, so they're bound to offer fresh Takifugu on the menu. I'll be in the alley before dawn when they get their fish delivered and steal one or two of the fish. The poison in the liver of a Takifugu is a powerful Tetrodotoxin, twelve hundred times more deadly than cyanide, and it would be impossible to trace the source. Yes, there's enough Tetrodotoxin in the liver of just one fish to cause a very quick and unpleasant death. Mixed with a transdermal compound, it would be absorbed through the skin leaving no marks. Pushkin would suddenly become violently ill vomiting, and collapse. Paralysis would soon follow then respiratory failure. Yes, that's the answer".

Borodin was in the alley before first light, and was able to steal one of the fish while the delivery men moved coolers of fresh fish into the kitchen door of the sushi restaurant. The handling of a Takifugu takes a practiced hand or the person doing the handling would be stuck by one of the many poisonous spines on the fish which could be deadly. He carefully extracted the poison from the fish's liver and intestines then distilled it increasing its potency many times. This step completed, he mixed the concentrated poison with a transdermal compound and poured the mixture into a thermos bottle he would put in his lunch box. This he could easily carry through the Kremlin's security as he reported for work at midnight that night. At ten minutes before midnight Borodin arrived at the Kremlin's service entrance where all service personnel entered and exited. The security detail checked his identification and he was instructed to remove his jacket, shoes, and to empty his pockets into a plastic tray similar to the ones used at major airports. He then moved through the body scanner and metal detector. He was cleared and had to wait a few minutes while his jacket and lunch box were searched and scanned. Finally clearing security, Borodin was issued a temporary pass and instructed to keep the pass in clear view at all times, and to stay in the areas assigned to him by the service personnel supervisor on duty. Borodin was assigned a list of offices he was to clean.

The offices were to be cleaned no later than three a.m. and General Pushkin's office was third on the list. He headed for the toilet before putting his lunch box on the shelf the cleaners used. He poured some of the poison mixture into a small plastic sandwich bag and put it in his jacket pocket, then put the lunch box on the shelf. Borodin completed the first two offices without speaking to anyone, and was followed to General Pushkin's office by a rather bored armed guard who stood in the doorway while he cleaned. When Borodin cleaned the coffee samovar and fine porcelain cup that the General always used, he brushed the poison mixture inside the samovar and cup including the handle. The mixture would dry, and when Pushkin had his cup of very strong coffee, as was his habit each morning as soon as he arrived at his office, the moisture from his fingers would turn the dried poison mixture back into solution and it would absorb through the skin. He would also ingest the poison from the cup and samovar. The strong coffee would mask the bitter taste and dilute the poison somewhat but he would get a sufficient dosage to kill him in short order. He completed the office and told the supervisor he was sick, and needed to go home.

He wanted to be out of the building before Pushkin arrived, just in case security closed the building after Pushkin was struck down.

Borodin left and waited in an ally with a clear view of the Kremlin's front enterance.

General Pushkin arrived at his office just after four thirty in the morning as was his custom. His secretary, Miss. Boc, had arrived at four a.m. sharp, prepared coffee and set the most important messages out on his desk for his review first thing.

"Good morning, Miss. Boc"

"Good morning, sir. Bit chilly this morning isn't it sir?" she said following him into his office.

"Yes, but most mornings are at this time of year" he said taking off his top coat and giving it to her.

She hung up his coat and poured him a cup of coffee carrying it to his desk by the saucer and setting it down for him. "You have a report from the embassy marked "MOST URGENT EYES ONLY" on top of the pile sir"

"Thank you Miss Boc. That will be all for the moment"

"Yes sir". She said, and withdrew closing the door behind her.

General Pushkin sat down and opened the "EYES ONLY" report from the Russian embassy. The report detailed the official complaint from the Italian embassy received the day before. The report made it quite clear that the Italian Special Branch and Interpol suspected the Russian army, and the KGB, of illegally conducting operations on Italian soil, and they would be demanding an explanation from the Chairman of the Presidium of the Supreme Soviet. Reading the report, he noted that the two men killed in Cortina d'Ampezzo were both active duty army currently assigned to General Vistin's personal security detail. "What the hell were these men assigned to Vistin's security detail doing in Cortina d' Ampezzo when Vistin's here in Moscow?" he thought.

Powering up his computer, he accessed the military personnel data base in the GRU system, and did a cross check of the names of the men killed in Cortina d'Ampezzo and the Russian's killed, along with five Islamic terrorist in the Berlin shoot out with the German Special Branch. The KGB was already investigating the Russian's killed in Berlin that had been identified as, Boris Sokolov and Anatoly Garin. The preliminary KGB report suggested that both Sokolov and Garin may have been in some way connected with the terrorist group identified as The Islamic Brotherhood for Jihad, but the report was inconclusive and ongoing.

"The Islamic Brotherhood for Jihad, the group that claimed responsibility for the killing of Paval Orlov, as well as the ones who tried to shoot down General Vistin's plane in Casablanca. Could they be trying to kill Vistin because he was in some way standing in their way, or because he is doing some sort of business with them?" he thought, remembering the note about betraying the brotherhood that came with Orlov's severed head. He continued reading the report and thought, "There'll be hell to pay when this gets to the Chairman, I need answers and quickly". He took a sip of coffee as he was reading and thought, "It's almost inconceivable that two former and two active duty Russian officers would be working with Middle East terrorist groups. This is simply unheard of." Delving further into the KGB report, he ran a cross check through the GRU system on all four of the men, and found one extremely upsetting link, all four men had served with General Vistin in Afghanistan and two were on his personal security detail.

He immediately sent an "EYES ONLY" request to the KGB Chairman of the First Chief Directorate Committee for State Security, Leonid Andropov, requesting an immediate meeting to discuss a most upsetting and potentially dangerous development and requested he bring all the information in the KGB report on the shooting in Germany with him to the meeting.

"I'll have to get as much information as I can from Andropov without telling him too much. Since the men involved were Army, it's more a GRU matter than the KGB." Pushkin thought.

A few minutes later Miss. Boc came over his intercom saying, "Excuse me sir, Mr. Andropov his here to see you."

"Thank you Miss. Boc, please show him in."

Miss Boc ushered The KGB Chairman in saying, "Chairman Andropov to see you sir." Then she retreated and closed the door.

General Pushkin said, "Thank you for coming so quickly Leonid. This is potentially a most serious matter. Please have a seat. Would you like some coffee while we talk?" he asked, as he poured some fresh coffee in his cup.

"No, thank you General; I'm limiting my coffee to two cups per day. My doctor says it's not good for my heart. Tell me, what is this serious matter you mentioned?"

Leonid Andropov sat in one of the leather visitor chairs and General Pushkin took his seat behind his large desk. "Leonid, I received a report from the Italian embassy that two Russian officers were killed in a shootout in Cortina d' Ampezzo last week, allegedly attempting to kidnap a Italian film star.

"Yes, I also received that report General"

"I understand that your department has an on-going investigation into the shooting in Templehoff earlier this month, and I'm wondering if these incidents could be in some way related. If they are in fact related, it could be a dangerous risk to State security. Tell me what your men have discovered regarding the Templehoff incident". Pushkin said.

"Well sir, the report is inconclusive at this time; but it seems that seven men were killed in that incident in Templehoff. Five of the men were identified as members of a Middle Eastern terrorist organization who call themselves The Islamic Brotherhood for Jihad, and two were Russian citizens who were identified as, Anatoly Garin and Borya Sokolov, both ex-Russian army officers. Identifying Sokolov was quite difficult; there was very little left of him to identify."

"Have you discovered what Garin and Sokolov were doing with these men from the terror group or who their target was?" Pushkin asked.

"We don't know their exact involvement, but the German Special Branch is said to have been conducting the rescue of a kidnapped Englishman"

"Who was this Englishman that the Germans would bring out the Special Branch, and that kind of firepower to rescue?" Pushkin asked.

"We don't have all the answers yet General. The Germans have put up a tight security screen around who the man was. It seems an English Physicist was kidnapped off a road in Zurs Austria some weeks ago, and we think this was the man who was rescued. We've questioned several people in Zurs and were told that they heard Russians were involved in that kidnapping, though we're still looking into who they might have been." Andropov told him.

"Do we have a name for this Physicist and what his specialty is"? Pushkin asked.

"No sir, not at this time. As I said, the Germans are keeping a tight lid on this."

Continuing, Andropov said, "When the German Special Branch team left the warehouse, after the terrorist had been neutralized and the Englishman rescued, the man Sokolov opened fire from an apartment at the end of the block and killed Garin, before a German Special Forces EC665 Tiger helicopter opened fire with a 7.62mm mini gun completely shedding the apartment and Sokolov. We've intercepted some CIA reports that they believe an organization of criminals known as Ophidian, could be operating in Russia, and that this Ophidian has been stealing and selling Russian built weapons to different terrorist groups including The Islamic Brotherhood for Jihad. It may be that Ophidian arranged the kidnapping and were going to sell the Englishman to the Brotherhood.

I think we must assume, until proven otherwise, that the Englishman was a nuclear physicist, and if this is so, the world would have become a much more dangerous place with these terrorist having a nuclear physicist in there custody and forcing him to create weapons for them. "

Pushkin was shocked and deeply concerned at the implications of what Andropov had just told him. "Have you been able to find out anything about this Ophidian organization? Who they are, and where to find them?" Pushkin asked.

"No sir. So far there is no intelligence on Ophidian, except the CIA believes that they may have also been involved, in what was reported at the time, as a gangland killing of a mafia boss named Valerio Drago, on the island of Isola di Pantelleria off the coast of Sicily.Three men were blown up in Drago's car. We've questioned several witnesses, and were told that two of the men killed in the blast were said to be Russian; but we have no proof of this or identification. All the bodies were burned to dust in the explosion and fire that completely melted the car and its occupants. The Italian police bomb squad said that the bomb used in the blast used Thermite. It was a very professional job sir."

"Thermite, my God, that burns at over four thousand degrees. It seems a bit of over kill just to take out a mafia boss. So there is no verification that the other two men were Russian?" Pushkin asked.

"No sir. Not enough left for an examination. We're also looking into a Russian citizen killed in Tempelhof just days before the shootout, one Gregor Delov, who died in a traffic accident. It seems suspicious that three Russians would all die in Templehoff within such a short time. We're looking for a connection between Delov, Garin, Sokolov and this Ophidian organization." Andropov told him.

General Pushkin sat staring at his desk with beads of sweat forming on his forehead and an ever tightening knot in his chest. He thought it was the realization of Russians acting with Middle Eastern Terrorist, and that General Vistin may well be involved.

"Thank you for your report Leonid. Please keep your men digging. We need to get to the bottom of this and soon. Have them redouble their efforts and uncover what Ophidian is, and where they're operating. As impossible as this may sound, there is some indication that General Vistin may be involved with Ophidian.

This is purely speculation at this time, but the men killed in Italy and Germany all served with General Vistin. If Vistin is involved with them we need to find proof that will stand up in a court of law. We can't let him know that we're investigating his movements, but we need to see if any other trails lead to him. Collect all the information you can pertaining to Vistin, trips, phone calls, emails, bank accounts any unusual purchases, the lot. We need information and proof of any allegations before I can take it to the committee."

"Yes sir, I understand the type information you need."

"That will be all for the moment" General Pushkin said without rising from his desk.

"Yes sir General. I'll put every available man on it at once. Are you alright General? You're not looking well sir". Andropov asked.

"Yes, Leonid, I'll be alright. This is a most upsetting business, and I think the implications are rather turning my stomach." Pushkin told him.

"Very well sir, if there's nothing else, I have much work to do." Andropov said and he left Pushkin's office.

General Pushkin was beginning to feel dizzy, and the tightness in his chest was getting worse, but he shook it off and pressed the intercom button saying, Miss Boc please ask the Chief of Directorate "K" to come to my office at once."

"Right away sir"

Within five minutes Miss Boc announced over the intercom that Major Alexander Ramius, Chief of Directorate "K" had arrived as ordered.

"Show him in Miss Boc." Gereral Pushkin said.

When Miss Boc escorted Major Ramius into Gereral Pushkin's office, the General did not rise to meet him. General Pushkin looked quite pale and was perspiring though the office was not at all warm.

"Are you feeling alright sir? You're not looking at all well sir." Miss Boc asked

"I'll be fine Miss Boc. That will be all".

"Yes sir. Please let me know if you need anything." She said as she left them.

"Major Ramius, please have a seat." Pushkin said.

"Thank you, sir. How can Directorate 'K" assist the General?" Ramius asked.

"This needs to be handled with the utmost discretion Major. I need you to investigate one of my officers who may be involved with a criminal organization known as Ophidian. This organization may be working with a Middle East terrorist group, known as, The Islamic Brotherhood for Jihad. I want round the clock surveillance of this officer, including listening devices placed in his office and home, as well as recording all calls."

"Who is this officer and where do we find him sir?" Ramius asked.

"Major, this cannot be handled today as it would have been in the past. We cannot just pick this officer up and question him in Lubyanka. Today we have to find sufficient evidence to convict him in a court of law. If in fact this officer is working with this criminal organization, we will have to prove it in court. There's another reason for discretion, this officer is high ranking with influential friends, and his family was very powerful within the party." Pushkin told him.

"I understand sir. Can you give me his name and position?" Major Ramius asked watching General Pushkin carefully.

Pushkin was sweating profusely and began to falter in his speech. He tried to rise from his desk but collapsed on the floor and became violently ill clutching his chest and struggling to breathe.

Major Ramius punched the intercom button and said, "Miss Boc get the doctor up here immediately, I think General Pushkin's having a heart attack."

Pushkin was beginning to go into violent spasms. Ramius came around the desk and said, "The doctor is on his way. General, give me the officers name while you can."

The doctor burst into the office with his nurse carrying an oxygen bottle and said, "Stand aside major. Nurse, get him on oxygen and see if we can stabilize him for transport to the hospital. An ambulance will be here in moments General." The ambulance crew arrived and strapped Pushkin onto a gurney as he was losing consensus. The doctor and ambulance crew rushed Pushkin into the elevator then loaded him into the ambulance. Miss Boc climbed in with them and the ambulance sped way.

Borodin watched as General Pushkin was brought out on a stretcher with an oxygen mask strapped to his face. Two attendants and a woman, he assumed was Pushkin's secretary, got into the ambulance and it sped away, siren wailing. Borodin walked slowly back to the apartment feeling very calm and satisfied that the commission was completed with the creative flair he insisted upon, even with such short notice. He would be leaving on the evening train two hundred thousand Euros richer.

Major Ramius said to the armed guard who had come in with the doctor to General Pushkin's office, "Sergeant, I want this room sealed, nothing is to be touched and no one is to enter until my men arrive. Is that clear, Sergeant."

"Yes sir, perfectly clear Major." The Sergeant of the guard said standing at attention.

Major Ramius went to Miss Boc's desk and phoned his secretary saying, "This is Major Ramius, I want a full investigative team to come up to General Pushkin's office at once, including Marco, our head toxicologist."

"Right away, but Major, Marco is not due to arrive until nine. I'll put in a call to him to come at once."

"Very well." Ramius said and hung up without further explanation. Then he looked at the General's appointment book and noticed that the KGB's First Chief, Leonid Andropov, had met with General Pushkin, just before the General had summoned him to his office. Ramius phoned Andropov and told him that the General had collapsed, and was on the way to the hospital. "Please come back to the Generals office Chief Andropov, we need to talk."

Chief Andropov arrived and was allowed to pass by the guard into the outer office to meet Major Ramius. "What's this all about major? What has happened to General Pushkin?" Andropov demanded.

"Let's talk in the General's office, but please do not touch anything, leave everything just as it is until my team arrives." Ramius said.

Once they were inside Pushkin's office with the door closed, Ramius said, "Chief Andropov, I was meeting with General Pushkin, he was telling me about an organization of criminals known as Ophidian that may be working with a group who call themselves The Islamic Brotherhood for Jihad. He said that he suspected that a high ranking Russian officer might be colluding with this group, but collapsed before he could give me the officer's name. I see from Miss Boc's appointment book that you had just had a meeting with the General. What did he want to see you about?"

"Major, I would need permission from the General to discuss what our meeting was about. What is his condition?"

Moving within a few inches of Andropov's face, Ramius said, looking into his eyes, "If we're talking about an officer who's gone rouge Mr. Andropov, who is obviously a threat to state security, you will tell me and right now."

"Major Ramius, do not forget to whom you are speaking. I'm the KGB Chairman of the First Chief Directorate Committee for State Security; you have no right to speak to me in this fashion. If there is a threat to state security, we will investigate it. If I feel we need your department, you will be brought in. If General Pushkin wants me to discuss the details of our conversation I will, but not until he tells me personally. Is that quite clearly understood, Major."

Ramius stood glaring at the Chief of the KGB and shaking with rage, but he knew at this point there was nothing he could do to make Andropov tell him the details of a private meeting with the General. "Understood, Mr. Andropov."

"Let's find out the Generals condition. It originally looked like a heart attack, but I'm beginning to think he may have been poisoned." Ramius said.

"Poisoned, here in the Kremlin? What makes you think so major?"

"He was telling me about this traitor and he began to sweat profusely, tried to stand and collapsed, then began to spasm and vomit. That would indicate poison Mr. Andropov. Did you eat or drink anything when you were here?" Ramius asked.

"No Major, the General offered me coffee but I declined."

"How did he seem to you when you first arrived?'

"He seemed fine, but towards the end of the meeting he was looking pale and beginning to perspire."

"Was he eating or drinking anything?"

"He was sipping some coffee from the samovar. We need to get a toxicologist up here and run a check." Andropov said.

"I have a team on the way, and have an emergency call into our head toxicologist. They should be here shortly." Ramius told him.

"I'm heading to the hospital to ascertain the General's condition. If the General was poisoned, as you suspect, have your men check his home, and car. Interview his driver to see if he stopped off anywhere this morning and of course a complete check of the office including the ventilation system. I'll let you know right away what the doctors have discovered." Andropov said.

"Call me at once if the General is conscious and able to speak Mr. Andropov, and I will be with him within minutes." Ramius said.

Arriving at the emergency room desk, Leonid Andropov identified himself to the duty nurse and said, "I need to see the doctor in charge, regarding General Pushkin, who was brought in half an hour ago."

"The General is in intensive care sir, under doctor Mishkin's care. Let me see if the doctor is free to speak to you." Realizing that she was in the presence of the Chief of the feared KGB, her anxiety doubled as she hurried to find the doctor.

Returning, the nurse said, "Doctor Mishkin will be with you shortly sir. He's with the General now."

"Take me to the General's room at once nurse." Andropov said eyeing her coldly.

"Yes sir. We cannot go inside, but you can wait outside the room." she said guiding down the hall.

Andropov paced up and down the hall outside the intensive care unit, after a few minutes, doctor Mishkin came out looking haggard.

"This is Mr. Andropov of the First Directorate for State

Security doctor. He is most concerned about General Pushkin's condition." The nurse said, then hurried away.

"Doctor, what is General Pushkin's condition? Did he have a heart attack or was it something else?" Andropov asked.

"General Pushkin's condition is extremely serious Mr. Andropov. We have done all we can, but frankly, whether he survives or not is out of our hands. He seems to have been poisoned by a very potent neurotoxin; we believe it could be in the Tetrodotoxin family based on the symptoms he experienced before he collapsed. We're running every test we have, but if it is Tetrodotoxin, there is no antidote and he will most likely parish." Doctor Mishkin said.

"Is he conscious? Can he speak? This is a matter of great importance to the state." Andropov told him.

"I'm sorry Mr. Andropov, he's unconscious, and may never regain consciousness. We can only hope and wait."

"Andropov walked back to the nurse's station and used their phone without asking, to phone Ramius. "Major, the doctor believes that General Pushkin was indeed poisoned. He is unconscious and not expected to survive. I'm on my way back to his office now."

Leonid Andropov knew very well that Directorate "K" was filled with vicious paranoids, who saw everyone as an enemy of the state, but understood the danger of not cooperating with them. He felt the German Gestapo of World War II and the old NKVD of Stalin's time had been gentle compared with Directorate "K". He wouldn't put himself at risk by withholding information from Ramius; but would need to be careful what he told him.

Arriving back at General Pushkin's office, Andropov was allowed to pass the armed guards, and saw a team of six Directorate "K" men inspecting everything within Pushkin's office, as well as the outer office, including Miss. Boc's desk with extreme thoroughness.

Major Ramius came to him immediately asking, "Do they know what poison was used or how it was transmitted to the General?"

"No major, at this time they know it was a powerful neurotoxin, possibly Tetrodotoxin, but they're still running tests. The doctor said that if it was in fact Tetrodotoxin, the chances of General Pushkin's survival, is very slim.

Ramius turned to the Directorate "K" head of toxicology, and said, "Marco test for Tetrodotoxin."

"Yes Major. Tetrodotoxin is extremely rare and very bitter, how the hell would he have ingested it without knowing it?"

"We don't know that yet Marco. Tell me, would strong black coffee mask the taste enough to have it go unnoticed?"

"If it was very strong coffee, perhaps it would. We'll test the coffee in the samovar and the cup he used at once for that toxin or any other" Marco said.

Ramius turned to the his team leader saying, "Captain, I want the security camera tapes for the last forty eight hours for this office checked with the cameras of the main entrance, and service staff entrance, as well as locker rooms. I want to know who was in this office, how they gained access, and I want it fast."

"Yes sir Major, I'll get them right away."

Turning back to Andropov major Ramius said "Mr. Andropov, in light of current developments we need to discuss the meeting you had with General Pushkin. I need to know who he suspects as a traitor."

"Of course major, under the circumstances we must begin a complete investigation." Andropov stood looking around the office trying to decide what to tell major Ramius. They were not sure that General Vistin was working in any way with Ophidian or The Islamic Brotherhood for Jihad at this point, but it was more than likely that, one or both of these organizations, had something to do with the poisoning. He knew that for any organization to get poison inside the Kremlin, and get it into the General's office, they would have to have an inside man with intimate knowledge of the Kremlin and its security measures. General Pushkin wanted legal evidence that would stand up in a court of law if General Vistin was guilty. If he gave Vistin's name to Ramius, Directorate "K" would kidnap Vistin, and torture him in the cells of Lubyanka with or without proof of wrong doing.

"We know practically nothing at this time Major. We only recently heard of Ophidian from intercepted CIA reports."

"Did General Pushkin tell you the name of the officer he was concerned was colluding with these criminals?"

"He was concerned that there may be a high ranking officer involved because of the two attacks on General Vistin, and the killing of the junior minister Paval Orlov. If Ophidian is working with The Islamic Brotherhood for Jihad, and arranged the attacks and the killing, they would have to have knowledge of the movements of both of these men that could only have come from within the Kremlin."

"That's true. The attacks and killings could be the work of the terrorist, but this poisoning was very sophisticated, and the work of a professional. This organization, Ophidian, would be more likely for this type job. Terrorist plant bombs and shoot up shopping centers, but generally don't go in for this of type thing. Did General Pushkin specifically say he suspected General Vistin?" Ramius asked

"No, not specifically, in fact The Islamic Brotherhood for Jihad has made two attempts to kill General Vistin. Why would they be trying to kill him if he's working with them? What was troubling General Pushkin, and why he was meeting with me, is that two of General Vistin's personal security detail were killed in Italy a few days ago, and they had no official reason for being there. Also, two of the men who were killed the shootout with the German Special Branch last month in Tempelhof, had been working with the terrorist and probably with Ophidian. Both had served with General Vistin in Afghanistan. General Pushkin felt there must be a connection and asked me to investigate both incidences."

"In that case I'll have General Vistin picked up at once for questioning." Ramius said.

"No major, General Pushkin specifically said not to do that. We have no evidence that General Vistin is involved. General Pushkin told me that we have to investigate General Vistin's activities, but to do so with the utmost discretion. General Pushkin said, if Vistin is in fact working with one or both of these organizations, we need to find proof that will stand up in a court of law. He was most insistent on that point."

"Very well Mr. Andropov. If that is what General Pushkin ordered, I'll get a team to wire his office and home with both listening devises and cameras. I'll also order round the clock surveillance of Vistin himself."

General Vistin had changed into his homeless clothing, knowing that the street people of Moscow noticed nothing, and no one paid the slightest attention to them. All they knew was the cold wind of extreme poverty, and the need for another drink and or fix. In this guise, Vistin would be invisible, and could follow Borodin back to the seedy one room apartment on Ulitsa Shchepkina after the ambulance had taken Pushkin away. He knew that Borodin would be drinking himself unconscious waiting for his time to depart. After about thirty minutes Vistin used the radio transmitter to activate the foam in the tube he had placed in the apartment's heater, now it was just a matter of waiting until the apartment was full of gas.

He thought about forty minutes or less would do. Just to be on the safe side he waited for forty five minutes, then using a call box at the end of the block, phoned the apartment. The phone began to ring, when the flint on the striker sparked, it ignited the gas filled apartment. The blast was so powerful it blew out the two front windows injuring several people on the sidewalk with flying glass and debris. A huge fire ball erupted from the blown out windows licking up the side of the building, as people screamed and ran for cover and the fire alarm bells rang. "So much for another loose end" Vistin thought as he walked down the alley and changed back into his uniform. He hailed a cab and headed for Sheremetyevo International Airport to catch a flight to Alakurtti Airbase near the Finnish boarder, and the first step toward freedom and a life of luxury.

When Mika arrived at the Kremlin in the morning, security was extremely tight. Everyone was being searched, and all brief cases and purses were emptied and completely examined. Inside there were armed guards everywhere, watching every move people made with intensity. She took the lift to her office on the third floor and there were guards in her office as well. She motioned with her eyes to her friend Niki, to follow her to the ladies room. Niki walked to the ladies room, and once inside Mika whispered "What the hell is going on? Aside from the armed guards, I saw KGB and Directorate "K" men everywhere on the way up".

"Early this morning they took General Pushkin out in an ambulance. It was thought at the time that he'd suffered a heart attack. Now it seems that he was poisoned and will most probably die." Niki whispered looking very afraid.

"They think General Pushkin was poisoned? Here in the building? Mika asked with a shocked look.

"Yes, they think so. Directorate "K" has taken all security tapes and are questioning anyone who was in the building between nine last night and seven this morning. The KGB is bad enough, but Directorate "K' scares me to death." Niki told her.

"I know what you mean. They scare the hell out of everyone. If they suspect you of anything, and they suspect everyone of something, you could find yourself in Lubyanka never to be seen again." Mika said meaning every word.

The day was going to be a long one and very stressful. During her lunch break, Mika took a walk along the Moskva, and was glad to be out of the tension filled Kremlin for an hour. She walked to a phone box and phoned Gregory at his hotel. Gregory was reading the afternoon edition of Pravda, when the phone rang. When he answered, Mika's voice was sweet as ever saying "Gregory, if you're free, let's have a drink in your hotel bar after I get off work, it's going to be long day."

He could tell something was amiss, but simply said, "Love to. How does six thirty sound?"

"Six thirty sounds perfect. A couple Gold Line martini's sound like heaven" She told him.

"Then I'll meet you in the bar at six thirty. It's going to be a long afternoon's wait" Gregory said, in a flirtatious way in case someone was listening.

"For me too, seeing you will give me something to look forward to. Oh, I need to get back. I hadn't realized it was so late, and my lunch hour is almost over. See you at six thirty Gregory" She said closing the line and hurrying back to her office. She didn't want to be late and draw any attention to herself.

Major Ramius and his team watched the security tape of the hall, and outer office to General Pushkin's office, from the time Pushkin left the evening before, until Major Ramius told Miss. Boc to call the doctor. No security cameras or listening devises were allowed in the General office. The only person to enter the office before Miss. Boc arrived at four a.m. was the cleaner, and the guard who stood at the door way but never entered the office. Turning to the head of his team Ramius said, "Dimitriy, I want the name and address of that cleaner in five minutes".

"Yes major. I'll get the cleaning crew supervisor from last night up here at once." Dimitriy told him heading down to the service office.

Within minutes the cleaning crew supervisor stood trembling before Major Ramius. Everyone knew of the fearsome reputation of Directorate "K" in general and Major Ramius in particular.

Ramius put his hand around the back of the supervisor's neck, gripping him tightly, and moved him in front of the monitor with the video of Borodin coming down the hall and entering Pushkin's office. Pointing at the screen he said to the supervisor, "I want that man's name and address and I want it right now"

"Yes of course Major, I'll get his card. Actually sir, that man is a temporary cleaner who just started last night. All his credentials were in order and he did a good job, but left early. He said he was not feeling well and the offices assigned to him were completed. He did a good job and....."

Ramius took the man by the shirt and pulled him to him saying, "Do you think I give a damn how well he did his job? Get me that name and address right now." pushing the man roughly into Dimitriy's grasp.

Dimitriy went to the supervisor's office and collected the temporary employment card telling the supervisor, "Stay here. Do not leave this office for any reason what so ever or we'll question you further in Lubyanka; do you understand."

"Yes sir, I understand and will wait right here sir." the man said, shaking in spite of trying to keep calm.

Dimitriy hurried back to General Pushkin's office and said

to Ramius, "The man's name is Vladimir Borodin, his permanent address is in Vilnius Lithuania, but the local address he used is a cheap apartment complex. Apartment number six Ulitsa Shchepkina, sir."

Ramius moved quickly for the door, grabbing his coat and hat on the fly, with Dimitriy right on his heels.

Ramius drove very fast for the amount of traffic in the area, and drove over the sidewalk scattering the pedestrians when the traffic was impassable. Arriving at the apartment on Ulitsa Shchepkina in less than ten minutes, he found the fire brigade beginning to roll up their hoses, and police keeping the crowd of spectators at bay. The apartment was a smoking ruin and completely gutted. There was an ambulance at the scene with a body covered by a sheet on a gurney being loaded in the back.

Ramius walked over to the ambulance and showed his identification to the policeman at the scene. He lifted the sheet but the body was so badly burned he couldn't tell if it a man or woman, let alone if it was Borodin, but he suspected it was. Turning to the policeman he asked, "Officer, what apartments were involved in the fire and how did it start?"

"There was a gas explosion in apartment number six about thirty minutes ago that spread to the two apartments above and to the one just next door, number eight. That man on the gurney was the only casualty, though several people were injured on the sidewalk sir."

"Was any identification found in the apartment?

"No sir, we're digging through the rubble, but it's all burned. We questioned several tenants and the manager as to who was living in that unit. The tenants didn't know; said he just arrived yesterday. The manager said the apartment was rented by the week, for cash, by post from Lithuania. That's no surprise in this area sir; this place is used by prostitutes and drug dealers by the hour."

Walking back to his car, Ramuis told Dimitriy, "Get me the coroner's report as soon as he has completed his autopsy of the body. I want to know if the fire killed him and anything they can discover about his identity. Tell the coroner this is his top priority, everything else can wait."

"Yes sir. Would you like me to drop you off at the Kremlin before I go to the coroner's office?"

"That will do. Just get me that autopsy report." Ramius told him.

Arriving back at his office at the Kremlin, Ramius was given a message to contact Yuri, the leader of the team assigned to watch General Vistin. Ramius phoned at once, "Yuri, what have you to report?"

"Sir, General Vistin is not in Moscow at this time. We had to ask through our informant in the GRU office, since we could not let anyone know we were looking into the General's movements. The informant said that Vistin is on state business but has not found out were at this time. I will move my team to Vistin's location as soon as we know."

"Very well Yuri, keep on it and find him. If he's on state business they know where and why. Tell the informant that it's vital that we locate Vistin quickly, but to be very discreet. If Vistin is guilty, he'll be on his guard. I want to be informed the moment he's located"

"Yes Major, I understand, and will contact you right away."

Gregory saw Mika when she entered the hotel lobby bar, as did every man there. She was as breathtakingly beautiful as before, but he could see a look of concern on her beautiful young face. As she joined him at the table in the far corner and gave him a kiss of greeting, he could see something more; he could see fear in her eyes.

"Ah Mika, you look lovely." He said, giving her a kiss and quick hug keeping the appearance of lovers meeting for a drink."

"Thank you Gregory. I don't feel lovely at the moment if I'm honest. It's been a very stressful day."

"Not to worry, it's going to get much better from here." She sat very close to him, and he signaled the barman to bring the two Gold Line martinis he had pre-ordered.

Their drinks arrived and Mika took a long sip. The fiery liquid helped calm her nerves and she said, "Thank God, I've needed that all day."

Sitting very close, Gregory put his arm around her shoulder and giving her a kiss on the cheek whispering "What is it? What's happened? You look very rattled.

"More than rattled my love, I'm downright scared"

She took both his hands in hers, and speaking softly so they were not overheard, told him, "General Pushkin was poisoned in his office by an unknown assassin and is not expected to survive. The KGB has been questioning everyone in the building since last evening, but it gets much worse. Directorate "K" is fully involved with the investigation. Their men have been questioning and watching everyone including me. If they blow my cover, I'll be taken to Lubyanka for interrogation, and no one ever comes back from there."

"Have they questioned you yet?"

"Yes, briefly this morning. They saw General Pushkin and me walking out of the building together last night on one of the security cameras. One of the Directorate 'K" agents questioned me as to what I was doing leaving with Pushkin, and insinuated that we were having an affair."

"That sounds about right. What did you tell him?"

"I told him the truth that General Pushkin and I just happened to take the same lift to the lobby, and due to the lateness of the hour, General Pushkin offered me a ride home. I thanked him but told him that I was meeting friends and was already quite late. The Directorate "K" man asked if General Pushkin had ever asked me out before. I said no, and that he had not asked me out last night, he was just being kind and offered me a lift home since his driver had the car waiting out front. "

"Was there anything else he wanted to know?"

"Yes. He asked why I had sent reports to both General Pushkin and Mr. Andropov that evening. I told him, that because the report was from the Italian embassy, and had to do with the death of two Russian army officers, regulations require that the head of GRU get a copy, that's General Pushkin, and the head of the KGB get a copy, that's Mr. Andropov, because of the foreign embassy being involved. He already knows why I sent them to both department heads; he was just trying to rattle me."

Gregory knew how serious she was, and what danger she was in. Her hands were perspiring and trembling as she spoke. "Do they have a suspect to Pushkin's poisoning?"

"I think so. All this is rumor, but the name Borodin was mentioned. This Borodin was a temporary cleaner who cleaned General Pushkin's office. When Major Ramius of Directorate "K" got the man's temporary employment card with his address, he was out the door with one of his men like a shot.

"The timing of this attack on Pushkin can't be a coincidence. Vistin knows the noose is tightening and that if Pushkin suspects that he's operating with Ophidian, he would be arrested, and suddenly Pushkin is poisoned. No, this sound like a Visitin move. Did they find this man Borodin?"

"Not really. I heard that when they arrived at his apartment, they found a burned out gutted apartment, and a roasted corpse."

"Yes, that's definitely got the Vistin touch. Do you know if General Pushkin got the information you put in the computer system leading to Vistin?"

"As I explained to the Directorate "K" agent, General Pushkin and I were riding the lift down to the lobby the night before he was poisoned. I told him that I forwarded an urgent message from the Italian embassy to him. He would have looked at them first thing in the morning. Just after he arrived, he accessed the GRU records file, and cross referenced the names of the men killed in both Germany and Italy. I'm sure he started investigating, but who knows if he had time to find what we placed in the system. We can only hope he did. He arrived at his usual time around four thirty and had a meeting with the Chief Andropov of the KGB about an hour later. Then Pushkin met with Major Ramius of Directorate "K" for just few minutes before he collapsed. Ramius told Miss. Boc to get the doctor and they took Pushkin out on a gurney, and took him to the hospital."

"Was Chief Andropov with him when he collapsed, or just Ramius?"

"As far as I know, only Major Ramius was with him." Mika told him.

"I think it's fair to assume that Pushkin did see the trail regarding General Vistin and Ophidian you put in the system, and that's why he did the cross check and subsequently called the meeting with Chief Andropov and Major Ramius." Gregory said.

"Do you know where General Vistin is now? Was he seen at the office today, after Pushkin was taken to the hospital?" He asked.

"No, General Vistin hasn't been in the office since last night."

"Can you find out where he went, without putting yourself in any danger by asking?

"I heard that he was out of the office on official state business. Where or what he's doing, I don't know and can't ask. The agents from Directorate "K" would want to know why a computer programmer was asking about where a General was and I would be found out. No, I can't do that Gregory." She said with a shaky voice.

"That's fine Mika. We don't want you to put yourself at risk. You've done more than enough. For the time being, just report for work as usual and don't ask any questions that may draw attention to yourself; but if you happen to hear something, let me know as soon as you feel it's safe to do so."

"Thank you Gregory", she said looking deeply into his eyes. "I think it would be wise if I could get out of Moscow for a while. The longer I'm in the office the better the chance Directorate "K" agents will start questioning me further."

"Do you have any vacation time available?" Gregory asked her.

"Yes, I haven't taken any vacation for the past three years, so I have almost a month coming to me."

"Ok, if it won't raise suspicion, due to the timing of the request, apply for your vacation and permission to holiday in the Lorie Valley in France for a couple of weeks. If you feel you're under suspicion, we can pull you out from there."

"I should be able to get the time off but I'll have to wait a week or so before I submit my request. Even though I would love to leave now, you're right; Directorate "K" would question me as to why I would pick this particular time to leave the country. Gregory, I'm really scared." She said meaning it.

"Don't worry, I'll arrange an emergency extraction team to pull you out within an hour's notice, but you don't want to use it unless there is no other option. Once we secret you out, you'll never be able to return to Russia, but we can do it if necessary."

"Thank you Gregory, that really does make me feel better."

She said squeezing his hand and looking deeply into his eyes. "I'll just go to work as usual until I leave for France, but I can't go anywhere near the GRU or KGB files in the computer unless they specifically order me to."

"That will do fine Mika. Just work as usual then go on vacation until this Pushkin thing blows over. And by the way, I'll make your hotel reservations and MI6 will pick up the tab." Gregory told her.

"Again, thank you for being here to help me Gregory"

"Let's order another round then head into the dining room for a bit of dinner before you head home. Everything will be alright, I promise." He told her.

Major Ramius returned to the Kremiln from the burned out apartment in a foul mood, and strode into General Vistin's office saying to Vistin's secretary,

"Miss Volga, is General Vistin available? I need to speak with him on a very important matter."

"No, I'm sorry major but General Vistin is away on State business."

"Where did he go and when will he return" Ramius said, with obvious impatience.

"He should return in a few days Major."

"Where did he go?"

"I'm sorry sir, but I'm not at liberty to say where he went since he's on official business." She told him.

Ramius could feel the rage building up inside him, but because he couldn't let anyone know that Vistin was under suspicion, he said as nicely as he could; "Miss Volga, it's really quite important that I get in touch with the General right away. As you know, General Vistin was attacked twice during a diplomatic trip not long ago, and was very lucky to have survived. We need to assign additional security to him on this, and any trips he makes, until we can eliminate the threat from these terrorist. The General is a very brave man and doesn't want more security, but we're very concerned about his safety. That's the reason I need to know where he is, so I can get some additional protection for him. So please, if it's not a top secret assignment, which I should not know about, I need your help in finding him."

Softening to his appeal, Miss Volga said "I understand major. The General would never admit that he needed more security, but I certainly see your point." She looked in her file and said, "General Vistin left this morning for a meeting with the commander of the Special Forces detail at Alakuritti Airbase, regarding supplies the commander feels his men need but are not getting. He should return in the next seventy two hours."

"Thank you Miss Volga. I'll get a detail from the airbase to keep an eye on him to make sure we get him back safely. Your help is most appreciated." Ramius said.

Walking into his office, Ramius told Dimitriy, "I want two agents on a plane for Murmashi Airfield, in Murmansk Oblast, within the hour. Vistin has gone to Alakurtti Airbase. Tell your men to acquire Vistin there, but not to let on that they're looking for him to anyone. Have them find him and shadow him until I signal to pick him up."

"Yes sir, Major. When you give the order to pick him up, are they to arrest Vistin, or find a way to bring him back without alerting him that he is under suspicion?"

"I'll have your men tell him that there's been another terrorist attack, this time at the Kremlin, and he's needed there at once. They'll tell him that due to the nature of the attack, and the attempts on his life in Casablanca and Aruba, they will be providing security for him during the journey." Ramius said.

"I'll send Ivan Nono and Mikail Markov as soon as I've briefed them on what's required. They're both competent men and have clandestine field experience." Dimitriy told him.

"Very well Dimitriy. Get going" Ramius said.

Ramius took the lift to the Chief of the First Directorate of the KGBs office and said to the secretary, "Major Ramius, to see Mr. Andropov.

"Yes major, let me see if he's free sir."

"Excuse me sir, Major Ramius of Directorate "K" would like a word." She said into the intercom.

"Please show him in." Andropov told her.

Ramius was shown into Andropov's office and the secretary retreated, closing the solid sound proof door behind her.

"Mr. Andropov, we believe the assassin was a temporary cleaner who listed his name on his employment card as Vladimir Borodin. We went to the address he listed as his residence to find an apartment gutted by fire, and a roasted corpse who we assume is Borodin, though they haven't conducted an autopsy yet for identification." Ramius told him

"How long had this man been living in the apartment?"

"The manager of the building said Borodin had just moved in and the apartment was rented by the week, paid in cash."

"Rented by the week and paid in cash?"

"Yes, it's the type of building that drug dealers and prostitutes use."

"Fools, that alone should have alerted someone who screens temporary employees to check his background further." Andropov said, with obvious disgust.

"You're absolutely right, he should have been thoroughly checked out. That's why I suspect an inside job, and Vistin is my prime suspect at the moment. He must have suspected that

Pushkin was on to his Ophidian connection and decided to have him eliminated before he could begin an investigation.

The killer would have had to have inside knowledge of the Kremlin security, and General Pushkin's habits and movements in order to arrange to poison him the way he did. Vistin had the information the killer would need, so I think Vistin set the whole thing up."

"That sounds like a plausible theory major, I agree. Have you assigned anyone to watch Vistin's office and home?"

"Yes of course, but according to Vistin's secretary, he left last evening for Alakuritti Airbase in Murmansk, ostensibly on state business. I think he knows that we're on to him and is making a run for it. I've just sent two agents to Murmashi airfield in Murmansk Oblast to find and shadow him."

"Excellent, I'll order a KGB car to be put at their disposal immediately. I'll also get some agents to watch for Vistin at the Finnish border." Andropov told him.

"Mr. Andopov, I'd like to get a copy of those CIA intercepts regarding Ophidian, to see what they suspect and what other information they may have acquired that we can use to bring this criminal organization down." Ramius told him.

"Of course Major, I have them right here. We also intercepted CIA communications between their U.S. Department of Justice and two banks, with accounts that the CIA suspects belong to Ophidian, in Switzerland and Aruba. Both are numbered accounts and have been receiving large deposits coming from several Russian companies and the Middle East. According to the Americans, there was a deposit of three hundred million Euros from a private bank in Egypt just hours before the shootout in Templehoff Germany."

"What banks are they?" Ramius asked.

"Banko de Aruba in Oranjestad is one, and the other is the Private Client Bank in Zurich."

"Have you sent any agents to look into these banks Mr. Andropov?"

"No not yet major. We just decoded the CIA intercepts this afternoon so I'm sending men to both Aruba and Zurich tonight. They all have banking experience, and will be able to get more information on who these accounts belong to. They should arrive by nine tomorrow morning."

"Very well, we'll keep an eye on Vistin. Alakuritti is very close to the Finnish border. If Vistin tries to cross the border, I'm having my men stop him and bring him back to Moscow. We can't let him cross or we may lose him." Ramius said.

"Agreed, but let's try to bring him in under some pretense that won't let him know we suspect him of anything, in case we're wrong." Andropov said.

"I've already given my people a cover story to get Vistin back here. But Mr. Andropov, we're not wrong, he's guilty and I'm going to have him."

"Let me make a call Major, please stay a moment longer."

Andropov phoned the base commander at Alakuritti saying, "This is the KGB Chairman of the First Directorate Committee for State Security, Andropov, has General Vistin arrived at the base yet?"

"Yes sir, he arrived this morning around ten thirty."

"Is he still there now, and is he available?"

"No sir, he was here for a couple of hours then left."

"You say he left, how, by plane or auto?"

"He took one of the base cars with diplomatic license plates sir."

"Commander, it's quite important that I locate him immediately. We need him to return to Moscow without delay."

"I don't know where he went sir. He didn't say where he was going and we didn't ask. When the car was ready he dismissed the driver we provided, saying a driver was unnecessary."

"Commander, you are aware of course, that regulations require that a driver be provided for all general staff officers."

"Yes Mr. Chairman, and we reminded the General of this, but he made it clear that he would be driving himself regardless of regulations"

"Are you in the habit of giving fueled cars with diplomatic license plates and no official driver, to anyone who wants one without asking where they're going, or when they're bringing it back Commander?" Andropov said with considerable heat.

"No of course not Mr. Chairman, but when a General says he needs a car, and orders the driver to stand down, we say yes sir, and provide the car. It wouldn't be proper for us to question him on why he needs it, or where he's going sir." the Commander said, trying not to say what an asinine question that was. But to insult the KGB Chairman can be a very bad thing to ones future indeed.

"Yes Commander I understand the problem, it's just very important that we get in touch with him. I want you to personally contact me the moment he returns. Is that absolutely clear commander?"

"Yes sir that is absolutely clear Mr. Chairman. I'll instruct the guards at the main entrance to the base to contact me while he is still at the gate and call you at once."

Andropov hung up the phone and turned to Ramius saying, "I believe your correct major, General Vistin is involved with Ophidian and may be on the run. The base commander just told me that Vistin took one of the base cars with diplomatic plates several hours ago, refusing the driver they provided, and did not tell him where he was going or when he would be back. A car with diplomatic plates could cross the Finnish border easily without being searched."

"Why do you think Ophidian would have arranged to have

General Pushkin poisoned? Vistin must have some heavy pull to get them to arrange a killing here in the Kremlin. And what purpose does poisoning Pushkin serve?" Ramius asked.

"If Vistin knows that the Italian embassy reported to our embassy that two Russian officers were killed trying to kidnap an Italian film star, he would know that the report would be forwarded to General Pushkin and me. General Vistin and General Pushkin dislike each other intensely, so Vistin would assume that Pushkin would begin an investigation of the men killed in Italy, as wells as the men killed in Germany, and find that they all served with him in Afghanistan. He would also discover that the two killed in Italy were on his personal security detail. With that connection, Vistin knew that Pushkin would order him to be questioned. If Vistin let that happen, and if he was suspected by the GRU, KGB or your Directorate "K", he would be put under guard and wouldn't be able to make good his escape. He had to act swiftly. By poisoning Pushkin, and making it look as though these terrorist had committed the act, our respective departments would be looking for terrorist, not him, giving him time to make his escape." Andropov told him.

"Let's assume that you're correct in your assumption, and he's going to try to cross the Finnish border to escape. Where would he go from there? He would need transportation and money. We must assume Ophidian will provide both." Ramius said.

"It would depend on how important Vistin is to that organization once he flees Russia. I would think he would have little value once he is out of the Kremlin and Russia, so they very well may just have him killed. I would." Andropov said, leaning back in his chair staring across the room at nothing in particular.

"As would I. Unless Vistin is Ophidian, and controls the money." Ramius said, rubbing his chin in thought. "If he is the head of Ophidian, than all those millions of Euros that have been transferred into accounts in Switzerland and Aruba are his, that's where he will run to before disappearing for good."

"Agreed, I'll get some men to cover the train stations and airports in Finland closest to the border, I don't think Vistin will want to go to deep into the country. We'll have to think of how he would plan such an escape in order to track him down." Andropov said.

"I'll get some men to cover the banks. My men should be arriving at Murmashi airfield in about an hour. I'll have them head towards the Finnish border and be on the lookout for the car Vistin is driving. If they spot him, I'll have them put our plan to bring him back into action." Ramius told him.

"Very well, I'll have a team of KGB watchers cover the border crossing with orders to stop Vistin and bring him back, using the same cover story. They're not to arrest him, but tell him that they are ordered to escort him back for his own safety." Andropov said.

CHAPTER FORTY FIVE

Kuoloyaryi Village near Finland

General Vistin sat in a small café, in the rural village of Kuoloyaryi, just ten kilometers from the Finnish border eating a lunch of rabbit stew, made with fresh rabbits raised by the owner, with white potatoes, carrots and onions all grown behind the cafe and a pint excellent Finnish lager. It was very rustic fare and he loved it. It reminded him of the good times he spent at his family's dacha high up in the Ural Mountains, along the banks of the Vetluga River so long ago. He had arranged to pick up false identity papers from the cafés owner, Ivan Stropenski who, as well as being an acceptable cook, was a master forger. Ophidian had helped to get Stropenski out of a five year prison sentence for forgery and helped him open his café. He had been on Ophidian's payroll ever since the day he got out of prison and owed them everything he possessed. Vistin had enlisted Ivan's services on several occasions for Ophidian operations, and he was well paid each time.

While he ate, he was thinking that things were going well so far with his escape. Everything about the escape plan had been meticulously planned years ago and now that it was being executed, there was nothing to do but let the plan work and watch his back. Vistin had contacted the owner of the Crescent Moon Shipping Line, Mr. Farzad Ahmadi, days before having Pushkin killed, and told him a favor was needed. Farzad had never seen Vistin, so he would not know it was Vistin himself that was on the run. Vistin phoned Farzad Ahmadi's private line at his offices in Bandar-e-Abbas, and told him that Ophidian had an agent that needed to disappear for a year or so, and that they wanted this agent to be made procurement officer on the tanker *Emperor of the East*. The agent would work aboard the ship for the next eight months to a year and that the ship's captain, Bijan Shah, was to treat him as he would any officer aboard his ship and ask no questions.

The Ophidian agent would rendezvous with the *Emperor of the East* at the port of Ystad in Sweden in six days, just three hours before the ship was scheduled to depart, as an emergency replacement for the ships usual procurement officer who had been hurt in an auto accident. Vistin would board the ship and sail the oceans under an assumed name letting his beard grow trimming it in the Iranian style for the next eight months to a year then leave the ship in Guangzhou and fly to France with false papers. Vistin already spoke English and Farsi so he would fit in. He planned to drive from Virojoki Finland, to the fishing village of Kotka Finland. There we would board a fishing boat the *"The Northern Lights"* which had been ordered to wait for Vistin's arrival and take him to Ystad Sweden, where he would board the *Emperor of the East*. After he finished his lunch he would cross the border into Finland and drive to Virojoki and his first step towards freedom.

As he was finishing his lunch, two KGB agents entered the café moving quickly to Vistin's table. The older of the two KGB men said, "Excuse me General Vistin sir. My name is Ivan Nono, of the KGB Finnish border station." Nono said, producing his identification card and showing it to Vistin.

Vistin glanced at the card and said, "Yes, what is it? Why are you disturbing my luncheon?"

"I apologize for the intrusion sir, but Mr. Andropov ordered us to locate you and escort you back to Moscow without dely. It seems that there has been a terrorist attack at the Kremlin, and you're needed."

"A terrorist attack at the Kremlin? What's happened?"

"I'm sorry sir, but we were not given the details; but Mr. Andropov said it is of the utmost importance that we escort you back safely. Mr. Andropov said that since these terrorist attacked your car and plane, that he wanted extra security for you in case they try again."

"Of course, let me just use the W/C and we'll be on our way." Vistin said

"Thank you sir, Mikail, bring the car around to the front door. I'll stay with the General" Nono said.

While in the W/C Vistin thought of simply shooting both KGB men, then head straight for the border, having the café owner dispose of the bodies. Thinking quickly he realized that the men must have been in radio contact with their base letting their superiors know that they found him, and were they were.

Changing his mind Vistin left the W/C, and walked with Nono out the front of the café to the waiting car. Mikail held the rear door open for the General, and then he and Nono got in the front and the sped away towards the airport.

Sitting in the back of the black Volga, as they drove down the highway toward the river bridge, Vistin thought, "I could just kill these two, but that would bring out more KGB hounds and they would know where I've gone. Whatever I do it had better be soon. I will not be getting on that plane."

CHAPTER FORTY SIX

MOSCOW

The Kremlin was abuzz with whispered rumors about who may have poisoned General Pushkin, and one of the whisperers told Mika that she heard that Major Ramius suspected that General Vistin, was behind the poisoning. This was an outrageous accusation, but she said she heard that General Vistin hated Pushkin, so he must have done it. She also said that she heard that Vistin was taken into custody near the Finnish boarder, and was on his way back to Moscow. Mika didn't necessarily believe her, because she had a tendency to exaggerate, but it was worth passing the information along to Gregory right away. Mika phoned Gregory on her lunch break from a call box around the corner from St. Basil's to arrange a meeting.

"Gregory, I should be off early tonight about six, are you free for dinner?"

"Sounds like the suggestion of the week. Would six thirty for cocktails at my hotel work, or would you like to suggest a good restaurant?" He asked wishing her request was for personal reasons, but knowing she must have important information to relay.

"There's an excellent steak house a few blocks from here on Ulitsa Varvarka just past St. Basil's Cathedral. It's been there forever, not fancy but the steaks are the best in Moscow, and they're wine list is excellent." Mika told him.

"Great, I'll meet you at the bar at six thirty then." Gregory said.

Mika arrived at the restaurant ten minutes late looking lovely, but tired.

"I apologize for being late Gregory, but with the heightened security inside the Kremlin, getting out of the building takes a long time."

"It's no problem Mika, you're well worth the wait." Gregory told her taking her hands and kissing her lightly. "What sounds good after a long day?"

"What are you having?" She asked, taking her seat at their table.

"Glenlivet, eighteen year old single malt; neat." He said.

"Perfect. I'll have the same, but with a splash of branch water. Also the shrimp cocktail here is the best in the city."

Gregory told the waiter, "I'll have another, and the lady will have the same with a splash of branch water. We'll also have two shrimp cocktails with our drinks, and then order dinner."

"Let's order dinner when he returns so we'll have more time to talk privately." he told her. They scanned the menu and he said, "I think I'll have the filet mignon Au Poivre, and roasted winter vegetables. What sound good to you Mika?"

"That sounds perfect. I'll have the filet as well, medium rare, but with the sauce Bordelaise and sautéed mushrooms."

The waiter returned with their drinks and shrimp cocktails, and Gregory said, "We've decided to order now."

"Very good sir,"

I'll have the filet mignon Au Poivre, rare and the roasted winter vegetables and the lady will have the filet mignon medium rare, with sauce Bordelaise and sautéed mushrooms."

"Excellent. Would you like to make a selection from our wine list sir?"

"Yes, we'll have a bottle of the Chateau Montrose 89'."

The waiter thanked them for their order and hurried away.

Raising his glass Gregory said, "Cheers, here's to a lovely evening with a very lovely lady."

They clicked glasses, and leaning in close he said, "As much as I wish this was just a dinner date, I suspect you have news"

"I wish it was just a romantic dinner as well, and someday it will be, but yes, I do have information or at least rumors, that I felt you should know about right away. I don't know how much of what I've heard in the Kremlin rumor mill is to be believed; but I thought I should pass it along. There are rumors aplenty, but one woman is the head of the steno pool, and seems to usually know what's going on behind the scenes. She said she heard that Major Ramius thinks that General Vistin arranged for the poisoning of General Pushkin, and that General Vistin is on the run."

"Well, that's certainly worth dinner, he said grinning. Do they have any idea where he has gone?" Gregory asked.

"His secretary said he was on State business and had gone to Alakurtti Airbase near the Finnish border, to meet with the Special Forces commander there. They said he took one of the base cars with diplomatic plates and dismissed the driver assigned and left alone." She said.

"That's an unusual breach of protocol for a general to be driving himself. Did the base commander resist?"

"I don't know, but what a general wants, he usually gets, with little argument from subordinates. Anyway, there's much more. She said the KGB agents looking for him found him and arrested him, in a café near the Finnish border, and were bringing him back to Moscow." She said breathlessly.

"If that's so, then Vistin is finished, and Ophidian has been beheaded. That's precisely what we were hoping to achieve." He said kissing her hands.

"You're right, if it's true of course." She said.

"It very well may be true. We planted very incriminating evidence for the GRU and KGB to find, so that's exactly the action we assumed they would take. Let's enjoy our dinner, and then unfortunately, I need to get back to London on the next available flight and try to get confirmation of this information. Remember, I still have an MI6 team ready to pull you out within an hour of your signal if you feel threatened" Gregory told her.

She sat quietly for a few minutes looking into her drink, then said, "Do you have to leave tonight? Couldn't we spend the night together and you could take the early flight back in the morning."

"Well, I suppose if the KGB have arrested him, and he's on his way back, a few hours more or less shouldn't effect things in London too much" he said, kissing her hands again and looking deeply into her beautiful eyes.

Gregory woke early the next morning. Untangling himself from Mika's warm embrace, he headed back to his hotel to grab his luggage and check out, with just enough time to catch the first British Airways flight to London.

CHAPTER FORTY SEVEN

VAUXHALL CROSS LONDON

The flight was bumpy but arrived at London Heathrow on time. Gregory took a cab directly to MI6 headquarters at Vauxhall Cross to report to Mobius. He arrived early in Mobius's outer office unshaven and feeling a bit shabby, still carrying his luggage. Miss Kent looked up surprised to see him, "Gregory, I didn't know you were back in England, is Mobius expecting you?"

"Good morning Kim. No, Mobius isn't expecting me. I wasn't able to let him know I was on my way back from Moscow by phone, because someone is always listening in on phone calls. Is he in?"

Checking her watch she said, "He should be arriving any moment. I assume you haven't eaten, so I'll have some extra pastries and coffee brought up."

"That sounds great Kim, thanks"

"So how is Moscow these days? I've never been there, but the old photos we used to see in school made it look rather drab."

"It's much more cosmopolitan than it used to be. You can get at great bottle of wine in almost every restaurant in the city, but it still has a long way to go to compare to London or Paris."

Mobius came in and didn't seem surprised to see Gregory. "Good morning Kim. Ah Gregory, I assume you just landed and have something that I need to hear. Come ahead" he said, walking into his office and waving Gregory to a seat.

"I apologize for my appearance sir, I didn't have time to change and shave this morning, and I had to hustle to make the early flight."

Miss Trent came in with a tray of fresh pastries and poured Mobius and Gregory a cup of steaming hot coffee, then left the office, closing the door quietly.

Mobius sat at his desk and took a sip of coffee and said, "So what's so important that you needed to come in without calling?"

"Well sir, I'll give you a brief synopsis of the past week. I met Max and she was able to input the data we gave her into both the KGB and GRU secure computer systems, so things were set. The morning after she inputted the data, General Pushkin was poisoned in his Kremlin office. They're saying it was The Islamic Brotherhood for Jihad. It sent all the security agencies onto a war footing; including Directorate "K". The KGB and Directorate "K" are in pure paranoid mode, so Max had to be very, very careful not to draw any attention to herself."

"Do they suspect her in any way?" Mobius asked leaning forward and looking quite concerned.

"No sir, she doesn't think so. But she is scared. I alerted an extraction team to be ready to pull her out within an hour if she raises the alarm."

"Good, good. She is a valuable asset and we must protect her. Continue." Mobius said, leaning back in his chair.

"Well sir, both the head of the KGB, Leonid Andropov, and Major Alexander Ramius of Directorate "K", are personally involved in the case. It seems that General Pushkin collapsed while he was in a meeting with Ramius, and I suspect the meeting was regarding Vistin and a possible connection with Ophidian. After Pushkin was taken to the hospital, Ramius viewed all security tapes and zeroed in on a temporary cleaner whose name is, or was, Vladimir Borodin, a Lithuanian. I say was, because he was found incinerated in the flat he was living in just hours after Pushkin was poisoned."

"If Vistin is behind the poisoning, and I'm sure he arranged it, then he is once again eliminating anyone involved with Ophidian. He's moving faster than we thought." Mobius said rubbing his chin. "Do we know where Vistin is now?"

"Vistin's secretary told Ramius that Vistin left on state business to Alakurtti Airbase near the Finnish border just after Pushkin was poisoned."

"Do you think he really went to Alakurtti on state business, or was that an excuse to get out of town?"

"No sir, he went to the base and met with the base commander, but then he took a car with diplomatic plates and left the base after excusing the driver assigned by the commander. Leonid Andropov had agents from the KGB Finnish border station look for the car, and it was reported that they found Vistin and have arrested him. Max said the word is they are bringing him back as we speak." Gregory explained.

"Well, if they do have him in custody and get him back to Moscow, he'll be a guest of Lubyanka for some heavy interrogation, before they put him on public trial for treason and crimes against the state. Then of course he'll be executed." Mobius said

"Yes sir that would be the best possible outcome. That's assuming that they get him back to Moscow. Vistin plans ahead and must have considered he would be questioned at some point, so he may have planned a way to escape the KGB if they caught up to him before he skipped the country."

"If he can escape the KGB, which won't be easy, we could lose him for good. I'll have some agents from our Finnish station in Helsinki, go to the border crossing nearest to Alakurtti, and have them check to see if the story of Vistin's being picked up is true. " Mobius said.

"We can't contact Max, because she is afraid she may be under surveillance. Do we have any other contracts in the Kremlin?" Gregory asked.

"No, unfortunately we don't. Let me contact the director at CIA, and see if they have anyone on the inside that can let us know if Vistin was brought in." Mobius said.

"Actually sir, let me contact Matt West in Langley. If they have anyone inside the Kremlin, he'll know, and he'll tell me without all the bureaucratic red tape of an official request." Gregory said.

"Very well, contact him as soon as you can." Mobius said.

"I'll call him as soon as he gets in. Also, I've given a lot of thought on how we might recover the art Vistin bought in Morocco. If we can do that, it would take several hundred million Euros out of picture, incase Vistin or Ophidian survives this. With West's help, I think we can pressure Theo Accola; the art dealer who was Vistin's buyer's agent, to turn the paintings over to us."

"What do you have in mind?"

"Well sir, I've roughed out a scenario that could work, but haven't worked out all the details at this time. On the flight from Moscow this morning I was thinking about how we might convince Accola to give us the art without MI6 being involved, but I still have some work to do on the plan." Gregory told him.

"Don't just sit there Gregory, you have a lot of work to do. It's going to take some pretty heavy persuasion to get the art dealer to give up one hundred thirty two million Euro worth of art, so get on with it man." Mobius said with a smile.

"I'm on my way sir."

Gregory went to his office and phoned Matt West, at CIA Headquarters Langley. Even though the hour was quite early in

Virginia, the phone was picked up on the second ring by a gruff voice, "West"

"Matt, do you ever sleep? Gregory MacNee here, how are things at CIA?"

"Oh just the usual things, terrorist plots, the worlds on the brink of disaster, the usual shit. This must be important to get you out of some lovely's warm bed at this hour of the morning. How and where have you been my boy?" West said jokingly.

"Actually, I've been in Moscow working with our agent there, implementing the plan to expose Vistin to the KGB and GRU that we discussed."

"Any luck with that?"

"It seems that we struck gold. Our contact put the data in the KGB and GRU computer systems and we thought we'd have to wait for some time for them to find the data, based on rumors we planned to spread. As luck would have it someone poisoned General Pushkin the next morning, in the Kremlin."

"Holy shit! You're telling me Pushkin was poisoned in his own office? That must have sent them into full on panic mode."

"Indeed it did. Pushkin collapsed during a meeting with Major Alexander Ramius of their Directorate "K".

"Ramius, that's one nasty sadistic bastard." West said with obvious disgust.

"He most certainly is. That's part of the reason I'm calling. Ramius got a line on the suspected assassin, a Lithuanian named Vladimir Borodin. They went to arrest him, only to find the apartment he was using gutted by fire, and the body of the man they suspected was Borodin incinerated, within hours of the poisoning so they were left with a dead end. A short time after they discovered the data we placed in their computers, the head of the KGB, Leonid Andropov and Ramius went to question Vistin, only to find he left hours before to head to a Russian airbase on the Finnish border. The KGB alerted their Finnish border station and two of their agents found Vistin in a small rural café. The rumor is that they have arrested him and are bringing him back to Moscow. This rumor is unverified at this time and our problem is; we can't confirm if this is true and need to know when he arrives at the Kremlin."

"Can't your man on the inside let you know?"

"No. She's afraid to contact us. Directorate "K" has questioned everyone, including her, and she feels she's under close surveillance."

"She you say; well that figures. Yes, I'm sure she is under surveillance, phone tapped and the whole lot." West said.

"What I was hoping, is that CIA has someone on the inside of the Kremlin that can let you know when Vistin is brought in, since we can't risk our contact."

"I'll get word to some of our operatives and have them contact me when he's brought in. No problem. Do you think they really have him?"

"We don't know. Vistin must have taken steps to protect himself, just in case the KGB got on to him. Just because they picked him up doesn't mean they'll be able to get him back to Moscow.

"That's true, he's been at least two steps ahead of everybody so far, and he won't hesitate to kill anyone who tries to take him. I'll get the word out and let you know. You said this is part of the reason you called. What else do you need?"

"I was thinking; how would you like to take a few lovely days in Zurich?"

"I'd rather take my Swiss holiday in St. Moritz. So what's happening in Zurich?"

"Let's meet in Zurich in two days. I'm working out some details to a plan that I think will get the art dealer, who's acting as Vistin's buyer's agent and custodian, to turn over the art work

Vistin bought, with the money from The Islamic Brotherhood for Jihad, to us."

"Damn! That would be quite a trick. How do you plan to do it?"

"I'll explain in two days time. I'll meet you at customs in Zurich International."

"I'll be there." West told him.

CHAPTER FORTY EIGHT

ZURICH SWITZERLAND

Thirty six hours later, Gregory checked into his suite at the Zurich Imperial hotel. After settling in, he phoned the Swiss International Private Client Bank and asked for the director.

"Director Boucher's office" the young woman said, in a professional tone.

"Good afternoon, this is Gregory MacNee from London. Is Director Boucher available?"

"Give me a moment sir; I'll see if he's available."

"Gregory, welcome to Zurich mon bon amie. I received a message from Miss Trent saying that you may be coming to visit us. How can I be of assistance?" Director Francois Boucher said.

"Francois, it's good to hear your voice my friend. If it's convenient, could you meet me for lunch at the La Trattoria restaurant on Mythenquai near the marina at one?"

"Could we make it just after one? I'll be in a meeting until twelve forty five, then I can come right over." Francois said.

"Not a problem, let's say one fifteen then."

"Excellent, I look forward to it. See you there." Francois said.

Francois Boucher was in his mid fifties, tall, with thick black hair just beginning to grey at the temples, and was always immaculately dressed for all occasions. He came from a wealthy banking family from Antibes France, and had been handling several All Empire International accounts for years. He was also MI6s man in Zurich for decades. Francois was always a very social chap, and had a way with the ladies that kept him on all the guest lists for the best parties. His position at the Swiss International Private Bank, and status in the social community, gave him access to wide variety of very confidential information.

Gregory rented a non-descript sedan from the rental agency at the hotel and drove to the marina for his appointment with Francois. Arriving at restaurant La Trattoria early, he requested a table on the terrace overlooking the marina, and sat enjoying the view of the sail boats, with their colorful sails, cruising on the crystal clear azure waters of Lake Zurichsee on this fine Swiss afternoon. Ordering an excellent bottle of chilled Swiss Chardonnay, and a plate of chilled mushroom caps stuffed with blue crab, he waited Francois to arrive.

Francois Boucher arrived exactly at one fifteen, and was led to Gregory's table by a lovely young hostess.

"Gregory my old friend, so good to see you again" Francois said, extending his hand.

"Always great to see you Francois" Gregory said, rising from his seat and shaking Francois's hand, guided him to his seat.

The hostess, with a fetching smile, said to Francois, "What may I bring you sir?"

Francois checked his watch and said, "I know it's a bit early, but it's such a lovely afternoon, that I think I'll have malt whiskey and branch water please."

"Thank you sir, would you like to see a menu now"?

"Not just at the moment thank you." Francois said.

"So Gregory; as nice as it is to see you, since Miss Trent alerted me that you would be coming to Zurich; I assume this is not All

Empire International business, but a bit more official." Francois said, keeping his voice low.

"Yes, it is, in a manner of speaking. I'm here to contact a fine art dealer here in Zurich, regarding some paintings he bought in Morocco for a man MI6 is very much interested in. The paintings were Impressionist master works valued at over one hundred thirty two million Euros. The money for the works came from a terrorist organization, The Islamic Brotherhood for Jihad, through a criminal organization known as Ophidian, operating out of Moscow. This organization, using shell corporations, recently transferred three hundred million Euros from a bank in Aruba to a bank here in Zurich. Did you hear about the transfer?"

"Yes. In fact I did hear whispers of a large transfer into The Private Client Bank a few weeks ago, but there was no talk of funds from terrorist. But, come to think of it, I have noticed KGB agents all over town, and they're keeping an eye on The Private Client Bank. Now that I think of it, I've also seen three or four dark skinned, well dressed men about the town, also watching the banks. I assumed they were wealthy chaps from the Middle East looking to hide a few hundred million here in Switzerland, but I haven't heard of any large deposits from that part of the world recently. Do you think they're from this terrorist group?" Francois asked, looking concerned.

"I'd have to assume yes. Both the KGB and The Islamic Brotherhood for Jihad are looking for the top man in Ophidian. His name is Nikolay Vistin, and he's a General in the Russian Army. The KGB and Directorate "K" are searching for him because he has gone rouge, buying and selling weapons from the breakaway republics through Ophidian. His organization is responsible for kidnapping a British Nuclear Physicist and at least half a dozen murders that we know of. I hadn't realized that The Islamic Brotherhood for Jihad had traced the money to Zurich. This is a very dangerous lot." Gregory told him.

"Rouge Russian Generals, KGB agents, Directorate "K" agents and Middle Eastern terrorists, not the sort of thing we're accustomed to here in Switzerland. Who is this art dealer?"Francois asked.

"The art dealer is one Theo Accola."

"Are the agents and terrorist looking for Accola as well?"

"I don't think the brotherhood knows about him or he would be dead. If the KGB wanted him, he would have be arrested and spirited off to Moscow by now. Do you know this Accola?"

"Well, yes. Not well, but I've heard of him of course. He owns the Accola Fine Art Gallery at the crossroads of Kernstrasse and Anwandstrasse. Nice little gallery, but they don't handle things like Monet and the other Impressionist Masters, mostly young French and Italian artist."

"What do you know about him, his business, personal habits, weaknesses, likes, dislikes, anything would help?" Gregory said"

"Theo Accola comes from a wealthy Jewish family involved in the diamond trade in Antwerp. He wanted nothing to do with the family business, so a rift was created between him and his family. In the end, they cut him off financially, so he came to Zurich and opened his art gallery, taking paintings on consignment from local artist.

He did rather well for a time, but then his habits got the better of him. You see, Accola has a weakness for drink, expensive cars, he can't afford, gambling, and beautiful young ladies; so it's not much of a stretch seeing him get into trouble trying to pay for one or both of the later of those weaknesses. There was talk that he sold several paintings as genuine that were fakes. The collectors that bought the paintings were outraged of course, but they didn't press charges, and the authorities couldn't prove it so he was never arrested, but his business suffered badly."

"Why wouldn't the collectors press charges if they bought fakes that had been represented to them a genuine?"

"In the art world, reputation means a lot to both the buyers and sellers. If word got around that a collector allowed himself to be swindled and sold fakes as genuine; his reputation as a collector would suffer, he would look like a fool to his contemporaries in the art world and his collections value would be damaged, so they just let it slide."

"I can see now how Vistin got his hooks into Accola. Gambling losses, costly dalliances with the ladies, and damaged business, would leave him open to an offer to act as Vistin's agent at the art auctions. Ophidian would have contacted him and offered a substantial fee for acting as agent. Accola would have jumped at the offer with no questions asked." Gregory said, staring out at the boats.

"What are your plans for Accola, Gregory? I hope you're not planning anything rough here in Zurich. The police and courts take a very dim view of anything that makes Zurich look bad to the financial world you know." Francois said, watching his friend closely.

"Oh no, nothing bad at all. In fact, I'm going to make him an offer that he can't refuse, and might just save his life and prevent any bloodshed here in beautiful Zurich. I'm meeting with a CIA agent here tomorrow evening, and we plan to explain to Theo Accola, why he should give the paintings he's keeping in a vault for Vistin to us." Gregory told him with a sly grin.

"Well good luck with that." Francois said raising his glass in a toast. "To get a man like Accola, who is in need of funds to live a lifestyle he can't afford, to turn over art to you worth at least one hundred thirty two million Euros will take quite a bit of talking."

"It may be easier than you think. I'll fill you in once it's over. Francois, it's always a pleasure to see you." Gregory said, rising and extending his hand to his old friend. "We'll get to together for a proper dinner when this business is complete. Please order whatever you would like, I'll take care of the check on the way out. I have business to attend to. Cheers my friend, and thank you for your help."

Gregory drove to a small café at the corner of Kernstrasse just across from the Accola Fine Art Gallery and went inside to use the public phone.

He phoned the gallery, and asked the young woman who answered, and identified herself as Miss Rousseau, if Mr. Accola was available. "I'm sorry sir; Mr. Accola is gone for the day."

"Gone for the day? Why it's just three fifteen. The gallery is open till five isn't it?" Gregory asked

"Yes sir it is. Mr. Accola is usually here all day, but he had business outside the gallery this afternoon. The assistant manager is available, if you would like to speak to him."

"No thank you, my business is with Mr. Accola. Will he be in on Thursday morning?"

"Yes sir, he should be. Would you like to make an appointment?"

"Yes. Please make the appointment for ten thirty in the morning, on Thursday for Mr. West." Gregory told her.

"Very well Mr. West, we'll see you this Thursday at ten thirty. By the way, we have limited parking in the underground garage. The entrance to the garage is just around the corner on Anwandstrasse."

"Thank you Miss Rousseau, You've been most helpful. I'll be there at ten thirty Thursday."

Gregory strolled past the gallery and looked at some of the art on display in the window. He could see what Francios meant about the art for sale at the gallery, nice, contemporary, but certainly not a dealer that would broker in the league of Monet and other impressionist masters. He took the short walk past the Private Client

Bank and noticed several KGB agents watching the bank from both sides of the street.

KGB agents were always easy to spot. They wore the same dowdy, cold war brown double breasted suits with brown fedoras, no matter what the weather or where they were. They might as well wear shirts with KGB printed on the back. Of course that was part of their strategy; the agents in the brown suits were making themselves obvious to un-nerve the subject under observation. They would have other agents watching as well that would just blend into the background; a young woman stylishly dressed window shopping, an old man sweeping the street, but watching, always watching. Gregory spent the next day watching the art gallery and followed Theo Accola to his apartment in a stylish neighborhood near the lake. Looking at the building and the neighborhood Gregory thought, "Yes, Accola does enjoy the finer things in life, but the gallery couldn't make the kind of money needed to live here. Either he inherited money, which is unlikely or Francios would have known and told me, or Vistin's money is paying for this."

The next morning Gregory drove to Flughafen Zurich International airport, and met Matt West at customs.

"Ah, welcome to beautiful Switzerland Mr. West, I hope you had a pleasant flight." Gregory said shaking hands with West.

"Oh yes, the flight was fine, and it's lovely to be here Mr. MacNee. Now can we cut the bull? It's been a long flight and I'm not in the mood for games. What's this brilliant plan and how does it pertain to taking down Ophidian?" Matt West said, obviously not in the best of humor.

"I was just joking Matt, come on and I'll explain on the way to your hotel"

"No sweat Gregory. Sorry, but the flight was full of screaming babies, bumpy and hot as hell. By the way, what hotel are you heading for? I never told you where I was staying. The CIA budget director for agents is cheap as hell these days, so she booked me into a low rent motel downtown since this was not official CIA business."

"Never fear my friend, Miss Trent back in London booked a room for you at the Imperial, at MI6's expense. Since you are doing us a favor, having your people get word to us on Vistin's return to Moscow, it seem the least we could do." Gregory told him.

"The Imperial, well, things are looking up already. As to Vistin, we've had no word about his arrival in Moscow yet. He should have been there yesterday, but intel is a little slow coming out of the Kremlin since Pushkin was poisoned. We'll just have to be patient. If they picked him up near the Finnish border he must surely be in Moscow by now."

"They probably have him stashed in Lubyanka, poor bastard, not that he doesn't deserve it. We have some people in the hospital that they took Pushkin to and they said that he didn't die, and should pull through. It was a close fought thing though; he was poisoned with a very rare Tetrodotoxin that's usually fatal. That Pushkin's a tough old son of a bitch." Matt told him.

"Glad to hear it actually. Pushkin is tough, but fair, and hates Vistin. They're going to skin Vistin alive when they get him back to Moscow. Anyway, the art dealer Vistin used to act as his agent, in the purchase of several impressionist master works at the sale in Casablanca, is one Theo Accola, and he has a gallery here in Zurich. Not only did Accola purchase the works for Vistin, he has them stored in a bank vault here in Zurich under his own name. I plan to convince him that the CIA knows about the purchase, and let him know that the money came from an International terrorist organization. That would make him an accomplice to doing business with international terrorist, and would land him in jail for twenty years".

***

During the drive to the Imperial, Gregory outlined his plan to convince Theo Accola to turn over the art work he purchased for Vistin in Casablanca to the French Government, The United States, and the British Government.

"I arranged an appointment with Accola, for tomorrow morning at ten thirty at the gallery under your name." Gregory told him.

"If this is an MI6 operation, why am I taking the lead? I thought I was singing back up on this one?" Matt asked, looking confused.

Mobius doesn't want my working for MI6 known, so you're taking the lead. I'll be representing Her Majesty's Government, but not as part of the intelligence community."

"Ok, so what's the plan?"

"We'll explain that the CIA and British Government know that he purchased several Impressionist master pieces from the fine art auction in Casablanca a few weeks ago, and that the money came from The Islamic Brotherhood for Jihad, through Nikolay Vistin. That, in and of its self, is an international crime for which he could go to prison for twenty years to life."

"Yeah, but I'm sure this Accola has covered his tracks well, and could just say he was simply hired by a wealthy buyer to act as purchasing agent. He'll claim that he had no reason to believe that Vistin was a criminal, and had no idea where the money came from. He'll hire an attorney to get him off the charges, and probably win."

"As a point of law that's true of course; but we have a couple allies that will scare the shit out of him and make him want to get as far away from those paintings as he can. We'll tell him that Vistin has been arrested by the KGB, and will be put on trial for high crimes against the state, which is punishable by death. We'll also explain, in very convincing terms, that if he doesn't cooperate with us, the information on who bought those painting, and who can access them, will be leaked to the KGB, who are in Zurich at this very moment looking for the money and any connection to Vistin. If we leak this information to the KGB, they will kidnap him and take him to Lubyanka. If they don't execute him, he'll spend the rest of his life in the gulag somewhere in a most un-pleasant area of Russia."

"Is the KGB here now?" Matt West asked.

"Oh yes. I was watching the gallery and the Private Client Bank and there were at least two brown suits watching. They're just waiting for Vistin, or one of his agents, to try to move the money. I don't think they know about the art yet, but they will once they get him to Lubyanka; you can make book on that. He'll tell them things they don't even want to know before he dies."

"That's for damn sure. I've heard about that prison, and their methods for extracting information. The interrogators at Lubyanka are sadistic bastards with no rules."

"I know. If the threat of the KGB isn't enough to get Accola to cooperate, we have the back up of The Islamic Brotherhood for Jihad. Our man here in Zurich says he's seen several Middle Eastern looking men here in Zurich, also watching the bank for anyone who tries for the money they gave Vistin for the purchase of Dr. Patterson, who we snatched back in Germany before the Brotherhood got their hands on him. We'll tell him that if the Brotherhood hears about the paintings that where purchased with their money, buy a Jewish art dealer, they'll be paying him visit post haste." Gregory explained

"Well that would certainly make most people give up the art. But one hundred thirty two million Euros is one hell of a lot of money to just walk away from. With Vistin out of the picture, Accola will know that the art is now his. He may think he could buy enough security people to protect him and become a very rich man." Matt said.

"It's possible. We'll just have to be so convincing with our argument, that he would rather give the art to us, rather than have the KGB and The Brotherhood looking to take him out." Gregory said.

The next morning, Gregory and Matt waited just up the block from The Accola Fine Art Gallery. Accola arrived at ten, and they noticed that he drove a very expensive Italian sports car that was well beyond the budget of any art dealers in the area. He got out of the car and walked to the gallery with a stunning young woman less than half his age. "That car didn't come from selling the paintings in his gallery, that's for damn sure." Gregory told West.

"Mostly cheap prints and stuff sold there?" West asked.

"No, I wouldn't say cheap; but certainly not the kind of art needed to afford that car, or the apartment he lives in. My contact here in Zurich informs me that Mr. Accola has a weakness for fast cars, gambling and the ladies, so the money to indulge in these vices must come from Vistin, or others like him." Gregory told Matt.

"Well let's go rattle his nice little world and see if we can get him to tumble to your plan." West said.

At ten thirty sharp they entered the gallery and were greeted at the door by the very elegant and sexy young woman who had arrived with Accola.

"Good morning gentleman, my name is Miss Rousseau. Are one of you gentleman Mr. West?" She asked

"Yes, I'm Mr. West; I have an appointment with Mr. Accola at ten thirty." Matt said.

"Let me see if he's available Mr. West. Would you gentleman care for coffee?"

"No thank you, Miss Rousseau. We're on somewhat of a tight schedule this morning, so please just let Mr. Accola know we're here." Matt said, in his usual brusque way.

"Yes, of course Mr. West." Miss Rousseau said, as she walked into Accola's private office without knocking.

A moment later, Theo Accola entered and said, "Good Morning Mr. West. I'm Theo Accola, how can I be of assistance this morning?"

"Good Morning Mr. Accola, I'm Mr. West and this is Mr. MacNee; do you have somewhere, a bit more private, where we can talk? What we have to discuss is of a somewhat confidential nature."

"Why yes, of course gentlemen, we can talk in my office. Please come this way." Accola said, shooting a quick quizzical look at Miss Rousseau. "Miss Rousseau, please hold my calls for the next fifteen minutes." Accola said, as he closed the office door.

Once they were alone in Accola's office, Accola said, "What paintings are you gentlemen interested in buying?"

"Well, as a point of fact, we're not interested in buying anything. Your life is in extreme danger Mr. Accola, and we're here to offer you a way to save it." Matt said, in his usual no nonsense style.

Accola eyed them carefully trying to figure out if they were joking, crazy or Mafia thugs attempting to shake him down for money. It was odd to find these criminal types operating in Switzerland, but not entirely unheard of. He'd heard of such a case several years ago, but the always efficient Swiss police were quick to arrest the perpetrators. "You claim my life is in danger gentlemen? Why would my life be in danger? Miss Rousseau isn't married is she?" Accola said with a laugh; trying to make light of the situation.

"Mr. Accola, we didn't come here to play games, so I'm going to come straight to the point." West said. "We know that you purchased several paintings by Claude Monet and Camille Pissarro among others at the fine auction in Casablanca last month. We also

know that the money that was used for the purchase of those paintings was supplied by a Middle East terrorist organization known
as The Islamic Brotherhood for Jihad. That is an International
crime, punishable by twenty five years to life in prison."

Accola sat there with a stunned expression on his face and
said in a shaky voice, "Yes, I bought the paintings you mentioned;
however they were not for me. I was acting as buyer's agent for a
wealthy patron of the arts. I have nothing to do with terrorism."

"Yes, we know who that wealthy patron of the arts is, Nikolay
Vistin. Vistin is also, or should I say was, a general in the Russian
army. He was selling weapons of mass destruction through a criminal organization known as Ophidian, to The Islamic Brotherhood
for Jihad, among others to be used against the United States,
Israel and Great Britain. He used the money these organizations
paid him for these weapons to buy valuable works of art through
you. That makes you and accomplice to helping fund International
Terrorism." West said, staring hard into Accola's eyes.

Accola had gone quite pale, and beads of perspiration appeared on his forehead, he swallowed hard and said, "But I had
no idea that Mr. Vistin was associated with the Russian military. I
thought he was just another wealthy art collector. Most of the very
wealthy people that collect priceless works of art don't want their
identities known, so they hire agents like me to do the bidding.

I knew nothing of terrorist or weapons, he paid me a handsome fee for the work and that's all."

"I'm afraid that's far from all Mr. Accola." Gregory said, speaking for the first time.

Accola stared at Gregory wide eyed and said, "No I swear, I
only acted as a buyer's agent, nothing more."

Gregory stood and said, Mr. Accola; let's take a walk to the
café down the block, and we'll show you something."

Accola stood up on weak knees and walked out of his office

saying, "Miss Rousseau; I'll be gone for about three quarters of an hour." The three of them left the gallery and headed down the block to the café across from the Private Client Bank. They took a seat at a table on the corner with a good view of the sidewalk on both sides of the street. Gregory ordered three coffees and a plate of fresh Danish pastries. They sat in silence until the coffee and pastries had been served then Gregory said, "Mr. Accola, Nikolay Vistin has been arrested and is on his way to Lubiyanka prison in Moscow. He'll be interrogated and forced to tell them whatever they want to know about his dealings with Ophidian, and terrorist organizations, before he's executed for high crimes against the state. He may or may not reveal anything about the paintings, that are held in a vault in your name, here in Zurich, simply because the Russian Government is more interested in his criminal activity stealing weapons and selling them and other high crimes against the state. They are however interested in the money he was paid, three hundred million Euros, by The Islamic Brotherhood for Jihad. If he doesn't tell them about the paintings in your vault and is executed, you become a very rich man. If he does tell them, you become a prisoner at best and quite dead at worst."

Accola realized with sudden elation what fortune had placed in his hands by Vistin's capture and execution. "With Vistin executed by his government, all the works in the vault belong to me. That's more money than I could have ever dreamed of having." he thought. But the thrill pasted quickly as he sat wondering exactly who West and MacNee were. Clearly they both knew all about his working for Vistin including where the art works were stored. He knew they didn't come here to tell him he was wealthy. "If all you say is true gentlemen, then why have you come here today, and why do you say my life's in danger? Exactly who are you gentlemen and why should I believe you." Accola asked, trying to show a bravado he didn't feel.

Gregory continued ignoring the question, "Mr. Accola, do you see those three men in brown suits on both sides of the street watching the bank? Those are KGB agents, sent here to watch the bank for anyone who tries to pick up the money Vistin has in his accounts or vaults. There are several more agents around that are less oblivious, but they're keeping the bank under surveillance from both the outside and inside. If anyone tries to access any account or box held by Vistin or Ophidian, they'll pick that person up as well as anyone else involved and take them to Lubiyanka for questioning. If Vistin tells them about the paintings they'll contact their agents here in Zurich, and they would pick you up within minutes of getting orders to do so, day or night, and you would be on your way to Lubiyanka. Mr. Accola, no one who's taken to Lubiyanka ever walks out free. They are tortured for all the information they know then killed, or sent to a gulag and disappear forever."

"If Mr. Vistin tells them about the paintings, I would explain that I was simply acting as a buyer's agent for Mr. Vistin, and turn the paintings over to the KGB and be done with the whole affair. Then they would have no further interest in me." Accola said, thinking of the other works of art Vistin had bought that he may be able to keep and sell.

Matt West said, "The KGB doesn't work that way Mr. Accola. They would assume, and they would probably be correct, that if you have the art bought in Casablanca last month, then you have other assets bought with funds supplied by Vistin and Ophidian. They would still take you to Lubiyanka and if they didn't kill you they would throw you into the gulag for having anything to do with a traitor to the state."

Accola sat staring at the table, perspiring heavily now and looking pale.

West continued, "That's not really the worst of it Mr. Accola. The Islamic Brotherhood for Jihad has a number of their fighters here in Zurich now also waiting for Vistin, or one of his agents, to take any of their money out of his account. At this moment, they may or may not know that Vistin has been arrested. We're quite certain that they have spies in the Kremlin that gave them Vistin's itinerary when he was in Casablanca, so they'll know soon enough. These are fanatics Mr. Accola, and at the moment very angry fanatics."

Gregory said, "You see, Vistin didn't deliver what The Islamic Brotherhood for Jihad paid Ophidian for. They didn't get their money back and feel that Vistin has betrayed them. For that, they only have one punishment, death. They tried to kill Vistin in Aruba by placing contact explosives on his state car while they were moving through traffic.

Vistin and one of his men escaped, but the driver was liquidated by the blast. Less than twenty four hours later they shot missiles at his plane as it was taking off from Morocco International airport. Only the remarkable skill of the pilots kept them from being blown out of the sky."

"Matt West said, "In order to find the name of the person responsible for Ophidian's theft of their money, they kidnapped a Russian Counsel Minister off the street in Almaty Kazakhstan in broad daylight, murdering his driver in cold blood. These photos will show you what transpired after they got the name General Nikolay Vistin from the Counsel Minister. These people don't play around Mr. Accola. The body on the bloody floor is that of the minister. They tortured him, and then beheaded him once they had the name. The next photo is the minister's head that was sent to the Kremlin in a box addressed to General Vistin. Obviously neither the KGB nor the Brotherhood know about the paintings yet, or you would already be dead, but they will find out if you don't agree to our suggestion as to what is to become of the paintings you hold in your vault."

Theo Accola looked as though he might pass out. He was pale and now sweating profusely. He tried to pick up his coffee but his hands were shaking so badly that he spilled it, then set the cup down and stared at West and MacNee near panic. "Who are you, and how can you help me?"

"I'm with the United States Central Intelligence Agency" West said, showing Accola his CIA identification. "Mr. MacNee, is a representative of Her Majesties Government in Great Britain; however not in the intelligence field. With our assistance we can get you out of this situation, with your head still attached."

Accola looked at the CIA identification near panic and said, "The CIA, The British Government, The KGB and Middle East Terrorists! I don't want anything to do with this or the paintings. Please gentlemen help me. Tell me what to do."

Gregory said, "What we propose Mr. Accola, is that you anonymously donate all the art works you purchased for Vistin, currently in your vault, to several great art museums in England, France and the United States, such as the Muse de Orsay in Paris, The National Gallery in London or the Tate, and The New York Metropolitan Museum of Art. Through my considerable influence with these museums, we can assure you that your name is nowhere in the records of the donations and our governments would waive any tax ramifications that there may be. The art would be available for the people to enjoy, and you would be out of this rather sticky situation."

"But what about the records of the sale, my name is on all the records as the buyer of these works? Surely the KGB and these terrorist would investigate and find my name as the buyer." Accola said.

"Matt West said, "The CIA will arrange to have your name wiped from the sale records and replaced by someone who does not really exist. You would be out of it Mr. Accola."

"If I agree and donate the paintings, what's to keep the KGB and the terrorist from kidnapping or killing me here. You said once they have the information from Vistin they would move against me quickly. What can you do to protect me here" Accola asked.

You'll close the gallery this evening and tell Miss Rousseau that you're going on an extended buying trip to the United States and the Far East. You'll ask her if she'd like to accompany you as your assistant, or she could take an extended vacation with pay, but she is not to disclose where you've gone, because some of the sellers are very keen on their privacy being protected. We can arrange for you to travel to London tonight, then on to the United States in two days. If you agree, we'll fly you to London on a special flight so you can't be tracked. As you said, the KGB and The Islamic Brotherhood for Jihad would investigate to see if Vistin was telling the truth. They would find no such buyer as Theo Accola on any of the records, and assume he had lied and would continue to look elsewhere.

In a month or so you could return and pick up your life and business where it will leave off." Gregory explained.

"Gentlemen, this is all happening very quickly, I must confess to being quite overwhelmed at the moment. I really don't know what to say" Accola said.

"We understand Mr. Accola; but as we've explained, time is of the essence in this case. Think about all we have told you and give us your answer by five this evening. We'll return to your gallery then, and if you decide to agree with our suggestion, be ready to leave the country by nine tonight." Gregory told him.

They left the café and walked back to the gallery. Both Gregory and Matt West shook Accola's hand and said, "Think hard about what we've said Mr. Accola. Your life does depend on what you decide. We'll see you this evening."

***

Gregory and Matt walked back to the rental car without saying anymore about the case. Once back in the rental car driving back to the hotel, safe from prying ears, Gregory said, "By the look on his face I'd say we made our pitch hard enough that he'll go for it."

"We'll know in a few hours. Once he's back in the gallery and feeling safer the thought of all that money will work on his mind. He may go for it, or he may go simple on us and keep the paintings." Matt said.

"That's true, and it's possible he'll try for the money, but I doubt it. The photos of Paval Orlov definitely shook him up. It would most certainly shake me up if I thought I might be next in line for that kind of treatment. I don't know how the Brotherhood could make it worse, but for a Jewish art dealer who tried to steal their three hundred million Euros, I'd bet they could think of something."

Arriving back at their hotel, Gregory attached his portable scrambler to the hotel phone and phoned Miss Trent back in London. "Kim, I need you to arrange a special MI6 charter flight from the Bimenzaltenstrass Private Jet Terminal at Zurich International for three passengers to Heathrow at 2100 hours tonight"

"No problem Gregory. Will you need security personnel at either end?"

"I shouldn't think so Kim. It will be me, CIA agent West, and one passenger who will need secure accommodations for two nights.

"Very well, I'll make all the arrangements. Your aircraft will be a Falcon 50 painted dark blue with a tail number ZZZ at the gate at 2100 hours."

"Thanks Kim. You're the model of efficiency as always."

"Cheers Gregory, we'll see you back in London tonight."

Hanging up the phone, Gregory said to Matt West, "Ok we're all set for transportation, assuming Accola goes for the deal. You'll be staying in Belgravia for two nights, and then escorting Accola back to New York City. Make sure he's safely ensconced at the suite Miss Trent will arrange for him at The Plaza Hotel in Manhattan."

"What do I do with him once we're back in New York? Do you have people there to take him or should I stay and keep an eye on him?" West asked.

"We'll have agents there to insure his safety, and make sure he completes his part of the bargain. We wouldn't want him to feel he's safe in the United States and go to grass taking any of the paintings with him. Our man from the National Gallery, Sir Jonathan Vanderveer, will arrange for the transfer of the anonymously gifted paintings to The Metropolitan Museum of Art. Accola and Sir Jonathan will meet the curator of the museum to arrange pickup of the painting when it arrives at JFK. Accola will be acting as an agent for the donator under an assumed name."

"Let's go for a drink at the terrace bar, and then we'll go see if Mr. Accola chooses life or death." Gregory said.

At four thirty they drove back to the gallery. Entering early, they found Theo Accola alone in his office. Walking in Gregory closed the office door and said, "Good evening Mr. Accola. So what have you decided?"

"Please have a seat gentleman." Accola said pouring three large glasses of scotch, and giving West and MacNee each one. Accola sat behind his desk and said, "After our discussion this afternoon I've decided that I want no part in the trouble Mr. Vistin has gotten into. I accept your suggestion, and will donate the paintings, as long as you can insure that my name is not on any documents."

"We can guarantee that your name will be taken off the records for any paintings you donate Mr. Accola." Matt West said.

"In that case, I'll donate Monet's, Water Lilly Pond and Nymphea's, to the Muse de Orsay in Paris as well as both Botticelli's. Camille Pissarro's, "Le Boulevard Montmare de Matine'e de Printemps, will go to the Metropolitan Museum of Art in New York. There are also two paintings by Joseph Mallord Turner, purchased by Vistin last year that will go to the National Gallery in London. I can give you the sale record for the Turner's so you can erase my name from them as well."

"I'll contact Langley and have it taken care of when we leave your office." West told him.

Gregory said, "It's important that Miss Rousseau be out of the picture here in Zurich, so the KGB and The Islamic Brotherhood for Jihad can't use her to find you. What has she decided? Is she going with you or taking a holiday?"

"She's decided to take a holiday on the island of Crete. I booked her into an elegant ocean front villa on Elounda Beach for three weeks. Hopefully this whole thing will be over by then. I'll join her there as soon as our business is concluded and we'll just stay out of sight for a few weeks." Accola said, with a grin.

"That sounds like a good plan, as long as she doesn't tell anyone where she's going." Gregory said.

"I've explained the buyers are very sensitive about their identification, so she won't mention anything about where she's going. She'll just tell her landlady that she has to go out of town for a few weeks on business, and ask her to look after her cat while she's away. So, what do we do now gentlemen?" Accola asked.

"You'll close the gallery and we'll all have a spot of dinner in the Gold Zimmer at the Imperial. I was hoping you would see sense and decide to go with our suggestion, so I made arrangements to fly you to London on a private jet this evening at nine. We'll stay with you to make sure nothing happens between now and then. We have you in a private flat in Belgravia for the next two days, while we arrange all the documents for the transfer of the paintings. Then you and agent West will fly to New York, to supervise the transfer of the paintings to The Metropolitan Museum of Art."

Arriving at the Imperial, Matt West was somewhat uncomfortable with the grand surroundings of the Imperials Gold Zimmer. He kept watch for any potential threats as they were guided to their table by the Maitre d'hotel. West said to Gregory, "Isn't this a bit flashy, when we're trying to slide this guy out of town quietly?"

"No, not at all. Business men, and men of power in Zurich, celebrate business deals in grand style all the time. We'll keep an eye out for the enemy, but just enjoy the evening." Gregory told him.

After a cocktail, they looked over the menu. West decided on the Sirloin Steak "Café de Paris" with pommes frites."I'll just keep it simple" he told Gregory.

"Order whatever you like Matt, it's our last night in Zurich for a while and my company's picking up the tab." Gregory told him.

"Steak is just fine." West said.

Theo Accola ordered the Rack of Lamb, with potatoes au gratin, while Gregory ordered the Chateaubriand with béarnaise sauce, and seasonal vegetables, and a bottle of Domaine de la Romanee Conti 85'.

"Excellent choice Mr. MacNee" Theo Accola said, very pleased by the wine selection.

"Well since you're donating some of the most valuable impressionist paintings for the people of France, England and the United States to enjoy anonymously, we may as well have a grand meal to celebrate." Gregory told him.

After dinner, the three of them shared a bottle of Veuve

Cliequot Ponsardin "Le Grand Dame". Checking his watch Gregory said, "Gentleman I believe it's time to head for the airport. We'll stop by your apartment Mr. Accola and pick up your things on the way.

They left the Imperial and picked up a bag Accola had ready, and then drove to the Private Jet Terminal at Zurich International. They cleared security and walked to the gate just as their jet was lowering the airstairs. The lovely, and oh so British, flight attendant welcomed them aboard and within minutes of buckling their seat belts the jet was airborne en route for London Heathrow.

CHAPTER FORTY NINE

LONDON

They arrived at London Heathrow's private jet terminal in just one hour forty minutes. Even though Gregory told Miss Trent that he didn't feel the need for security to meet them at Heathrow, she had a service car and driver there to meet the plane just the same. The MI6 driver took the three of them to a luxurious flat in the Belgravia area of London that the service owned, and maintained as a safe house for important people. All the domestic staff, butler, chef, chambermaids, etc. were all fully trained and armed MI6 service personnel there to see to the guests needs, but mainly to provide top level security. Once they were inside Gregory said, "Mr. Accola, agent West will be staying here in the flat next door, and we have security agents in the building to make sure you're safe until you fly to New York the day after tomorrow. Simply touch five on your phone to order food or drink and anything else you may require. Please don't leave the flat. I don't think the KGB or the Brotherhood know about the paintings yet, nor do they know you've gone to London, so you should be fine here. We don't want to take chances since we've guaranteed your safety. In the morning, I'll arrange all the required documents for your signature to allow the legal transfer of the art works from your bank vault to the designated museums."

"Will you be coming back here Mr. MacNee, or am I going

to meet with your man, Sir Jonathan Vanderveer, at the National Gallery?" Accola asked him.

"I'm not sure yet. When I meet with Sir Jonathan in the morning, he'll let me know how we're to proceed. Well goodnight gentleman, I'll see you tomorrow." Gregory said.

The next morning at seven thirty, Gregory met with Sir Jonathan Vanderveer, in Mobius's office at Vauxhall Cross.

"Getting these Turner's is quite a boon for the National Gallery Mr. MacNee, a magnificent gift." Sir Jonathan said.

"Yes, at least there's been some good to come out of this whole affair with Ophidian. You remember the two Monet's and the Pissarro that were sold at the fine art auction in Casablanca, last month when we were there?" Gregory asked.

"Of course I remember them. Extremely valuable works, sold for over to one hundred thirty million Euros." Sir Jonathan said.

"Well, the two Monets and the two Botticellis will be going to the Muse de Orsay in Paris, and the Pissarro will be going to the Metropolitan Museum of Art in New York City. The Turner's were a bonus. It's of the utmost importance, that the name of the man donating these paintings not be found on any records relating to the past ownership, sale, or the donation. The names used on all documents will be pseudonymous, but is completely legal, according to our top legal authorities." Gregory told him.

"But such a magnificent gift, why anonymously?" Sir Jonathan asked.

"I'm sorry Sir Jonathan. The details are of a top security nature and cannot be discussed." Mobius said.

"Of course Mobius, I understand. What do you need from me?" Sir Jonathan asked.

"We need you to provide us with all the legal documents for the signature of the current owner, in order to transfer the ownership of the art from his vault at the Private Client Bank in Zurich, to the museums named. We also need you to arrange the actual transfer from the bank to the museums." Gregory told him.

"That's not a problem at all gentlemen. Our legal department will assemble all the required documents by late this afternoon, let's say four this evening. " Sir Jonathan told them.

"There is one other thing Sir Jonathan. We need you to go to New York City tomorrow, and make all the arrangements for the transfer of the Pissarro to the Metropolitan Museum of Art. The Americans will require you to be there in person. It's a technicality of American law. The CIA, and their Department of Justice, have instructed the museum to accept the paintings without knowing the name of the benefactor. The museum has to agree, however, they are insisting that you are to be there in person.

I know how you dislike travel Sir Jonathan, so we've arrange transport on a MI6 special flight, as well as The Edwardian Suite at The Plaza Hotel on fifth avenue in Manhattan. You'll have limousine transportation during your trip so as not to inconvenience you too much." Mobius told him.

Sir Jonathan sat there looking a bit upset then said, "Your right Mobius. I don't like travel at all, but if it's necessary, then I accept. Let's hope this is the last trip for some time. First Casablanca last month, now America, this is not good for my digestion at all."

"Very well then, it's all arranged. Miss Trent will arrange your departure and have a car ready to pick you up at the time you specify. Thank you for your help in this matter Sir Jonathan." Mobius said, shaking Sir Jonathan's hand warmly.

"Again, thank you for all you've done Sir Jonathan" Gregory said shaking his hand. "You've been a tremendous help to me. We'll have dinner at my club as soon as you return." Knowing Sir Jonathan was a true connoisseur of fine wines and cognacs he said, "I understand they've just received a very rare bottle or two of Hennessy Ellipse. We'll sample a bottle if you'd like."

"Hennessy Ellipse, you say. Well, that just might make the trip worthwhile. I'll look forward to it Gregory." Sir Jonathan said with a smile.

"I'll see you at your office this evening at four, with the gentleman who will sign all documents for the transfer." Gregory told him.

CHAPTER FIFTY

Near the Finnish Border

With agent Mikail behind the wheel, the black KGB Volga kept a steady speed of just under sixty kilometers per hour, as a light rain began to fall. Agent Boris Nono phoned his headquarters to say that they were escorting the general back to Murmashi Airfield, and that he would be airborne within two hours. General Vistin sat watching the shadows lengthen as the early evening sun dropped behind the rolling hills along the heavily forested area. He sat straight and upright, not having said a word to either of the young KGB agents since getting in the back of the car. They were approaching one of the few scenic look outs on this stretch of road. Several cars were parked along the side of the road, with four men and three women enjoying the view of the steep drop off into the ravine, where the river frothed and churned far below. There was a large fuel truck coming in the opposite direction, having just cleared the narrow bridge, when Vistin drew his Makarov PM .380 pistol, firing through the thin seat, he shot Mikail through the heart. Mikail's body jerked the wheel to the left sending the Volga straight into the path of the oncoming fuel tanker. Vistin rolled from the back door hitting the pavement hard. The driver of the tanker attempted to avoid the oncoming Volga without success. The tank began to skid into a jackknife as the cab slammed into the Volga pitching the vehicle, and the terrified Nono, off the side of the road and down the steep drop into the ravine. The truck continued out of control over the edge and down into the ravine, collecting two of the three parked cars, and all the people that were looking at the view just a few moments before. As all the vehicles and bodies crashed down to the bottom of the ravine, the heavily loaded fuel tank broke in the middle showering the area with eleven thousand gallons of petrol. The fuel covered everything on the hillside and when it came in contact with the hot engines of all the vehicles, it erupted into a fire ball that reached three hundred feet into the air.

The scene was like looking into the very mouth of hell. The flames started a raging forest fire that continued to spread. Vistin just managed to roll out of the path of the trucks massive wheels and lay dazed and bleeding in the bushes on the opposite side of the road. The heat was so intense that the trees, and his uniform, began to smoke as he pulled himself into a ditch behind some large boulders for some protection from the searing heat. He tried to get to his feet, but collapsed face down in the dirt. Using one of the boulders to steady himself, he stumbled towards the last remaining car on the side of the road, choking in the thick acrid smoke, and falling several times on the way. The intense heat blistered his face as he finally managed to reach the car and got inside burning his hands on the hot steel of the door handled.

"If this thing doesn't start, I'm dead for sure." Vistin thought as he twisted the key with intense pain shootng through his burned fingers. The engine came to life with only one twist of the key. Vistin shoved the car in gear and spinning the wheels wildly, pulled out on the highway heading back to the café. He drove as fast as he was able with burned hands. The heat had also burned his eyes, and he was having a difficult time seeing where he was driving, but he had to keep going.

"If I can make it back to the café, Ivan can patch me up and get me over the border into Finland. I must get out quickly now, the accident will draw law enforcement from all over and I will be caught." He thought, as he drove.

The drive back to the café seemed to take hours even though it was less than fifteen minutes. Vistin pulled the car around the back of the café where it could not be seen from the road, and stumbled in through the kitchen door. Ivan heard the kitchen door crash open and came running in with a stout club he kept under the bar for when local drunks got out of hand. He was shocked to see Vistin leaning on the wall bleeding and filthy.

"Jesus Christ Nikolay, what the hell happened? Did those men beat you up?" Ivan asked, coming to Vistin's aid.

"No, those were KGB agents sent to bring me back to Moscow. I killed them both and escaped, but there was a terrible accident about twenty kilometers up the road. This whole area will be swarming with law and emergency vehicles in just a few minutes and of course more KGB. I need to get cleaned up, and you have to get me over the border now, before they close the border crossing." Vistin told him.

Ivan led him into a small bathroom, and began to clean and bandage the cuts on Vistin's face. Vistin recoiled in pain from the burns on his face and hands. Nikolay, I need to get you to a hospital, you need a doctor badly, your face and hands are badly burned and you probably have some broken bones."

"No doctor or hospital. Just get me over the border to Kotka, as quickly as you can." Vistin told him, shaking his head rapidly. "Get the clothes and my leather satchel out of the boot of the car with diplomatic plates outside, I'll never get across the border in uniform like this."

Ivan went to the car and found the clothes and the satchel, and brought them inside, then continued to bandage Vistin's burned hands.

"I have an idea how we're going to get you through the border. Your face is bleeding and burned; I'll wrap bandages around your head to stop the bleeding. You can change into some farm clothes I have, and I can take you through in the old lorry in the back that I use to pick up supplies for the garden. We'll tell the guards that you were injured in the accident down the road, and that I need to get you to the hospital right away. If we move quickly, we can get through before the law is there in force. "Don't worry, it'll work Nikolay."

"Very well, let me get changed. Bandage my face and we'll go" Vistin agreed.

Once Vistin was bandaged and changed, Ivan hid the government Volga with the diplomatic pates, in a shed in the farm area of the café. Then he helped Vistin into the back of the lorry where he could lay flat on some straw, as they headed for the border crossing. Ivan knew the border guards well, he crossed the border into Finland for supplies in the lorry several time per month. When they arrived at the border Ivan said to the guard, "Kimi; there was a terrible accident involving a tanker truck at the lookout twenty kilometers from my café. Mika here, who helps me in the garden, was burned badly and was lucky not to have been killed in the crash. I understand there were several cars and people involved, but he's not in condition to tell me more. I need to get him to the hospital fast."

"Yes Ivan, we heard about the accident on the radio. Does he have his papers so he can cross the border?" Kimi asked, looking concerned at Vistin lying in the back of the lorry, moaning.

***

"Of course he does Kimi, he crosses six times a month, but at the moment he's badly injured and burned. I didn't think to get his papers when he arrived at the café. I'm just trying to get him to hospital before he dies." Ivan reached across to Kimi and handed him his papers, here are mine. Kimi, he doesn't have much time, I have to go."

"Shouldn't we call an ambulance for him?" Kimi asked.

"God All Mighty Kimi! There's no time to wait for an ambulance to get here. That would take thirty to forty minutes each way. I can have him there in less than thirty minutes, if you'll just let us go." Ivan said, looking desperately at the Finnish guard.

Kimi looked at Vistin lying in the back of the lorry, dirty, disheveled with bloody bandages on his face and hands and said," Damn, it's against regulations, but go ahead Ivan get him some help before he dies."

"Thanks Kimi." Ivan said has he slowly accelerated away from the border crossing.

Ivan drove for about ten kilometers before he pulled over to the side of the road, out of sight of the border crossing. He got out and checked on Vistin.

"Nikolay, are you going to be able to make it to Kotka? It's a good twenty five kilometers of slow driving."

"I'll make it Ivan. Just keep going for God sake."

"Ok Nikolay, but we'll need to get another vehicle soon. If the border guard phones the hospital, and asks if a burn victim arrived in the back of an old lorry, they'll tell him no. Then he'll alert the police and they'll start searching for us." Ivan told him.

They drove on for another ten kilometers when Ivan spotted a small service station with several delivery vans parked in the lot. The station was closed, and if any of the vans were in running order, he could hide the lorry in the back and steal one of the vans for the remaining drive to Kotka. He broke the window on the back door of the station and found the keys to all the vans hanging on a board. One set of key was on the board marked "Completed". He took the keys, and found the correct van. After he got Vistin settled in the back, he moved the lorry to the rear of the station and quickly took the registration plates off, and all the vehicles papers out of the glove box. This would buy a little time while the station owner and police tried to find out who the lorry belonged to.

Ivan drove out of the station carefully, and headed for the fishing port at Kotka, thinking, "I won't be able to go back to the café, so I need to find a way out of town as soon as Vistin is gone."

"You know Nikolay, I won't be able to return to the café or my home. The police will have been notified that I took someone over the border without papers and never arrived at the hospital where we were supposed to be going."

"I know Ivan, don't worry. Ophidian will take care of everything. Just lay low for a few days and we'll arrange things for you." Vistin told him

When they were just a kilometer or so from the fishing port, a police car pulled in behind them and turned on his lights. Ivan knew that he was not speeding, so the van must have been reported stolen by someone he didn't see when they took it.

"Nikolay, we're being pulled over for the love of God. What should I do?"

"Just relax Ivan, and go along with whatever the officer tells you to do. I'll take care of him if things go wrong." Vistin said, unlocking the passenger side rear door and sliding his Makarov pistol out of his leather satchel, grateful that he thought to bring it, but hoping not to have to use it with burned hands.

Ivan pulled to the side of the road and watched the police officer walking up to him and looking at the back of the van.

"Good evening officer. Is there a problem?" Ivan asked
innocently.

"Your brake lights are not working and the registration plate is
expired. May I have your driver's license and registration please?"
The office asked in a very matter of fact tone.

"Let me get my license. I just borrowed the van, mine broke
down. They didn't tell me the lights weren't working." Ivan said, as
he pretended to look for the registration papers.

"I see, if you'll give me the registration papers please."

"I'm sorry; they don't seem to be here officer. Like I said, I just
borrowed the van from a friend."

The police office handed Ivan back his driver's license noticing, that it was issued in Russia and said, "I'm sorry Mr. Stropenski,
but I can't let you continue in this vehicle. In Finland, it's illegal to
operate a vehicle on any public road without proper registration
and all lights and signals in working order."

Vistin had been listening to the conversation, and knew things
were going badly. He knew that the officer would radio the vehicle
registration tag number to his head quarters, and if the vehicle had
been reported stolen they would be arrested. He would be caught
and turned over to the KGB. If that happened, the KGB wouldn't
bother taking him back to Moscow this time. They would just
shoot him and be done with it. He silently slid open the side door
and climbed painfully out, with his Makarov pistol in his hand,
and came around from behind the van.

"Officer, how am I to get to my friends home if I can't drive the
van? Once I get there I'll give it back to him and tell him about the
lights and registration." Ivan pleaded.

"I'm sorry sir, but I can't let the van back on the road. I'll call for a taxi and a tow truck". As the officer was turning to go back to his police cruiser to call for the tow truck and taxi, Vistin shot him in the face killing him instantly.

"Quickly Ivan, get his body into the trunk of the patrol car before someone comes along." Vistin shouted.

Ivan got out of the van visibly shaken, and dragged the dead officer back to the police car, opened the trunk and dumped the dead man inside. Slamming the trunk lid he said, "Oh sweet Jesus Nikolay, this is just going from bad to worse. Now I'll be wanted for murdering a police officer. They'll never stop looking for me now and I'll never make it out of the country. What am I going to do?"

"Stop worrying and get hold of yourself Ivan, damn you. This will work out fine. You'll just be coming with me and we'll be out of the country in a few hours.

Vistin pulled his leather satchel from the van, and quickly collected Ivan's identification and the vehicle registration paperwork, then closed and locked it. Limping painfully back to the police cruiser he told Ivan, "I have a boat waiting to take me out of the country, they'll have room for you my friend."

Ivan drove the police cruiser to the small fishing port and parked it in an empty dilapidated old warehouse. Vistin took his satchel and walked painfully to the fishing boat, "*The Northern Lights*" that had been ordered by Ophidian to wait for his arrival, and to obey his orders without question.

Seeing Vistin's condition the mate helped him aboard saying, "Are you o.k. sir? You look pretty rough. Let me take you to the doctor."

"Take this man to a cabin, and then take me to the captain immediately." Vistin snapped at the mate.

The captain saw Vistin and Ivan come aboard, and met them in the passageway.

"Welcome aboard sir, we were becoming a little concerned. You were due several hours ago." The captain said.

"Cast off and get underway at once Captain." Vistin ordered.

"Yes sir. But where are we going? I'll need to tell the harbor control office where we're headed." the Captain asked, a bit surprised at Vistin's appearance and hostile attitude.

Vistin looked at the captain, barley able to control his rage at this fools asinine questions and said, "Fishing captain, this is a fishing vessel is it not? Tell them we're going fishing! Once we're in international waters, in about five hours, you'll be given further instructions. Other than the call to the harbor masters office, telling them we're going fishing, you will not use the radio without my express permission. Is that understood Captain?"

"Yes sir, perfectly understood." the Captain said, wondering what the hell he'd gotten himself involved in. It had been a slow fishing season, money was tight, and Ophidian had offered enough to pay the overdue bills and keep him going until the following season, so he jumped at the offer. Now he wasn't sure that was the best idea.

Turning to the mate Vistin said, "I'll need fresh clothes and a hot meal as soon as possible. Show me to my quarters and send the doctor to me immediately."

The mate returned with fresh clothes and the ship's doctor at the same time, wanting to distance himself from this particular VIP guest. "Your dinner will be brought to your cabin in about twenty minute's sir." The mate told Vistin.

Vistin curtly nodded acknowledgement to the mate as he turned to leave the cabin. "Doctor, these dressings need to be changed." Vistin said, raising his hands and indicating his head."

The doctor took a pair of shears from his bag and cut off

Vistin's bandages saying to himself, more than to Vistin, "First and second degree burns on hands and burns and lacerations on the face and forehead. They're not too bad, but I'll bet they hurt like the devil." The doctor had more sense than too ask what happened, he knew this man was on the run and had been told not to ask any questions.

"Yes they do doctor, so please get on with it."

The doctor cleaned and redressed Vistin's hands, and put a smaller bandage on the laceration on his head. He then gave him some pills saying, "Take these and they should take the edge off the pain."

"Thank you, doctor. That will be all." Vistin said, dismissing the doctor.

Vistin took the pain pills and ate the greasy fried fish that the cook had sent up from the galley. After finishing the barely edible meal, he decided to sleep for a couple of hours before completing the next phase of his escape. He was startled awake by a sharp knock on the cabin door. Sitting bolt upright with his pistol in his hand, immediately alert, he said, "Come!" The captain entered and said, "We're in International waters now sir. Do you have a course?"

"I'll meet you on the bridge with the co-ordinance in a few minutes Captain and I'll have need of the radio"

"Very well sir, I'll see you on the bridge." The Captain said as he turned and left the cabin.

Prior to his flight from Moscow, Vistin had sent a flash message to Farzad Ahmadi and had ordered the tanker, *The Emperor of the East,* to put to sea at once. He gave Ahmadi the co-ordinance and said that the ship was to wait until he arrived. *The Emperor of the East* was now on station, and waiting for Vistin's arrival. Many of the crew aboard were ex-Iranian fighters and were used to just doing what they were told without questions, so there was no issues with having the ship waiting in International waters to pick up Vistin.

Vistin climbed up to the bridge and took a sheet of paper from his leather satchel with the co-ordinance that was their new destination, and handed it to the captain. "Captain, we will rendezvous with a large vessel at these co-ordinates as soon as possible. Making your best speed, when will we arrive?"

The captain went to the plotting stations and worked out the ETA for the rendezvous, "The sea is smooth, so running at full speed, we should arrive in just over two hours fifteen minutes sir." He told Vistin.

"Very well, make full speed Captain. Now, I need to use the radio to send a message to the ship with our ETA."

"Of course sir, it's just over here. You can select voice or text only on the same frequency by flipping this switch."

"Thank you Captain." Vistin typed a coded text message to the captain of *The Emperor of the East* telling him of their ETA to his position, then turning to the captain said, "Again captain, no one is to use the radio without my express permission."

The captain gave a curt nod in response, and Vistin left the bridge.

Vistin walked down the companion way to the engine room, and seeing it un-occupied, slipped inside and took two C-4 plastic explosive charges with timers from his leather satchel, and hid one beside each of the fifteen thousand gallon diesel fuel tank inlets. He set the timers to detonate in three hours, then walked back to the bridge to keep an eye on the crew.

The captain's calculations were quite accurate, and in just under two hours the massive bulk of the *"The Emperor of the East"* was growing larger through the dense fog. Right on schedule, the "*The Northern Lights*" came along *The Emperor of the East's* port side, where the pilots boarding ladder had been rigged in place. Taking his leather satchel Vistin said, "Captain, all the funds have been transferred to your account as promised by Ophidian". Indicating Ivan he said, "You're to take this man to the Port of Tallinn, in Estonia and drop him there."

"Yes sir."

Speaking to Ivan as they left the bridge, "I've arranged to have you picked up at the Port of Tallinn and flown to Paris. All your expenses will be covered by Ophidian, so just lay low and have some fun. Thank you my good friend."

"Thank you, Nikolay. Take care of yourself, and get in touch with me when it's safe to do so." Ivan said.

" Good luck sir." The captain said, as he guided Vistin to the side so he could leave the ship."

As Vistin was about to jump to the pilots boarding ladder on *The Emperor of the East,* he said to the captain, while looking him straight in the eyes, "We will be monitoring all radio emissions for the next twenty four hours. If you use the radio, Ophidian will be notified and you'll never live long enough to spend the money. Do you understand captain?"

"A bit shocked, the captain said, "Yes sir, I quite understand. Don't worry; we won't use the radio unless we're sinking". The captain said, then turned and left Vistin to the rest of his journey, whatever that may be, thinking "That's the last time I get involved in this kind of shit. I'll stick to fishing."

As soon as Vistin was been reported aboard by the seaman there to assist him, *The Emperor of the East* got underway, quickly disappearing into the fog with no scheduled stops until China. The two ships went their separate ways and Vistin headed for the bridge of *The Emperor of the East*. None of the crew seemed to take any notice of the new arrival, as he went into the captain's sea office. Vistin was watching the radar scope tracking "*The Northern Lights*" and at precisely three hours from the time he set the C-4 timers, the blip for "*The Northern Lights*" disappeared from the scope. There were no radio calls or emergency signals. It just disappeared into the deep.

Returning to his cabin, Vistin poured a large glass of vodka, and flopped down in the old leather chair, sore and exhausted thinking, "That's done. What is it the pirates in the cinema like to say? Oh yes, Dead men tell no tails. Soon I'll be free of the KGB and can begin to rebuild my organization"

CHAPTER FIFTY ONE

VAUXHALL CROSS LONDON

"**W**e received a flash message from Max last night."Mobius told Gregory.

"Is she all right sir?" Gregory asked, looking quite concerned.

"Yes, she's fine. Things have calmed down somewhat at the Kremlin over the past few days. She said that Vistin never arrived after his arrest. It seems there was a bad accident involving the KGB car taking him to the airport, as well as three other cars and a heavily loaded gasoline tanker. The report said there were no survivors. Vistin, the two KGB agents, the tanker driver and seven other people were all killed."

"Did they recover Vistin's body?" Gregory asked.

"No. They haven't been able to recover anyone from the scene of the accident. All the vehicles went over a steep cliff into a ravine. The tanker exploded, incinerating everyone and starting a forest fire that they haven't been able to get under control yet."

"Until we hear someone has made a positive identification of Vistin's body, we must assume the son of a bitch caused the accident and got away somehow." Gregory said

"I've sent three agents to Finland, to go to the scene of the accident and find out all they can. They'll also question the Finnish guards at the border crossing, to see if anything unusual has happen that day other than the accident. We'll continue to check railway stations, airports and harbors to see if we can get a lead on him, assuming he survived, but it's very doubtful he did. For the moment the KGB said their closing the case on Vistin. They will continue to investigate Ophidian, to see if they have anymore operatives in Russia or any Soviet countries according to Max." Mobius told him.

"Well, I won't believe he's dead till they see and identify the body as his. I swear this bastard has nine lives. Our plan to have the KGB zero in on Vistin and his Ophidian organization was solid, and was moving along better than we had hoped with the poisoning of General Pushkin. They had him, and now he's slipped the noose. Christ; I've heard it said, if you want God to laugh out loud, tell him you've got a great plan, well so much for my plan." Gregory said, pacing back and forth around the office.

"Steady on now Gregory. We'll have to assume he's dead for the moment. Either way, Ophidian is finished. In fact, the mission was to destroy Ophidian and neutralize Vistin; not kill him. If he's dead or alive the mission was an overwhelming success. Ophidian's cover is blown to the KGB, their money is being confiscated by the Russian Government, the paintings that Vistin bought with the terrorist money are safely in the hands of the worlds great museums, their top operatives have been neutralized, and their head, Vistin, is either dead or on the run. You and your team have done outstanding work on this very complicated case." Changing the subject suddenly, Mobius said, "I want you to take a few days off, then be prepared for a two week joint MI6-CIA training conference in Langley Virginia, at what they lovingly call The Farm."

"We're having a joint training conference with the Americans sir?" Gregory asked, with a shocked expression. "Foreign intelligence services have never actually trained together successfully in the past, as far as I've been told."

"That's not actually true, though it is a widely accepted rumor. The CIA director and I have been discussing how well you and your team worked with the CIA agents to crush Ophidian so quickly and effectively. Oh, by the way, agent Waxman is doing well, and will make a complete recovery from the wounds he received in Germany. He'll be tied to a desk for another month, but then he'll be cleared for field work again. Anyway, the CIA Director and I have decided that with special rapid response teams from MI6 and CIA, sharing up to date intelligence information, and having trained together in both small unit tactics and all weapons currently used by NATO and the Soviets, we will be a more effective force against this growing trend towards International Terrorism." Mobius told him.

"Well sir, I can't argue with the logic of having teams from both services train together, but will the Americans really share intelligence information with MI6? In the past, the rivalry between services had made the rivalry between Oxford and Cambridge look mild." Gregory said.

"I don't really know. It was tried during the war and worked out well. Of course, once the war was over, things tended to go back the way they were before the shooting started in earnest. Well, the Director and I have decided to give it a try anyway; so you head for Virginia in five days." Mobius told him.

"Very well sir. I think I'll go over to Finland and see what I can find out about the accident and Vistin, before I go to Virginia." Gregory said.

"No, you won't Gregory. The Ophidian case is closed for the moment." Mobius said with finality. "I want you rested and ready to work with CIA next week. Byron Hill, Connell Baines and Susan Jamison will be there as well."

"Yes sir. Gregory said; knowing that when Mobius said no, that it means no, and that's an end to it. "Will the four of us be traveling together?"

"No, Byron Hill is already there working with their demolition experts. Susan and Connell will be flying out this evening. After they've trained with their CIA counter parts, both teams will train as one unit once you arrive. Six weeks after your training ends, the CIA teams will come here and train at Fort Monckton in Portsmouth, then at the special SAS facility the Scottish Highlands. Now, go get rested up Gregory, this trainings going to be a bitch." Mobius said

"Yes sir. Thank you sir. I'll pick up Matt West and Theo Accola, and meet with Sir Jonathan at the National Gallery to complete the final paperwork for the transfer of the paintings then head home." Gregory said, leaving the office.

His chauffeur Pierre, was waiting; holding open the rear door of Gregory's Bentley; parked in the "Absolutely No Parking – Tow Away Zone" when Gregory walked out of MI6 Headquarters at Vauxhall Cross, from the Albert Embankment entrance. He looked at the car, and the Absolutely No Parking sign and thought, "Unbelievable, no matter how many times I tell him to wait else-where where parking is allowed. Oh well, what the hell." Climbing in the back seat Gregory said, "We'll be going back the Belgravia flat to collect Mr. Accola and Mr. West, then take us to the National Gallery."

"Very good, sir". Pierre said, with his usual excessive formality as he closed the door.

The big Bentley pulled silently out into the traffic on Albert Embankment and merged with the flow of vehicles crossing the Lamberth Bridge into central London, then on to the flat on Wilton Crescent in Belgravia. The traffic was light for early evening, and they made better than expected time back to the flat.

***

Gregory said to Theo Accola, "Everything's been arranged for the transfer of the Monets, Botticellis and the Turners. We will be meeting with Sir Jonathan at the National Gallery at four. Once the paperwork is completed and signed; you and agent West will go back to the flat, then fly to New York City to complete the transfer documents for the Pissarros to The Metropolitan Museum of Art. Once that's done; you're free to go wherever you like."

"I think I'll head over to the Isle of Crete to soak up the sun and keep Miss Rousseau company. I wouldn't want her to get lonely. I don't mind saying I'll be damn glad to put this whole situation behind me Mr. MacNee." Accola said.

"I'm sure you will. I'll have my office here in London make your travel arrangements by private jet from New York's JFK International to Nikos Kazantzakis Airport on Crete; that way no one can track you, even if they knew you were in New York, so you'll be perfectly safe to enjoy the sun in Crete and Miss Rousseau's ample charms." Gregory told him.

Pierre drove the three of them to the National Gallery with Gregory and Theo Accola relaxing in the rear seat. Matt West preferred to ride shot gun up front as he liked to put it. They arrived at Sir Jonathan's office precisely at four o'clock and, not surprisingly, Sir Jonathan's staff had all the necessary documents ready for signatures. Theo Accola signed the name of Wu Hong Ling to each of the documents transferring ownership of the paintings to the Musee d' Orsay in Paris and the National Gallery in London. Wu Hong Ling was the name the CIA had instructed the art dealer who held the auction in Casablanca to use on the purchase documents.

Wu Hong Ling was not a real person; but a creation of the CIA, with all the documentation of a man's life, records of birth, education and even marriage and divorce. He was a wealthy eccentric multi-millionaire who was supposed to live in Hong Kong, but no one had seen or heard from him personally in years. The fictitious Wu Hong Ling owned many homes but was a total recluse so he was a safe bet for the CIA to use incase the KGB or The Brotherhood for Jihad came looking. While Theo Accola signed the documents, Gregory said to Matt West, "So, have you been told about the joint training at the farm?"

"Yes, I just heard about it last night when I phoned in my evening report. I've got to tell you I'm not at all thrilled. I'm not in that kind of shape anymore, too many years in the field." Matt said.

"That bad is it?"

"Let's just say it won't be anything like a holiday at the Imperial in Zurich."

"Bloody hell, boot camp again is it? Oh well; duty is duty. When Accola is through, Pierre will drive you both back to Wilton Crescent. Tomorrow you'll fly out on an MI6 special flight at 0930 in the morning. A CIA car will meet you at the private jet terminal at JFK and take you to The Plaza Hotel in Manhattan. You'll meet Sir Jonathan at the Metropolitan Museum of Art the next afternoon, and Accola will sign all the required documents. After that, take him back to the private jet terminal at JFK. He's heading to Crete on the same MI6 Falcon 50 that will take you both to New York. Then we're done with him."

"Have your people heard anything about Vistin?" Gregory asked.

"They reported that there was an accident involving the KGB car brining Vistin in, and several other vehicles, including a tanker truck. As far as they know, there were no survivors." West told him.

"We got the same report. According to our source, the Kremlin is assuming Vistin was killed in the crash. Unless new information surfaces after they can inspect the remains of those in the crash, they're closing the books on Vistin and Ophidian, at least for now."

We're also putting Vistin on the back burner. Mobius said MI6 will continue to watch for him but we need to move on to other assignments, based on all the information we have." Gregory said, looking disappointed that he didn't have proof of Vistin's death.

"The CIA Director feels the same way. Oh well, off to boot camp I suppose." Matt said.

Sir Jonathan's assistant escorted Theo Accola out of the office and said, "All the required documents for the transfer of the Monets, Botticellis and Turners have been signed. We'll arrange for a special security team to pick up the paintings from the bank vault in Zurich, and transport them to the Muse de Orsay and the National Gallery within forty eight hours."

"Well that's all for today Mr. Accola. My driver will take you and Mr. West back to Wilton Crescent, and then you'll fly to New York City in the morning. You made a wise choice Mr. Accola. In future I'd suggest you may want to investigate anyone, who wants to employ you as a buyer or sellers agent more carefully. Have a safe trip, and enjoy Miss Rousseau's company in the sun." Gregory said shaking Theo Accola's hand.

With the business of the paintings completed, and the Ophidian case closed, Gregory took a cab back to his home on Grosvenor Street in Highgate London to enjoy a few of Anatole's excellent meals and a soft bed. Then he would begin to prepare for the intense training to come in the United States. "Well, if it doesn't kill me I'll be in much better shape when it's over, and it may just prevent me from getting killed in the field". He thought, riding in the back of the cab.

CHAPTER FIFTY TWO

LANGLEY VIRGINIA USA

T he Global Airways flight from London Heathrow to Washington Dulles airport was smooth and uneventful. Gregory flew in a few days early and took a hotel near the sprawling CIA Headquarters complex in Langley, so he could be rid of the jet lag before training started. The scale of things in the United States always amazed him. You could fit MI6s Vauxhall Cross building in just one of the CIA complex parking lots. Everything in the U.S. was on a grand scale, highways, shopping malls; even grocery stores were massive by European standards. He knew that the training would be tough, but also realized that he was being trained by some of the top professionals in the world at what they do. They would have hand to hand combat training from the United States Marines Force Recon experts, demolition training using the most up to date explosives and techniques by the United States Navy SEAL team instructors, and electronic surveillance by the CIA's own top people. "Yes, the training will be tough, but the best available." He thought.

Gregory met with Matt West three days later at CIA Headquarters.

"So Matt, did everything go to as planned with Theo Accola and the Metropolitan Museum of Art?"

"Sure. We met with Sir Jonathan and the curator of the

museum, and they accepted the paintings as planned. They seemed dubious about it, but they couldn't pass up a gift of that nature, whoever it came from. As long as they had our assurance that the paiting was not stolen of course. Our Director assured them there were no improprieties. That, along with Sir Jonathan's assurances, and now and they're happy with their new treasure. "West told him.

"Is dinner with John still on?" Gregory asked.

"Sure is. We're meeting at seven thirty at one of the oldest and best restaurants in Washington D.C. Knowing your taste for the finest; we'll have one last good meal, before two weeks of hell begins."

Matt and Gregory arrived at the famous, The Old Ebbitts Grill, just before seven thirty. The restaurant had been a Washington D.C. landmark for well over one hundred years, and had the reputation for having some of the finest food in the city. They met John Waxman at the bar, and then took a table for three in back of the restaurant. Gregory ordered a fine 21 year old Glenlivet neat. Matt decided to say with his usual domestic draft beer, and unfortunately, John explained that because of the medications he was still taking, he would be drinking only mineral water. They had an outstanding meal and tried not to talk shop too much.

"Matt's kept me up on the development of the case after I was shot up, and tells me that the Ophidian case is closed and Vistin is out of the picture." John said to Gregory.

Leaning into the table and keeping his voice low, Gregory said, "Well yes, for the time being at any rate. The Ophidian organization is out of business, at least for the moment, but until we get confirmation of a positive identification of Vistin's body, we can't be sure Ophidian is finished. Because of the fire at the accident scene, it could take some time to recover the remains of the victims of the crash, and still longer for positive identification of the bodies. That would give Vistin time to go to grass somewhere in the world, if he's still alive. We'll just have to keep our people watching for any sign of him and wait."

They enjoyed a sumptuous meal, starting with the famous Blue Crab and Artichoke dip, followed by Oysters Rockefeller all around. The main course was served, with Gregory having the Jumbo Lump Crab Cake and an excellent Chardonnay. John enjoyed the Grilled Fresh Atlantic Salmon while Matt, being Matt, said the Barbequed Baby Back Ribs would do just fine, a full rack of course. They finished with a delicious warm peach cobbler with rich vanilla ice cream on top and coffee.

"I'd love a good cigar and port right about now, but of course most restaurants in America these days don't allow smoking. Oh well, since Cuban cigars are illegal here, I might as well pass anyway." Gregory said.

"I didn't know you smoked" Matt said with surprise.

"Well actually, I smoke very little; but I do enjoy a Cuban Cohiba Behike 52, along with a forty year old vintage Hine Port after a particularly fine meal. But since there is no smoking here, I'll just finish with a Remy XO, and a double espresso."

"Ok your lordship, enjoy it because in less than nine hours it'll be cold baked beans, water and sleeping on the hard ground. We need to report in at the farm at 0530 tomorrow morning." Matt said.

"In that case, we probably should be pushing along to the hotel for some shut eye. John, it's been great seeing you again, and I'm glad to see you healing up so nicely. Take care of yourself my friend." Gregory said, shaking John Waxman's hand.

"Good seeing you as well Gregory. Enjoy the farm. Matt, I'll see you in a few weeks, if you survive the good old farm." John said.

"Don't you worry, I may be old and fat, but I'll survive and come back leaner and meaner." West said with a laugh shaking his friends had.

Matt and Gregory arrived at the reception desk at 0500 feeling a bit delicate from too much rich food and too many drinks, but they were there and ready to learn. Matt wasn't kidding about the accommodations. Each room had six surplus army cots and a foot locker for their gear. "By the feel of these cots, they must have been surplus World War One issue. Oh well, this is boot camp after all." Gregory thought.

The days were long, starting at 0430 with calisthenics and a ten mile run. Class room training from 0700 till mid day, then weapons training in the field. It was as tough a training regimen as he had ever experienced, including his Royal Navy training.

"As tough as this is, the time spent learning to become proficient with the latest U.S., NATO and Warsaw Pact weapons, as well as explosives and surveillance techniques, were well worth it to be a more efficient field operator for MI6 in this increasingly dangerous world." Gregory thought.

The last day of training was finally over, and in true American style they had a huge BBQ, with chicken, hamburgers, hotdogs and copious amounts of cold beer. All the training teams felt like brothers by the time it was all over, and were ready to head back to their respective assignments.

Byron Hill, Connell Baines and Susan Jamison decided to stay for a few extra days to see some of the sights in Washington DC and Virginia, while Gregory was scheduled to fly back to London Heathrow that next evening after meeting with the CIA Director.

"Walking down the jet way to Global Airways flight seven and taking his seat in the first class section, Gregory could feel the fatigue of the past two weeks catching up to him and was thinking,

"Dinner and some sleep on the eight hour flight would fit the bill just fine."

The young couple seated across the aisle from Gregory, were clearly excited. "Is this your first trip to London?" They asked Gregory.

"Oh no, I was born there and lived there all my life. Now I'm just guessing mind you; but you're newlyweds on your way to England for your honeymoon?" He said with a smile.

Oh God, does it show that much? We were just married this morning." She said, holding tightly to her husband's arm with a look of great happiness.

"Well congratulations to you both. I wish you a long and happy life together." Gregory said, meaning it, but feeling the stab of pain he always felt thinking of when he and Octavia were the newlyweds just starting out, all full of joy and the promise of a long happy life together, that was not to be.

They both thanked him for his good wishes. After the flight attendant asked everyone to please buckle their seat belts, she began the emergency procedure instructions. Just a few minutes later Global flight seven took to the sky for the long flight to London and home. Gregory never would have thought that the happy young couple, as well as almost everyone on the plane, would soon be dead, with only himself and a few others surviving the night.

Waking up in the hospital, six weeks after the crash of Global Airways flight seven, Gregory knew that he had been blessed by God to have survived. But he dreaded the long months of recovery in the hospital.

CHAPTER FIFTY THREE

LONDON

Steppings firmly believed, that Gregory would recover more quickly and completely in the large family home on Grosvenor Street in Highgate London. Once old Steppings made up his mind to see to Gregory's recovery, there was no shifting him. To him, Gregory was that ten year old boy again who so desperately needed him, after his parents had been killed in a traffic accident in Hong Kong just after his tenth birthday. He wasn't that far off the mark with that feeling either. Gregory could barely move, and couldn't walk yet. After having one of the guest rooms on the ground floor converted into a hospital room, Steppings had all the necessary equipment brought to monitor Gregory's condition during his recovery. The door to Gregory's guest room was removed, as well as the doors to his study, library, kitchen and in-formal dining room for easy wheel chair access. The bathroom door was widened and the shower modified so Gregory could bathe in privacy. He began to recover quickly being at home, just as Steppings had predicted.

Gregory's physician, Stephanie Bond, would stop by every afternoon to check on his progress, and just help him pass the time. He was improving rapidly and began morning workouts in his gym, and took long walks in the afternoons. He was somewhat concerned that over the months of recovery, his relationship with Stephanie was becoming more than a doctor patient relationship.

She had no knowledge of his working for MI6, and it was imperative that it stayed that way. His working for MI6 was one of the most closely guarded secrets in the English Intelligence community. To her, and the rest of the world, Gregory MacNee was simply the wealthy Chairman of the Board of All Empire International.

Stephanie Bond was in her late twenties, extremely intelligent and beautiful, with chestnut hair, deep brown eyes, a fantastic figure and a quick wit.

They would take long walks together in the Green Park and lunch at his club.

They were sitting in the library by the fire one rainy evening, enjoying an excellent Mouton Rothschild, when Gregory said, "Stephanie, would you join me for dinner this evening? It's getting to be that hour, and I can't think of anyone I would rather dine with".

"I'd love too" she said, I hadn't realized it was so late. What are we having"?

Gregory rang for Steppings, who arrived immediately and silently, saying "Yes Sir"?

He arrived so silently, in fact, Stephanie started.

"Steppings, Miss Bond will be joining me for dinner this evening. Please tell Anatole, to use his imagination with dinner tonight.

"Very good, Sir" Steppings said, gliding silently out of the library.

"How does he move so quietly" Stephanie asked.

"I don't know, he's always been that way. Perhaps he's had Ninja training."

Stephanie laughed, "So what are we having for dinner?"

"Actually Stephanie, I'm not sure what we're having. Whenever Anatole uses his imagination though, it's bound to be something extraordinary".

"So who is Anatole?" she asked.

"Why, Anatole's my chef of course. He's been with me for years. He's a graduate of Le Cordon Bleu you know." Gregory said with a knowing grin.

"Is he really, a Cordon Bleu? Good Lord Gregory, I can't wait" she said.

Seated in the formal dining room, they discovered Anatole's inspiration was Japanese for the evening. The first course was Snow Crab Ceviche; the sweetness of the crab balanced with the tang of lime juice and heat of the peppers, paired with a properly chilled Pino Grigio from the Friuli Venezia Giulia region of Northeastern Italy, delicious. Next, he gave them a piping hot Lobster Toban Yaki; rich with lobster, mussels, clams and scallops, in a spicy red miso sake broth with garlic crostini on the side and ice cold Asahi Super Dry beer, a perfect combination for a cold rainy evening. They finished the meal with fresh fruit tacos, made from caramelized Gyoza with mixed fresh fruit and lime zest, accompanied by flutes of Perrier Jouet Blason Rose' Brut Champagne.

"My God Gregory, that was fabulous. I just love it when Anatole uses his imagination. For such light dishes I'm completely stuffed." She said.

They moved into the library for warmed snifters of Remy XO by the fire. She wanted to stay and be with him all night, but she knew that Gregory had not been able to be truly close to a woman since the death of his wife and son. "It will happen if it's meant to" she thought.

"Thank you for staying Stephanie, it was a lovely evening. We'll do this again very soon. I know you have the early shift at the hospital, so I'll have Pierre drive you home". Gregory said

Walking together to the car, Stephanie said, "I can't tell you how much I've enjoyed today. It was truly wonderful. I'll have to find some way to pay you back".

Holding each other close, and then sharing a long passionate kiss, Gregory said, "It was a wonderful day, because of you. Next time perhaps you won't have to work, and we can have Anatole fix us breakfast. He does that rather well too".

As the car moved off in to the rainy night, he thought, a bit uneasily, "I think I may be falling in love with her, never thought that would happen again."

Over the next few months they spent wonderful days and nights together. They decided to take a weekend trip to Paris, staying in one of the beautiful suites at the elegant Hotel de Vendome in the first Arrondissment, just across from Jardin de Tuileries. Spending pleasant afternoons strolling along the Champs-Elysees, enjoying the many fine restaurants, and doing a bit of shopping at the designer shops in that area, the trip was very relaxing. On the final day of their visit they met Stephanie's favorite Aunt, Elinor Sheriden for lunch at the Musee d'Orsay.

"Aunt Elinor studied at the Sorbonne Institut d' Art et d' Archeologie, and is considered one of the foremost authorities on the French Impressionist period. She works with the Societe Nationale des Beaux-Arts as a consulting expert. I thought it would be fun to meet here at Musee d' Orsay while we're in Paris. I know you'll like Aunt Elinor." Stephanie said, taking him by the arm and guiding him to her table.

Stephanie's Aunt Elinor was an impressive woman to say the least. She was in her early fifties, tall and statuesque with graying hair, piercing pale blue eyes and a welcoming smile.

"Good afternoon Aunt Elinor, I'm so glad you could make it today." Stephanie said with a smile.

"I was happy to rearrange my schedule. It's always delightful to see you mon cher." Elinor said, rising and giving Stephanie a warm hug.

"Aunt Elinor, this gentleman is Mr. Gregory MacNee, the man I told you about"

"It's a pleasure to meet you Monsieur MacNee." She said sweetly offering her hand, "Please sit here next to me."

"It's a great pleasure to meet you Madame Sheriden" he said taking her hand gently. Stephanie's told me all about your work here in Paris." Gregory said

"I've been most fortunate being able to work in a profession I'm passionate about, and live here in the center of the artistic world. Stephanie has told me of your terrible experience in the plane crash. It was a miracle you survived. I must say that you look like you've recovered beautifully from you injuries, which I understand from Stephanie were quite severe. It must have been a horrifying experience." Aunt Elinor said with a look of genuine concern.

"To be honest, I don't remember much about the crash itself. Yes, there have been nightmares, with disjointed images; however that's all fading with time. But that's all in the past now, and today I'm enjoying the company of two lovely ladies on a beautiful afternoon in Paris. What more could a man ask for. As to my recovery, it wouldn't have been possible without Stephanie." He said giving Stephanie's hand a squeeze.

"Before we head over to the gallery, tell me Monsieur MacNee, have you been interested in the Impressionist for long?" Elinor asked.

"No actually, not so very long at all. An associate of mine, Sir Jonathan Vandeveer, is the Curator of fine art at the National Gallery in London, and got me interested in Impressionism during a trip to Morocco earlier this year. There was a fine art auction at the Museum of Fine Art in Casablanca and we attended. Sir

Jonathan showed me some extraordinary works and I found that Monet was my favorite. But I must confess, I know very little about the period or the artists themselves. Perhaps you know Sir Jonathan?" Gregory asked.

"I have heard of him of course, but I've not had the pleasure of meeting him yet. As to the Impressionist Period, a brief history will increase your enjoyment of the works we'll be viewing this afternoon. The mid ninetieth century was a time of change, as Emperor Napoleon III rebuilt Paris. At the time, the Academie des Beaux-Arts or The Academie, dominated French art. They preferred works of historical subjects, religious themes and portraits that were carefully finished and realistic, with subdued and restrained colors. There was no interest in still life or landscapes with vivid colors and bold brush strokes.

In the early eighteen sixties, Monet, Renoir, Sisley and Bazille, studying under Charles Gleyre, discovered that they shared an interest in painting landscapes and contemporary life, rather than historical and mythological content. They preferred vivid colors and bold brush strokes evoking the impression one sees of a scene. They were of course considered radicals in their time and both the Academie and the public were hostile to their methods. However, the public gradually came to believe the Impressionist captured a fresh vision.

Their principal dealer in Paris, Monsieur Paul Durand-Ruel, helped keep the movement alive by showing their works in New York. The American collectors embraced the new method. Once they were interested, the Impressionist works began to command large prices that the Americans were willing to pay. But I could go on for hours. Let's go view some of these beautiful paintings. In fact Monet's "Water Lilly Pond and Nympheas" were just recently donated to the museum by an anonymous patron of the arts. What a magnificent gesture." She said.

***

They enjoyed a wonderful afternoon at the gallery ending the evening with a fantastic meal at the fine restaurant high up in the Eiffel Tower, with stunning views of the city. Relaxing on the train back to London, Gregory said, "I really enjoyed meeting your aunt Elinor. She does have an amazing knowledge of art, and I can also see where you get your sense of humor. She made the gallery much more interesting by explaining the artist motivation in their work and telling stories about the artist themselves. Maybe we could get together again in Paris, or perhaps she can visit us in London".

When he arrived back home in Highgate; Steppings said, "While you were away sir; Mobius phoned and asked if you could come to the office for a meeting as soon as it would be convenient for you."

"Very well, I'll give him a call." Thank you Steppings."

This wasn't a meeting he was looking forward to. He would have to tell Mobius, that if he were to marry Stephanie; he would have to resign from the service. He wasn't at all sure he wanted to resign, but Stephanie couldn't know about his work with MI6. This was a day he had wanted to put off as long as possible but, he phoned Miss Trent and arranged for a meeting with Mobius after lunch the following day. His sleep that night was restless, and he woke early and took a good five mile run through the Green Park to try to clear his mind and be ready for his meeting with Mobius. Pierre drove him to Vauxhall Cross and he arrived at Mobius's office at one fifteen. Walking into the outer office, Kimberly Trent came around from her desk and gave him a big hug saying, "Gregory, it's so good to have you back. The old place just hasn't been the same without you. I've missed you."

"Thanks Kim. Actually, it's good to be back. I've missed you too."

She touched the intercom and told Mobius that Gregory had arrived.

"Show him in Miss Trent." Mobius said.

"Ah Gregory, you look well and fit, please have a seat." Mobius said.

"Thank you sir, I'm about ninety nine percent recovered, just some weakness in my lower back, but it's coming along fine."

"I hope you had a splendid time in Paris, you look well rested."

"It was very relaxing sir. Stephanie and I saw Monet's "Water Lilly Pond" donated to the Muse de Orsay by Theo Accola, and I stopped by the National Gallery and saw the Turners."

"Do you feel fit enough to be put back on the active duty roster if you're certified by medical?"

"Well, yes sir, I feel fit enough. However, I have some personal issues I have to decide on before I can resume my duties here at MI6. You see sir, Stephanie and I have become more than close over the past several months. In fact sir, we have discussed the possibility of marriage in the future." Gregory told him.

"You haven't mentioned your association with MI6 to her I assume."

"No sir, of course not. In fact that's the bulk of my dilemma. Since she can never be told of my working for MI6, I would have to resign in order to marry her, and I'm not sure I'm ready to do that."

"Well your resignation would be a great loss to the service, and to your country. You're the finest strategist we have, and a top field agent. Your position at All Empire International allows you access to places no other agent could have, so it would indeed be a great loss for us if you elect to resign.

However, all of us in Her Majesty's service with MI6 fight those who would take away our freedom and our right to a happy and productive life. That being the case, you've more than earned a right to that happy life. Take as much time as you need to decide what is best for your future. If you decide to marry Stephanie, God bless you both, she's a wonderful woman." Mobius said.

"Thank you sir, I really do appreciate that. I'll give it a lot of thought over the next few days and let you know what decision I've come to. By the way, did they ever recover the remains of the crash in Russia involving our friend Vistin?"

"It took over four days and some heavy rain to put out the forest fire started by the crash. The rain was badly needed, and helped to put out the fire, but unfortunately, the rain caused a mud slide at the crash site because all the ground cover had been burned away.

They had to clear away tons of mud and rock to get to the wreckage which has taken many weeks due to the terrain. They finally did recover some human remains among the burned and twisted pieces metal of the vehicles, but they had been so badly incinerated that it will take forensic experts quite some time to identify any of them." Mobius told him.

"So basically we're still in the same boat as before my accident. We don't have any positive proof Vistin is dead."

"That's correct. We don't have any proof from the crash site so we don't know if he escaped. Our agents have been combing the area for any information and have come up with one or two curiosities. They checked with the Finnish border guards on duty at the time of the crash and one of them said that a man, who owned the café that Vistin was arrested in, drove across the border in an old lorry with a man who he claimed worked for him. He said the worker was injured in the fire and needed immediate medical attention. The man's face and hands were bandaged and he looked bad, so they let him pass without proper papers so he could get this man to the hospital before he died." Mobius told him.

"Did they check with the hospital to see if it was Vistin?"

"Oh yes, but when they checked with the hospital, they were informed that the injured man had never arrived." Mobius said.

"This is beginning to sound more and more like Vistin escaped." Gregory said.

"In fact it does, but we have no proof one way or another. The Finnish police found the lorry at a service station where a utility van had gone missing, then they found the van abandoned on the road to Kotka. It seems the van was pulled over for out of date registration tags the day of the accident in Russia.

The officer did not report back into his station at the end of his shift, so an investigation was started to locate him. They found the police car in an abandoned warehouse near the docks several days later with the body of the police officer, who had been shot in the face, in the trunk. The area was searched for the driver of the lorry, assuming he had switched vehicles to the utility van and killed the police officer, but no one was found. The only thing our people found out that was odd was that a fishing boat named *The The Northern Lights* when out fishing the same evening as the accident, and has not been heard from since. The Swedish Coast Guard had searched thousands of square miles but found nothing. They contacted all ports within the fuel range of *The Northern Lights*, but the vessel has not shown up anywhere. It seems that *The Northern Lights* simply disappeared into the night, and if Vistin was on it, he's disappeared as well."

"Could he have transferred to another ship at sea then sank *The Northern Lights*?" Gregory asked.

"Of course it is possible, but we have no way of knowing at this time. If in fact he did survive, was aboard *The Northern Lights,* and transferred to a ship at sea; he could have gone anywhere. So for now it's a dead end. Again, as far as Ophidian and Vistin are concerned, the case is closed. If we hear of someone fitting Vistin's description anywhere in the world, we will look into it, but for now it's time to move on to new business. I need to assign teams of specialist operators to several situations ongoing in China, as well as several hot spots in Africa, by the beginning of next week, and your expertise would be quite valuable. Please consider what you want for your future, and let me know as soon as possible. If you decide to stay on we could use your talents on these assignments." Mobius said.

"I understand and will give you my decision within three days." Gregory told him.

"Very well then, I'll talk to you in three days." Mobuis said shaking Gregory's hand.

Sitting in the back of the Bentley as Pierre drove back to Highgate; Gregory's mind was spinning with the weight of the decisions that had to be made, quite soon. When he arrived home he walked into his study and he took a large Saint-Louis Chrystal double old fashioned glass from the bar, and poured a solid four fingers of 18 year old Glenlivet single malt. He felt the whisky would calm him and help him make his decision.

Lying on the leather sofa staring at the ceiling, Gregory tried to weigh all the possibilities. Was Stephanie really the one, should he follow his heart with Stephanie, or his life long career with MI6. Did he really want marrage and a family or was he still drawn to the intensity of defending his country with the secret service.

This was without a doubt the most difficult decision he had ever been forced to make, since one could not exist with the other.

"One can't simply resign from MI6, and then come back if they get bored with civilian life. If you resign, you're out for good." He was thinking. After ruminating on the choices for some time, his head began to hurt. It was just too much to think about. Decisions on what action to take on a mission, no matter how serious, had always come easily. On a problem of such personal significance, the answer was just not coming.

***

Steppings knocked on the study door, then entered saying, "Please excuse the interruption sir, but there is a Miss Sophia Gambini on the line asking to speak to you, if you're available. She has phoned several times while you were away. What would you like me to tell her, sir?"

He felt his heart skip a beat and his pulse quicken at the mention of Sophia's name. He was sure, that after the attack in Cortina d' Ampezzo, he would never hear from her again. Closing his eyes, Gregory took a deep breath, trying to appear calm, and after a long moment said, "Ask her for a number where I can reach her. Tell her I'm in a meeting and will phone her as soon as possible."

"Very good, sir." Steppings said, closing the door silently behind him.

Gregory drained the last of his glass of Glenlivet, and walked over to the bar for a refill. Leaning heavily against the bar, he said to the ceiling, "Sophia, oh my God! Problems never come singly; God's definitely laughing out loud with this one."

Made in the USA
Columbia, SC
22 December 2020

29677236R00231